BABIES IN WAITING

Meet Louise, thirty-eight; Toni, twenty-six; and Gemma, eighteen . . . they are all expecting babies in September. And they are all discovering that impending motherhood is more than a little overwhelming. Finding their way onto an online forum, they discover fellowship, friendship, way too much information and — ultimately — one another. Meeting in real life, they set out to face the highs, lows, secrets and revelations of pregnancy and the first months of motherhood together. But one of the women is keeping a secret that will test their friendship to its very core . . .

ROSIE FIORE

BABIES IN
WAITING

Complete and Unabridged

CHARNWOOD
Leicester

First published in Great Britain in 2012 by
Quercus
London

First Charnwood Edition
published 2012
by arrangement with
Quercus
London

British Library CIP Data

Fiore, Rosie.
    Babies in waiting.
    1. Large type books.
    I. Title
    823.9'2–dc23

    ISBN 978–1–4448–1337–1

Published by
F. A. Thorpe (Publishing)
Anstey, Leicestershire

Set by Words & Graphics Ltd.
Anstey, Leicestershire
Printed and bound in Great Britain by
T. J. International Ltd., Padstow, Cornwall

This book is printed on acid-free paper

For Ted.
Written because of, and in spite of you.
Love you, small boy.

THE FIRST TRIMESTER

Louise

Sitting on the loo, blue penguin pyjama bottoms around her ankles, Louise stared again at the pregnancy test in her hand. The blue cross was very much still there. It wasn't going anywhere. Pregnant. Who would believe it? Here it was, the baby she'd always dreamed of, but at the wrong time, in the wrong circumstances, and totally and utterly with the wrong man. The irony wasn't lost on her. One stupid night with Brian. Just one, stupid, drunken shag, and now this. If she were a different woman, she'd have burst into tears and rung her mum or her best friend.

But Louise's mum was dead, and she wasn't the sort to have a girly best friend. Anyway, it was a work day, and a busy one. She couldn't sit on the loo all day. She had to get to work, get on with the day and think about all of this later. She certainly couldn't think about it at work, not today, not with the branch managers' meeting and Brian pretending to ignore her across the table. Although she thought they'd been discreet that night in Manchester, she was pretty sure everyone knew. Barrett and Humphries was too small a company. Until now, Louise hadn't given the gossip machine much thought. She hadn't really cared. All her energy had been focused on treating Brian with icy professionalism.

She turned on the shower and switched on to autopilot. She went through into her bedroom, laid out her clothes for the day on her bed and stripped off her pyjamas. She showered quickly and efficiently, blow-dried her short, dark-red hair, and dressed in a maroon suit, with severe lines which flattered her slim, tall figure. She ate a quick breakfast of fruit, yoghurt and muesli and then rapidly applied her minimal make-up, just mascara and lipstick. Her briefcase was already packed, her keys and sunglasses in their usual place by the front door. She rinsed out her bowl, looked around her tidy kitchen and was out of the door fifteen minutes after she'd done the pregnancy test.

It wasn't until she'd eased her little car out of her quiet road and taken her place in the traffic queue heading towards the town centre that she let herself switch on her brain again. Suddenly, she began to shake. What was she going to do? Clearly, she couldn't have it. She could just imagine the looks at work as she started to show. Barrett and Humphries was as progressive as an old-fashioned Yorkshire printing firm could be, and she knew they appreciated her skills and professionalism. But if it came to a choice, there was no doubt Brian would win. He was older, more senior, a partner. She'd be out on her ear quicker than you could say 'discrimination lawsuit'. Yes, she could probably fight it, but did she really want the humiliation of having her mistake made public?

No, there was no doubt, she'd have to have an abortion, and she most certainly couldn't have it anywhere around here. Even if she went to a hospital three towns away, Sod's Law said she'd

4

bump into some colleague, or a friend of a friend. Even York didn't seem far enough. No. She'd go to London, stay with Simon and get it over and done with as quickly as possible. Edward, her boss, had been nagging her to use up her annual leave. She could take a week or so and be back as if nothing had happened.

As she inched forward in the traffic, Louise decided that going to work was a really stupid idea. She'd be in a world of her own, pale and worried. She might say something silly in the branch managers' meeting, and Brian would give her his heavy-browed look across the table. He'd think he made her nervous, and that she was carrying a torch for him. There was no way she was going to put herself through that. Pulling into a convenient loading zone, she grabbed her mobile and rang her PA. She made an excuse about a domestic emergency, a burst pipe and a flooded kitchen, and said she'd do her best to be in later. She deftly nosed back into the traffic, made a swift three-point turn in a side road and headed home. Simon wouldn't be in his office till ten. She'd ring him then, and then go online and find a clinic in London. With the decisions made, the trembling stopped and she felt like herself again.

But two days later, she still hadn't done what she had set out to do. She just didn't feel she could tell Simon everything on the phone or in an email. Eventually, she rang him and asked if she could come down and stay for a few days, saying she'd missed him and was having a few days off work. That done, she set about making the necessary arrangements. She rang a clinic not far from Simon's flat, and the woman she had spoken to seemed to think they'd be able to fit her in for an appointment at fairly short notice.

★ ★ ★

She got into London at about four in the afternoon. Simon was a fairly senior civil servant, and she knew he'd clock off at exactly five thirty. She had a key to his flat, so she popped to the nearby supermarket, bought a bunch of flowers, a bottle of wine and some dinner ingredients and let herself into his riverside apartment.

As always, her brother's home was perfect, and the vases of flowers discreetly dotted around were much nicer than the ordinary supermarket blooms she'd brought. She opened the fridge and saw he'd stocked up because she was coming: the shelves were packed with cheeses, pate and gorgeous salad ingredients, as well as several bottles of good white wine. She smiled. What else had she expected? He was such a perfectionist. She unpacked the simple groceries she'd brought and put the kettle on. As it came to the boil, she heard his key in the door.

'Lou! It's fabulous to see you. And the kettle's on! Best sister in the world. Won't you make me a little green tea, please? I'm parched.' He swept into his bedroom and kept up a stream of chatter as he changed out of his suit and into pressed chinos and a crisp sky-blue shirt.

Louise always marvelled at Simon's personal

reinvention. He'd completely lost his Mancunian accent, and spoke in a crisp, transatlantic one instead. He'd spent time and money learning to dress well, and he paid attention to grooming: his hair, skin and nails were always perfect. When she remembered the miserable, scrawny teenager he'd been, hiding his thin body in awful, shiny tracksuits, slouching and picking at his bad skin, she was so proud of him. They'd grown up just outside Manchester, in a grey little suburb. Simon had worked hard at school and as soon as he could, taken off for the south to study. He'd got a grant to read Social Policy at LSE, and had built a life and a career for himself in London. She supposed she'd always known deep down that he was gay, and that their lovely but conservative parents would never understand that. But in London he could openly live the life he chose. Once their parents died he'd been more open about his lifestyle. He'd had a couple of long-term relationships, but wasn't seeing anyone at the moment. Jokingly he'd said to Louise that his social life was too busy for a relationship.

She loved him to bits, but in a funny way, she felt distant from him. He'd worked so hard to make his shiny, wonderful life, and she often wondered if there was space for his slightly hectic, very northern sister in its designer perfection. She knew Simon well enough to know these worries were in her head, not his. He was always loving, rang her often and kept asking her to come down and stay with him. She didn't accept his invitations as often as she might have:

between work and her studies, things had been ridiculously busy over the last few years.

Their other sister, Rachel, lived down in Surrey with her banker husband, Richard. Simon didn't like Rachel's suburban lifestyle, so they didn't often see each other — he felt they really had nothing in common. Because he was so cold about his relationship with one sister, Louise was grateful that he made such an effort to keep her in his life.

She hadn't told him about Brian . . . it had been a momentary lapse, an out-of-character mistake she wouldn't want to admit to. And now, here she was, bringing all her horribly messy baggage to his doorstep. Her stomach lurched. Simon might need something a bit stronger than green tea to get him through what he was about to hear. She took one of his nice French bottles of wine out of the fridge, opened it and filled two large glasses to the brim.

He came out of the bedroom, smiling and turning back the cuffs on his shirt. He kissed her warmly on the cheek, noticing the glasses. 'Wine! Much better than tea. Come and sit down.' He led her into the living room and they curled up in opposite corners of the big squashy sofa.

'Cheers, dear,' said Simon and took a big gulp of his wine. Louise raised her glass, but the smell of the wine was so strong that it brought on a flood of nausea. She put the glass down on the coffee table and smiled brightly at her brother.

'So how's work? Any plans for the summer? Ooh! How are Eric and Julian?'

Simon looked at her curiously. 'Fine, possibly

Rhodes, and they're very well, thank you. Considering getting married in the autumn. They send their love.'

'Oh, send mine back, and say congratulations.' Louise knew that there was a slightly manic edge to her voice. They carried on chatting, but the conversation was stilted and halting. He asked about work, and she told him about the cutbacks they'd had and the people she'd had to let go. He kept looking at her really closely, which made her shift in her seat. How the hell was she going to bring the conversation around to what she needed to say?

She wished she could manage a big slug of the wine to calm her nerves, but the smell of it (wafting over from the coffee table . . . so powerful . . . had there ever been a glass of wine that smelt so strongly?) was making her mouth fill with saliva, and not in a good way. Suddenly, she knew for sure that if she moved suddenly or coughed, or opened her mouth to speak, she'd be sick. She felt a fine sweat break out along her hairline. Simon peered at her intently. 'Lou, are you all right?' he asked. She managed a weak nod. He kept staring at her. Out of the blue, he gasped: 'Oh my God, you're pregnant!'

She didn't stay to hear any more, but bolted for the bathroom. When she came out, pale and smelling of mouthwash, ten minutes later, Simon had got rid of the wine and made cups of fruit tea. She edged shamefacedly into the room and sat back down, wedging herself tightly into the corner of the sofa.

'I was half joking, but then I saw your face.

You are, aren't you?'

She nodded. 'How did you know?'

'Well, the vomiting was a giveaway, but also, it's not like you to be slow with the wine.'

'Cheek!' she said weakly.

'Well, it's true! You usually inhale your first glass and pour another while I'm still genteelly sipping. But the main giveaway was the boobs.'

'They're bigger, aren't they?'

'Dear God. The Met Office has put out an alert for two missing weather balloons.'

Louise began to giggle, then hiccup and then cry. Simon knew her too well to hug her. He got up and fetched tissues, moved her teacup closer to her hand and didn't speak until she stopped.

'So, are you going to tell me whose it is?' he asked gently.

The story just spilled out.

'It's a guy called Brian, from work,' she began.

'Have you been seeing him for long?'

'I'm not seeing him. It only happened once, on a business trip. It was a mistake.'

'Ah, accidental sex. I've heard of that. Sorry. I don't mean to make fun. But is he so awful? Would you not want him in your life?'

'Well . . . ' said Louise slowly.

'Oh,' said Simon, and she knew he understood.

'The thing is, well, it started at a conference we had a month or two ago. You know how hard I was studying for the MBA. I mean, I hadn't been out partying for as long as I can remember. So we went away on a team-building event in

Derby, and, well, I was in the mood to let loose
. . . within reason, of course.'

'And then?'

'Well, there were twelve branch managers and about the same number of assistant managers on the weekend, and we spent the Friday night at a murder-mystery evening in this lovely Edwardian hotel we were staying in. We all had to dress up as different characters, and everyone got into the mood quite quickly. We all drank quite a lot. I had to dress up as a 'femme fatale' in a silky, black 1920s dress, and believe me, I got plenty of attention.'

'I can believe it,' Simon smiled.

'I just laughed it off . . . I've always worked with big groups of blokes, so I've seen every clumsy move in the book. Most guys will give it a go when they've had a few. But Brian was different. He just kept to himself. His role was a gambler, and he acted his part quite seriously, and then he just sat quietly in an armchair while everyone else played all sorts of drinking games and got more and more raucous. I knew who he was, of course, he's one of Barrett and Humphries' most successful managers. We'd met a few times, but I'd never really had a conversation with him.'

Louise took a sip of her tea and carried on. 'I know when to stop drinking . . . '

Simon raised an eyebrow. 'In a work context I do!' she protested. 'I'm always very professional. Anyway, at about ten I switched to tea, and I found myself sitting next to Brian in the corner of the room. There's this woman, Natalie, who runs the Bradford branch, and she was kneeling down on the floor with her hands behind her back, trying to pick up a cereal box with her teeth. She's pretty loud at the best of times. She's got a laugh that could rattle glass, but after she'd been drinking all night she was quite a sight to behold.'

Simon giggled at this, but didn't interrupt. He nodded so that she would carry on.

'So I laughed and I turned to Brian to say something, but he looked so serious, I didn't know what to say. He's a big guy, about six four and hunky, with this really unusual auburn hair. And then he turned to look at me, and his eyes were the most piercing blue I'd ever seen.'

'Oh God,' Simon said.

'Exactly. So he stared at me for a second and then he said, 'I can't take any more of this. Shall we go to the bar and get a drink?' What was I going to do? I said yes. So as we walked out, one of the North Yorkshire managers, a big, red-faced bloke, yelled, 'Oi, Brian! You don't get to just walk off with the best bird at the party.' And Brian said, 'You're right, Gerald, I don't. You see, she's a co-worker, not a bird, and we're off to the bar to talk shop.' The blokes all laughed, but I was still impressed.

'We went to the bar and he got us each a good brandy, and then we talked through some of the issues I'd been dealing with since I took over my branch. He made some very useful suggestions, and he told me some of the methods he used in his own branch. He really knows his stuff, so I was very interested to hear what he had to say. Then, when we'd finished talking, he walked me

12

back to my room, and said goodnight without touching me, and then went off to his own room.'

'Playing the long game,' said Simon.

'You're such a cynic.'

'Am I right?'

'Well . . . '

'Carry on with the story.'

'Well, the next day, we did all sorts of physical games and an assault course. Obviously I'm quite fit, and, let's face it, a bit slimmer than most of the blokes, so I did okay, and we had a mock awards ceremony that night, and I got a special mention. So that night was even more drunken than the first one, but somehow I kept noticing Brian, and he was alone and quiet again. I found myself sitting next to him again and chatting. He was easy to talk to, but that night, he seemed a bit preoccupied. He kept stopping in the middle of sentences, and looking into the distance.

'After a while I asked him if he was okay, and he said, 'Yes. Just, you know. Family stuff.' I didn't want to pry, but he still looked so serious that eventually I said, 'Everything okay?' And he said, 'Well, no. I'm . . . er . . . well, I'm about to leave my wife.' I said, 'Really? I'm sorry,' and I tried to sound compassionate and professional, as a colleague should, but inside I was thinking . . . interesting . . . veeeeeery interesting indeed! Anyway, he told me that his wife, Lisa, had some problems with depression, and alcohol. If it weren't for the kids . . . '

'He's got kids?' Simon said, alarmed.

13

'Emily is ten and Charlotte is eight. Anyway, he started telling me how awful his marriage was and how he couldn't carry on, though his kids mean the world to him. They didn't love each other, and they hadn't . . . you know . . . for years.'

'Of course they hadn't,' Simon said cynically.

'I'm just telling you what he said. It was very convincing at the time. He just stared at me with those blue eyes and said, 'She's just drifted further and further away, and I've tried everything. Arguing, counselling for her, counselling for us as a couple . . . medication . . . I miss her, but it's just not possible to get her back.' And then he looked like he was going to cry. I didn't know what to say. I reached out my hand to pat his arm and he grabbed it and held it tight, like he was drowning. And then he said, 'So this is the end. When I get back from the conference, I'll tell her. And within a fortnight, I'll have moved into my own place.' And then he squeezed my hand and said softly, 'Thank you. Thank you so much for listening. I haven't told anyone that before.''

Simon actually snorted at that. Louise sipped her tea and nodded.

'Anyway, a week later, the company won this big prize at an awards ceremony in Manchester. All the managers went along, there was a lot of champagne, and flirting . . . and well, then there was falling into bed. As soon as I woke up the next morning, I knew it was a mistake. I mean, I might have had a moment of madness, but I'm not permanently dumb. I knew I'd been fed a

14

line. He wasn't going to leave his wife, and I wasn't interested in being his bit on the side. So I said goodbye very politely and left.'

'How did he take it?'

'He didn't get the message at first. He kept ringing me up and texting me . . . he sent me a mobile number, different from his usual work number, and said he thought we had something special going. Then we had our usual fortnightly managers' meeting. I avoided him while we were all getting coffee outside, but he hung back so he could walk into the meeting room with me, and as we went through the doorway, he slid a finger up the sleeve of my jacket and stroked my wrist. It was sexy, but way too risky for me, so I sent him a text that afternoon and said I didn't want anything to do with him. He sent one back calling me some not very polite variations on the term 'cock tease', and we haven't spoken since.'

Louise took a big breath. 'So here I am, Simon love. Thirty-eight, and pregnant by a married man.'

Simon shifted in his seat, then said quietly, 'Sorry to ask this, but didn't you use anything?'

'Of course! We used a condom, but . . . '

'It broke?'

'I know, I know, oldest cliché in the book. I didn't have anything with me . . . I wasn't planning on sleeping with a co-worker, as you can imagine. And I suppose that one had probably been in Brian's wallet for some years. He told me he was sure it would be fine.'

'But . . . '

'Well, obviously not so fine now, is it?'

'So, how far along are you?'

'About eight weeks. I want to get it over and done with as soon as possible.'

'Well, you've got a good few months to go yet, you know, I mean you're not even starting to show yet, and . . . ' Simon stopped cold. 'Oh my God. You mean . . . '

'I've got to get rid of it, Si. You know I do. How can I go through with this and carry on with my life?'

'Get rid of it?' He looked completely horrified, and as he repeated the words Louise heard how awful they sounded.

'It's not an old car or something, Lou. It's a baby.'

'Don't say that. Please don't say that. I have to think of it as an inconvenient clump of cells or I won't be able to do it.'

Simon opened his mouth to say something, thought better of it, then nodded. There was a long silence. He smiled weakly at her.

'Now you've thrown up, do you feel better? Shall I cook, or should we get a takeaway or go out?'

'Out,' said Louise. 'Out is good.'

They went to a busy pizza place in Canary Wharf, where the music, chatter and plate noise meant they didn't have to talk much. By the time they got back to Simon's flat, Louise was dead on her feet. She kissed him goodnight, brushed her teeth and fell into a deep and dreamless sleep in Simon's cosy spare room.

In the quietest part of the night, she jerked awake suddenly. London's ever-present orange

16

glow lit the room. She'd never got used to the way it didn't get properly dark there. She glanced at the bedside clock. It was 3 a.m. Then, with a shock, she realized Simon was sitting on the edge of her bed, watching her. She struggled to sit up. In the half light, she could only see the wet glow of his eyes. She waited for him to speak.

'Don't do it, Lou. I beg you. I've been sitting up for hours, arguing with myself, saying that it's your decision, that you have to do what's best for you, that the circumstances are terrible.'

'Simon, I . . . '

'Please, let me say my bit. I've been practising in the sitting room for hours. Then you can shoot me down.'

She nodded.

'The circumstances *are* awful, it's true. Your job, what people will say, what that wanker Brian will say . . . and yes, before you interrupt, he *is* a wanker . . . '

Louise had no choice but to smile and nod.

Simon continued. 'But this is a baby, Lou. An actual, real human being. He or she exists. They didn't pick the circumstances, but it's happened, and right now, the inconvenient bundle of cells is growing. It's got a heart, did you know that? And legs and arms . . . it's got wrists!'

'How do you know . . . ?'

'I looked on the internet. There are pictures. You should see them.'

'I shouldn't. I really shouldn't.'

For the first time, Simon's voice became firm. Up until now, he'd been really gentle with her.

'I think you should. Lou, I'm your brother. I know deep down you've always wanted a baby. And now you have one. It might not be fathered by the man you'd choose if you were in your right mind, it might mean some big life changes, but it's still a baby. Your baby. And you know what? If you came to live in London, it could be our baby. Little Sprog Holmes, raised by Mummy Lou and Uncle Simon.'

'Simon . . . '

'Just think about it, okay? I would never have forgiven myself if I hadn't said my piece. I'll love you and support you whatever you do, but just . . . think about it.'

And then he was gone.

★ ★ ★

When Louise woke up in the morning, Simon had already left for work. He'd printed pictures out from a baby website and left them on her bedside table. They showed a funny, curled-up little prawn with starfish hands. Under the picture, Louise read: 'Congratulations — your embryo is now called a foetus, which means 'offspring'.'

Louise lay back down and let the tears come. She wished she'd never told Simon. It just wasn't fair. He'd made this so much harder. It just wasn't possible. How would she support a baby? If she moved down to London, she'd have to leave her job. She could hardly get a new job, several months pregnant, and even if someone would take her on, what would happen then?

18

She didn't want to take three months' maternity leave and then go back to work, leaving a tiny baby in some overpriced crèche. She had savings, that was true. Quite a nice little nest egg, but if she spent that . . . well, what financial cushion would she and the baby have?

She got up slowly and went through to the kitchen. From experience she knew Simon would have left a pot of coffee warming, and she was starving. She seemed to have escaped morning sickness — her nausea came on in the late afternoon.

Simon had left her coffee, and a little platter with a fresh croissant, butter and a selection of jams. Louise thought, not for the first time, that if he weren't her brother, she would marry him. At the very least, he should run a hotel. He knew how to make guests feel totally pampered. She sat nibbling on the buttery pastry and wondering how to go about her day. She'd imagined that she would be off to the clinic first thing, but Simon had taken the wind out of her sails. She wasn't at all convinced by his argument, but she did feel she had to give the whole subject more thought. At that moment, her mobile bleeped. Simon had sent an email.

Hello, lovely.
Hope you slept okay. Please take today to think about what I said. I know money will be your first concern. Please use my computer to do any sums you need to do and remember that my offer to be a part of this is serious. I will contribute financially and I

19

will always be there.
Love you lots.
S.

It seemed like as good a thing to do as any, so Louise fired up Simon's MacBook and crunched some numbers. Her house in Yorkshire was mortgage-free: what would happen if she let it out? What could she reasonably expect to get? What if she sold it? She looked up a couple of estate agents in her area on the internet, then rang them. She told them where her house was and asked them to estimate both rental income and a possible sale price. They dithered and iffed and butted, but in the end she had the numbers she needed. Next, where would she live? She loved Simon and knew that his offer to help was genuine, but she didn't see a place for a baby in his spotless bachelor home. Even if he said it was okay, she wanted to believe that at some point he would meet someone and fall in love, and a resident sister and squawking infant would make that very difficult indeed. Also, they were in their late thirties, both set in their ways. Far too late to set up home together. She knew she wouldn't be able to live as centrally as he did, so she used a property website to look at the rental cost of two-bedroomed apartments in the outer suburbs of London. Coming from up north, she was horrified at the cost, but she entered the numbers in her spreadsheet, and added costs for council tax, food and other regular expenses. Once she had finished, she left the flat and took a long walk along the Thames. She stopped for coffee, then walked some more. She stopped somewhere else on the river for lunch. By then she was tired and her feet hurt. She found a nearby cinema and sat through an afternoon showing of a really soppy romantic comedy. She was one of three people in the cinema, and the only one under sixty. It was exactly the brain popcorn she needed, and she switched off totally for the two hours of the film. Leaving the cinema, she decided to pamper herself and hailed a black cab. The cost was eye-watering, but the trip back to Simon's flat was painless and speedy.

When she got upstairs, Simon was already there, stirring a pasta sauce that smelt of basil, tomato and luxury, and listening to classical music. He kissed her absent-mindedly on the cheek and directed her to the fridge to get a drink.

She loved it that they didn't need to talk. She poured herself a fruit juice and sat on a stool at the kitchen counter, vaguely paging through the newspaper. Simon put a saucepan of water on to boil and took some beautifully yellow fresh pasta out of the fridge. Yes, it was excellent the way they could sit together in silence. Louise turned the page of the newspaper and stared unseeing at the words on the page. She sipped her fruit juice and sneaked a look to see if Simon was watching her. He wasn't. He was carefully slicing cucumber, humming softly along with the music. Ah yes. Companionable silence. So soothing. So refreshingly unusual, so, so *annoying!*

'Oh Christ, just ask!' Louise burst out.

'Ask what?' Simon asked, innocently.

21

'If I'm keeping it.'

'Keeping what?'

'Keeping it. Keeping the . . . the baby. My baby.' As she said it, Louise felt something give gently in her heart, and the tears began to flow.

Simon stepped around the counter and wrapped his arms around her.

'Well, old girl, there's my answer.'

'What?' she hiccupped.

'You called it 'my baby'.'

'I know. It's all your bloody fault. You made it real. I tried to turn it into an inconvenience . . . a problem I could manage, but you came along with your pictures and your plans. Then I started looking at numbers . . . and let me say right now I really, really can't afford to do this and your niece or nephew is going to grow up in rags and sleeping in a drawer . . . '

'Not if I have anything to do with it. I'll buy it John Lewis' finest crib. Promise.'

Louise hugged him harder. Then she spoke quietly. 'When I started thinking about it as a possibility, I couldn't unthink it. He or she is real now. I'm going to do it, Si. I'm going to have this baby. I'm terrified, totally terrified, and I have a million problems and no solutions, but I'm going to be a mum.'

'And what about . . . ?' Simon said carefully.

'Brian? I don't know. I'll have to tell him. But I don't want him involved in any way. I know he won't want to be, but I want him to understand that I won't ask for anything from him.'

Simon nodded. Whether he agreed or not, he clearly wasn't going to say. 'Well, first things first, you're going to eat your dinner. Get your strength up, as Mum used to say,' he said, giving her one last squeeze and taking the saucepan to the sink to drain the pasta. 'Then we'll sit down and look at numbers together and see what I can do to help.'

★   ★   ★

A couple of hours later, they sat side by side, staring at the computer screen. They'd been over the possibilities time and time again. They'd made a few plans, but things still looked pretty bleak for Louise.

'It's going to be tight and no mistake,' said Simon.

'Really?' said Louise tensely. 'Looking at this, it looks like my choice is rent or food.'

'I keep telling you, I'll give you money . . . '

'Si, I can't take your money. If, like you said, when I first move down here I can stay with you, that'll be a big help. But I can't be your charity case.'

'You're not a charity case. You're my sister. And that's my niece- or nephew-to-be.'

'I know, I know, but you have your own future to think about. You might want to travel. You might get a great new job offer. Who knows? Mr Right might be just around the corner.'

'Rubbish.'

'Not rubbish! And if he is, I don't want you to miss out on opportunities because you're financially and emotionally tied up with me and my problems!'

'But . . . '

'No buts. I'll stay with you for three months. Just long enough to get me on my feet one way or another. Then I want you to be the best uncle in the world. But that's it, okay?'

'Can I still buy the crib?'

'You can still buy the crib.'

'And lots of cute outfits?'

'Go crazy. The cutest you can find.'

'And can I be at the birth?'

'Are you mad?'

'Not at the business end. Good Lord. I've made a lifestyle choice never to view women from that angle. I'm not about to start now. But I could stand at your head and say encouraging things and mop your brow.'

'It's not a film, Si . . . it's messy. There'll be blood and screaming.'

'There'll be no screaming! You're made of tougher stuff than that. You can maybe purse your lips a little bit.'

'Well, let's both learn a bit more about the whole thing, and then we'll decide. To be honest, I don't know the first thing about babies, or giving birth or pregnancy for that matter.'

'Really?' said Simon, 'I thought at your age . . . '

'Thanks a lot. You thought I'd have lots of friends having babies?'

'Well, I suppose so.'

'I'm sure women my age are popping them out all the time, but not my friends. Actually, most of my friends are men anyway, and the ones who do have children don't really talk

24

about them a lot. I'm a working woman, Si, not a member of some yummy-mummy Surrey set.'

'Oh Lord,' Simon said suddenly.

'Oh Lord what?'

'Speaking of Surrey yummy mummies, or not mummies as the case may be . . . '

'Rachel,' Louise said soberly.

Rachel was the youngest of the Holmes siblings. She'd studied Media at university and worked for a short time in marketing for an investment bank, before marrying the richest, handsomest banker on the trading floor. She'd then immediately given up work and stayed at home in Richard's Surrey pile, waiting to fall pregnant with the first of the three perfect blond children that she would spend her life raising. She filled her days with charity work and volunteered as a classroom assistant at the local nursery . . . all things she could drop at a moment's notice as soon as she conceived. Unfortunately, ten years later, there was no sign of the blond children. Rachel had undergone every test under the sun. Richard had been shunted off to have his sperm count checked. There was nothing physically wrong, yet Rachel could not get pregnant.

Both Simon and Louise didn't have much to say to a sibling who had never really worked. She had no idea of the day-to-day realities of earning a living, having to save for something you wanted, or being too busy at work to listen to a twenty-minute-long description of some-thing a cute child in the nursery she worked at did today. Rachel was quite clever enough to know they found her boring. She also knew Simon and Louise were very close and she was horribly jealous of their easy and intimate relationship. She wooed Simon constantly, playing on the fact that he lived so close to her, and she patronised Louise whenever they spoke, not so subtly implying that Louise was well on her way to becoming a dried-up spinster, or a hairy-legged, feminist ball-breaker.

And now, this had happened. Louise had achieved the one thing Rachel couldn't do without even trying. Not only that, but Simon was closely involved. There was no doubt about it. Rachel was going to be devastated.

'Yes, Rachel,' Simon said. 'I didn't tell you this before, because, frankly, we've had one or two other things to discuss. But she heard you were coming down to see me, so we're expected for lunch on Sunday.'

'Bugger.'

'Exactly. Do we tell her?'

'And have her go on at me for the whole meal? No thank you.'

'Or she could find out later, and work out that we knew when we were there for lunch and didn't tell her?'

'Would she care?'

'Would she? She's got nothing else to think about. Babies, fashion, gossip and family drama. Even if there wasn't drama in this situation, she'd make some.'

'So what's your suggestion?'

'Tell her. Tell her everything with the minimum of fuss and give her lots of details. It'll

26

keep her busy for a while. If you like, you can pretend I don't know and you're confiding in her first.'

'She'd never buy that.'

'No, you're right. You two have never been joined at the hip.'

'I'm sure I can make it sound like I need her help too, though.'

'Good call.'

Louise laughed suddenly and clutched Simon's arm. 'Good God. I don't believe I have to go to lunch with Rachel and Richard and endure a major family trauma, and I can't even drink!'

★   ★   ★

That Sunday, Louise and Simon took the train down to Oxshott. Richard roared up to the station in his 4x4 Porsche and whisked them along the winding roads back to the house. Rachel, as always, had created a perfect social setting. They walked into the house to be met with the scent of lilies and roses. She'd arranged a huge bowl of flowers in the entrance hall. Moving into the living room, the smell of roast lamb wafted to meet them, and soon that was blended with a waft of Rachel's expensive perfume as she swept out to kiss them. She was very slim, Louise noticed. Her hair was an expensive shade of blonde and her skin was polished and much more bronzed than you'd expect for a chilly January.

'You look lovely,' Louise said. It was true. She liked to dress smartly and stay in shape, but even with all the time and money in the world, she'd never have Rachel's expensive elegance.

'Thanks, Lou. You look . . . fine,' Rachel replied. She turned to kiss Simon. 'Hello, gorgeous brother.'

'Drinks?' Richard boomed, rubbing his hands together. He and Rachel liked to play very traditional couple roles. He'd never dream of setting foot in the kitchen, and she wouldn't have poured a G & T if her life depended on it.

'A gin for me, please, Richard,' Simon said quickly.

'And I'll just have a fruit juice,' said Louise. Richard looked at her as if she'd just made fun of his golf game. 'I'm on antibiotics. Teeth,' she explained. He relaxed a little, although he was still clearly horrified that someone would miss out on a pre-lunch tipple.

'And a sherry for me, darling,' Rachel chipped in. 'Simon, you must see the blinds I had made. The most perfect shade of duck-egg blue.'

Richard got the drinks, and Simon walked around the living room with Rachel, making the right noises about the additions to her decor. Louise stood slightly awkwardly in the middle of the room, trying not to get in the way. Their plan was that they'd wait till lunch was underway before dropping their bombshell. They'd decided that if Richard had a few drinks in him and Rachel had been softened by an endless stream of compliments about her home and food, the fallout might not be too ghastly. Still Louise found herself wishing it was all over already. She had a sick feeling low in her stomach, as if she was waiting to see the headmaster.

Simon and Rachel had finished their grand tour and Richard had placed drinks in everyone's hands. 'Cheers, dears!' Rachel said brightly and raised her glass. 'Lovely to have you both here, for once!'

Just as Louise opened her mouth to reply, the doorbell pealed.

'They're here!' Rachel trilled. 'Let them in, Richard!'

'Who's here?' Simon asked as Richard went to open the door. He exchanged a quick glance with Louise. This was an eventuality that hadn't even occurred to them . . . other guests.

'Our dear, dear friends, David and Samantha Hamilton,' Rachel explained. 'David is Richard's boss, and they play golf together *all* the time. So Sam and I are golf widows and console each other . . . although we're on quite a few of the same committees!'

So this was an aspirational lunch . . . Rachel and Richard were showing off for the boss and his wife, and Simon and Louise had been invited to provide some family colour.

David and Samantha came in, with Richard rubbing his hands behind them like a toadying Dickens character. David was tall, with a mane of silver hair that he wore a fraction too long, and a handsome, if slightly hard face. Samantha was blonde and Louise suddenly saw where her sister's polished new look came from: she was trying to be a Samantha clone. There was air-kissing, introductions and drink-pouring, and everyone sat down in the living room. Simon squeezed Louise's hand surreptitiously. Their announcement would obviously have to wait. Rachel rushed off to bring in trays of appetisers, and Richard and David started teasing each other boringly about golf.

'So! David!' Rachel said brightly, as she handed him a blini with caviar. 'This is my sister I've told you so much about. She's quite the career girl! She works at a printing shop.'

'Actually, I run a branch of a printing company,' Louise said, hating herself for rising to the bait. The way Rachel had said it, it made her sound like she tottered about photocopying things for people. 'We're one of the largest high-volume printers in England. Barrett and Humphries?'

David nodded dismissively, and carried on telling a story to Richard about someone called Binky and some futures. Louise wished heartily she could slurp up an enormous glass of wine to make the afternoon go quicker. But there was no wine for her, and the meal seemed to go on forever. Rachel kept bringing out course after perfectly made course, and making slightly barbed comments at Louise while fawning over her guests. Louise toughed it out, teeth gritted, determined to stick out the meal and get a chance to chat to her sister on her own. But she soon had to admit defeat. There was no way they'd be able to outstay the Hamiltons — David and Richard had gone on to cigars and brandy, as if they were members of the Victorian gentry. So an hour or so later, Louise and Simon managed to excuse themselves, making excuses about her early start.

They were both quiet on the train on the way home. Simon broke the silence when they got back to the flat and were curled up on the sofa with cups of tea.

'Honestly, what ghastly people. If that's what Rachel is aspiring to, then I . . . ' He ran out of words.

'I know. And all that sucking up she and Richard were doing. Eurgh.'

'Still, I wish we'd had a chance to tell her,' Simon said sadly.

'I know. I have to go back home tomorrow morning, and I don't want to leave it till I come back. She has to hear it from me.'

'I know, love. I wish I could do your dirty work for you, but if I tell her, it'll just give her something else to be upset about.'

'I'll ring her tomorrow. No. I'll email her.'

'Email her?'

'I'm a coward. She can't cry at me over email.'

'But she can then ambush you with a phone call.'

'Well, I'll have to deal with that if it happens. Made my bed, lie in it, et cetera, et cetera. I'm going to take flack from a lot of people for this choice; I might as well start now.'

'Oh, sweetheart,' Simon said, hugging her. 'I know I talked you into this. I hope you don't feel . . . '

'Come on. You don't really believe you could talk me into something I didn't want to do?'

'Are you saying you might be a little bit stubborn, sweet sister?'

'Like you're a little bit gay?'

'Fair enough. As long as you're sure.'

Louise grinned at him. 'Do you know what? I know it's mad, but I've never been surer about anything in my life.'

★ ★ ★

The next morning, she caught a 6 a.m. train back to Leeds, and was at her desk by 9 a.m. She had a raft of work emails to deal with, but she decided to get the Rachel one out of the way first, before she lost her nerve.

'Dear Rachel and Richard,' she wrote (she had to; they shared a home email address).

Thank you so much for a lovely lunch yesterday. It was good to meet your friends and the food was wonderful as always.

(That was all very formal and correct, just what Rachel would like. Now how to carry on? How do you take a deep breath in email terms, she wondered? Best just to press on.)

I have some news which I had hoped to share with you yesterday, but as it's a family matter, it didn't seem the right time as you had other guests. I'm pregnant. I was in a relationship that has ended, so I will be raising this baby as a single mother.

(No need to share the details of Brian's marriage, the extreme brevity of their 'relationship' or the fact that he currently had no idea about his impending fatherhood, she decided).

> Simon has been very supportive, and I
> plan to come down to live in London
> before the baby is born.

(And before the pregnancy begins to show and all of Yorkshire is gossiping.)

> I know this must come as a surprise. I
> haven't told anyone else yet as it's early
> days, so please don't spread the word.

She sat staring at the screen for a very long time and tried to think of a way to end the email. 'Be happy for me'? How could Rachel be happy for her? 'I hope you'll enjoy being an aunt?' That just rubbed it in that she wasn't a mum. In the end, she just wrote 'Love, Lou' and hit Send before she could change her mind.

She was madly busy for the next three hours or so, working through all her emails, catching up with her staff and checking paper orders for the magazine print run coming in that afternoon. She spent an hour or two on the shop floor, making sure everything was running as it should, then, as she was starting to feel a bit dizzy, made herself go to the caff opposite and eat a bacon roll.

When she got back to her desk, she saw there was an email from Rachel. She read it, then read it again. She was going to get back on a train, go round to her sister's house and disable the exclamation mark on her keyboard.

Dearest Lou!
OMG!!!!!!!!!!!! I cant believe you got a
BFP!!!!!!! I didnt even know you were
TTC!!!!!! I'm soooooo thrilled for you and
the daddy. Phone me soon!!!!! I want to
hear all about it.
((((((((((((((((hugs))))))))))))))))
Rach

Disable the exclamation mark and possibly the
brackets as well. (What *is* that? A hug? Via
email?)

She read the email again. To be honest, she
didn't understand a word of it. BFP? TTC? What
were these? Political organisations? And what
was the bit about 'you and the daddy'? Clearly
she'd chosen to ignore the information that
Louise was no longer with the father. Rachel
knew not to ring her during the working day
— Louise wouldn't pick up, as she was usually
too busy. But she had no doubt that she'd come
home to two or three messages on her mobile
and a blinking light on the answering machine.

She would have to deal with Rachel later. The
email after it was from Edward, the general
manager. Her new and urgent priority was the
Macintosh report. She had to have it checked,
proofread and off her desk by 2 p.m., or there
would be hell to pay. It was just . . . well, that
tiny little baby, no bigger than a sultana, made
her feel so damned sick every afternoon. Well,
never mind. She'd just have to ignore the nausea.
Work to do. The Macintosh report waits for no
sultana. If only her stomach would stop roiling

34

and filling her mouth with bile, like she was on a rowing boat on the sea. She could not, would not, be sick at work. No way. Too humiliating. Too much of a giveaway. Too late.

She managed to walk rather than run to the Ladies, her lips tightly pursed, and dashed into a cubicle. To her relief, there was no one else there. Her bacon roll came up quickly, followed by a few agonising minutes of dry heaving, through which she prayed that the bathroom would remain empty. Finally, it stopped. She flushed and came out to face her own horrifying reflection: damp hair, smudged mascara, swollen lips . . . and the equally unwelcome vision of Deidre from HR, who peered at her curiously.

'Oooh . . . not well, are we?' Deidre said, in a cutesy, wheedling tone.

'I'm fine,' Louise said briskly, going to the basin and turning on a tap to repair the damage. 'Dodgy bacon roll.'

'From the caff?' Deidre looked horrified. Deidre was not a small girl. The caff was her spiritual home.

'Yes,' Louise said firmly, and, she hoped, finally. She folded a paper towel and wet it, using it to mop up the worst of the panda eyes. She combed her fingers through her hair: it was short and straight, and this temporary repair would have to do. She desperately wanted to rinse out her mouth, but she was damned if she was going to do that with Deidre staring at her. Not one to take a hint, she hadn't moved.

'Can I get you anything, Louise? A glass of water? An antacid?'

(A gun? Louise thought.) 'No thanks, Deidre, I'm fine now. Really. I'd just like a minute . . . '

'Of course,' she said, still not moving. Then Louise caught Deidre's eye in the mirror. It was as if she could see the cogs creaking in Deidre's not-very-bright mind. She could see Deidre adding the vomiting to what she had no doubt heard about Louise's fling with Brian. She saw Deidre glance at her breasts, then look up guiltily and catch her eye again. Then Deidre turned away and went quickly into a toilet cubicle, locking the door behind her.

Louise went back to her desk and sat very still, feeling her heart pounding in her chest. She hadn't imagined the gossip would start so soon. But now she could just see Deidre sitting in the staffroom with her packet of smoky-bacon crisps, whispering to Ethel from Accounts and one or two of the shopfloor boys. It would be a matter of hours before it crossed the branch barrier and someone in Brian's branch, or, God forbid, Head Office, got wind of it. She needed to get out . . . out of Barrett and Humphries, out of Leeds, as quickly as possible.

She thought about ringing Simon in a panic and explaining what had just happened. He'd tell her she was being paranoid, that she was seeing spies round every corner. Deidre couldn't possibly know, and she could speculate all she liked . . . nobody would believe her. She was a notoriously unreliable gossip. And anyway, who was to say Louise wasn't in a relationship with someone else? They didn't know. That's what Simon would say. She took a deep breath. She didn't need to ring him . . . just thinking about speaking to him had calmed her down. It would all be fine.

★ ★ ★

That evening, she got home to a long, breathless message from Rachel on her answering machine. She couldn't face talking to her, so she sent a text saying thanks for the good wishes, but she would be out all evening and couldn't chat. She knew that the following evening was Rachel's yoga night, so she had a day or two's grace.

Work carried on as normal. She kept an eye on Deidre from HR, but she didn't seem to be watching Louise too closely or looking too suspicious. Louise began to relax. She knew that the next step was speaking to Brian. She didn't have the courage to ring or email him and ask to meet. That Friday was the branch managers' meeting. She had decided she would corner him after the meeting and ask to go for a quick coffee. She'd tell him then, with the minimum of fuss. She'd do it in a public place, so he couldn't yell at her, and so she couldn't get over-emotional and cry.

She arrived at Head Office early. She'd dressed carefully in a navy suit that she knew looked good: professional, but not sexy. As she got out of her car, Stephanie, who was the new assistant manager at Brian's branch, pulled into the parking lot. She waved enthusiastically at Louise, who felt obliged to wait, so they could go in together. Stephanie was tall and blonde, with a wide toothy grin and a tendency to talk a lot and very animatedly. She was not the companion Louise would have chosen that morning, but she plastered on a smile and nodded while Stephanie rattled on about the monthly figures and the big contract she and Brian had just signed. Reception soon filled with management from all the branches, and everyone chattered around her. Stephanie went off to talk at someone else, and Louise poured herself a cup of tea and waited in a corner. She saw Brian arrive, and saw him glance at her and frown. He was wearing a crisp, ice-blue shirt and he looked very handsome. She felt a little tug . . . this man was the father of her child. Maybe things would be okay. Maybe he would want to be involved . . . how she couldn't imagine. But maybe they would find a way. She wanted to go to him then. But she hung back.

That was how she saw what she saw. Edward's PA opened the doors of the conference room and they all began to file in. Brian and Stephanie walked in together and Louise was just a few steps behind. As they got to the doorway, she saw Brian reach out and slide a finger inside the cuff of Stephanie's jacket and stroke her wrist.

Louise stopped dead. She felt like someone had punched her in the stomach. Someone behind her bumped into her, and there was a flurry of apologies and laughter which carried her into the meeting, Somehow, she didn't know how, she made it through the meeting and even gave her report in an even, clear voice. As soon as they finished, she made an excuse about an urgent phone call, ran to her car and sped away.

As soon as she got back to her branch, she shut her office door, then opened the filing cabinet. She had her employment contract on file, and she took it out to go through it carefully. She was enormously relieved to see that her notice period was only a calendar month. The contract did include a restraint of trade, but that only stipulated she couldn't work for another printing business within a fifty-mile radius of Leeds for the next year. She'd be able to get a job in London, if anyone was mad enough to take on a pregnant single parent.

Well, sooner rather than later, she said to herself. She pulled the computer keyboard closer and began to type:

Dear Edward,
It is with great regret that I tender my res-ignation with immediate effect . . .

She put in some gumph about a change in family circumstances and the need to be in London — that was roughly true — the baby was her family, after all — and signed off saying how much she'd enjoyed working at Barrett and Humphries. That was entirely true. She'd loved the challenges of her job: climbing the ladder, getting her own branch to run, making it one of the most successful in the group. She would miss it, and she would miss her staff, even tiresome Deidre from HR. No time for sentimentality, though. She printed the letter, signed it and popped it in an envelope. She'd drop it off at

Head Office on her way home. Once the envelope was sealed, she felt an odd sense of relief, as if the plan was now in motion.

She knew Edward wouldn't just accept her resignation, so she was prepared for the call she received at home as soon as she got in that evening. She'd worked out a list of things to say: yes, her family definitely needed her. No, she couldn't be persuaded to stay. No, it had nothing to do with dissatisfaction, she was very happy in her job. No, more money would not make her change her mind. Edward paused, and she could practically hear him arguing silently with himself before he finally, hesitantly said, 'It's not . . . a man, is it, Lou?'

'Definitely not,' she said, keeping her voice steady. She had no idea what gossip Edward might have heard, but the less she said, the less she could incriminate herself.

'Good,' said Edward, sounding relieved. He wasn't one to pry about emotional issues, so she knew he'd rather not have asked the question at all. He certainly wasn't going to pursue the matter. 'Well, Louise,' he said seriously, 'I really am gutted to see you go. Truly I am. If there's anything I can do . . . you know . . . to help you find your feet down south, just let me know.'

'Thanks, Edward,' Louise said, genuinely moved. She hadn't expected that. 'Well, if you do hear of anyone looking to hire someone, let me know. My . . . er . . . family commitments will be quite heavy, so I'll be looking to work predictable hours, not too much travel, that sort of thing.'

'I'll keep an ear to the ground,' Edward

promised, and rang off.

So this was it. A month from now, she'd be heading for London . . . jobless, homeless and pregnant. She felt so, so afraid, and suddenly, irrationally, she wished Brian was there. She wished he wasn't a faithless, immoral slug of a man, but instead was single, sexy and desperately in love with her. And she wished, more than anything, that she could share this life-changing experience with the father of her child. And then she began to cry.

Edward had rung the minute she walked through the door, and now, through the tears, she noticed that her answering machine was blinking away like mad. Rachel. She'd put her sister off for days and days, but she had to face up to it and speak to her. Not quite yet, though. She sniffed and looked around for a tissue to wipe her eyes and blow her nose. But before she could find one, the phone rang again. And as soon as she picked it up, Rachel began talking.

'Oh my goodness! I couldn't believe it when I opened the email with your amazing news! That's just brilliant. You must be so excited. Have you decided where the baby will be born? Have you made any antenatal appointments yet? I'm really happy to come up to Leeds and go along with you. Wait till you have the first scan, it's so amazing to see your little darling on the screen . . . '

Rachel drew breath and Louise took the opportunity and cut in.

'Slow down! I haven't had any appointments yet, and I'm coming down to London in four weeks, so I'll register with a doctor and organise everything then.'

'Oh my God, are you crying?'

'No.'

'Lou, I've been your sister for thirty-four years. I know what your voice sounds like when you're crying. What's happened? You're not spotting, are you?'

'I'm fine, just a bit tired, that's all. Listen, Rach, this isn't a great time . . . '

Louise felt instantly guilty. She was always busy when Rachel rang, it was never a good time, she always said she'd ring her straight back, and she almost never did. Rachel was obviously thinking of making a fuss, but she thought better of it. If Louise was pregnant and emotional, she'd go easy on her. She was clearly trying to sound smiley, easy and encouraging.

'I know, I know . . . you're busy. Just tell me the basics and I'll let you go.'

'I'm pregnant, that's as much as I know.'

'How many weeks?'

'Nine, now, I think.'

'You think? Are you not sure? When was your last period? Are you still so regular? Because it can make a difference to your due date, you know, if your cycle is shorter or longer.'

Louise felt stretched to the limit. She didn't want to have a girly chat with her sister. She was tired and anxious and over-emotional, and she needed to absorb what she'd seen in the meeting-room doorway that morning. But Rachel was trying so hard, and this must be so difficult for her. She shouldn't be mean. She really shouldn't. She'd just have to bite the bullet and answer the question she knew was coming.

'And . . . the daddy?'

'We're not together, Rach.'

'So you said in your email . . . but what does he think?'

'About what?'

'About being a dad? About your moving away? How will he have access? Have you made maintenance arrangements? I've heard the Child Support Agency is much better now at chasing deadbeat dads.'

'Rachel . . . I . . . ' Oh boy. She really, really hadn't wanted to get into this. But unless she was going to come up with a pack of lies that she'd have to remember, it was probably easiest just to tell the truth.

'I haven't made any arrangements because I'm not sure I'm going to tell him. That's one of the reasons I'm coming down to London. We broke up, there's no future. He probably never needs to know.'

'Louise! You can't do that! What about when your baby's a teenager and wants to go looking for his or her dad. What will happen then?'

'Well, then . . . I don't know.'

Rachel was talking again, very fast and in a very shrill voice, but Louise couldn't listen to her. Not any more. Not right now. She cut her off mid-flow. 'This is very early days, Rach. I still have a lot of stuff to work out. I know that. Please stop bombarding me with questions, okay?'

'I'm not bombarding you, I'm only trying to — '

'I know, I know! Okay? Can you just give me a bit of time? A few days to sort my head out. And then I'll try and have answers to some of your very valid questions.'

'All right,' said Rachel, slightly soothed. 'I'm just going to ask one more question.'

Louise sighed. 'What?'

'Are you taking folic acid?'

'Folic what?'

'You need to be taking folic acid to stop your baby getting spina bifida. And at your age, you need to find out if they do the triple test in your area or if you need to go private.'

'The what? Triple test? Stop talking medical talk at me!'

'I have to! There's stuff you need to know and be thinking about right now. There's no time to waste. Your baby's in its most critical stage of development right as we speak. Listen. I'm emailing you the address of a website. It's got everything you need to know . . . and also a great forum section if you want to chat to other mums online.'

'I'm not really one for online chat . . . '

'Whatever. Don't use that part if you don't want to. But there's loads of information that you might find useful. Trust me. I'm going now. Love you, okay?'

And Rachel was gone.

Toni

It was a normal Friday evening in. James watched the footie with his feet up on the coffee table. I'd sat at the dining-room table with my laptop. We didn't chat much; we often don't in the evening. But it was comfortable and nice. Then the match finished, and James stood up and stretched.

'Coming to bed then?' he said.

'Um . . . not right now. I'll be there in a bit.'

He came to peer over my shoulder. 'What are you doing?'

'Oh . . . just chatting,' I said, minimising the window on my laptop.

'Sexy chat?'

'Don't be silly. It's, um . . . it's just a work thing. I won't be long.'

He kissed the top of my head and headed for the bedroom.

Well, I just lied to my husband on two counts. What I'm doing is definitely not for work, and in some ways, I suppose you could say it *is* sexy chat. Except on the site I'm chatting on, it's called BD or DTD. And for your information those aren't acronyms for something really kinky and illegal. Confused? Me too. Let's go back a step, shall we? To this afternoon.

This afternoon, I had to go to the gynaecologist. You see, I've been having some issues with my periods. I know what you're thinking . . . three paragraphs in and already we're in the area of Way Too Much Information. I've just always had really irregular periods . . . sometimes two in a month, then nothing for three months. It's been going on for years, really, and I didn't do anything about it for ages. But eventually I went to the doctor, who referred me for tests and scans and blah, blah, blah, all of which led to me sitting opposite this gynaecologist who looked worryingly rather like my dad.

He looked at the pages on the desk in front of him for a really long time, and then he looked up at me, over the top of his specs. 'I'm afraid the news is not too good, Antonia,' he said seriously. Wow . . . really like my dad after I'd had a less-than-excellent school report. He'd full-named me and everything. Everyone except my parents has always called me Toni. 'Not good?' I said, and my voice sounded a bit high and squeaky.

'No, Antonia, not good at all,' he said, and looked down at his notes again. The man was definitely a fan of the extended dramatic pause. He looked at me again.

'You have primary ovarian insufficiency, Antonia,' he said, and instead of hearing what he was saying, I found myself wishing he'd stop using my name in that slightly condescending way. He paused again, and I realised I was supposed to say something. All I could manage was, 'So?' Not very articulate. But there you are. Not so good under pressure, me.

'It's not going to get any better,' he continued. 'You're likely to experience menopausal symptoms within the next few years, and those may be

46

quite severe. Your fertility is already significantly compromised, and every year that passes, that's going to decrease.'

Whoa. My fertility? I'd come to see him because I was sick of never knowing when I was going to come on. Fertility? That was a problem for women in their forties. Not women like me. Who on earth would start going on about fertility? Well, actually Dr Dad did. And he was still talking about it and I'd missed something crucial. What was he saying?

' . . . would suggest you get on with it.'

Now I'd missed the important bit because I hadn't been listening. 'I'm sorry?' I peeped.

He frowned at me. He'd obviously run out of time and decided to skip the pauses and cut to the chase. 'I see from your notes that you're married. If you're planning on having children, I'd say you should do it sooner rather than later. Within the year, if possible. Before it's too late.'

Well, I heard that. I thanked Dr Dad and headed back to the office. I had a busy afternoon ahead . . . a press release to write, three meetings and a conference call with Seattle. I didn't ring James and tell him. He'd known I was going to the doctor, but I hadn't gone into detail about why. To be honest, I wasn't ready to tell him what I'd just heard. I needed to get my head around it. Children within the year? Wow.

Were we planning on having children? Well, of course. Dr Dad was right, we are married, but we're still pretty young. I'm twenty-six and James is twenty-eight. Most of our friends, the ones who are in relationships, are just starting to move in together, and none of them have kids. We'd agreed when we got engaged that we wanted a family one day . . . but that was very much the point. One day. A lot was going to happen before that. I wanted to move ahead in my career. James was aiming to be a senior designer or junior creative director within a few years. We were still toying with the idea of a year out to travel. And of course we'd have to scramble a few rungs up the property ladder from our tiny little house in a not very posh bit of Surrey before we started popping sprogs. 'One day' was eight, maybe ten years into the future. Not this year. Not now.

So back to this evening. James had gone to bed, and I was sat digging around on the net. Primary ovarian insufficiency. 485,000 hits on Google. Endless websites listing the symptoms and causes. Well, from the sounds of it, Dr Dad was right. It seemed I was in the minority of women with this ovarian-insufficiency thing to have any eggs at all, and they were going off as I sat there.

That morning, before I'd gone to the doctor, if you'd asked me what I really wanted, I would probably have said a skinny latte. A new handbag. A holiday in Greece. More sleep. Slimmer ankles. Now, all I could think about was the baby I was probably never going to have. And I wanted it. So, so badly. More than anything I've ever wanted in the world.

I wasn't tired. I was wide awake, and I didn't want to go and lie in bed next to James, because I knew I'd end up waking him up and telling him the whole story and I needed to think about it a bit more on my own first. So I carried on surfing the net. I started looking for a website for women like me. Women who might be thinking about maybe getting pregnant, sometime soon, maybe. If they could.

I'd had enough medical information, so I skipped all the NHS fact-based ones, and googled 'baby'. Not very clever, but it seemed to work. There seemed to be thousands of sites. I picked the first one that came up. There were frankly baffling numbers of articles about everything to do with making babies, being pregnant, looking after babies . . . and then a huge forum section with thousands of women talking about these things in great and lurid detail, using all sorts of confusing terms and initials.

There were hundreds of groups and threads, and I dug around a bit and settled on one called 'TTC'. That's trying to conceive, for the uninitiated, which is what I would have been if they hadn't explained it in brackets after the acronym. It took me a few goes to work out that DTD means Doing the Deed, which I know is how babies are made, but BD took a bit longer. Then someone spelled it out . . . 'Babydancing.' Ah. Cute. Well, that made me feel a bit sick. Then there were all kinds of complicated explanations to do with taking your temperature and working out calendars of ovulation, and then highly technical discussions about fertility drugs. It was making my head swim. It seemed as if you needed a PhD in science to do this baby-making

49

thing. How can that be? There are billions of people in the world. They were all babies once. It just can't be that hard to make one. And let's face it, for at least two girls in my year at school, it wasn't difficult at all . . . they managed to do it, even though they couldn't do Maths or Science for toffee.

But if Dr Dad is right, it's going to be very difficult for James and me. My dried-out, old-raisin ovaries were well on their way to their sell-by date and if we didn't BD with all speed, we'd end up one of those old childless couples who have allotments or collect china dogs.

I turned off my laptop and crept upstairs. I peeked into our bedroom, and James was fast asleep, starfished across the whole bed. I stood and watched him for a bit. He was so handsome, even when he was asleep. Sometimes, when we meet in town, and I'm waiting for him in a station or restaurant and he walks in, I find myself thinking 'Wow! What a foxy bloke!' in the instant before I recognise him.

I went into the bathroom, showered quickly and brushed my teeth, then crept into bed next to James. He didn't wake up when I got in, but instinctively turned over and curled around me in our normal sleeping position. James' arms always make me feel safe. For the first time since I left the doctor's office, I felt like things might just be okay. Maybe you're wondering about James and me. I mean . . . he really is fit, and I'm, well, I suppose I'm okay-looking, but I don't stop traffic. I'm short and blonde, tending towards the curvy if I don't keep an eye on my weight. I've been told I'm cute and bubbly, and I know I have okay skin and big green eyes. I'd much rather be statuesque and sexy, but there you are. You get what you're given. James on the other hand, is a grade-A hunk. We've been married for a year and a half, together for four years.

We met at work — we'd both been hired as interns by a big advertising firm, straight out of uni. It was James, me and four other people of the same age. We were going to be working all the hours that God gave for Tube fares and lunch money, and we were supposed to count ourselves super-lucky. We all met up sitting in the all-white lobby of the agency. There were two other girls, and by the time I got there they were sitting either side of James, talking really quickly over one another, trying to impress him. He was leaning right back, his arms folded over his chest. He had curly blond hair, cut very short, and a face that looked like it had been carved out of marble. Really. I know that sounds like something out of a Mills & Boon, but it's true. He's stunning. But I was in my surly, intellectual, I-hate-everything-anyone-else-likes phase, so I immediately decided I wasn't impressed by him. Urgh, I told myself. One of those vain guys who thinks he's God's gift.

Then he caught my eye, and did a comedy one-two sideways glance at the girls either side of him. One was flicking her hair like a mad thing, and the other had surreptitiously undone another button on her top. He smiled a bit, and then, and I'm not kidding, he winked at me!

Honestly, I think my mouth fell open a bit. No one our age winks. It's something my grandpa did, or sleazy blokes in *Carry On* films. But James winked at me. He still does it, and I have to say, four years later, I still find it funny, but in a really endearing way. It's like his way of saying 'inasmuch', and the way he watches *Springwatch* every year. Under his cool, well-dressed exterior, despite the fact that he's a brilliant graphic designer, and even though he's into really good music, he's a tiny, weeny bit geeky and middle-aged.

Back to that day four years ago. I decided then and there I wasn't going to fancy him. He was too cool. Too handsome by far. And he winked. Anyway, I had a boyfriend.

I was still going out with my uni boyfriend, Gavin. We'd lived together in a shared house when we were at university, and I thought we'd find a place together in London as soon as we could afford it. But in the meantime, he'd moved back in with his mum. As she did all his washing and cooked three meals a day for him, he was in no hurry to go anywhere. Gavin thought I was a mug for doing an unpaid internship. His employment strategy involved sitting on the sofa watching *Murder She Wrote*, playing computer games and hoping someone would miraculously offer him a job he couldn't be arsed to apply for. To be honest, by the time I met James, I think I was already going off Gavin a bit, but I was never going to admit that to anyone, let alone myself.

I got to like James a lot in the three months of our internship. He'd studied graphic design and he was good. He worked very hard and did a lot of extra hours. It was soon clear he was the most talented of all the interns, but he was never pushy and know-it-all about it. I was trying to be a copywriter, and while I really enjoyed my time there, I wasn't much good at it. Copywriters have to be able to write devastatingly clever things in three words, and I'm not very concise. I ramble on a bit, to be fair. You might have noticed. I put the experience to good use though . . . the agency name looked great on my CV. I went on to do a short course in PR and press liaison and then got a job as a junior at an international PR firm . . . and I'm still there, although I'm a few rungs up the ladder now.

I digress. Anyway, we finished the three-month internship, and on the last day, they offered James a junior designer's position. It so happened that my birthday was the same week, so we all went out for drinks to celebrate the triple: me turning twenty-two, the end of our time together and James' job offer. Because of my birthday, Gavin grudgingly said he would come out with my work friends for the first time. He came to join us in the pub in Holborn. Typically, he was very late, so we were all a few drinks down already, and chattering away.

Gavin had the sulks from the moment he arrived. He barely spoke to me at all and didn't speak to anyone else. He just sat in the corner, frowning into his pint, then got up suddenly and left without saying goodbye. I chased after him, and caught him outside Holborn Station. 'What's the matter with you?' I demanded.

'What's the matter with me?' he yelled. 'What's the matter with you? Simpering away at that bloke who thinks he's God's gift, giggling about straplines. You're such a cliché. You're not the girl I fell in love with.' And with that, he stormed off through the barriers into the station.

I was just speechless. There was so much wrong with everything he'd said. Firstly, 'You're not the girl I fell in love with' is such a fucking cliché. And if we were lobbing accusations about clichés around, what about him? Lolling on the sofa, thinking the world owed him a living because he had a 2:1 in Politics. Well, that's what I would have said if he'd stuck around to hear me rant. Secondly, James doesn't think he's God's gift . . . (although I conveniently forgot that it's *exactly* what I'd thought when I first met James). And lastly . . . lastly I don't *simper*!

I poured all this out to James when I got to the pub, between viciously necking glasses of wine. I was so furious. I'd had such a great day, and before Gavin arrived like the ghost at the feast, I'd been having a great time in the pub. I paused to draw breath, and was about to have another huge gulp of pub Chardonnay. Suddenly, James put his hand on my wrist.

'Toni, I'm going to ask you three questions, and you have to promise you'll answer them completely honestly.'

'What is this, like Truth or Dare?'

'I'm serious. Completely honestly.'

'Okay.'

'Promise?'

'Promise.'

'Question One. What is your dream?'

'Just one?'

'As many as you like.'

'To write. To travel. To make a difference. God, I sound like a Miss-World contestant. I don't know. I'm only twenty-two. I want a life that's extraordinary, and I want to share it with someone who feels the same.' Bear in mind I was quite spectacularly drunk by then. There was probably quite a lot of wild hair and arm-waving that went with that little speech.

'Question Two. Is that someone Gavin?'

'Yes. No. It was once. Probably not any more. No. It's definitely not.' That was quite a scary thought, and for a moment, I thought I might cry. I put my glass down. 'Excuse me,' I said unsteadily, and went to the toilet. I washed my face, combed my hair and put some lipstick on. I don't know many crises that aren't made better by combing your hair and putting some lipstick on. So I didn't love Gavin any more. After three years together, that was huge. Gavin was my most serious, well, to be honest, my *only* serious relationship. What would happen if we broke up?

I didn't want to think about the implications of that. It was just too scary. So I did what any right-thinking girl would do. I went back out into the pub, bought two flaming sambucas, drank one, gave one to James and asked him to take me home with him.

When we woke up the next morning, I expected to feel terrible . . . awkward with James, ashamed of myself, awful about cheating on Gavin. But to my surprise, I felt quietly happy.

55

James seemed pretty happy too . . . in fact he was happy twice more that morning. Later, as we sat eating toast in his kitchen, I remembered.

'You never asked me Question Three.'

'No, I never did.'

'What was it?'

'I'm not saying.'

'Come on!'

'No . . . It would have been okay in the pub when we were both pissed. But now it'll just sound cheesy.'

'I don't mind cheesy. In fact I love cheesy. I've got cheese on my toast. See?'

That made him laugh, but then his face went serious again. 'I'm not going to ask you now. But I will ask you Question Three one day. I promise.'

Two years later, on my twenty-fourth birthday, he handed me a beautiful dark blue box that he'd designed and made himself, with the words 'Question Three' printed on the lid. Inside was an antique sapphire ring. When I'd stopped crying and said yes, I said to him, 'You were never going to ask me that in the pub all that time ago. You hardly knew me.'

'I know. It was mad. You would have thought I was a psycho or it was a line. But I kind of knew, even then, that this was forever.'

Soppy, I know. But that's James. And I think I'm bloody lucky to have him.

★ ★ ★

We woke up late on the Saturday morning, made love, went back to sleep, and then woke up and went for brunch at our favourite Italian coffee shop. I put all the thoughts about my doctor's appointment to the back of my mind, and concentrated on enjoying a romantic morning with my lovely husband. James bought the papers and we split them between us, reading slowly, sipping our coffees and nibbling on almond croissants.

Two tables away, there was a couple with a baby and a little boy of about three. The baby was sitting in a high-chair and the dad was spooning some neon gloop into its mouth. Its face was covered in the orange stuff. The little boy had a toy car, which he kept bashing really loudly on the table. The mum was trying to get him to eat some toast, but he just kept pushing her hand away. She looked like she hadn't slept in weeks. She definitely hadn't brushed her hair and she had a biscuit-coloured handprint on the back of her shoulder. Worst of all, she and the dad hadn't said a word to each other for the whole meal. It was like they operated next to each other, but not with each other, if that makes sense. I couldn't stop watching them.

Then the little boy got up a really good head of steam with the car-on-the-table bashing, and James sighed. He turned around and glared at the family, then snapped his newspaper like a grumpy old man and turned away again. Well, that was all it took. I burst into tears. Now I have to admit I am a bit of a cryer . . . by that, I mean I snuffle and tear up when I watch the proposal episode of Friends (every time), and I need to take tissues when we go to a wedding. But I don't think James has ever seen me sob uncontrollably before. He looked very alarmed indeed. He immediately put his paper down and came to sit beside me on the banquette.

The whole story poured out, about the doctor and my rubbish ovaries, and how we had to have a baby right away but I didn't want to end up not brushing my hair. Admittedly, it was a bit of a muddle and it took about fifteen minutes of patient questioning from James before he'd got all the facts straight. Once he understood, he nodded, motioned to the waitress and ordered us more coffee. Then he took my hand in his and he said, 'Okay.'

'Okay? Okay what?'

'Okay, let's start trying. We know we want kids, and if it's going to take time, we'd better get cracking. We might do things in a different order, but it doesn't mean we can't still do all the things we dreamed of. We'll just take our baby backpacking round Thailand with us. In fact, the baby can go in the backpack! It's all very convenient.'

I managed a sniffly laugh, and hugged him. James always managed to make the most complicated things simple.

The idea of trying for a baby seemed a bit odd . . . I mean, James and I have always had a lot of sex anyway (yes, yes I know . . . too much info again). So, really, all that happened was we stopped using condoms. We agreed that we'd just carry on as normal for the first year, and see what happened. After that we'd start taking temperatures and things and consider fertility drugs. We both imagined it would be a good two or three years before I got pregnant.

James and I had agreed not to tell our families or friends that we were trying, or that we were expecting problems. 'We've got quite enough pressure as it is,' James said. 'I don't need your dad coming round asking if we're shagging often enough.'

I laughed at that . . . the idea of my conservative, north-London-dwelling, professor father saying 'shagging' was too silly for words.

I felt bad not telling my close friends. I have two best mates. Robyn and I made friends at nursery, and we went the whole way through school together. She works in travel now, and she's a bit of a hellraiser: she's always off on some jaunt across the world, bungee-jumping or skiing or white-water something-or-other. And my goodness, she can drink! Even James is a bit scared of Rob when she's on a Friday-night mission. Then there's Caroline: we met at uni and she's twenty-six going on forty-five. She's got much further in her career than I have: she's the head of PR for some mega investment bank in the City and she's always on her BlackBerry dealing with the *FT*, and averting huge PR disasters. Fashion is her thing, and she has items of clothing that cost more than our sofa. Rob and Caro both love James, and they were very happy when we got married (and, I might say, the best bridesmaids you could imagine . . . my hen-do . . . *wow!* But that's another story). But still, kids are definitely not on the radar right now for either of them.

Caro has a boyfriend . . . Piers. He's a banker (naturally), but they seem to communicate electronically mostly.

They're certainly nowhere near moving in together, let alone getting married or having kids. She hates them anyway. I can just imagine Caro's 'I smell dog-poo' face if I told her I was trying to have a baby. When we go out, she always sighs and growls if there are kids around. James calls her 'Herod' because she wants to kill all the children.

And Rob, well, Rob is too busy having fun and shagging her way alphabetically through the nationalities. There's no time for kids right now in Robyn-world. Kids would get in the way of extreme sports, and they'd need to go to bed when she was trying to drink tequila shots off a salsa dancer called Paulo. She's always said she wants them one day, but for her I think one day is ten years or maybe more in the future. She'd fall over in shock if I told her we were trying for a baby now. James was right. I'd tell them when, and if . . . there was something to tell. Not before.

It wasn't like I didn't have support . . . I kept visiting the baby website, and reading the threads about trying to conceive. I didn't post . . . I didn't have a story to tell yet, and I had so much to learn. There were lots of women who'd been trying for five years and more. Lots of them were on fertility drugs, had undergone IVF, or had had miscarriages. It was a bit like having a thousand really close friends . . . I got to know the names of many of the regular posters, and they'd let us know when they were expecting their period to start. Together, we'd count the days, and if they didn't come on when they expected, they'd start wondering whether they should take a test. Every now and then, someone would excitedly post that they'd had a BFP (it took me ages to work out that this meant Big Fat Positive), and there'd be hundreds of congratulatory messages. The women who managed that then left the TTC group and went to join a group with other women whose babies would be due in the same month as theirs. It was like a graduation.

I found myself logging on every evening at home, then, when I got more involved, I'd log on at lunchtime at work too. I lived through a rollercoaster with Pink–Girl32, who'd been trying for a year. She was about to start fertility drugs, but then out of the blue had a BFP. We wished her well, and she went off to join a birth group, but a few days later she was back, having had an early miscarriage. The doctor had advised her and her partner to try again immediately, and that's what they planned to do. Then I picked up on the story of Curvy–Sue and her husband, who had finally saved enough for their first round of IVF. Everyone in the group had gone through the drugs and the egg harvesting with her. I first read one of her posts the day after she had had her embryos implanted. I read back through the threads she'd posted on, and found myself totally invested in her story. Along with everyone else, I counted the days until she could do a test, then cheered for her when one of the embryos stuck. I had all this ahead of me, and I felt happy that these women, or others like them, would be there to support me when the time came.

I didn't even notice that I'd missed a period. Well, strictly speaking, I hadn't . . . I only have about six a year. That's one of the symptoms that sent me to the doctor in the first place, so it didn't occur to me to count the days of my cycle like the other woman in the TTC group did. Also, it was Christmas . . . we were dashing out to parties and going down to Sussex to spend time with James' mum, then dashing to Hendon to see my dad. We were having sex a lot, but I certainly wasn't thinking . . . well, anything really. The first thing I noticed was that my breasts were really sore. I was in the shower, and they felt lumpy and hot and incredibly tender. I decided that it was because my period was coming, making my hormones go all funny. Two days later, I woke up and went into the kitchen. James had brewed a pot of coffee.

'Want some?' he said.

'Yes please,' I yawned. But when he put the cup in front of me, it smelled vile. 'Eurgh,' I said. 'Is this a new brand of coffee?'

'No, it's the same one we always buy.'

'It smells disgusting!'

James sniffed my cup. 'Smells normal to me.'

I poured it down the sink and made myself tea instead. Later, on the Tube, I found myself noticing other smells. The perfume of the woman next to me was overpowering. A guy standing up near us reeked of cigarettes. Out on the street, near my office, I was hit by the diesel reek of a passing bus.

I got to work and had to rush to the loo to pee. That'd be that big mug of tea I drank. But by 11 a.m., I was off to the bathroom for the third time. Angela, who sits at the desk next to mine, never misses anything. She notices if I buy a new skirt, or wear my hair slightly differently. I promise you, she has no life. She couldn't resist commenting. 'Off to the loo again? Upset tummy, is it? Or cystitis?' She has no understanding of boundaries either.

'No, I just seem to be peeing a lot today.'

'Oooh!' she shrilled. 'Maybe you're in the club!'

'Yeah, right,' I laughed, and headed for the Ladies.

As I sat on the loo, I thought about it. What a ridiculous thought. I couldn't be. We'd only been trying for a few weeks. I had shrivelled-up old-woman ovaries. But I was showing a lot of symptoms . . . No. That's ridiculous. It couldn't possibly be.

But the idea wouldn't go away, and at lunchtime I found myself wandering around Boots, and, accidentally on purpose, ended up in the pregnancy-test section. There was quite a selection, so I ended up buying three different types: a double pack of the Boots own-brand cheap ones, and two different digital ones that flashed up how many weeks you were in a little window. I wouldn't use any of them now, of course, but I might as well have them for a few months' time.

I left them in my handbag and tried not to think about it. I had a busy afternoon at work and a lovely, peaceful evening at home with James. But the next morning, I woke up half an hour before the alarm and lay in bed, thinking. There was no harm in trying . . . I mean . . . it would be an experience. Like most women, I've had the odd scare, but I'd never done a pregnancy test I actually wanted to be positive. I got up quietly, fetched the Boots bag from my handbag in the living room and went to the bathroom. I opened one of the cheaper tests and read the instructions. It wasn't rocket science . . . pee on the end of the stick and wait two minutes. If the test was negative, one line would come up in the window. If it was positive, two lines would form a cross.

I sat on the toilet and did the necessary. I knew it would take two minutes to register, but I looked at the test to see I'd peed on the right bit, as it were. In the window, I could see a faint blue cross. That couldn't be right. I hadn't waited the two minutes yet. It must be faulty. I put the test down and read through all the instructions again. It didn't say anything about a cross coming up immediately. By then, two minutes had passed and I looked at it again. The cross was now properly dark blue. I couldn't believe it. I sat there for quite some time. The cross had come up so quickly, it must be a mistake. There must be something wrong with the test, or I had done something wrong. I would have to do another test, but unfortunately, I was all out of pee to do it with.

I went to the kitchen and made myself an enormous mug of tea. Could I be? It seemed unbelievable. From what the doctor had said, it was a total long shot that I would ever get pregnant. It was supposed to take years, if we ever managed it at all. It must be the cheap pregnancy test. It had to be faulty.

Halfway down the cup of tea, I needed to pee again. This time, I used one of the digital tests, and it took an excruciating three minutes before it popped up a result. 'Pregnant', it announced emphatically, then helpfully added 'Two-three weeks'.

As I sat on the loo, speechless with disbelief, I heard the alarm go off in the bedroom and James groan and roll over to my side of the bed to switch it off. He got up and shuffled into the kitchen. There was no point in speaking to him before he'd had his first cup of coffee. He wouldn't be able to tell me his own name before that, let alone deal with my startling bombshell. I decided to have a shower. I wasn't avoiding the issue, just giving James a bit of time to wake up.

I showered, washed my hair, shaved my legs, moisturised all over and plucked a few stray hairs out of my eyebrows. I wanted to be ready. Then I made a dash into the bedroom to get dressed. Well, I didn't want to tell James wearing just a dressing gown. But what do you wear to tell your husband you're pregnant? I was standing in front of the wardrobe in my underwear, trying to choose a dress, when I heard James go into the bathroom. The bathroom, where two positive pregnancy tests were lined up on the countertop next to the sink.

'James!' I yelled, and ran through to the bathroom. I pounded on the door. 'Come out! I need to . . . ' I hadn't thought this through. What could I possibly need to do so urgently? I'd just come out of there. 'Come out!' I yelled again in desperation.

James opened the door slowly. He had the digital test in his hand. He didn't say anything. I stood looking at him, dressed only in pants and a bra, my wet hair dripping down my back.

'I was going to tell you . . . ' I stuttered.

Eventually he spoke. 'But we only just . . . '

'I know.'

'And I thought you couldn't . . . '

'Me too.'

'But I don't understand how . . . '

'Me neither.'

He looked at the test again.

'Fuck me.'

And, predictably, I burst into tears.

We didn't really have time to talk about it. We both had to get to work. I calmed down and dried my hair and managed to get dressed and organised and ready to leave. James kissed me and hugged me hard before he dashed off to the bus stop. He hesitated in the doorway and then said, 'I love you, okay? This is huge, but we'll work it out.'

That made me feel a bit better, but in another way, it made me feel worse. It was huge, but what was there to work out? We'd set out to get me pregnant, and I was. Granted, we'd banked on two years and it had taken two weeks, but this was the desired outcome, wasn't it?

I went to work, but it would be a lie to say I worked. My boss was out at a meeting all day, and I didn't have anything too urgent to do, so I spent most of the morning on the baby website, reading stories of women trying to do what I'd done, against all the odds, more or less by mistake. I'd never posted, in fact I'd never signed up or given myself an online alias. At about midday on a whim I registered on the forum, giving myself the username PR–Girl. Hesitantly, I started a thread headed 'Unexpected BFP'.

Hi,
I've been a lurker here for a while, never posted before. I'm twenty-six and I was diagnosed with POI a few weeks ago.

(I didn't need to spell out what that was . . . there were loads of other women who had it and the women who spent their time in that group were versed in every pregnancy-related acronym under the sun).

This morning, I did a test, and it seems I have a BFP. This is the last thing we expected . . . we thought it would take years, if ever. I'm excited, but so, so scared.

I didn't know what else to say. In fact, I wasn't sure why I had posted at all. I pushed my chair back and sighed loudly. When I looked up, Angela was staring at me. Sometimes, she gave me the creeps . . . it was like she was watching me like a spy. Didn't she have work to do, for God's sake? You might think I had work to do, but there was no hope of that, not that day. I thought for a minute longer, then I sent a quick text to James. 'Lunch? Tx.'

My office was in Holborn and James' office was a ten-minute walk away in Covent Garden. We didn't often get a chance to have lunch together: he'd have to work through, and I was frequently out of the office or lunching with clients. He fired back a text within two minutes. 'Sure. Jack's at 1? Jx.'

For the first time that morning, the tumble-dryer that had been churning in my stomach stopped moving. I'd go and have lunch with my husband. We'd make sense of this together and everything would be okay.

I got to the sandwich shop ahead of James and grabbed our usual table in the back corner. Jack, who knew us well, brought me a tuna-and-salad on wholewheat and a cheese-and-pickle on white for James, without being asked. The smell of my sandwich made me want to heave, but I was really hungry, so I switched sandwiches. James would have to eat the tuna one and like it.

James rushed in fifteen minutes late, dropped a kiss on the top of my head and slid into the chair opposite me. 'I'm starving,' he said, grabbed the sandwich and took a huge bite. His eyes widened. 'Yuck! This is yours,' he said, and pushed the plate across the table towards me.

'I swapped. Sorry, didn't get a chance to tell you. I can't eat the tuna. It smells awful to me.'

He looked put out. 'Well, thanks for telling

me.' He looked at his watch. 'Shit. I've only got a few minutes. I haven't got time to get Jack to make another.' He started eating the sandwich in big bites. I was a bit surprised about the 'only got a few minutes'. He'd been fifteen minutes late to meet me after all. It seemed if we were going to talk, we'd have to talk quickly.

'So, how are you feeling?' I said tentatively.

'Oh, it's been a mad busy morning. A new brief came through — a billboard for a deodorant campaign. Ed and I have till four o'clock to scamp up three concepts.'

'I meant about . . .'

'Oh.' He took another huge bite. 'I don't know, Tones. I mean . . . I'm a bit in shock, I suppose.'

'In shock?' I felt a knot in my stomach. That wasn't the response I was hoping for. Joy, yes. Excitement, definitely. But shock? Shock sounded not good at all.

'Well, I mean, it kind of changes everything doesn't it?'

That sounded a bit better. It did change everything. I had a million thoughts I wanted to share. After all, there'd be a new person in our relationship . . . we'd be a family now. We could have the baby in our little house for six months or a year or so, but after that he or she would need their own room. We'd have to think about buying a bigger house . . . if we'd conceived one so easily, could we think about having more than one child after all? I was about to start sharing some of this, but James was still talking.

'I mean, we've got that snowboarding trip

69

booked for April. I suppose you won't be able to go now.'

There was so much wrong with what he'd just said, I didn't know where to begin.

I ended up just saying, 'Snowboarding?'

'Yeah, I mean, I've been really busy this morning so I haven't had a chance to check the terms and conditions of the trip. Maybe someone else could have your air ticket, if the name change isn't too expensive. Alex — or Dave, maybe. He was keen to go.'

I was really, really tired of bursting into tears in front of my husband. It would have been just too pathetic to do it again, so I just got up and left. I heard him say 'Tones . . . ' in an exasperated voice as I walked out of the door, but I just put my head down and kept walking. I knew he wouldn't follow me. He was too busy. He had scamps to produce and an air ticket to Andorra to auction.

When I got back to the office, it was a ghost town. Everyone was out for lunch. Even Angela had wandered out into the watery winter sunshine to stalk another one of her co-workers. I sat down at my desk. I was really hungry — I had only had a couple of bites of the cheese sandwich. I couldn't face going out again to get something, so I rootled through my desk drawers and found a box of slightly stale cereal bars, left over from a week when I'd tried to break my afternoon-Twix habit by eating something healthier. It had failed when I'd read the ingredients and calorie count on the cereal-bar box and realised I was getting more sugar and fat

70

in the healthy bar than in the good old-fashioned choccie. I was eating for two now, I reasoned, and munched my way through three of the chewy granola monstrosities. They made me horribly thirsty, so I went to the vending machine in the office kitchen and got myself a Diet Coke. I gulped half of it walking back to my desk, then a thought struck me. Hadn't I read somewhere that caffeine was bad for unborn babies? And surely a meal of cereal bars wasn't what was required to sustain a tiny, growing embryo. I typed in the URL for the baby website immediately, planning to look for an article on nutrition for pregnant women.

A notification popped up: 'You have twenty-seven replies to your post'. Twenty-seven? How could that be?

I clicked on the link and there they were. Twenty-seven personal messages expressing joy and excitement at my pregnancy. All of them were full of love and encouragement from a group of women I had never met or even spoken to. Some of them were quite poetic (if a bit greeting-card-ish): 'Congratulations . . . you're about to embark on an amazing journey'. Some verged on the illiterate: 'OMG that's grate!', and almost every one contained a rather confusing collection of brackets: '(((((((()))))))))'. It took me till message twelve to work out that it meant sending a hug, and I only worked that out because Lucy_19 wrote '(((((((((HUGS)))))))))'.

Well, then I did cry. This bunch of complete strangers had been kinder, more understanding and more excited for me than my own husband.

It was too ironic for words. I typed an incoherent thank you, then went to the bathroom to wash my face and fix my make-up. It took a while to mop up the tears . . . they just seemed to keep coming . . . but eventually I managed to splash my face with cold water and reapply eye make-up and lipstick. I felt better and worse at the same time. Better, because someone had said that what was happening to me was something miraculous and worth celebrating. Worse, because it was totally the wrong someone.

Somehow, I made it to the end of the work day. It was an odd feeling . . . I'd never not wanted to go home before. I'd always been eager to leave and get back to our little house and see James. I dragged my heels polishing and rewriting a short and very simple press release, packing up my things, visiting the loo one last time. By the time I got in the lift, it was twenty minutes later than I would usually have left.

When I got downstairs, I was about to turn left and head for the Tube when I spotted James sitting on the wall opposite our office front door. He was holding the most enormous bunch of flowers.

He stood up and walked hesitantly towards me. 'I was an idiot, Toni. I'm sorry. I never thought I'd be the kind of bloke who had to buy flowers to say sorry for being an idiot. But I am. Will you take the flowers? And my apology? Please?'

What could you say to that? I took the flowers, and slotted into my place, tucked under his right arm, and we walked to the Tube together.

Once we got back home, he was Mr Caring. He made me sit on the sofa and brought me a cup of tea. Then he sat on the coffee table and held both of my hands.

'What can I do?'

'What do you mean, what can you do?'

'I'll be honest, Tones, I'm completely freaked out. I just wasn't expecting this to happen so . . . fast.'

'Me neither.'

'And maybe I'd be able to get my head around it better if I had stuff to do.'

'Well, there's nothing to do yet . . . I suppose I should go and see the doctor, make sure everything's all right . . . work out when this baby will be born.' I could have sworn I saw the colour drain out of his face. 'That's what it is, James. A baby. If nothing goes wrong, in nine months or so we're going to have a baby. Get used to it.'

'I know . . . it's just . . . ' I could see him thinking whether he should say what he was going to say. He decided to go for it. I wish he hadn't. 'Well, I expected to have more than nine months of my life left.'

'Of your *life?* It's not a death sentence.'

'I know. But everything about our lives is going to change. I just wasn't prepared — '

'*You* weren't prepared? I'm the one who's going to blow up like a balloon. I'm the one who's going to have to give birth. And I'm pretty sure it won't be you taking a year out of your career to look after it!'

I tried to get up and walk away but he caught

hold of my hands again.

'I'm sorry, I'm sorry. I keep saying the wrong thing. Please forgive me.' He rested his head on our joined hands and sighed. I sighed and stroked his hair. 'This is ridiculous, James. We can't spend the next nine months in a cycle of you saying something awful and then me getting upset and then you begging for forgiveness. For one thing, I don't have enough vases.'

He looked up at me and smiled. I continued. 'I know this is mad. But it's happening. We'll just have to get used to the idea. It'll be a bit of a steep learning curve. I've been going on this baby forum online, and I've learned such a lot from the women I've been chatting to.'

As soon as I said it, I regretted it.

'A forum? Really? Can I go on it too?'

'It's not really . . . for guys.'

'What, so it's like a secret women's group? Where you all bitch about your husbands?'

'No, James,' I said exasperated. 'But they do get quite graphic about what they're going through. Do you want to know about some pregnant stranger's piles? Or constipation? Or discharge? Didn't think so.'

'No, you're absolutely right. I'll take an executive summary from you.'

I felt stupidly relieved. The baby website was my thing. I didn't want to share it with him. Then it occurred to me that this was the first thing since we'd been serious about each other that I hadn't wanted to share with James.

'Give me a job, though,' James said. 'Let me rub your feet or something. I feel helpless. I want

74

to do something to help you.'

'Well, I definitely don't need my feet rubbed. It's not like the baby weighs very much yet.'

'How big is it?'

'I don't know . . . just a few cells so far, I think.'

'Well, there's *something* I could do. I could go and get us a book. A baby book that would tell us all the stuff we don't know.'

'That's a great idea. The bookshop on the high street doesn't shut till eight. You nip down and I'll get dinner started. Oh, and love . . . can you buy me some caffeine-free tea?'

James grabbed his coat and keys and ran out of the door. I popped some jacket potatoes in the oven and put some beans in a saucepan. Maybe not the healthiest of dinners. I'd grate some cheese and make a salad too. That would add some other food groups.

James was still out, so I fired up my laptop and checked my personal email and Facebook. Then I logged on to the baby website, just for a moment, to check if my post had had any more replies. There was one more post on my thread. It was from somebody called BlondeAmbition.

Hi PR–Girl,
Your story really touched me. I'm so happy for you and your OH

(I'd learned that that meant 'Other Half', a blanket term for husbands, boyfriends and life partners).

I've been so worried about my relationship with my OH. He's been pulling away from me, and I think he's getting restless. He's my whole life, and I can't imagine being without him. I know that people say a baby won't fix what's wrong in a relationship, but I truly believe that if I get pregnant, it will bring us closer. We haven't started trying officially, but I think we will soon. Has your pregnancy made you and your OH stronger together? Do you think we . . .

I couldn't read any more because I heard James on the stairs, so I closed the window immediately. I had to laugh . . . had it made us stronger together? We'd rowed more today than we had in the last four years. I was shutting down my computer like a guilty pervert caught watching porn. My husband was more worried about snowboarding than impending fatherhood. Had it made us stronger together? At this rate, we wouldn't make it to the end of the week!

James had a bag with three different kinds of tea in it, and an armful of books. 'I didn't know which one to buy, so I bought them all. Firstly, I had a look at this one, and I learned you're four weeks pregnant, not two. You take the start date from the first day of your last period . . . I know you don't have regular ones, so you estimate fourteen days . . . anyway . . . it's four weeks, not two. I got this one, which is all about nutrition in pregnancy, and let me tell you there are *loads* of things you can't eat. And I got this one, which shows you how the baby looks at different stages.' He opened the book at a page headed: 'Two weeks after conception'. There was a picture of a tiny blob. 'It looks about the size of an apple pip, doesn't it?' said James, putting an arm around me. Then he gingerly put a hand on my stomach. 'Hello, Pip. I'm your dad.'

Maybe we would be okay after all.

Gemma

Gemma's weekly schedule was pinned above her desk, neatly typed, and colour-coded with highlighter. On Mondays, Tuesdays and Thursdays, she was at school until four, then in the dance studio until six thirty. She had Wednesday afternoons off from school, but then she almost always had tennis practice or a match. Friday afternoons were set aside for course work or doing some extra reading. On Saturdays she had dancing and on Sunday mornings she taught a beginners' class for little kids at the tennis club. She barely had time for friends — she tended to chat to them on Skype or twitter rather than socialise in person. She definitely didn't have time for a boyfriend. Not this year, not now. But then . . . but then . . . along came Ben.

Gemma's best friend Lucy's parents went away to their house in France one weekend, and Lucy threw a party. She'd made the mistake of issuing an open Facebook invitation, and the house was overrun. Luckily, it wasn't one of those parties that end up in the newspaper because the house gets trashed . . . it was just around a hundred kids, all drinking and dancing. Most of the guys were from the boys' school, the brother school to Lady Grey's. Lucy and Gemma didn't know most of them, but the atmosphere was festive and unthreatening and everyone seemed to be having fun.

An hour or so into the party, Gemma went into the kitchen to get another drink. Ben and a group of his mates were sitting around Lucy's mum's scrubbed oak table, playing a drinking game. She and Lucy had both noticed him when he'd arrived at the party . . . he was the best-looking guy there. Tall, slender, with longish straight black hair (probably not his natural colour), and bright blue eyes, he had a slouching, casual grace that showed he knew he was good-looking and that girls would notice him. And they had. Gemma had seen quite a few groups of girls huddled together, giving him sideways glances. He didn't seem interested, though. He was concentrating on the complicated game he was playing with his three much less hot friends.

Gemma took a can out of the fridge and poured it into her glass, then added a splash of vodka. She only drank vodka and Diet Coke. Anything else had too many calories. She leaned against the fridge door and watched the game for a while. It seemed very complicated . . . something to do with coins and pointing with your elbows, but after a few minutes, she suspected that the lumpy boys were losing on purpose so they'd have an excuse to down their drinks. Ben was playing more seriously, as if he really wanted to win, and after ten minutes or so, when all the other boys had drained their glasses three or four times, his was still full. The liquid was clear . . . tequila? Neat vodka? Whatever it was, Gemma was sure the other guys would be throwing up within the hour.

79

And sure enough, one of the boys suddenly lurched up from the table, clapped his hand over his mouth and looked around wildly. Gemma reached over and pulled the kitchen door open and he dashed outside. She heard him retching over Lucy's mum's herb garden.

Ben looked up from the table and smiled lazily at her. 'Lightweight,' he said, jerking his chin at the hapless hurler. 'Do you want to play?'

'OK, but I'll stick with the drink I've got, thanks,' she said, as she slid into the vacant chair.

It wasn't the most romantic beginning, but what happened afterwards was. They went out into the garden together, where loads of kids were sprawled on the lawn chatting and smoking. Ben led her to the summerhouse, and they sat side by side on the patio swing and talked and talked. They discussed cinema and books. Surprisingly, he had broad tastes in films, not just the action/superhero stuff most guys seemed to like. They'd both recently read *1984* and thought it was mind-blowing. Ben wanted to tell her about all his favourite bands. Gemma wasn't that into music, so she ended up nodding a lot. He took his iPod out of his pocket and chose a track, then took her arm to draw her closer so they could each have one of his earphones. He left his hand on her arm and then slipped his hand into hers. Gemma could barely hear the music, the blood was pounding so hard in her ears.

When the song finished, he gently took the earphone from her ear, turned her face towards him and kissed her. Even though he had been drinking, his breath was sweet and biscuity, like a child's. It began to rain, and the kids who were sitting on the lawn made a run for the summerhouse. They all piled in, stumbling and laughing, and several shrieking girls flopped on to the swing next to Ben and Gemma. Ben took her hand and led her out onto the lawn. The rain was soft and not at all cold. They walked towards the house, but there were people spilling out of the kitchen door and the French windows . . . it was clear the house was crammed. Ben drew her under a tree, away from the lights of the party, took her in his arms and began to kiss her again. They hadn't said a word. Gemma could feel the tiny cool drops of rain on her cheek, and the soft warmth of Ben's lips on her own and she knew she would remember this moment forever.

Things seemed to change really fast after that. Ben rang and texted her several times a day. They met up whenever they could and spent hours in parks and cinemas, whispering and kissing. A week after they met, he took her for a walk and seriously, gravely, told her he loved her, and asked her to be his girlfriend.

She thought her schedule had been full before, but now she realised it had been empty. Suddenly, without warning, Ben rushed in like the sea and filled every moment of her day. When she wasn't with him, he was all she thought about. She played the Spotify playlists he had made for her over and over. She couldn't sleep or eat properly. Her stomach fluttered with nerves and excitement all the time, and she felt slightly sick. She only felt properly alive when she was with him. It was like the world was suddenly more brightly coloured. They had silly names for one another and a million private jokes. She had never felt so close to another human being. She felt warmed by him, and she wanted to touch him all the time. It was just like a film or a song. It really was.

Up until now, it wouldn't have occurred to Gemma's parents that she was old enough to have a boyfriend, or even that she might want one. As far as they were concerned, she was still their good girl, always working at schoolwork, ballet or sport, friendly with Lucy, Iris and Sophie, girls from the same sort of upper-middle-class families as her own.

She had had some problems, granted . . . there had been the short patch when she'd stopped eating, really. It wasn't an issue, she'd just wanted to stay slim enough for ballet, but her mum had made her go and see a shrink for a while and he'd made her keep a food diary. She'd put on a few pounds to keep them happy, and it had all blown over.

So now she looked like the perfect daughter — active, beautiful and perfectly well behaved — which gave her parents carte blanche to carry on with their extremely busy lives. Her father did something in the City that meant he left for work at seven and was seldom home before ten at night. He was out playing golf most weekends too. Her mother didn't work, but seemed never to be at home. Between hair, nail and facial appointments, gym, charity and social events, she would never have been able to find time for a job.

Gemma knew that all her friends thought her life was perfect. She was an only child, living in a big house. Her parents drove great cars, and her father had already promised her a new Mini convertible when she passed her test. But the friends had no idea how lonely it was. They seldom ate meals together: her father was never home for dinner and her mother was always rushing somewhere. They lived on M&S ready meals, eaten separately in the enormous kitchen. They certainly never watched TV together, or went out as a family. Gemma couldn't really remember the last time she'd heard her parents having a conversation. They seemed to pass by one another, exchanging bits of information occasionally. It wasn't like they hated each other or that she thought they would get divorced — far from it. More like they just didn't see each other — as if the other one was invisible.

She didn't set out to introduce Ben to her parents — it would have been quite difficult. It wasn't as if she could invite him for a family dinner — they didn't do dinners like other families did. And she definitely wasn't ashamed of him. It wasn't as if he came from a dodgy background or anything . . . far from it. His parents were divorced; his dad was a university lecturer and lived in New York, and his mum was a lawyer. His older sister was at Cambridge. He and his mum lived in a big, very modern house about a mile from Gemma's house. It wasn't even as if he was one of those sullen teenage boys who slouch around and say nothing . . . she knew her dad would hate that. Ben was personable, well-spoken and handsome. She'd seen him with his mum's friends, and he was very charming to adults. It was almost as if . . . well . . . they'd really approve of him, and that was why she didn't want them to meet him. The relationship was her own private thing, and she didn't want Ben to be 'Gemma's lovely boyfriend', who her mum could gossip about at the beautician's, and her dad could be condescending about to his golf mates.

But a few weeks after they started going out, he came round and they were sitting in the kitchen when her mother breezed in, en route from one appointment to another. She saw Ben and raised one perfect eyebrow. 'And this is . . . ?'

'Mum!' said Gemma, scrambling to her feet and dropping Ben's hand like it was burning her. 'This is Ben.'

'Ben . . . ?' Samantha said, extending a slim hand.

Ben stood up and smiled his devastating smile. 'Ben Norman, Mrs Hamilton. So pleased to meet you.' He shook her hand. 'You have a lovely home. Thank so much for letting me come round.'

But Gemma's mum had spent too much time around charming men, including her own husband, to be won by easy compliments.

'Yes, nice to meet you too, Ben. I'm sure Gemma's dad will also be very interested to meet you.'

And sure enough, he was. It seemed, to Gemma's surprise, her parents actually had had a conversation about her, because the next evening her father came into her room and asked about Ben. He suggested that she invite Ben round for tea that weekend,

'Tea?' Gemma asked incredulously. 'We never have tea.'

'Well, we're having tea this Sunday. I want a look at this boy.'

Ben took it in his stride. Gemma didn't like to think how many girls' houses he'd been invited to for tea before, because he agreed like it wasn't surprising at all. Where he'd failed with Samantha, he succeeded with Gemma's father. Within minutes, they were chatting about rugby and cricket and David was offering Ben a beer. It turned out David knew someone who knew Ben's dad, and in the world of men, it seemed that was enough for them to get on like a house on fire.

At the end of the afternoon Gemma walked with Ben to the bus stop. 'Thanks for doing that,' she said hesitantly.

'No problem,' he said, giving her a squeeze. 'I'm good at parents. They love me. And they have no idea what I have planned for their lovely daughter.' And checking they were well out of sight of the house, he kissed her deeply and stroked her breasts through her shirt.

When she got home, David rumbled something about Ben being a splendid chap and went off to his study. Samantha sat quietly at the kitchen counter, reading a magazine. She didn't say anything. Gemma went to the fridge to get a drink, and when she turned back her mum was staring at her.

'What?' she asked defensively.

'Just . . . be careful, darling, won't you?' said Samantha brightly, and went back to her magazine.

★ ★ ★

Gemma was about fourteen when she worked out that her father had other women in his life. He just wasn't all that worried about hiding it. He'd get a phone call on his mobile and his voice would change and go all honeyed and fake, then he'd leave the room to take the call. He'd tell Samantha he was going out to play golf at the weekend, then drive away, leaving his golf clubs in the hall. Gemma reckoned that if *she* had worked it out, her mother must definitely have worked it out. But her mother just didn't seem interested . . . or didn't seem to care. Gemma had wondered about it for a long time, and couldn't understand it. If she thought about Ben with someone else her stomach tied itself into a knot of pain and she wanted to scream. How could her mother bear it? She wished she could ask her, but she knew exactly what would happen. Her mother would give her an especially blank stare, open her blue eyes very wide and say, 'I can't imagine what you're talking about. Now I have to go, sweetie. I'm very busy.'

Her mother was always very busy. Maybe that was why her father had to look for other women . . . women who weren't quite so busy and wanted to pay him some attention. Women who could find the time for him. The only hint that his behaviour touched her mum at all was that on the evenings her dad was 'out' Samantha would have several very large glasses of wine with her ready meal. She'd often leave most of the food, but she could finish off a bottle of wine easily on her own.

★   ★   ★

After a few weeks, Ben and Gemma's kissing and touching started to get serious. Gemma knew he wanted to have sex with her. She knew without a doubt that she loved him, and he told her all the time that he loved her, so if that was what he wanted, she'd do it. There was no way she could go to their family doctor and ask to be put on the Pill, and Ben had said he didn't like condoms and didn't want to use them. He'd suggested they go to his doctor, at a busy practice close to where he lived.

'You can go there and say you're my cousin or something,' he said. 'Come on, Gem. It'll be easy.'

To be honest, to Gemma it had sounded terrifying, but if it would make him happy, she wanted to do it. Ben forged a letter from his mum saying Gemma was a niece who had come to stay for a few months. He made it all sound so easy. He made an appointment and then walked with her to the doctors' surgery. At the glass doors, however, he stopped.

'See you later. Text me when you come out,' he said, not meeting her eye.

'What? Aren't you coming in with me?'

'Nah,' he muttered. 'They all know me in there. You'd better go alone, it'll look weird otherwise.'

She wanted to cry, but they'd come so far, and she didn't know how to say that she wasn't brave enough to do it alone. She went into the doctors' waiting room, gave her name and sat down. Through the glass doors, she could see Ben walking away quickly across the playground opposite. The waiting room was bright and cheery, but very busy, filled with harassed-looking mothers and toddlers and sick-looking old people. She was terrified that someone who knew her family might walk in at any time, so she kept her head down and stared at her phone in her lap. She willed it to ring or beep, willed Ben to change his mind and come back and sit with her, but it didn't happen.

She had to wait for forty-five minutes. She was too upset and apprehensive to read any of the magazines scattered around the waiting room. The long wait gave her time to think about what had happened. Surely if she was actually Ben's cousin, he might have come to the doctors' with her? If she was new in town, or something? It wouldn't have looked that odd for them to have sat in the waiting room together. She had a creeping, sneaking feeling he might be a bit of a coward, but she put the thought out of her head. This was the boy she loved. He loved her too. He'd said so. This was just a little hiccup, and they'd be fine.

The long stay in the waiting room was by far the worst bit of the experience. When her name was finally called, she was ushered in to see a harassed woman doctor, who barely looked at her. Gemma hesitantly said that she wanted to go on the Pill. The doctor nodded, brusquely took her blood pressure, typed quickly into the computer and printed out a prescription. She was obviously hugely relieved that this appointment had been so simple, and was already watching the door, hoping Gemma would leave quickly so she could make up some time on her overrunning schedule.

Gemma took the hint and left. There was a pharmacy nearby, so she went in and got the first three months'-worth of pills. She sat down on a low wall, read the leaflet and took the first tablet. Only then did she text Ben.

Sex the first time was uncomfortable and a bit scary, but he'd seemed to love it so much she felt encouraged, and after a few times it got better and she started to enjoy it more. Afterwards, they'd lie for ages and giggle and talk. Gemma loved this bit best of all.

'Let's run away,' Ben said one day. 'Just you and me. We'll get a grotty little studio flat somewhere and I'll work at Tesco to support you and keep you in ballet shoes.'

'Ballet shoes?' laughed Gemma.

'You can stay home and dance around our tiny flat like a fairy. And I'll come home all tired in my Tesco uniform, with bags of dented cans of beans and you can make me meringues.'

'Out of beans?'

'I'm sure you'll think of a way to do it. You're very clever. And we'll sleep on the floor because we're too poor to get a bed.'

'I'm not sleeping on the floor,' Gemma said firmly. 'You can get a bed from Tesco Direct with your staff discount.'

'Ooh,' said Ben. 'She's a nagging wife already!'

She got a little thrill when she called her his wife, but she knew better than to say anything about it. Instead she said hesitantly, 'I'm sure we can do a bit better than a nasty studio flat. I've, um . . . I've got some money in trust from my grandma, which I'll get when I'm eighteen.'

'Me too!' said Ben, sitting up, suddenly excited. 'Mine's enough to get a car and pay the first year's insurance. My mum and I are going to start looking for one as soon as I pass my test.'

'Mine's . . . um . . . a bit more than that.'

'How much more?'

'Well, not enough for a house, but definitely enough for quite a nice one-bedroom flat. Or a not so nice two-bedroom one.'

'Wow!' Ben whistled, suddenly impressed. 'You can be my sugar mommy!'

Gemma giggled. 'I'm only three weeks older than you.'

'Doesn't matter. I'm seeing you in a new light. Well, change of plan. You buy the flat, and then go out to work as a high-powered business lady, and I'll stay home and look after the kids.'

'The kids? Now we're having kids?'

'At least six,' he said, pulling her close to him. 'Let me show you how babies are made, sugar mommy.'

And after they'd had sex again, Ben sat cross-legged on the end of the bed and played his guitar for her. He had a lovely, soft, husky voice, and he sang softly as he played.

Lying in his bed, watching his lovely profile, Gemma thought she'd never been so happy in her life.

A few weeks later, he got the chance to play a few songs in a local bar, as the first act in an open-mic night. Gemma sat in the front, beside herself with pride, and filmed every minute on her phone. There weren't a lot of people there, mostly Ben's mates, but he got a great response, and set up a Facebook fan page. Slowly, the number of fans climbed from ten to fifty, and then two hundred. He wasn't a big star, just popular among the local kids, and he started to get a lot of attention from other girls. Gemma went to all of his gigs and glued herself to his side as soon as he stepped off stage. She saw other girls whispering and looking at her, and she knew they were saying she was the paranoid, psycho girlfriend, but she didn't care. Ben was hers and it was going to stay that way. He laughed and chatted to people with her by his side. He didn't talk much to Gemma, in fact he almost seemed to ignore her, but still. She was his girlfriend and that was what mattered.

One Friday night, Ben played his biggest-ever gig. She'd spent the evening glaring at girls who tried to talk to him and by the end of the night she was ragged with tension. Eventually he extricated himself from his crowd of tittering fans and they left and he walked with her to her bus stop. He was a bit merry and in the mood for sex, and when she said no and that she had to go home because she had ballet first thing on the Saturday, he shrugged and walked off, leaving her at the bus stop without saying goodbye. She cried herself to sleep that night.

It was a good thing she had a busy day the next day . . . it meant she couldn't fall apart. Her mother gave her a lift to the ballet studio on the way to some charity planning meeting. She spent the whole journey talking to someone about flower arrangements on her mobile phone, so Gemma didn't have to make conversation.

Once she got to the studio, she went into autopilot. She'd been coming to studios like this since she was five, and the process of changing, doing her hair and warming up came automatically. She took her place at the barre and the class began. They weren't supposed to talk, but the girls were practised at whispering conversations in the moments when the teacher was at the other end of the line. Behind Gemma, two girls were catching up on the events of the night before.

'So . . . Nat . . . Josh Morris . . . ' murmured Eleanor between clenched teeth.

'Yeah. So?' Natalie was slender, with unusually large breasts for a ballet dancer. She had thick dark hair that coiled like serpents and her eyes were black and heavily fringed with long lashes. Gemma knew that boys loved her and were desperate to go out with her. She'd seen them clustered around Natalie at parties, clowning around, trying to get her attention.

'Josh Morris . . . ' Eleanor repeated. 'Mm-mm-mm. He's fit.'

'He's all right,' Natalie said.

'Are you going to see him again?' Eleanor asked, but at that moment, the teacher came back to their end of the row to correct Eleanor's arm position and push Gemma's knee out further. When she'd moved away again, Eleanor came back to the subject. 'Well? Are you?'

'God, Eleanor . . . get a life. I don't know. I haven't decided yet. I don't really care, to be honest.'

'Did he ask for your number?'

There was no answer, but Gemma could imagine the eye-rolling glance Natalie had given Eleanor. What guy wouldn't ask for her number? Eleanor hadn't finished prying, however.

'So what did you do with him? I mean . . . I saw you kissing, but after that?' They all had to move out into the middle of the floor then, so Gemma never got to hear what Natalie and Josh Morris had done — if she had revealed anything to Eleanor, that was.

Later, when she got home, she went up to her room to do homework. Her mother was still out at her charity meeting and her father was playing golf. She sat on the bed and thought for a moment. How did Natalie do it? How did she achieve that effortless confidence? Gemma had heard girls pretending to be indifferent about boys before, but she could always tell they were pretending . . . playing it cool. But Natalie hadn't been pretending. She genuinely didn't care if she never heard from Josh Morris . . . who, from Eleanor's respectful tones, was clearly considered quite a catch. It was, Gemma thought, because Natalie was totally, completely comfortable in her skin. She knew who she was, and she knew she was all right.

Lucy, when she and Gemma had been close, had been the same. Lucy loved to talk about herself, and Gemma had often found her self-centred pronouncements irritating . . . 'I'm such a perfectionist,' Lucy would say. Or she'd eat a big sandwich after school and say, 'I'm always hungriest in the late afternoon . . . it's just the way I am.' But who was Gemma? Which way was *she*? She started getting ready to do her homework. She laid all her books and pens out on her tidy, empty desk, and then looked around her tidy bedroom. Was this who she was? Neat handwriting in carefully covered notebooks? Her ballet certificates in a row on the wall? Her tennis trophies? The cork board covered in snapshots of expensive family holidays and shots of her laughing with her friends, who all looked very much like she did? And that damned colour-coded schedule that ran her life, week by week? Yes, that was the shell, but what was inside? When Gemma looked within herself, she was frightened. It seemed to her as if she was empty. As if there was nothing at her core.

For six wonderful months, being Ben's girlfriend had defined her. But somehow, without her having done anything, things had changed between them. His musical success had changed him, made him more confident, and Gemma felt she couldn't keep up. It just seemed as if he was bored with her. She knew he'd seen her as a trophy in the beginning. He told her all his friends thought she was hot, but maybe that wasn't enough any more. He had a big social crowd now, and he was always working on a new musical project, collaborating with someone on a recording project, playing a gig with someone else. At first, he'd talk to her all about it, but she'd get upset if any of the names he mentioned were girls' names, so after a while, he stopped telling her.

It wasn't as if her life away from him was very interesting . . . all she did was study, dance and play tennis, so she had very little to talk to him about. She'd ask about his day at school and he'd grunt, or say 'Fine.' So mostly, they'd have sex, or if they weren't having sex, they'd sit together listening to music, or she'd watch him play games. He never played his guitar for her any more. Lately, when she rang or texted and suggested coming round, he'd started making excuses. They were spending less and less time together.

Gemma worried about it constantly. She couldn't get to sleep at night, she woke early, she couldn't eat. Her course work had started to slip, and for the first time since she was six years old, she missed ballet for an entire week.

She didn't really have anyone to confide in: Lucy had said from the beginning that she thought Ben was a bit of a player, and she didn't like him. Gemma knew it was just because she was jealous, so she'd stopped talking to Lucy about him and they'd drifted apart. She'd neglected all her other friends since she'd been going out with him, so she had no one she felt close to. Ben was her boyfriend, her best friend, her world, and the only person she wanted to confide in . . . and she couldn't.

Then there was a further blow. Gemma's Pill prescription ran out after six months and she had to go back to the doctor for a check-up to get another. She went back to Ben's surgery, but to her relief she didn't see the care-worn GP she'd seen before. Instead she got a locum, a young Asian man.

He asked a few cursory questions, then took her blood pressure. She saw him frown, turn to his computer and check the notes, and then he pumped up the cuff again. 'I'm afraid your blood pressure is definitely up.'

'Is that a problem?'

'It's not good, certainly. I don't think your contraceptive is agreeing with you,' he said briskly. 'I'd like you to stop taking it immediately.'

Gemma was alarmed. 'But can't I just go on another pill?'

'I wouldn't recommend it. In cases like yours, we often recommend the contraceptive implant. It's inserted under the skin of your upper arm. You can have it in for up to three years, and you won't have to remember to take the Pill. Many women find it preferable.'

'Fine. Can I get it done now?'

'It's a clinical procedure. It can't be done in a normal consultation. You'll have to book in for the next available slot at the clinic.' He checked his computer screen. 'That's in three weeks' time.'

'And until then?'

'Well, in the meantime, you'll need to take additional precautions.'

When Gemma told Ben they would have to use condoms in the short term, he sulked. 'I hate them,' he said. 'I suppose we don't have any choice, though.' He didn't ask Gemma about her blood pressure, or if she felt ill at all.

It just seemed to be another reason for him to be annoyed and impatient with her.

Late one overcast Wednesday afternoon, she texted Ben as she left school to see if he wanted to meet up. After an hour, she'd not had a reply, and she started to walk towards his house. As she turned into his road, she saw him walking up ahead, deep in conversation with a short, dark-haired girl that she didn't recognise. She stopped and took a sideways step behind a tree. Ben wasn't touching the girl, but he was looking down into her face and laughing at something she had just said. Gemma couldn't remember the last time Ben had laughed with her.

Ben and the girl stood for a while and chatted on the pavement, then both took a step apart, as if they were parting ways. Ben reached out and punched her shoulder softly and affectionately. The girl said something, laughed and tossed her head. Then she walked away. Gemma turned and walked back the way she came. She didn't hear from Ben that day, or the next, or for a week after that.

Just when Gemma had begun to tip into the blackest despair, Ben seemed to soften towards her. He texted her and they met up in the park.

He didn't talk much, but he held her hand as they walked around. It made Gemma feel a bit better, but as soon as they parted the anxiety returned. Maybe she'd bored him. Maybe he hadn't talked because she was so dull. She wished she knew what to say to make him laugh like the short, dark girl did. He'd never ring again. Then what would she do? She spent hours in her room, telling her parents she was studying. But in reality, she was lying on her bed, staring at her mobile, willing it to beep or ring.

Then he rang her and invited her to come around for dinner for his mum's birthday. That had to be a good sign. She wanted to be able to stay the night with him, so she told her mum she was sleeping over at Lucy's and spent ages getting ready. She wore her best jeans and a pink hoodie Ben had once said he liked. She spent ages straightening her hair and getting her make-up just right.

Ben's mum, whose name was Hannah, had cooked great bowls of pasta and made lots of salads. She had invited a few friends — women like her — in their late thirties and early forties, successful, assertive and forceful. The conversation was loud and often quite rude. Everyone talked over one another and the table was so full of food that there always seemed to be a bowl being passed around.

Gemma was completely intimidated. She moved her chair as close to Ben as she could. She'd put a few strings of pasta on her plate, and filled the rest of it with lettuce leaves, and she used her fork to move the food around. She kept

98

her head down and let her hair hang over her face. As the wine glasses were refilled, the banter got louder. Ben, who had known these women all his life, gave as good as he got. Hannah's friend Sarah was sitting on the other side of Gemma. She was something very senior in a media company, and she was a tall, big woman with a terrifying smoker's cough and a voice to match.

She leaned over Gemma and poked Ben in the arm. 'So, pipsqueak,' she rasped, 'this your girlfriend?' She didn't wait for an answer. 'You should put a tag on her or something. If she turns sideways, you'll lose her. You must have to wrap yourself in bubble-wrap in the bedroom . . . you'd lacerate yourself on those hipbones!' She leaned over and peered at Gemma's plate. 'Good lord, darling, you'll fade away if that's all you eat!' She grabbed a bowl of potato salad and added a massive dollop to Gemma's plate. She leaned across the table and ripped a hunk off a loaf of garlic bread and balanced that on top. 'Now you don't leave the table till that's all gone!'

Gemma looked at her plate, horrified. There was no way she was going to eat all of that. Especially not in front of Ben. She mumbled something about the loo, and left the table.

She went upstairs to the bathroom next to Ben's room and shut the door. She checked her make-up and tidied her hair. How long could she stay in there? Until they cleared the plates? Or at least until Sarah had drunk a few more glasses of wine and decided to ignore her. She couldn't stay away too long . . . knowing those women, they'd start speculating loudly about what she was doing in the bathroom. This was a nightmare. She'd have to go back out there. She washed her hands, then decided she should flush the toilet for authenticity.

As soon as she pushed the handle, she heard a wail from Ben's room. As she opened the door to step out, one of the women pushed by her and went into the bedroom. She heard her say, 'There, there, Lily. Don't cry. It's just a strange place. You're at Auntie Hannah's, aren't you?' The woman, whom Gemma remembered was called Patti, came out of the bedroom carrying a chubby baby girl. The baby had rumpled blonde curls and cheeks flushed with sleep. She had one fat little arm wrapped around her mother's neck, and with the other hand was rubbing her face in bewildered grumpiness.

Gemma followed them back into the living room. She realised she needn't worry about anyone noticing her or what was on her plate: all the women were too busy fussing over the baby. The poor sleepy little thing was being passed from woman to woman. They were all asking Patti about her eating and sleeping . . . did she have any teeth? Was she sitting up properly yet? Lily looked increasingly miserable, especially when gravelly Sarah bounced her energetically on her knee. 'Who's a gorgeous girl then?' she rasped, putting her face close to the baby's. She probably reeked of smoke and wine too. Lily's little face crumpled and the corners of her mouth turned down like a comedy clown's. She drew breath in and began to wail. The women all laughed, like this was the funniest thing they'd ever seen. Patti leaned over and took her back from Sarah.

'Silly girl. Want to go to your Uncle Ben?' Patti dumped the baby on Ben's lap. To Gemma's surprise, Ben wrapped his arms comfortably around her. The baby stopped crying immediately, rested her head on Ben's chest and put a fat little thumb into her mouth. She looked at everyone else in the room with big eyes, blinking slowly. Within a few minutes, she had closed her eyes and was sleeping quietly in his arms. Gemma could barely breathe. She had never loved Ben as much as she did in that moment . . . he looked so masculine and tender, gently holding the beautiful baby girl.

Gemma hadn't had much to do with babies: as an only child, she had not experienced the arrival of younger siblings, and as Samantha and David didn't go in for extended family occasions, she barely knew any of her cousins. She stared and stared at Lily and couldn't believe how tiny and perfect she was: her fat little hand, with its impossibly tiny pearly nails, resting on Ben's arm, the flushed curve of her cheek, her candyfloss hair. She leaned close to Ben and smelt the sweet scent of Lily's baby shampoo. She was desperate to hold her, but she was much too shy to ask if she could. She made do with lightly stroking the back of Lily's hand. She had never felt such soft skin.

Ben held Lily until Patti and the other women were ready to go home. Patti gathered up a big bag of baby stuff, then handed Ben a blanket. He wrapped it gently around the baby and carried her out to the car. Gemma helped Hannah to clear plates and put them in the kitchen.

'Well, that was all right,' Hannah commented, loading plates into the dishwasher.

'It was lovely, thank you,' said Gemma. 'Let me do that. You shouldn't work on your birthday.'

Hannah needed no further persuasion, and she poured herself a glass of wine and sat down at the counter. She was a bit drunk, and clearly in the mood to get chatty. 'You're a super girl, Gemma. Really. Haven't seen so much of you lately. It's nice to have you back among us.'

Gemma didn't know what to say, so she nodded and kept rinsing plates and loading them into the dishwasher. But Hannah continued to talk. 'Ben seemed a bit funny when I asked him to invite you. I hope things are all right with you two.' Mercifully, she didn't seem to expect a response to this. She raised her glass to Gemma. 'Anyway. I hope you had a nice time.'

'I did, thank you,' Gemma said, but she felt sick and cold. So Hannah had invited her. It hadn't even been Ben's choice. He'd obviously just gone along with it.

When he came back, he was smiling. Hannah said good night and went into the bathroom. Ben sat down on the sofa and put his arm around Gemma. 'Do you need to go home?' he asked.

'No, I can stay if you'd like me to,' she said hesitantly. She didn't know what she'd do if he

102

said no . . . her parents thought she was sleeping at Lucy's, so she could scarcely go home. What would she tell them?

'Nah. Stay. You're all right,' he said. He pulled her nearer and started stroking her upper arm. Gemma knew what that meant. He wanted sex. That was fine with her — if he wanted to have sex with her, maybe he did want to be with her, and that was all she needed to know.

The sex was quick and urgent, and over quite soon. Afterwards, they lay quietly side by side in Ben's bed. Gemma turned on her side and looked at Ben's profile. He was staring up at the ceiling, and she could see his jaw working as if he were grinding his teeth. Almost against her will, she said, 'What are you thinking?' and immediately regretted it. What if he were thinking he wanted to break up with her? But Ben turned on his side and smiled his devastating grin.

'I was just thinking that was amazing and I'd like some more of the same, please. I've got a twelve-pack of condoms here, and the night is young!'

He started to pull her closer, but Gemma resisted. If there was a window when he was going to be nice to her, maybe they could talk, try and regain some of the easy intimacy that seemed to have leaked slowly away.

'So Patti's baby really likes you,' she ventured.

'Yeah . . . babies usually do like me. I've got loads of cousins, and lots of my mum's friends have had babies. Babies are cool.'

'Really? Don't they just scream and stuff?'

'I suppose sometimes they do, but if you play with them they're usually okay. They giggle and it's pretty cute.'

'I don't know anything about babies,' said Gemma. 'But Lily is so beautiful. All that blonde hair. Like a little fairy.'

'She reminds me of you,' said Ben. 'I bet you were the most adorable baby. I looked like a bald frog.'

'I bet you didn't.'

'I bet you I did. No hair, big goggle eyes . . . it's amazing I'm as gorgeous as I am now.'

'You *are* gorgeous,' Gemma said shyly.

'I am, aren't I? And so are you,' Ben said, stroking her back lightly. 'We would have awesome babies.'

Gemma couldn't work him out. One minute he was cold to her and ignoring her, the next, he was talking about having babies. He sent such mixed messages all the time. Tentatively, she said, 'We used to talk about a little house, or a flat . . . just you and me and our six kids.'

He laughed lightly. 'Did we? Six kids? Wow.'

It made Gemma sad, the way he said it, as if he hadn't been there for the conversation. As if she'd had it with someone else. Another Ben. But then he said, 'I can think of worse things than having babies with you.'

He kissed her then, and his tongue insistently nudged her lips apart. Clearly, the time for talking was over.

Much later, when Ben had gone to sleep, Gemma lay in the dark and allowed herself to imagine . . . to picture having Ben's baby.

104

Having a baby with someone tied you to them for life. She wouldn't just be Ben's girlfriend; she'd be the mother of his child. And on top of that, she'd have a baby. Her own little angel, like Lily. Someone who was all hers, who was her own family. She and Ben would laugh and joke again, and the perfect blonde baby, with her hair and Ben's amazing eyes, would bring them closer together. They'd buy a little flat, like they'd talked about, and they'd eat dinner together every night. They'd take the baby to the park and have picnics. And when the baby got bigger, Gemma would be there to pick her up from school every day, and when Ben got home he could read her stories.

But of course it couldn't happen. It was crazy. They were so young. And it wasn't as if their relationship was going all that well. When she thought about it she wanted to cry. It was like she'd had a perfect dream, and then someone had woken her up. She curled around Ben's sleeping back. He sighed in his sleep and she put an arm over him and hugged him tight. She would give anything . . . anything at all, to be the mother of Ben's baby.

She left Ben's early because she was supposed to go to a ballet class, but in the end, she didn't go after all. She went home, told her mum she'd eaten something dodgy at Lucy's and got into bed. She needed to think about the night before and what it had meant. It seemed very significant, almost as if she'd had a vision, a glimpse of a possible future.

She rolled over on to her front and pressed her

face into the pillow. There was an ache in her gut, like period pain, and a constant fluttering, like a million butterflies. Over and over, she thought about Ben saying, 'I can think of worse things than having babies with you.' Why would he have said that if he didn't mean it? Could it work? Could it? Could she have found a way to be happy and complete, to have a life she'd never dreamed of imagining before?

When Samantha came home later, she seemed surprised to find Gemma downstairs, busy in the kitchen. 'Hi, Mum!' she said, her eyes sparkling and her cheeks pink. She'd spent the last hour making a big lasagne for dinner. Her mother stared at her, bemused. 'Good grief, Gemma. You must be feeling better. My goodness . . . you cooked! I brought some stuff home from M&S . . . I didn't expect — '

'I know! But I finished my history course work, and I felt like cooking. Besides, I thought it would be nicer for us to have a real dinner. I knew you'd probably get in too late to cook. Did you buy any salad ingredients?'

'Yes,' said her mum. She looked suspicious. 'This isn't like you at all, Gemma. It's all I can do to get you to eat, usually, let alone cook.'

'I know. But I think that's going to change now. I'm not going to study dance full-time or do the teacher's exams, so that's sort of it for my dancing.'

'My,' said her mother faintly. 'I suppose I hadn't thought of that. You shan't be doing ballet all the time any more.'

'No,' said Gemma. 'And with all my

. . . studying . . . I'd like to start eating really healthy food.'

Samantha still didn't seem convinced. 'I'm sure it's just another of your teenage fads, but I have to say I'm very pleased that you want to eat better. Even if it's only this week.'

'Is Dad coming home?'

'He'll be in any minute. He rang me from the golf club to say they'd finished and were just having a few drinks.'

'Right. Well, I'll set the table!'

Gemma bounced into the dining room and started laying out cutlery and table mats. She felt ridiculously happy. She had a plan now. If her parents knew what it was, they would be utterly horrified. Her friends at school would turn up their noses in disgust. Her teachers too. But she knew that it was the right answer for her.

For months, she'd been putting off thinking about finishing her A-levels. If she was completely honest with herself, she just couldn't imagine going to university. She knew she wasn't ready, that it was very likely she wasn't cut out for it. Her parents were convinced she'd be taking up one of the offers she'd had to study English at a top university: St Andrew's, or Durham. But she had no desire to. She just wasn't excited about the idea of further study. There really wasn't anything she wanted to learn more about. And most of all, she didn't want to live far from home, away from Ben.

But now she didn't have to. Because she was going to talk to Ben about starting a family — and doing it soon. If they had a baby together, they would never be apart again. Ben could still go to university, as long as he chose one in London. It was the perfect solution. She'd be a young mum. Even if she got pregnant really quickly, she'd still be eighteen before the baby was born, and that wasn't embarrassingly young. It wasn't chavvy young or anything. When her child was eighteen, she'd only be thirty-six. And the emptiness she'd always felt, the coldness in her centre would go away when she had a child to love. She was born to do this.

She set out wine glasses beside her parents' places and put out a juice glass for herself. Her parents thought it looked good to let her have a glass of wine at dinner if they ate out: they always said it was how the Mediterranean people raised their children. But now she was planning to fall pregnant, there'd be no drinking. There'd be healthy food, lots of sleep, and, as she'd learned from the internet that afternoon, folic acid. She planned to go down to Boots the next day to buy some. She'd make sure she'd been taking it for a few weeks before she and Ben . . . oh, it was all so exciting!

She heard her dad come in through the front door. 'Samantha?' he boomed, his voice echoing in the hall. She heard her mother's heels clicking on the floor, and then she heard them talking to one another in low tones. She hoped it was just one of their standard rows, not a summit meeting about her making dinner.

Her father came into the dining room and absently kissed her hello. 'Gosh! Look at all this!' he said indulgently, as if she was six and had just

108

done a finger painting. 'Your mother tells me we're all eating dinner together.' He didn't sound wildly enthusiastic, but Gemma gave him her brightest smile.

'Nice for a change, isn't it, Daddy?'

'It is, sweetheart, it is,' he said. 'Let me go and wash my hands.'

Gemma went back into the kitchen and got her lasagne out of the oven. Her mother was making a salad, and together they took the food through to the dining room. Gemma filled the wine glasses and, on impulse, put two candles on the table and lit them. Her mother smiled. 'Looks lovely, darling.'

They both sat down and waited. There was no sign of her father. Gemma got up and went out into the hallway to call him. He was standing by the front door, talking on his mobile. She heard him laugh softly. Then he heard her footsteps and turned. His face froze for a second, and then he turned away and spoke even more quietly into his phone. Gemma went back into the dining room. 'He's on the phone,' she said flatly.

'Well, we can't let your lovely food get cold, dear. Let's start without him.' Her mother sounded completely unfazed, and her face registered no expression at all. But whether that was Botox or inner peace, Gemma had no idea. Her mum filled her wine glass, drained it and filled it again. Gemma felt nauseous and miserable. She had seen the expression on her father's face: guilt and pride and shame and something else all mixed up. Whatever happened, she never wanted to see that expression on Ben's face. Their life together was going to be different from this, that was for sure. She served herself a great lump of lasagne and began to eat.

★ ★ ★

Somehow, the moment to talk about having a baby just never seemed to arise. The more Gemma thought about it, the surer she was that it was what she wanted. Yet, somehow, the way things were with her and Ben, there just wasn't ever a good time to bring it into the conversation. To be honest, they weren't talking much anyway.

If she allowed herself to think about it, she might have thought that Ben was losing interest in her. If she texted him, he took ages to text back. When she went round to his, more often than not he'd sit playing some violent game on his X-Box for hours, and she'd just have to sit beside him in silence. They hadn't gone out anywhere together in weeks, but he never missed his Saturday nights out with his mates. He seemed to be getting bored with her, and the more sweet, easy-going and sexy she tried to be, the less interested he seemed to be.

She felt desperate. She wished she was one of those girls who could just walk away, play hard to get, refuse to take his calls, and turn him down when he finally put down his X-Box controller and pulled her to him. But she wasn't that girl. Ben was her world, and he knew it. She knew that there were loads of girls who'd be ready to take her place as Ben's girlfriend at a

110

moment's notice, and the thought of having to see him out somewhere with someone else made her feel sick.

Still, he always wanted to have sex, and it seemed to her that that was the only time they really connected. When they were in bed, he was passionate and focused only on her. She often thought that if they were going to have the conversation about starting a family, after sex would be the time to do it. But Ben either fell asleep very quickly, or got up because he had somewhere to be or something to do. The days of lying in bed and cuddling and talking were over.

One Friday evening, Ben had a gig at a bar in Islington. It was a chilly night, and an icy breeze cut through Gemma's jeans and jacket. She wanted to cuddle up to Ben, but when she looked at his face, his expression was forbidding and she didn't dare to. They stood side by side at the bus stop, shivering. Ben had no coat, and he huddled inside his tracksuit top, leaning against the side of the bus shelter, staring at the corner shop opposite. Gemma felt nauseous. He looked as though he'd rather be anywhere but with her. She was too scared to say anything. Then the door of the shop opened and the short, dark-haired girl she had seen with Ben all those weeks ago came out carrying a pint of milk. She glanced up and saw Ben and Gemma. Her lip curled and she turned and walked quickly away. Gemma turned to look at Ben. His eyes followed the dark-haired girl, and a storm of emotions crossed his face. Before Gemma could pluck up the courage to ask him who the girl was, or what

111

had happened between them, the bus came and they had to get on it. Ben's mate Liam was on the bus and they sat at the back together. Ben and Liam chatted and ignored Gemma.

It was Ben's best ever gig. There was a big crowd, and he got an amazing response. When he came off stage, the promoter came to him and congratulated him. 'You did a great job,' he said. 'Here's twenty quid. We'd love to have you here again.'

It was the first time Ben had been paid for a gig and he was jubilant. He'd borrowed an ID from someone who was at college and ordered drinks for himself, Liam and Gemma. It was a raucous, fun night, and Gemma was quite drunk. Liam's mum came to pick them up and dropped Ben and Gemma off at Ben's house.

Ben was all over her the moment they got out of the car. 'Can you stay?' he whispered, kissing her and sliding his hands over her body. 'My mum's away on business. We've got the whole house.'

'I can't really . . . ' Gemma said doubtfully. 'I said I'd be home.'

'Text your mum. Please,' he groaned, pressing himself against her. 'Tell her you're at Lucy's. I beg you.'

Gemma took out her phone and sent her mum a quick text. As soon as she finished typing, Ben dragged her into the living room and started to pull her jumper off over her head.

'In here?' Gemma said.

'Look,' Ben replied and pointed to the enormous floor-to-ceiling mirror that hung opposite the fireplace. 'I want to watch us.' He pulled her boots off and took her jeans off her and then stood her in front of the mirror in just her underwear. 'Oh, Gem . . . ' he groaned. 'You're so hot.'

She had never seen him so excited. In seconds, he had pulled off his own clothes, and laid her down on the thick carpet. He lay on top of her, and she felt him start to slide into her.

'Ben, wait!' she said breathlessly. 'We haven't got a condom.'

'I know,' he said, his eyes glazed with lust.

'But what if we . . . I mean . . . we could . . . ' As she spoke, she felt Ben slide all the way inside her. She looked seriously into his eyes. 'Do you want to, Ben? I mean, I really do, but do you want to — '

He was thrusting and panting. 'I want to, baby, I do, oh God . . . I want to — '

'You want to have a baby?' Gemma gasped, but as she said it, Ben came hard, yelling and arching away from her, and she wasn't totally sure he had heard her.

She didn't know how, but she knew, in that instant, that they had done it. They'd made a baby. And sure enough, two weeks later, her period, which was always on time, didn't come. She waited two more days, then took a bus to the next village. She didn't want to buy a pregnancy test in the local chemist: the pharmacist had known her all her life, and besides, there was too good a chance of bumping into someone she knew, or worse, one of her mother's friends.

She went home and locked herself in the

bathroom. She knew before she did the test that it would be positive, but when she saw the little blue cross appear she began to shake uncontrollably. There was no going back. Well, there was a way out, but she wasn't even going to give that a moment's thought. She would never do that.

She'd read up on the internet and knew she was about four weeks along. She knew about the risks of miscarriage, and it seemed best to get through the twelve-week danger period before she told anyone, even Ben. It seemed to her if she were twelve weeks pregnant, properly pregnant, everyone would have to take her more seriously. It wouldn't be hard to keep it a secret . . . she was used to keeping everything to herself. Ben never really talked to her, and her parents definitely didn't. She kept her conversations at school to the purely superficial, talking about course work, ballet or parties. They were revising for exams, so luckily it wasn't a big social time.

Once she knew she was pregnant, she didn't want to keep on sleeping with Ben. She still texted him every day, but when she went around to his place she tried to avoid having sex. She knew all the books and websites said it was fine to have sex, but she was pretty sure that it couldn't be good for the tiny baby in there to have all that bumping and thumping going on. Ben got pretty ratty when she kept making excuses. He'd snuggle up to her, but when she said that she was too sore after tennis, or that she would have to go soon to get home, he'd slump back on his side of the sofa and reach for the

X-Box controls. Things between them got even more strained, and, although he never said anything, Gemma knew he was wondering why she kept coming round if she wasn't going to sleep with him. It was only for a few weeks, she told herself. Once everything was out in the open and he knew about the baby, things would be brilliant.

THE SECOND TRIMESTER

Toni

James was crying. The only time I'd seen him cry before was when he asked me to marry him, but here he was, sobbing like a baby. I was surprised. I mean, I knew I'd cry. With my hormones as they are at the moment, I cry if my shoelace is untied. He was absolutely fine, just sitting there, holding my hand, but then the woman put the wand thing on my tummy and the fluttery, wooshy sound of a rapid little heartbeat filled the room. I felt him grip my hand tightly and I looked over and his eyes were all red and teary. Then the woman said, 'If you look here, there's a little foot.' At first it just looked like we were peering into a snowstorm, but as she pointed bits out on the screen, I started to be able to see. I saw a round head and the long string of beads that made up the spine. She took all sorts of measurements and then she printed out a set of three little photos for us, printed on funny shiny paper, like the kind you got in old-fashioned fax machines.

I'd seen sonogram pictures before . . . they all looked the same, and if someone at work showed you one, you had to smile politely and pretend you could see what it was, or that there were features you could identify. But now we had our own, nothing was more fascinating than those three little bits of paper. I knew we'd stare at them for ages, scan them and post them to

Facebook and email our friends and family, and generally be the sonogram bores we'd laughed about.

We went to sit in a coffee shop and stared at the pictures like they were priceless relics. 'It looks like it's got your nose,' James said.

'And look at those long legs! Just like you,' I pointed. It was the twelve-week scan, so too early to tell the sex of the baby, although we still weren't sure if we wanted to find out (well, I was, but James said he didn't want to know). The best part was that our baby was there at all, and seemed to be perfect. Although I'd had a bit of morning sickness, had done six or seven positive pregnancy tests and had all sorts of other typical symptoms, I don't think I'd quite believed it until I'd seen that fuzzy little figure on the screen. But there he or she was. Toes, fingers, a little turned-up nose. A tiny, perfect person.

Yes, yes, I know this probably bores you too. I know billions of people have done this before. I know it's not a unique miracle, but it was to us . . . and I suppose it is for every first-time parent. I knew that the girls in my birth group on the baby website would get excited with us. We'd all been counting down the days until our twelve-week scans, and we'd all cooed enthusiastically over the pictures as people posted them. For a few, the twelve-week scan had brought heartbreak, when there'd been no heartbeat, or the baby hadn't grown beyond a little bean and had died.

I'd come a long way in the eight weeks since I'd found out I was pregnant. The first few weeks, I admit, had been a little crazy.

I knew nothing. Less than nothing. It was ironic . . . I'd learned all sorts of things about how to fall pregnant, but nothing at all about what would happen when I actually was. I went for a walk around Mothercare one Saturday, and found I was staring at all sorts of unfamiliar objects. I had no idea what they were for. I saw women fill trolleys full of stuff: fluffy stuff, clothes, gadgets, toys . . . How can something so small need so many things? Are these women all suckers? Or did we actually have to go out and spend thousands of pounds on equipment we never knew we needed?

On top of that, I realised I had no clue what was actually going on inside my body. I knew about morning sickness, and I figured the sore breasts were part of the hormonal changes, but what was actually going on in my uterus? So, the next day, Sunday, when James had gone to play five-a-side football, I sat down with the baby book he had bought.

Half an hour in, I was nervous. Within an hour, I was terrified. Two hours later, and I was feverishly googling spina bifida, and by the time James came back, I was kneeling in front of the fridge, wearing rubber gloves and chucking half the contents into the bin.

'Good grief,' he said, dumping his kitbag on the floor and kicking off his muddy boots. 'Has pregnancy turned you into a domestic goddess? What are you doing?'

'Cheese,' I said madly rootling around in the back of the fridge.

'Do you want some? Is this your first craving?'

'No, no cheese. I can't eat any cheese ... I might get listeria and the baby might die. And no pâté either. And what about that night last week when I had three glasses of wine with the team after work? We need to go to the supermarket and get spinach.'

James gently took my arm and got me to stand up. He kicked the fridge closed. 'Love, you'll be fine. You've always eaten pretty healthily, and I'm sure you'll carry on doing that. We'll get you all the vegetables you want, but you don't have to chuck out my Belgian pâté ... You don't have to eat it, and it's not actually a threat to the baby, just sitting there in the fridge. And you can eat cheese, just not ones with rind or mould, or made with unpasteurised milk.'

I nodded, and sat down on one of the kitchen chairs. But then I noticed.

'Your boots!' I gasped.

He looked a bit exasperated. 'What about them?'

'They're covered in mud.'

'I know, I know ... I'll clean them. Sorry. I'll even wash the floor.'

'It's not that ... what if you got cat poo on them? I could get toxoplasmosis.'

He didn't even say anything that time. Just looked at me for a long moment.

'I'm a total hysterical crazy, aren't I?'

'You've just got information panic overload. You know not to believe everything you read on the internet about most things ... why are you freaking out about this?'

I thought for a long time. 'Because everything else in my life that I've done, I've really only been responsible for myself. Now I'm sharing my body, and I'm responsible for someone else's *whole life!*'

That statement shocked James into silence. He sat down opposite me at the table and took my hand. 'You're right. I hadn't thought of that,' he said quietly. And, of course, that made me cry again.

'Come on, squirrel,' he said gently. 'Let's go and sit in the living room.'

We went through and he settled me in his arms and held me quietly until I stopped sobbing.

'I can't take it, James. I can't be scared for nine whole months . . . and then for every minute of every day when we have this tiny, helpless thing to look after. This is too big.'

'I know this sounds an obvious thing to say, but people have been doing this for thousands of years,' James said. 'It seems hard, but it can't be that difficult.'

'I wish my mum was still around. I'd ask her how she managed,' I sobbed.

'I could ask my mum,' said James hesitantly.

His mum lived in Sussex, and we both felt a little guilty that we didn't see her more often. She was sweet and terribly kind, and she'd always been very nice to me. She wasn't the typical mother-in-law at all. Eileen was a stay-at-home mum, and she was good at all the mum things like cooking and baking, and she did amazing birthday parties for James and his brothers. I knew she was over the moon she was going to be a grandma again (one of James' older brothers already had two kids), but I hadn't actually spoken to her.

I thought about it for a bit. 'I'd like to ring her if that's okay.' James looked at me, really surprised. In all the years we'd been together, I don't think I'd ever rung his mum of my own accord.

'Okay,' he said, encouragingly. Before I could talk myself out of it, I grabbed the cordless phone and speed-dialled her. Eileen answered in that old-fashioned way, with the last four digits of her telephone number.

'Seven eight one two?'

'Hi, Eileen, it's Toni.'

'Toni! How lovely to hear from you! How are you feeling?'

She was so polite, she managed to keep all surprise out of her voice, and responded purely with warmth. It made me want to cry again.

'I'm doing all right, Eileen . . . still a bit of morning sickness, but apparently that's a good sign that everything's doing what it should.'

'Not too tired? I was so exhausted in those first few weeks with James I didn't know what to do with myself!'

'No, so far so good, I'm not falling asleep at my desk or anything.'

'Oh good,' she said, with a little upward inflection, and then she left a little gap of silence to give me the chance to say whatever it was that I'd rung to say. She was very good like that. I launched straight in before I could bottle it.

124

'Eileen, I know you're going to think this is crazy, but would you mind if I asked you a question?'

'Of course not, dear.'

'Were you scared?'

'Scared?'

'When you fell pregnant. When you had the boys. Were you scared? Because I'm absolutely terrified about everything, and I don't know if that's normal. Then I start worrying about stress hormones affecting the baby, and I get more scared because I'm scared being scared will hurt my baby.'

'Oh my goodness,' she said, then she thought for a while. 'Well your generation definitely has a lot more information than we did . . . and you get a good deal more fiddling about from doctors and nurses.'

I had to smile at 'fiddling about' . . . she said it with such prim distaste. She spoke again.

'We didn't have any of your ultrasound scans or growth charts or anything like that, and if we were lucky, we only had Dr Spock to refer to.'

'The Vulcan from *Star Trek*?'

'No, dear, that's Mr Spock.' Eileen had raised three sons, she was very culturally literate about these things. 'No, Dr Spock was the childcare guru of my day. But to be honest we just did things the way we thought best, or the way our mums showed us. And we managed. Or at least, I think we did . . . my boys seemed to turn out all right.'

I looked at James sitting on the sofa, his blond head bent, trying to be supportive without eavesdropping, and I remembered all the little things he'd been doing for me in the last few days.

'I think your boys turned out fantastically.'

'I can't stop you worrying, Toni, but maybe the best thing to remember is this. Worrying won't change what happens. It's not like a work project where you can take steps to fix something. That baby is inside you and growing, and either he'll be fine and grow perfectly, or he won't. Not much you do is going to change that.'

'Within reason.'

'Within reason, of course. I'd suggest you stay off roller-coasters and you don't consider rodeo as a new career path.'

'I'll keep that in mind.'

'Now I know with Lesley, she read far too much on the internet and got on to all those chat forums, and she knew her risk factor for this, that and the other thing. And you know what? She got herself in a right tizwaz, and the babies both turned out fine.'

Lesley was James' eldest brother Peter's wife.

'But Lesley also had a miscarriage,' I pointed out.

'As did I, Toni. In fact, I had two. You'll find most women who have children will have had at least one. I'm not promising you this pregnancy will go perfectly, or that you definitely won't lose the baby. I'm just saying worrying about it won't affect the outcome. So maybe it's better not to worry.'

What she said made such total, perfect sense. I couldn't do it, of course. I was already too wound up, too involved. I'd already found too many things to worry about. But Eileen's calm, practical view of things made me feel much better.

I said goodbye, and then went back and curled up in the crook of my husband's arm on the sofa. That night, we made love for the first time since I found out I was pregnant. James was gentle and careful. I still felt weird, like my body wasn't quite mine, but I managed to enjoy it. We'd get through it somehow, these strange nine months. Somehow, this baby and James and me would make it.

★ ★ ★

I'd listened to most of Eileen's advice, especially the bit about there being no point in worrying. But I didn't stay off the internet. I'd got totally addicted to the baby website, especially the forum. We used an online calculator to work out when our baby was due . . . 14 September, according to the dates we'd estimated. Someone had started a group for mums having babies in September, and I joined it. It was such a relief finding a bunch of women going through all the same things I was . . . and the discussion was really no-holds-barred. Cystitis, constipation, husbands who'd gone off sex . . . whatever people were going through, they shared in a big way. It was hilarious. I found myself having discussions I'd never have had, even with my closest friends, with a bunch of complete strangers. Maybe that was what made it easier.

I told them about having to plan a pee break into the middle of my morning Tube journey, and loads of people wrote back and said they had to do it too. One of them even confessed to wearing old-lady incontinence pants. I soon got to know some of the screen names . . . some women obviously had a lot of time to post, and commented on nearly every discussion thread. There were lots who write their posts in text-speak or with lots of awful misspellings ('should of' just made me want to scream), but some girls' posts were really witty and interesting to read.

I suppose I got a bit too caught up in it for a while. I'd check the site first thing in the morning before I left for work, then again when I got to work, then again at lunchtime and if it got quiet in the afternoon in the office I might sneak on to see if anyone had posted anything interesting. Then while James watched telly in the evenings I'd spend another hour or so online. At first, I told James a lot of the things I read about, but after a while, if I started a sentence with 'You'll never guess what I read on the baby website today', his eyes started to glaze over. To be perfectly fair, I knew it was a bit much to ask for him to be interested in the day-to-day lives of a bunch of women he'd never met (although neither had I). It was like having two hundred new, very close friends. Linda–Q, who lived in Lincoln, was always online, and every lunchtime she'd start a thread about what she was cooking for tea. We'd all respond, and it was a bit like we were all sitting together in the same office. The website also made me feel like I wasn't so weird for being a young mum . . . in fact by most people's standards I was average to quite old at twenty-six! There were lots of mums who were twenty and younger, often having their second or third babies. There were also some older mums . . . one whose first child was eighteen. She'd been on her own for years and then met a lovely guy in her late thirties, and now she was having a new baby. Her son was the same age as some of the mums she was chatting to, but everyone seemed to get along and find something in common, no matter how different we all were.

I really wished that I was having the same sorts of experiences in real life (or IRL, as we called it on the site), but that wasn't the case. We'd been very careful not to tell anyone but close family until the twelve-week scan, but once we'd got over that hurdle, we started telling our friends.

Well, Robyn was just furious. We had a proper row about it. 'Fucking hell!' she said when I told her. She slapped the table top in the coffee shop, making the two old biddies at the next table jump. It seemed like a bit of a strong reaction to the news, but I let it go. I chattered on about the scan and took out the pictures, but I could see her building up a proper head of steam, and, being Rob, she didn't wait long to let rip. 'So you're telling me now?' she said sharply. 'How long have you known?'

'About . . . um . . . eight weeks?' I sounded a bit timid, I know, but Rob can do that to you.

'And you've spoken to me how many times in those eight weeks?'

'A few. Quite a few. Look, I'm sorry, Rob . . . I
. . . we weren't ready to tell anyone.'

'We. Being you and James.' She said this a bit
snidely, as if my relationship with James couldn't
possibly be as important as my friendship with
her.

'Yes.'

'Does Caro know?'

'No. Just my dad and James' mum. You're the
first other person I've told.'

She nodded then and leaned back and folded
her arms. She wasn't satisfied, but at least she
wasn't yelling.

Robyn doesn't stay cross for long, though.
And she's insatiably curious, so she was soon
asking a million mad questions. 'So what does it
feel like?'

'What does what feel like?'

'Being pregnant, numbskull. Can you feel it
moving around?'

'No, it's still much too small.'

'It's really freaky. You've got a whole other
person growing inside your body. It's like *Alien*.'

'Thanks, Rob.'

'Wow . . . imagine it bursting out of your belly
button, all teeth and mucus . . . '

'You do know how babies are born, don't
you?'

'Yeah. I don't really want to think about that,
thanks.'

'That's because you don't have to do it.'

'No, but you do. Sucker! So do you have lots
of weird cravings? Do you want to chew the
wallpaper and eat coal? Wow . . . imagine if it's a

boy. You've got a penis growing inside you! That's grotesque! And if it's a girl, you've got two twinkles. They'll call you two-twinkle Toni . . . '

After an hour or so of this, I was exhausted . . . half from laughing at her total lunacy, and half because even though she was trying, she just really, really didn't get it. It was like I was a lab experiment she was staring at through a plate-glass window, not her friend going through something big, but really quite normal.

Now Caro tried, I'll give her that. Despite her allergy to children, she pretended to be excited at first and asked slightly more sensible questions. But she soon lost interest and wanted to talk about holidays or going clubbing. I'd known all along that this wasn't something I'd be able to share with her, and that was OK.

James told me when he told his footie mates, he got a lot of teasing about his life being over, and how he'd been tricked into fatherhood by the old ball-and-chain. His close friends, Alex and Dave, seemed to be thrilled for him, but, like Rob and Caro, they were nowhere near becoming parents themselves, so their interest was a bit academic.

I'd never been a massive drinker, but I really like to go out and be sociable, so I saw no reason for our lives to change on that front just because I was pregnant. I could still chat, I could still dance, and I was a world-champion eater once the morning sickness died down. So for a few weeks after we'd had the twelve-week scan and told all our mates, we tried to carry on our lives pretty much as we used to.

Nothing's ever simple though, is it? Firstly, anyone and everyone appointed themselves boss of me. I'm not kidding. People I hardly knew: new girlfriends of friends, the barman in our local, some old geezer we often see in the Italian down the road . . . as soon as they knew I was pregnant, they'd keep an eye on what I was eating and drinking.

'Is that water?' someone would ask suspiciously. As if I would sit in a public bar quaffing a pint glass of neat vodka.

'No prawns for you!' said a waiter with a cheeky grin when I tried to order a seafood salad for dinner. And, 'Isn't it late for you to be out?' from an oh-so-concerned girl I hardly knew when James and I walked into a bar. For God's sake! It was 9 p.m.!

It made me want to dig my heels in and keep going out, but I was fighting a losing battle. You see, I finally had to admit to myself that it just wasn't as much fun any more. There's nothing duller than being the sober one in the pub sipping lime and soda, while everyone else gets pissed and raucous. Drunk people think they get wittier and funnier as the night goes on, but that's only true if their only audience is other drunk people. To the sober people, they just look stupid. I also learned that drunk people have no sense of personal space. After the second or third evening we'd spent in a pub when someone had lurched and bumped into me, and someone else had leaned too close and breathed beery fumes into my face while telling me a very boring, very long story, I decided that, for now at least, my party days were over. It wasn't for long, though, I kept telling myself. Once the baby was born and sleeping through the night, we'd get a babysitter and I'd be out and partying with the best of them! I wasn't dead, I was just going to be a mum.

Even if my two best friends weren't totally on the same page, I had my new online friends and a whole wide world of fascinating baby and pregnancy things to learn about, but James had a big hole in his social life.

'You go out tonight without me,' I told James one Saturday evening. 'It's no fun for me. I'll wait at home like a good little wife.'

'But I'll miss you,' he said, putting his arms around me and kissing my neck. 'Going out is no fun without you.'

'It's no fun *with* me, pumpkin,' I said. 'I spend my time perched on a bar stool, sipping my soft drink, worrying about how I'm going to get through all the people to go to the loo *again*, and hoping nobody's going to elbow me in my bump. I don't have a nice time, and I don't want to spend the evening sulking or pulling on your sleeve, asking you to take me home. Go! Have fun. And come home to me and tell me stories of your wild adventures.'

But, that night, he didn't go out. He stayed in with me and spent the whole evening drinking wine and flicking between channels on the TV. He got himself into a completely foul mood by the end of the evening, and stomped off to bed in a massive sulk. I got into bed a few minutes later and curled myself around his broad back. I knew he wasn't asleep. I thought about it for a while, and then I whispered in his ear.

'Love, you should just have gone out, you know,' I said. 'It wasn't a test or a trick . . . I really don't mind.'

He thought about it for a while, then he said, 'I know. But what kind of dickhead goes out on the lash and leaves his pregnant wife at home alone?'

'The kind whose wife told him to go?'

'Yes, yes . . . but it just looks bad.'

'To whom? I don't care. I bet Alex and Dave and the guys don't care. And it's not like you were going to go to a lap-dancing club and come home at four a.m. with some girl's thong dangling from your ear. You were going to Hoxton for a few drinks.'

I knew he was smiling in the dark. 'So, the thong dangling from my ear. That would be a bit of a no-no?'

'It would be frowned upon by the wife department.'

'I'll bear that in mind.' Then he turned over and took me in his lovely warm arms.

★ ★ ★

After that, he would go out one night at the weekend, and often for a few drinks one night during the week. I was quite happy for him to go, although a little part of me wished he wouldn't come home so happy, clearly having had a fabulous time without me.

If our friends were a bit odd about my being

134

pregnant, work was worse. All the wrong people, i.e. scary Angela, were really excited. My work friends, the ones who were the same age as me, were a bit like my non-work friends . . . they pretended to be interested, but having babies really wasn't on their radar. Most of them were still single and interested in advancing their careers above all else. As soon as word got out that I was pregnant, some of the more obvious ones started circling like sharks.

One Tuesday morning, a girl called Naomi, who works on medical and pharmaceutical accounts, cornered me in the kitchen while I was making myself a cup of caffeine-free tea and a bowl of porridge.

'Toni!' she said, and her over-friendly voice set my bullshit radar going. We don't work on any of the same accounts, and we've probably only ever crossed paths in the loo or at big staff parties. We'd not spoken two words to each other in the years we've both worked there. 'I heard your happy news, congratulations! When is it due?' she gushed.

'September,' I said warily.

'Wow . . . just as the Christmas campaigns launch!' She sounded heartbroken for me. Then she added, ever so innocently, 'Who'll be looking after your cosmetics accounts?'

I laughed and walked away, but I was furious. I've worked really hard to get where I am, and I know it's a competitive industry. Someone would obviously have to look after my accounts while I'm on maternity leave, but I'd be back and no mistake.

I've always been really close to my boss, Kate. She's only a few years older than me, and, of everyone, I would count her as my closest friend at work. We went out for lunch that day, and I told her the story about Naomi. 'It's outrageous!' I said, viciously chopping at my Caesar salad. 'They all seem to see it as a signal that it's open season on my clients! It's like I'm not even dead yet and they're picking through my clothes. I mean, I know I'm not going to die, I'm going to go on maternity leave and come back.'

'Are you, though?' Kate said.

'Am I what?'

'Going to come back.'

'Of course I am. Don't be silly! I'll take six months or so, we haven't quite worked it out yet, and then I'll be back.'

'And put your baby in a nursery from eight in the morning till six at night? I don't think so.'

'What are you saying?' I said, trying to stop my voice shaking.

'Come on, Toni, how many women have you heard about who go on maternity leave and never really come back to work? They want to work part-time, then they get pregnant again with the second one . . . I just . . . ' She stopped herself and shook her head. 'Never mind.'

'You just what? What were you going to say?'

'I can't say. I'm your boss.'

'You're also supposed to be my friend. What were you about to say?'

She hesitated, then said, 'I just didn't think you were that sort of girl.'

'What sort of girl?' I felt close to tears now.

This wasn't the supportive, friendly girl-chat I'd been expecting when we decided to go out for lunch.

'The sort who would throw it all away when you were still in your twenties.'

'You're right,' I said. 'You shouldn't have said it. I'm going to go now, and pretend you didn't say that, as my friend or as my boss.' I stood up.

'Toni, I'm so sorry,' she said quickly, and I could see a look of panic in her eyes. But it wasn't because she'd hurt a friend or because what she'd said was wrong, it was because it broke every HR rule in the book and she was worried I'd throw a gender discrimination lawsuit at them.

James was out at client meetings, so I rang Robyn to have a rant about what Kate had said as I walked back to the office.

'I hate whining,' I said. 'But this just seems so unfair. I love my job. I had a career path. I'd have loved to have waited till my mid-thirties to have a baby. Another two years in this job and a few years as an account manager and I think my position would be much more secure.'

Robyn's nothing if not direct. 'So why didn't you wait?'

'Because the doctor told us that it was now or never. My crap ovaries are shutting up shop, so we had to choose. Conceive straight away, or maybe never have kids.'

It takes a lot to shut Rob up, but that did it. She was quiet for quite a while. 'Do they know that at work?'

'No. And it's really none of their business.'

'You're right. But if people knew that they might not be so quick to judge.' And I knew in that moment she'd been doing some judging of her own and was now feeling rotten about it. 'Seriously, Tones, I didn't really understand before. Now I get it. And I'll help you as much as I can. I'll babysit and everything.'

I imagined Robyn tearing down the road with my baby strapped to her bike carrier like a parcel, and I managed a smile. It was the only one that day.

When I told James that evening about Kate, he was furious. 'You *should* sodding sue them!' he raged. 'How dare she say something like that?'

'Because she believes it. She thinks I'm going to throw my career away and become a yummy mummy and pop out sprogs for the rest of my natural life.'

'Well, that's ridiculous. She should know you better than that.'

'She might have a point, though.'

'What? What do you mean?' James looked panicked.

'Well, I have to say, the way people have behaved at work hasn't made me feel like they really care about me. And Kate is right . . . I don't want to go back to work when the baby's six months old and leave it in some horrible crèche for ten hours a day. Also, do you know what childcare costs?'

'I haven't a clue,' James said.

'I looked it up on the baby website,' I began, and he started to roll his eyes. I ignored him and kept talking. 'We're looking at up to four hundred pounds a week. If I look at what I bring home, I'd be working to pay for childcare, for my Travelcard and lunch at work, and that'd be pretty much it.'

'Four hundred quid a *week*?' James went a little bit pale. 'There has to be a cheaper way. Most people wouldn't be able to afford that, surely. How do they manage?'

'Well, a lot of people don't live in the south-east, for a start. It's a lot more expensive here. And maybe they have family to lend a hand. A grandma or a sister helps out. I don't know.'

'Well, we don't have that option. Your mum's no longer with us, and my mum's miles away in Hove. It's not really practical to take a baby down to her there every day.'

'No.'

'So what do we do?' James looked at me expectantly.

'I don't know, James! I don't have all the answers. Ideally, I don't want to go back to work before the baby's a year or so old, and even then I don't think I want to go back full-time. What's the point in having a baby if neither of us ever see it?'

'Fair point,' James said. 'But we can't afford this house without your salary. We're a bit screwed, really.'

We sat side by side on the sofa in miserable silence. 'We didn't really think this part of it through, did we?' said James after a while.

'Well, it did happen very fast,' I said, stating the obvious. 'I suppose we just thought we'd have more time.'

'More time for what? To win the Lottery?'

'I know. It seems impossible. But we'll find a way to make it work. We have to. You can't un-knock me up now.'

'Well, I'll look at some numbers over the next few days,' James said. 'Let's see what we can do.'

James has always been the money brain in our relationship. He works out budgets and puts money away in savings accounts and tells me how much we have to spend on a holiday each year. I knew he was the right person to solve this problem.

It took him a little while, but one evening a few days later, he asked me to sit down in front of the computer with him. He had a whole spreadsheet laid out, which just made me nervous. It looked so formal.

'Okay, Tones, this is what we have to do. Here are our expenses, here's what we have coming in if you take a year off and get statutory maternity pay after the first twelve weeks.'

I may be no good at finances, but even I could see that the first number was bigger than the second one.

'So what do we do?' I asked.

'Well, we need to cut some costs,' James said. 'So, for example, we spend a lot on entertainment. If we cut down on nights out and takeaways, we can trim a bit there. Shopping in a cheaper supermarket will help too. I'm giving up my gym membership, and I think you should too.'

'I don't mind for me . . . I won't be able to go at all soon, but why should you give it up?'

140

'I go about once a week, so it costs me about a tenner a time. I'll go running instead. That's free.'

'Are you sure?'

'Well, we have to economise somewhere, and we still have to eat. Luxuries will just have to go for now. Some costs will decrease while you're not working, like your travel, but the baby will cost something too. Nappies aren't free.'

'That's true.'

'I've also been asking around, and I think I could get a bit of freelance design work. We're not supposed to moonlight, but everyone does it, and we could certainly do with an extra few hundred quid every month.'

'But you'll have to do that in the evenings!'

James sighed and looked at me. 'We have to do something, Tones. Somehow we have to get these two numbers closer together.'

'Maybe I could take on some freelance writing, or do some PR stuff for local companies. I don't know what the rules are with maternity leave, but I'll see what I can do.'

'That's great,' said James, then he gave me a quick one-armed hug. 'Come on, Toni, we'll make it work somehow. We always do. How hard can it be?'

Louise

She tried to tell Brian. She tried twice, in fact. She sent a text message to the private mobile number he'd given her, saying, 'Can we meet up? Need to talk.' She got no response. There was no way of knowing whether he'd discarded the SIM and got a new one to communicate with Stephanie, or whether he was ignoring her. As she'd already seen that he'd been too lazy to come up with a new secret sexy signal, Louise suspected he was just hoping she'd go away. But she tried again. She sent an email to him that could have been construed as a request for a work meeting, but she knew he would know was not.

He got his PA to respond, saying he was currently too busy to meet with her, but would be happy to look over any documentation she wanted to send. She considered peeing on a pregnancy test and posting it to him.

In a funny way she felt relieved. The thought of speaking to him made her feel sick. Seeing him touching Stephanie the way he had touched her made her feel even worse about that night in the hotel. She'd never imagined that she was the first, or the only woman he'd seduced, but it now it was obvious that she had just been one in a string of his conquests. It made her feel foolish, and she didn't like that at all. As far as she was concerned, she'd done her level best to contact him and tell him what had happened. He wanted nothing to do with her, so she would remove herself from the company and from his life, and hopefully never, ever have anything to do with him again.

Once she set the wheels in motion, it all happened really quickly. Andrew, her second-in-command, had been put in charge of her branch while they recruited a replacement. She'd spent the last few weeks handing over all her responsibilities to him. He was young, only in his late twenties, but he was ambitious. He'd be just fine as a stand-in, and Louise said privately to Edward that he could do worse than consider Andrew as a permanent replacement for her.

She hadn't expected to feel very emotional about leaving, but she found she was absolutely gutted. She had put heart and soul into building her branch and she felt devastated that she seemed to be so dispensable. By the time it got to the last few days, she was really just hanging around the office, watching Andrew deal efficiently with every aspect of management. Her team took her out for dinner on the last night. They tried very hard to press cocktails into her hand, but she told them she was on antibiotics and stuck to the Diet Coke.

She sobbed when she got home that night, like someone had died. She had moved to Leeds to take up the position at Barrett and Humphries, and because she had been studying and working so hard, she'd made few, if any, friends outside of work, and certainly no one she was as close to as she was to her team. She was full of guilt that none of them knew why she was really leaving, and she felt sad she couldn't share any of her sorrow, excitement and terror with them. She felt like she was running away into the night and going into hiding. She wouldn't be able to come back and visit, wouldn't even be able to stay in casual contact with these people. In the dark, early hours of the morning, it seemed like an enormous, terrible price to pay for an uncertain future.

On the domestic front, things had run suspiciously smoothly. She had handed over the care of her house to an estate agent, who rented it out to a doctor who had come over from Canada to work at a local hospital. She did a massive clear-out and threw away loads of stuff, then packed the rest and put it in storage. In the end, all she had to do was pack her clothes into two suitcases, put three pot-plants on the back seat of her car and drive down to London.

As she passed the Gateway service station in north London, she breathed a sigh of relief. This was it. She was here, for better or worse. As far as she knew, no one in Leeds suspected that she was pregnant. She hadn't bumped into Brian before she left, thank heavens. Although, on reflection, he had probably put a lot of effort into making sure it hadn't happened. If all went smoothly, he'd never, ever know that he was a father again. Louise would be a distant memory, someone he'd known a long time ago and lost touch with. It was for the best. It really was. And when the baby grew up and had questions, well . . . well they'd cross that bridge when they came to it.

She navigated her way through central London, which was relatively quiet since it was a Sunday, and pulled up outside Simon's building. She buzzed him and he rushed down and helped her carry her things up to the flat.

'Is this all?' he asked, surveying her neatly packed bags and the three plants, now sunning themselves on the windowsill.

'My furniture and most of my stuff is in storage in Leeds. It was cheaper than putting it in storage in London. If . . . when I find a place, I'll go up and fetch it. But for now, I'm a nomad.'

'Wow. How are you feeling?'

She chose to answer the question as if he was asking about the pregnancy, not her emotional state. 'Well, I'm thirteen weeks now . . . the nausea's finally going, and I actually feel really great. I saw a doctor in Leeds, Rachel nagged me until I did, and I had a first sonogram. Everything's fine.'

'You had a sonogram?' Simon was very excited. 'Any pictures?'

'Of course,' Louise laughed. She opened her handbag and took out the pictures, which she had tucked away in her purse.

Simon peered at them closely. 'That is the most beautiful white fuzzy blob that I ever saw. Hello, niece-or-nephew!'

Louise smiled. 'It is beautiful, isn't it? I can't quite believe it's in there. But it is. Today, it's about two and a half inches long and completely fully formed. It's even got fingerprints.'

'Really?' Simon peered closer at the picture.

'You can see all that?'

'No, silly. I've been reading. Rachel sent me a link for this baby website, and there's loads of information. I didn't think I'd get into it, but I'm totally hooked. I've learned loads!'

'So you're looking after yourself?'

'Eating all the right things, taking supplements and getting enough sleep. Promise.'

'That's what I like to hear,' Simon said approvingly. 'Now, what would you like to do, lady of leisure? Late lunch? A walk along the Thames?'

'Ah, you call me lady of leisure. I call myself a jobless bum. I've had lunch, thanks. I stopped on the way down and ate. But a walk would be lovely.'

They left the flat and strolled arm in arm along the riverside path. It was a cold, clear day and the tide was out, so the Thames was lying very low. Seagulls squawked overhead. 'So, jobless bum, eh?' Simon said after a while. 'Any progress on the job front?'

'Not really. To be honest, I haven't really looked. Just getting myself down here was about as much as I could manage. Also, I'm not sure whether it's really ethical to go looking for a job I know I can't stay in for more than a few months.'

'Well, you wouldn't be eligible for maternity pay, but I do know a prospective employer can't discriminate against you because of it. They can't even ask you about it in the interview.'

'Yes, but they're perfectly within their rights to hire another candidate and say they were better qualified . . . even if their only qualification is a flat belly. I know I'd have hesitated to hire a pregnant woman at Barrett and Humphries.'

'Fair enough, but you won't know till you try.'

'I know,' said Louise. 'I'll start job-hunting tomorrow. But now I'm cold. And the baby wants a hot chocolate.'

'Oh, the *baby* does?'

'It's all for the baby. I'd be happy with a glass of water, but it's demanding chocolate. And I have to give it what it wants. I'm selfless like that.'

'Well, conveniently, there's a coffee shop just around the next bend.'

'Maybe the baby knew that.'

'A genius and it hasn't even been born. Takes after its Uncle Simon, I see. Does the baby need whipped cream on its hot chocolate?'

'And possibly a muffin. For sustenance.'

★　★　★

She was miserable for the first week. It wasn't so much homesickness as, well, work-sickness. She really, really, missed her job. Every morning, she woke up and mentally ran through her preparations for work, her commute, and imagined what she would have done that day. She fought the urge ten times a day to ring Andrew and check up on various projects. Finally, she had to give herself a stern talking-to. She had left. She was no longer running the branch, so it was no longer her concern.

She then spent the next few weeks sending out

her CV to large-scale printing firms in the south London area. Once she had a job and went looking for her own place, she wanted to be close to Simon, and within a reasonable distance from Rachel, so she researched firms that fitted into the right sort of geographical area. She was careful to mention in every covering letter that she was pregnant . . . she didn't want to come to an interview and face their polite horror when they saw her tummy. She needn't have worried, however: the silence that greeted her deluge of post and emails was resounding. She rang Deidre from HR in Leeds and got the names of a few recruitment firms in London specialising in the printing industry, but when she spoke to the recruitment agents, they were far from encouraging. When she sent in her CV, they made very enthusiastic noises, but as soon as she told them she was pregnant, they started muttering about the economic climate and saying they couldn't make any promises.

Simon was away every day at work, but Rachel was desperate to spend time with her . . . desperate enough to leave Surrey and come into town to meet her for lunch. 'It's ridiculous,' Louise told her. 'They're so excited to hear about my skills, but as soon as they realise I'm knocked up, they can't get off the phone quickly enough.'

'But do you have to work?' said Rachel, picking at her salad.

Louise looked at her as if she was speaking Chinese. 'I would have told you if I'd won the Lottery. I mean, I have a bit of income from renting out my house, but it's not enough to survive in London for very long. I don't want to just blow all my savings. Anyway, I *want* to work. I didn't spend all these years studying and gaining experience to throw it all away.'

Rachel hesitated. 'But what about . . . '

'Rach, if you're going to have another go at me about the father, I'm going to leave. I'm not asking him for help, and that's that.'

'Does he even know he's a dad?'

'No. I tried to contact him before I left Leeds, but he wouldn't talk to me. It's over between us, and he wants nothing to do with me. And to be honest, I really, really don't want him in my life.'

'What if he finds out?'

'He's not going to find out. He's hundreds of miles away. As far as he's concerned, I'm a blip in his past . . . a little interlude, and now I'm gone, I'm sure he'll never give me another thought.'

'It's a big decision to make for someone else,' Rachel observed.

'Who, the baby?'

'No, the man . . . Brian, is it? You know, Louise, I'm not a feminist . . . '

You don't say, Louise thought.

' . . . but I think if a man forced a woman to have a child against her will, people would be up in arms. It can't be right to do it the other way.'

'It's not against his will. It's just without his knowledge,' Louise said flippantly, but her voice sounded unconvincing, even in her own ears. 'I'll think about telling him. Okay?'

'Okay,' said Rachel. 'Now, do you want to share a dessert?'

'I want to share a dessert with myself and my unborn child. Pregnancy makes me greedy. Come on, Rachel, I know you haven't eaten a whole dessert since 1995, but break out! Live on the edge. You know you want to.'

★ ★ ★

Another week of sitting at Simon's kitchen counter sending out CVs and Louise was beginning to despair. She tried to stay motivated, tried to get up every morning and treat looking for a job like a job, but it became more and more difficult. She spent a lot of time on the baby website, and she started reading the posts in the discussion forum section of the site. There was a group for women having babies in September, so she joined that. Many of the women seemed much younger than her, and their preoccupations were very different from hers, but she did find some of the posts about symptoms useful. There were a couple of people who wrote regularly who seemed closer to her age, or at least as if they were educated, professional women she might have something in common with. She started to look out for their posts. She hadn't posted herself or replied to anything yet, but with time on her hands, she found herself checking in on the site several times a day. She set up an account and called herself Northern–Bird. Then, one day, she saw a post that really resonated with her. It was from someone called PR–Girl, and was titled 'Mixed Blessings?'

I am so, so excited to meet my LO,

(Louise knew this meant Little One. It was a bit cutesy, but it was the shorthand everyone on the site used for babies-to-be)

don't get me wrong. But being pregnant does seem to have made my life more difficult and complicated.

Anyone else feeling really quite lonely? I thought getting pregnant would bring me closer to people, but I feel like I'm losing all my friends. None of them are in the same place as me, and some of them, my boss at work, for one, think I'm 'throwing my life away'.

Then the whole thing is also putting pressure on my marriage: my OH is worried about money and how we'll afford time off for me to stay home with the baby. We both earn pretty good salaries, but we're going to have to cut back a lot to manage. I don't understand how anyone can afford to have a baby, let alone more than one. We live just outside London, by the way.

It was touch and go whether I'd fall pregnant at all, so I am truly excited to meet my miracle baby. But it looks like precious and valuable things come at a price.

The post was signed 'Txx'. Before Louise could think about it, she was typing a reply.

151

Dear Txx,

Our situations may be very different, but I really know what you mean. My pregnancy wasn't planned and I'm doing it on my own. I've moved down to London from the north and given up a very successful job. Right now, I don't have one to replace it. I've had to leave a whole life and friends behind. I also already love my baby-to-be

(she couldn't bring herself to write LO)

and can't wait to meet him/her, but there are days, like today, when the price seems high. There are just so many unanswered questions about our future. I'm not used to that, and I'm scared.

She thought for a while, then signed the post 'Lou'.

She kept an eye on the thread for the rest of the day. A couple of other women posted. Most of them said things like 'Can't really relate, but sending hugs ((()))', and one posted something a little critical, that suggested women who were pregnant with healthy babies should just be grateful. PR–Girl, or Txx, whoever she was, didn't post again on her own thread.

The next morning however, when she logged on, there was a 'friend request' from PR–Girl and a personal message.

Hi, Northern–Bird (Lou, is it?),
Thanks so much for your reply. You made

152

me feel like I wasn't alone; I had a very bad day yesterday, and seeing your reply when I got home made me feel a lot better. You said in your post that you've just moved down to London . . . so thought you could maybe use a friend to chat to. I might be able to help with some suggestions about coping in this big, horrible city.

Anyway, hope you'd like to be friends. Drop me a line sometime.
Toni
xx

Louise smiled and accepted the friend request. A new friend, at the safe distance created by being online, sounded like just what she needed.

She stopped getting up at eight and started sleeping in a bit every day. The pull of the sofa and daytime TV was also strong, and there was a bookshelf in Simon's spare room with piles of detective novels that she'd never had time to read because she'd always been too busy working. So it happened that when the phone finally rang, she was dozing on the sofa in a pair of tracksuit bottoms, with a Val McDermid mystery open on her bump.

'Louise?' a male voice with a northern accent said. For one horrible moment, she thought it was Brian. But then he said, 'It's Edward.'

Her ex-boss. Louise struggled into a sitting position and tried very hard to sound as if she hadn't just woken up. 'Edward! How nice to hear from you.'

'Listen, I'm ringing on the off chance you haven't been snapped up yet. How's the job hunt going?'

'Oh, you know . . . ' Louise said. God, she sounded intelligent. She just wasn't awake enough to lie with breezy conviction. Edward waited for her to expand on this clever statement. In the end she came up with, 'I'm looking at a number of possibilities. Nothing concrete yet.'

'Well, I've just had a call from an old college mate of mine. Adam Harper. He's got a banner-printing business down in Surrey and he needs someone at short notice. It's a small operation, nothing like you're used to, but if you'd be in a position to help out an old friend of mine for a few months, I'd be most grateful.'

Now Louise was awake. 'A few months?'

'Yes, the mad old bugger's had a chance to go sailing round the world on one of those tall ships. He'll be away for four or five months and he needs someone to mind the shop while he's out of town. I think he might want you to live in his house too, while he's away, if that's at all possible.'

Louise said calmly, 'Edward, could you hold on for a second?' she put her mobile on mute, put it down on the coffee table and did a crazy, bum-wiggling dance around the room. Then she picked up the phone again. 'Sorry, someone on the other line. Well, I'd certainly be interested. Could you give me this Adam Harper's details?'

Now this was worth getting dressed for! She showered and put on clean clothes, then wrote a covering email and attached her CV. She had it

154

ready to go in her drafts folder, then she picked up the phone, offered up a little prayer, and rang the number Edward had given her.

A young woman answered the phone. 'Harper Graphics, good afternoon!' she said in a breezy Australian accent.

'May I speak to Adam Harper, please?' Louise said, in her most businesslike tone.

'No worries!' the girl chirped, 'I'll get him for you!' There was a moment's silence and the receiver clunked down on a hard surface. 'Adam!' Louise heard her yell. It didn't sound like a very professional operation. She heard footsteps approaching, and Adam Harper came on the line. 'Hello?' he barked. His voice was deep and gravelly, with a faint Scottish accent. Louise introduced herself and explained that Edward had suggested she contact him. She launched into her professional patter about training and experience, but he cut her off. 'If Ed recommended you, that's good enough for me.'

'I'll send you my CV by email . . . '

'Yes, yes. When can you get down here? This afternoon?'

'Well . . . ' That came as a bit of a surprise. Should she play hard to get? Imply she was too busy just to drop everything? On second thoughts, Adam Harper didn't sound like a man who'd be impressed by corporate game-playing.

'How long will it take me on a train from London?' she said.

'About an hour. I can pick you up from the station. Trains run every half an hour from

155

Waterloo at twenty past and ten to.'

She did a rapid calculation. 'Right, well, I'll see you at the station at three twenty then,' she said briskly. Adam seemed to be happy with that. She told him what she looked like and they rang off. She sent off the email with her CV, although she doubted he'd bother to read it. It wasn't until ten minutes later that she realised she hadn't told him she was pregnant.

She rushed around, packing her briefcase, changing into a suit and doing her hair and make-up. She dashed off a text to Simon, telling him she was going down to Surrey for an interview and would be back later, then trotted down the stairs and out of the building. She'd already decided to splurge on a cab to Waterloo: there was no point in getting hot and dishevelled on the Tube if she could avoid it.

She bought a coffee and a newspaper, found the train without a problem and was on her way. Only then did she relax and allow herself a little laugh. Edward had rung her a little after midday. It was now two thirty and she was on her way to an interview which could solve all her problems in one fell swoop (what was a fell swoop, she wondered? Well, whatever it was, it seemed she had one and it was doing its job).

The train ran mercifully on time, and forty-five minutes later, she stepped off it on to the platform at Chertsey. Adam Harper had told her to look out for a Land Rover and she scanned the parking lot for 4x4s. Then she heard a roar, and a rattly old olive-green Land Rover, which must have been at least twenty-five years old, came barrelling into the parking lot and stopped at the station steps. The driver's door burst open with a creaking groan and a tall, rangy man stepped out. 'Louise?' he said.

'Adam,' she replied, and went to shake his hand.

He was at least six foot three. Louise herself was tall, five nine, but she found herself looking up into his bright blue eyes. Despite the wintry weather, he was tanned (that would be the sailing, she thought), and his thick and curly black hair was going grey in that splendid silvery way that only seems to happen to men. He was undeniably gorgeous.

This is ridiculous, she thought. I'm here for a job interview, and I'm staring at this man like he's the hero of a romantic novel. Was she doomed to be attracted to men she worked with? This was becoming a habit. She stood up straight, took a deep breath and put on her most formal tone. 'Mr Harper. Shall we go back to the shop so I can show you my CV?'

He smiled (Oh no, Louise thought. He has a dimple. That's just not fair. Be professional. Be professional. Don't be intimidated by him. Imagine him naked. No! Definitely not! Under no circumstances imagine him naked! Oh, he'd be lovely naked. Did the tan go all the way down?). ' . . . vinyl and wide fabric banners for exhibitions and displays, for indoor and outdoor.'

Oh God, he was talking business and she was thinking saucy thoughts. He'd turned back towards the Land Rover and was walking. She followed him, arranging her face into an

157

attentive expression.

He drove fast, but well, and within a few minutes they were out in the countryside. He chatted about the scope of the business. Outdoor display work was new to her: she'd focused on large-volume publications, but she soon realised they spoke much the same language. He needed someone who could keep an eye on scheduling and budgeting, make sure the necessary materials were in place for upcoming jobs and listen to the staff when they had problems. All of this she could do.

Ten minutes more and they turned off the main road on to a small avenue fringed with tall trees. The road curved to the left, and then she spotted a sign beside a big pair of iron gates: Harper Graphics. Adam turned in and drove up the well-kept driveway. He pulled up outside a lovely, low, stone farmhouse, and jumped out of the driver's seat. He came round to open Louise's door.

She had unbuttoned her coat in the warmth of the car, and, as she stepped down from the high seat of the Land Rover, her back was arched. Adam, facing her for the first time, saw the small but unmistakable bump. She saw him arch an eyebrow, then he turned away and motioned to her to follow him. They didn't go into the house, but walked round it. Behind the house was a courtyard. Two vans with the Harper Graphics logo were parked outside the large sliding door of the barn. They went in, and the noise of the large printing presses was deafening. There were three or four guys on the floor, and they raised a

158

hand in greeting to Adam as they walked through. They crossed the floor and went up a flight of stairs to an upper level. There was a glass-fronted office suite, and Adam opened the door for her to go in. Thankfully, once they were inside with the door closed, the noise was largely muted.

In the outer office, there was a tall, leggy blonde of about twenty-two, typing at great speed on her PC. 'Hi there!' she said brightly. Her accent told Louise this was the Aussie girl who had answered the phone when she rang.

'Anita, this is Louise Holmes,' Adam said.

'Hi, Louise!' said Anita with Australian enthusiasm, and leapt up to shake Louise's hand vigorously.

'I'm hoping Louise will get us out of this fix and look after the business while I'm away,' Adam said.

'Fantastic!' Anita said, and she seemed so genuinely thrilled that Louise did believe it truly would be fantastic.

So far so good, Louise thought. Adam Harper seemed to be keen to have her. She didn't think for a moment that he was a pushover, but he did seem to think she would be doing him a favour. He didn't need to know how desperately she wanted this to work out. She decided to play it cool, but professionally, and try not to give anything away.

They left Anita and walked through to Adam's office. His desk was piled high with paper. Louise was sure he was one of those people who could put his hand on any piece of paper at a moment's notice and knew exactly what was going on in the chaos, but it wasn't the way she liked to run things.

He asked her to sit down and offered her a drink. 'Just water, please,' she said, and he stepped back into the outer office to get it. She opened her briefcase and took out her neatly bound CV and laid it on the desk in front of her. Adam came back in and handed her a glass of iced water.

'So when is it due?' he asked quietly. Her hand shook uncontrollably, and a large splash of water landed on the front page of her CV. Hoping he hadn't noticed, she wiped her hand over it, but the ink instantly ran and smeared.

She took a deep, shaky breath. 'Well, this is going well!' she smiled. So much for cool and professional. She wanted to kick herself, and she felt a blush rising up from her collar.

Adam looked at her steadily. His expression gave nothing away. Then he said, 'Don't worry about the CV. I printed the one you emailed. I've seen it already.' Then he left a long pause, and she knew he was waiting for her to answer the question.

'Um, it's due in September. Around the beginning of the month.'

'Well, I'm due back mid-August, so that should work,' he said calmly. Then he sat down at the desk, shuffled through the untidy stack of papers before him and pulled out her CV. He spent the next twenty minutes questioning her closely about various aspects of her experience. She was right. He wasn't a pushover, and he'd paid careful attention to everything she'd written in the covering email and her CV. It turned out he was going to give her a proper interview after all.

She answered thoughtfully and concisely. She could see he had a finely honed bullshit detector, and that there was no point in trying to baffle him with numbers or statistics. He asked very direct questions without being aggressive, and he listened carefully to everything she said. After several weeks out of a corporate environment, she found the conversation quite a challenge, but she relished it.

After he'd worked through her CV to the end of her time at Barrett and Humphries, she steeled herself for the next question.

'So why did you leave Barrett and Humphries?' he asked.

'Family commitments,' she said, hoping her tone suggested she didn't want to expand on this. 'I needed to be based in or near London.'

'Would this work for your . . . family commitment? Not too far away?' Adam asked and then glanced up at her with his piercing blue eyes.

'I would think so.'

'It's not a permanent position, I hope you understand that. I mean, I feel bad that I'll be booting you out just as you . . . '

'Pop?' she said mischievously.

'Indeed. Pop. Now, it would suit me best if you lived in the house . . . firstly because if we're working double shifts, it's best to have a manager on the premises. Even if you're asleep, you'd effectively be on call if something went wrong. And secondly, there's . . . well, there's Millicent.'

161

Louise was confused. Was she supposed to know who this was? 'Millicent?' she asked tentatively. 'Is she an . . . aunt?'

He tried to look dignified. 'Millicent is an elderly and slightly temperamental Siamese cat. She runs the house. She decides who sits where, who sleeps where and she always eats before I do. If I put her in a cattery when I'm away, she'll break out and then hunt me down and hurt me. So I need someone who'll put up with sharing a house with Millicent and being ruled by her. For my own safety, really.'

'Wow. She sounds scary.'

'You have no idea. I hope you're not allergic to cats.'

'No. I've never had one myself, but I rather like them.'

'And your husband?'

'My . . . what? Oh, God no. I mean . . . er . . . I don't have a husband. Or a boyfriend. It's just me.'

He nodded, looked down at his papers and tapped his pen a few times. It was the first time Louise had seen him looking disconcerted.

He changed the subject then and began to talk about the trip he would be taking. 'Every year, there's a series of Tall Ships Races around the world. It's a way to get young people into sailing, and it's an amazing adventure for them. A friend of mine needed someone to be a responsible crew member for a few months. I was going to say no, I mean, I've got a business to run, but then I thought, why the hell not? My kids are teenagers and don't need me on a daily basis,

Millicent will manage without me as long as someone gives her her Iams and stays off her cushion in the sun . . . so why shouldn't I?'

'Why shouldn't you indeed? It sounds like the chance of a lifetime.'

'I thought so. You know, nobody gets to their deathbeds and says, 'I wish I'd printed more giant banners advertising university open days.'' He gave her a crooked smile.

'I imagine nobody does.'

He hesitated for a second. 'Look, Louise, I tend to go with my gut instincts, and even though we've only just met, I think I could trust you to do a good job running this business. Edward's recommendation means a lot, and I've seen nothing to make me change my mind.'

'Even . . . ?' she gestured at her belly.

'If you're healthy and you look after yourself, it shouldn't make a difference to your ability to manage the business. I'm guessing you're about sixteen weeks?'

'Seventeen, but well guessed!' she said, surprised.

'So, if you were nauseous, you're probably past it. This is the easiest bit of pregnancy, and there's a good team here to give you back-up. You wouldn't be alone. You can turn to Anita and the guys at any time, they all know the business backwards. My print-floor manager, Alan Shuster, is also a great guy. He's not nearly as experienced as you are, but he can step up and take over if anything . . . '

This made her really uneasy. 'I'm not a charity case, Adam. I am up to this job, I assure you,' she said, and her voice was sharper than she meant it to be.

'I wasn't suggesting you were. If I didn't think you were up to it, I wouldn't be offering it to you. But I have to be practical. If you get pre-eclampsia, or the baby comes early, and I'm somewhere in the mid-Atlantic, to put it politely, I'm screwed. For both of our sakes, we need to know you're properly supported.'

There really was nothing she could say to that. He was being utterly reasonable and more than generous.

'Do I take it that you're offering me the job?' she asked.

'If you'd consider accepting it. I know we need to talk about money . . . '

'Mr Harper . . . '

'Adam.'

'Adam . . . if I'm living in your house, my major expense is covered. So, let me come to the table and say my needs are reasonably modest.'

He smiled. 'Wow. I've never had someone try to talk me down in a salary negotiation before.'

'I don't want to feel that . . . '

'I'm doing you a favour? I'm not. I'll have access to email even when I'm at sea. I'll be checking in regularly, and we have monthly targets set for the business. If you're not doing the job I expect you to do, I'll know.'

After that, he took her to look at the house. It was a lovely old farmhouse with uneven flagstone floors and low ceilings. It was clear to Louise that he lived there alone: only one bedroom looked lived in, and while everything was comfortable and clean, the decor was functional and spare and very male. Millicent lay on a cushion on the window-seat in the living room and opened one azure eye. She gave Louise a witchy glare, but when Adam went over and scratched behind her ear, she stretched and arched, let out an eerie, humanoid Siamese meow and gazed up at him adoringly.

Business concluded, they had a cup of tea sitting at the big table in the farmhouse kitchen. They chatted about the printing business, and Adam told her a few funny stories about Edward in their college days. She felt very comfortable in his presence. It had turned into a most unexpected and wonderful day.

After what seemed like a few minutes, she glanced toward the window. It was pitch dark outside. 'Good grief! What time is it?'

He looked at his watch. 'Six o'clock, nearly.'

'I really should be getting back. My brother will think I've been abducted.'

He stood up. 'I'll run you to the station.'

'Are you sure? I can call a taxi . . . '

'Don't be silly.' Now, suddenly, he was all business. 'We'll need to meet several times more before I go, and that's in a fortnight. Can you email me a list of free dates?'

She was well beyond playing hard to get at this point. 'It would be easier to email you my not-free dates. I'm due to have lunch with my sister tomorrow. I could cancel that. Other than that, I'm yours. I mean . . . I'm available.' She really should stop talking. Job interview rule 101: do not flirt clumsily with the man who is about to offer you a job and a home. Luckily, Adam seemed to have missed the double entendre.

'That's fantastic. I'll get Anita to set up meetings with Alan and the work team, our major suppliers and our sales guy. She'll try and get them into as few days as possible so as not to waste your time.'

'That's . . . great,' she said, somehow a little deflated. She'd hoped to see more of him in the two weeks before he left on his travels.

As if he had read her mind, he said, 'I'll be running around like mad getting ready for the trip, but I hope we can spend some more time together . . . sorting out the details.'

'Yes,' Louise said. She didn't really trust herself to say more.

He drove her to the station, and when she got on the train, she could still feel the warm pressure of his handshake. Ridiculous. Utterly ridiculous. It must be a mad flush of pregnancy hormones, making her come over all unnecessary at the sight of a handsome man. It was a very good thing he'd be away when she was living there. She'd only embarrass herself.

She rang Simon from the train and told him the bare bones of her day, and by the time she got back to the flat, he'd cooked a delicious risotto and chilled a tiny half-bottle of champagne. 'Have a sip, go on,' he said. 'It's not every day you get a job and a home.'

'It isn't, you're right,' she said, and she savoured a few mouthfuls of the crisp, icy bubbles.

'So tell me everything. What's the place like?

166

What's the house like? What will you be doing?'

'Slow down! It's really lovely. It's not far from Thorpe Park, on what must have been an old farm. Adam lives in the farmhouse, and the printing presses are in the barn behind. They do large outdoor print, so not what I'm used to, but most of the principles are the same. Adam's built the business from scratch . . . he started it after he left college.'

'Wow . . . sounds great.'

'It really is. Adam says he's thinking of expanding into exhibition stands next year, but he needs to build a relationship with a construction firm. It all sounds really exciting.'

'And the house?'

'It's okay . . . very male and functional. Adam's got this old Siamese cat called Millicent. I'll have to look after her. She hates me already, but she adores him.'

'I'm guessing she's not alone,' Simon said wryly.

'What do you mean?' Louise was already pink. She hoped Simon would assume it was the wine.

'You've got a really bad case of mentionitis.'

'Of what?'

'Mentionitis. You've managed to say 'Adam' about five times in the last two minutes. Dr Simon diagnoses a case of the crushes.'

'Oh my God. I know. I have to get my hormones under control. But it's very difficult.'

'Is he very hot?'

'In an Eric-Bana-meets-the-Croatian-doctor-from-ER kind of way. With an Edinburgh accent.'

'Oh dear. That's bad.'

'I know. Thank God he'll be hundreds of miles away, climbing the rigging of a tall ship.'

'With his shirt off, getting all bronzed and muscly?'

'Stop it, Simon! I have to work for this man!'

'So is he married?'

'My guess is that he's divorced. He mentioned teenage kids, and he certainly knows all about pregnancy, but he definitely lives alone. After all, if there was a wife, he wouldn't need me to live in his house, would he?'

'All right, Miss Marple. You really have thought this through!'

Louise was serious for a moment. 'I really liked him, Si. Yes, he's very attractive, but he also seems to be a really good man. Reasonable, fair, kind to his cat . . . I haven't met a nice single man in years and years. Why now? Why when I can't do anything about it?'

'Well, you can't do anything now, but there's no reason why you can't fantasise . . . and when he comes back . . . '

'When he comes back, it'll be to evict me from his house. I'll either be the size of said house, or I'll have a tiny baby and my stomach will be flapping around near my knees. Along with my tits.'

'You paint such a sexy picture.'

'Sorry. But I have to accept my dating days, such as they were, are over.' She cupped her tidy little bump with one hand. 'This has to be my priority now.'

'It doesn't mean you have to be a nun.'

'No, but it's a moot point anyway. He didn't

168

show any sign of being attracted to me, and that's no big surprise. He's not going to pull a move on a knocked-up bird while he's interviewing her for a job, is he?'

'That's true. Even if he fancied you rotten, it would be a bit sleazy.'

'It would. Either way, it's been an amazing day. I've got a job, and got somewhere to live for the next few months.'

'Not bad for an afternoon's work.' Simon yawned and stood up. 'I'm going to have a shower, sweetie. I'm thrilled for you.' He dropped a kiss on the top of her head and went off to the bathroom.

Louise wandered over to her laptop and switched it on. She had a few automated response emails from recruitment firms. She was thrilled to be able to dash off a quick response to them all, saying she'd found a position. They'd done nothing to help her. She was very glad none of them would be earning a commission from her good fortune. She sent a very thankful email to Edward. Somehow, she managed to resist the urge to pump him for information about Adam.

Then she logged onto the baby website. It seemed there had been a very heated discussion about giving birth with or without pain relief. There was one post with over three hundred replies, and more kept popping up while she read them. She got caught up in reading the arguments, so it took a while to notice that there was a personal message waiting for her. It was from Toni.

Hi there . . .
Sorry to be a stalker, but I've not seen you
on here today. Just wanted to check you
were OK.
Txx.

Louise smiled. It was so nice to have a friend,
even if it was a digital one, who cared where she
was. She typed a reply, filling Toni in on her
eventful day. She didn't say anything about being
attracted to Adam. After all she didn't know Ton
. . . no reason to spill her guts to her. But it was
great to be able to write down that she had a
good job and somewhere to live, at least for now.
On impulse, she added her email address to the
message. They could move their chat away from
the site that way.

She then composed a short, polite and formal
email to Adam, thanking him for meeting with
her and giving her the opportunity to work with
him. She summarised everything they had
agreed and asked him to confirm the terms in
writing. Putting things on a professional footing
between them made her feel a little more secure.

She slept better that night than she had in
months, and the next day met Rachel in a
riverside cafe for lunch. Rachel was excited, and
duly asked all the wrong questions — 'Are you
sure you have to work? Will you be able to take
days off so we can go shopping for baby things?
You won't have to lift anything heavy, will you?
What about poisonous chemicals?' Louise
answered them all patiently, and in the end,
Rachel seemed happy, especially about the fact

that Louise would now be living just a few miles away. Louise patiently explained that it was a normal office job and that she'd be working normal office hours, and wouldn't be constantly free for lunches and shopping.

Their food came and they started to eat. Then Rachel suddenly said excitedly, 'Ooh, you'll never guess what!'

'You're right, I never will. What?'

'Do you remember David and Samantha? You met them at our place when you and Si came for lunch.'

'Richard's boss and his wife? Very posh?'

'Yes, well, maybe not so posh. Their teenage daughter's pregnant!'

'Really? How old is she?'

'Oh, she's eighteen, but not at all the sort you'd expect to get pregnant . . . one of those blonde, skinny ballet girls, good at everything and a bit superior. Apparently she's got some bad-boy-musician boyfriend who got her up the duff. David's about to explode, he's so furious.'

'I'm sure. After all that expensive private schooling, that probably wasn't the return on his investment he was expecting.'

'Samantha just couldn't cope, so she's gone off to some posh spa near Cheltenham for a rest cure.'

'Really? Sounds like something out of a Jane Austen novel. Did she get the vapours?'

'No, I think she got the gin . . . Richard said she was at some work cocktail party and she was a real embarrassment, telling anyone who'd listen how her daughter had failed her and it was

171

all David's fault. He packed her off the next day.'

'My goodness!' Louise said. 'Well, it sounds like it's all happening down in leafy Surrey.'

'Anyway, Richard mentioned to David that you're pregnant too . . . '

(I bet he did, Louise thought. Sucking up to the boss . . . 'Oooh, my wife's sister's also a disgrace, pregnant and alone') ' . . . and David said maybe you could talk to Gemma.'

'What?' Louise said, alarmed.

'Maybe you could come down this weekend and meet Gemma and talk to her. About being pregnant and stuff.'

'Gemma's the daughter,' Louise said, playing for time.

'Of course,' Rachel said, impatiently. 'So will you come? Samantha's going to be away for another few weeks at least, so David's going to bring Gemma round to ours on Sunday afternoon. For tea.'

'For tea,' Louise repeated weakly. 'Gosh, that sounds fun. So tell me, Rach, what is the well-dressed hostess serving to the knocked-up adolescent and the middle-aged single mum this season?'

'There's no need to be mean,' Rachel said snippily. 'I'd consider it a big favour if you came. And so would Richard.'

To be fair, Louise didn't give a toss what Richard thought. But she found herself saying, 'Okay. I'll come. Can Simon come too?'

'I already asked him, but he said he was busy.'

I bet he did, Louise thought.

'Listen, I'd love to sit and chat all afternoon, but I have to go. I've got a step class at gym.

Sunday at three then?' Rachel asked.
'Sunday at three.'

Subject: Guilt, Guilt, Guilt

Dear Toni,
Why does everything have to be so
damned complicated? I don't know if I
told you about my sister before . . . she's
three years younger than me, and you're
never likely to meet two more different siblings. I'm tall and dark, she's petite and
blonde (although that's now courtesy of
her very expensive colourist). I went to
uni, and I've worked all my life. She got
married as soon as she could and gave up
work to be a corporate wife. And of
course, the ultimate irony is that I've got
knocked up by mistake in my late thirties,
and she's been trying for a baby for years
with no success. There are plenty of reasons for me to feel bad about my situation,
but for some reason, this is the thing that
makes me feel worst.
    I know, I know. I didn't do it on purpose,
but I still feel like I have to make it up to
her in some way. So I say yes to anything
she asks me to do. So we've just been out
for lunch and she asked me to go round for
tea on Sunday . . . her husband's boss's
teenage daughter (yes, I know it's complicated, keep up) is pregnant, and no one
knows what to do with her. Solution — ask
another pregnant woman to speak to her.

Me. Yes, I know it's mad, you know it's
mad, but in Rachel-land, it makes sense. So
I'm driving to Oxshott this weekend to
counsel a pregnant teenager. Any ideas as to
what I should say?
   Hope you're okay, by the way, and
please excuse the massive brain dump.
Ignore it if you like.
Lou
X

Subject: Re: Guilt, Guilt, Guilt

Dear Lou,
I'm normally rubbish at advice, but I heard
something on the radio the other day that I
think might help a bit. It was all about the
principle of limited good. Apparently in
some primitive societies (and Oxshott's
definitely one of those), they believe that
there's only so much good fortune in the
world. So, for example, if you get a nice new
car or job or date with George Clooney, it
means *I* can't have a nice new car or job,
and Mr Clooney will give me the shove.
Now in civilised places like Kingston (more
developed than Oxshott, we like to think),
we know that that isn't true. Your good fortune doesn't cancel out my good fortune,
unless we're going for the same job or bloke
(so scratch the George-Clooney thing
above, it doesn't make sense at all).
   Maybe that's a bit intellectual, but think
about it this way. If you weren't pregnant,

Rachel wouldn't be pregnant in your place. I'm going to type in caps now for emphasis, but I'm not shouting . . . I just want you to know IT'S NOT YOUR FAULT.

I told you I have primary ovarian insufficiency. It means I had to try and fall pregnant immediately, even though James and I weren't really ready to start our family. It probably also means that I can only have one child. But that's nobody else's fault. And I don't want to spend the rest of my life jealous of women who had carefree years in their twenties and got to go further in their careers, or women who get to have four lovely kids. Because IT'S NOT THEIR FAULT.

You've got plenty of things on your plate right now . . . don't beat yourself up about things you can't change. But it's still a good thing to go and meet the poor teenage girl. She's probably really frightened and freaked out. She could do with hanging out with someone who isn't going to judge her.
Love
Txx

Subject: Re: Re: Guilt, Guilt, Guilt

Dear Toni,
Thank you, thank you, thank you. Your advice is brilliant, and makes perfect sense. From what you say I'm guessing you're still in your twenties . . . wow . . . you're

going through an awful lot at a compara-
tively young age, and you sound so sorted
when you talk about it. I'll try to take your
advice . . . as you say guilt is really a
wasted emotion. Thanks again and chat
soon. I'll update you after Surrey Sunday.
Love,
Lou
Xxx

Gemma

The twelve-week mark came and went, and Gemma still hadn't found the courage to tell Ben. Then, one rainy Saturday afternoon, it all came to a head. He'd been really quite sweet that day: they'd gone to see a film, which they'd both laughed at a lot, then come back and he'd made them each a jacket potato with beans and cheese. Gemma ate it all: she was hungry all the time now, and she knew her waistline was thickening.

After their meal, they were sitting on his bed, watching some videos on YouTube on his computer. He slipped an arm around her waist and started stroking up and down her side. She didn't say anything, but she stiffened up a little and moved away from him slightly. Out of nowhere, he snapped. 'Why do you keep coming here?' he said sharply.

'What?' She knew this had been coming, but she was caught off guard.

'Well, you don't want to sleep with me any more. So, what, do you want to be, like, friends?' He sneered when he said this, as if it was the most ridiculous idea.

'No! I mean, I want to be with you, Ben. I love you.'

They'd told each other they loved each other in the beginning, when things between them were new and exciting. But he had stopped saying it a long time ago, and because he had, so

177

had she. Saying it out loud sounded shocking, and Ben shrank back as if she'd slapped him.

'But . . . Gemma, I dunno. I mean . . . things between us have been kind of weird lately. I've been thinking, and . . . This isn't working. I think we should break up.'

She wasn't surprised to hear him say it, and amazingly, she wasn't upset at all. Very calmly, she said, 'Things are about to change, though. I've got amazing news. I'm pregnant. We're going to be a family.'

The silence was terrible. It just went on and on. Ben's face went a strange pasty colour, and sweat broke out on his forehead. Then, suddenly, he stood up and walked out of the room. A few seconds later, Gemma heard the front door slam. His mum was out, so she was left alone in their house. She didn't know what to do so she stayed sitting on Ben's bed for another hour or so. He didn't come back, so eventually she got her things together and left. She walked slowly to the bus stop, looking out for him along the way, but there was no sign of him. It was starting to get very cold and dark. Eventually she had to get on a bus and go home.

When she got in, her parents were sitting together in the living room. Her dad was reading the paper and her mother was watching some home-decor show on the television. It was a rare show of family togetherness. Her dad looked up when she walked in. 'Hello, pumpkin,' he said vaguely. 'It's a bit late. Did Lucy's mum give you a lift home?'

'I'm pregnant,' Gemma said. For the second

time that day, there was an awful, unending silence. She kept standing in the middle of the living room rug, with both of her parents staring at her. Finally, her mother said, 'I beg your pardon?' in the faint, polite voice she used when she thought shop staff were being rude to her.

Gemma said it again.

'You can't be!' her father exploded. 'That's insane. You're a child!' Then his face darkened. 'Is it that little bastard Ben? I'll cut his bloody balls off, so help me.'

There was a lot of yelling then. Gemma tried to tell them that everything would be all right, but when her father asked if Ben knew she was pregnant, she had to admit that she'd told him and he'd walked away. Then her father blustered some more, and yelled about how never mind the balls, he'd bloody kill Ben when he got his hands on him, and Gemma's mother burst into tears and went and poured herself an enormous drink. It all felt like an episode of some horrible soap opera and Gemma wished very much that it would all be over. She'd known what they would say and how they would shout. She'd always known it would be like this. But they couldn't make her have an abortion. She was eighteen. Ben would come to terms with it and everything would be fine. She just knew she had to stay calm through the screaming stage.

In the days that followed, it got uglier. Her father got hold of Ben's mum, and they both came round to the house for a 'meeting'. It all started with icy politeness, but soon there was mud-slinging from both sides. Gemma's dad barked at Ben, who stayed sullenly silent, Hannah got defensive and told David to shut up. David had never been told to shut up by a woman, so he yelled at her and she yelled back. She was a lawyer after all, so she did some good yelling. Throughout all of this, Gemma's mother drank and cried, and Ben sat on the sofa, his arms folded and his handsome face crumpled like a sulky child's.

Things really weren't turning out the way Gemma had imagined. Ben had said he wanted to have babies with her. But now he'd just become a six-year-old who hid behind his mum's skirts. He hadn't spoken to her at all since she told him — all conversations seemed to happen between their parents. She'd wanted to take him up to her room to talk, but her father had started yelling again and said he forbade it. Gemma said, 'Why? I can't get any more pregnant, can I?' But apparently it wasn't a good time for a joke.

The next day, Ben texted her. 'Meet me at mine this afternoon', it said. No kisses or any of his usual silly banter. Gemma knew it wasn't going to be good news. She caught the bus after school and went to his house. He opened the door when she rang the doorbell and walked back into the house without saying anything. She followed him into the living room, where he sat down on the sofa. She sat on an upright chair opposite. It felt like a job interview, or going to see the headteacher at school.

'I'm not going to ask you if you did this on purpose,' Ben said, and Gemma was shocked to hear his voice shaking, like he was going to cry. It made her furious.

'Did this on *purpose*? You were there too, you know. Remember the night of your Islington gig? When we had sex right there?' She pointed at the Persian rug.

'Yes, but . . . '

'I said we didn't have a condom, and I asked you if you wanted to make a baby and you said yes . . . '

'I was drunk!' yelled Ben, red-faced. 'I wanted to have bareback sex. I would have said yes to anything!'

Gemma stared and stared at him. She couldn't speak. In the long silence Ben finally started to look ashamed. When he spoke again, his voice was quieter, but still angry. 'I'm not going to say I want you to get an abortion, because I hate the idea of a baby dying. But this . . . this thing is not fair. This is my *life*.'

'It's my life too . . . ' Gemma began.

'But you had some choice about this. I've got none.'

What a whiny brat he was. There seemed no point in yelling about how unfair that statement was, so Gemma waited.

'I'm eighteen years old and now I'm going to be a dad, and that's all there is to it. My mum says I have to face up to my responsibilities, so now, even if I get to go to uni, I can only go to one in London. And I have to get a job so I can give money towards the baby.'

'You don't need to worry about money . . . I've got my inheritance . . . '

181

'That's what I said, but my mum says it's my baby, and it would be wrong not to support it.' He sounded so bitter and angry, it made Gemma feel quite ill.

'Anyway, I just want you to know that I'll do what I have to do, but what I said before you sprung this on me still stands. I don't want to be with you. As far as I'm concerned, we're broken up.'

'Fine,' said Gemma. She got up to leave. Ben didn't stop her, and she walked out calmly, and went straight to the bus stop. Fortunately, a bus came almost immediately, and she was on her way home ten minutes after she had got to Ben's house.

It was odd. She had thought that that would be the worst moment of her life, breaking up with Ben. But it wasn't. She really didn't like the bitter, selfish little boy he'd turned out to be. If Ben grew up and turned into a halfway decent man, maybe there'd be a future for them. If not, well . . . she'd manage without him. She had her baby, and she'd be fine. The tiny little person inside her womb had become her strength and her purpose. She was amazed at how calm and together she felt. After years of feeling unsure of herself, of feeling invisible, like she didn't have a place in the world, it was novel to feel so strong, so independent. Maybe becoming a mum was all it took to grow up. She wished she had someone she could explain it to, but as there was no one, she spent hours in her bedroom, hand on her stomach, talking quietly to her baby, her best friend-to-be.

In the next few weeks, her mum's drinking really got out of hand. Gemma came down one morning to find her mum sitting at the table with a glass of red wine next to her bowl of muesli. When Gemma walked in and glanced at the glass, Samantha laughed harshly and said, 'Yes, sweetheart, this is your fault.' Then raised the glass and drank deeply. It was a day or two after that that her father drove Samantha off to the 'spa' in Cheltenham.

Word got out at school that she was pregnant. She wasn't sure how . . . she didn't tell anyone. But someone heard that her mother was in a drying-out clinic, and someone else heard why, and within days people were whispering as she walked past them. She knew that at other schools, there were lots of teenage mums. But it wasn't the sort of thing that happened at Lady Grey's. Girls from Lady Grey's went to Cambridge or Oxford. It was a bit sensational if someone opted for Durham. They didn't get pregnant at eighteen and skip university altogether.

Looking from the outside, things really couldn't be worse. Her mother was a drunk, Ben was a king-sized wimp, and her dad was crashing around shouting and looking like he was brewing a stroke or a heart attack. But Gemma didn't care. All she cared about was the tiny light she felt glowing inside her. She was going to be a mother, a real, loving, caring mother. This baby would be hers and hers alone (seeing as Ben didn't look like he was going to be much of a father), and Gemma would never, ever feel empty or alone again.

So, somehow, all the yelling and ugliness just passed her by. She floated through her days at school, wrote her exams and did her work in a happy haze. She thought she'd better finish her A-levels . . . naturally she wouldn't be going to university that year, if ever, but she would probably need to have some qualifications to be able to support her baby in the years to come. Her granny's money wasn't going to last forever. As the baby was only due in late September she had plenty of time after she'd finished to get ready for the birth.

There was another strange and unexpected bonus — with her mother gone, her father seemed to think he shouldn't leave her alone, so he seemed to have cut back, or maybe even stopped his extra-curricular love life. She hadn't seen him sneaking off to make mobile phone calls for weeks. He came home at a reasonable time after work every evening and was home for the whole weekend.

He didn't have a clue what to do with her . . . he didn't know what to talk about, or what she liked to do. She'd decided to give up tennis, so her weekends were really quite free. They went to the cinema a few times, but if he picked the film, it was usually some blockbuster violent thing and she was bored, and if she picked a romantic comedy or a drama, he spent the film restlessly shifting in his seat and looking at his phone. He took her out for a few insanely expensive dinners at very posh restaurants in London. She enjoyed that, especially because she got to dress up, but they had nothing to talk about, so they would end up picking at their food in silence.

One weekend, about two weeks after her mother had gone to the clinic, her father knocked on her door. It was Saturday morning. 'Listen,' he said abruptly, 'we've been invited for tea by a work colleague of mine. Tomorrow.'

'Okay . . . ' Gemma said dubiously. That didn't sound like fun at all, sitting in a room sipping tea with a sweaty, red-faced banker huffing and talking about the FTSE. Still, she didn't want to say no and make her father angry when they were living in a state of relative peace. He saw her indecision though. He gave a tight smile. 'Relax. They're not old fogies like me,' he said. (Who says 'fogies' any more? Gemma thought.) 'Richard works for me and he's quite young, and his wife's even younger. Rachel. Lovely girl.' Oh no, thought Gemma. She was being dragged off to see one of her father's tarts. They were going to play happy families at tea while her father played footsie under the table. She's rather go and see the sweaty banker she'd imagined . . . rather FTSE than footsie, any day.

But she'd said yes, and she'd have to go. Well, there was no reason to make it easy for him. She got dressed with care the next day. She chose low-rise jeans that just skimmed her hipbones, then put on a very sheer white jumper. Her bump was very small, but because she was so slim it was unmistakable. Let's see that strumpet Rachel get sexy with her dad while his pregnant teenage daughter looked on.

185

She couldn't have been more wrong. They arrived at Richard and Rachel's place just after three. There were two silver 4-by-4s in the driveway, and parked behind them, a shiny little red hatchback. When Rachel opened the door, Gemma was surprised to see that she looked just like a younger version of Gemma's mother . . . a little too thin, with carefully styled and coloured blonde hair and subtle make-up. She smiled brightly and said, 'Hi! You must be Gemma!' She used a cutesy voice, as if Gemma were six, or mentally retarded. That was when Gemma knew this was a pity visit, and that Rachel already knew she was pregnant. Richard came to the door too, and greeted Gemma's dad like an enthusiastic puppy. What an idiot, Gemma thought. She knew how much her father hated people sucking up to him. He'd told her over dinner about how he hated the toadying little twits in his office. This was going to be a disaster of an afternoon.

But there was another surprise to come. They walked into the living room, and Rachel said, 'Gemma, this is my sister, Louise.' She said it in a special tone, as if she was giving Gemma a gift. Sister Louise was sitting on the sofa with her back to them, and when she stood up and turned Gemma saw she was pregnant, not hugely so, but a little further along than Gemma herself was. Louise was tall, much taller than her sister, with a slim, muscular build. She had dark, reddish hair which she wore cropped short, and she had a lovely wide mouth that looked like she smiled and laughed a lot. Gemma glanced quickly at Louise's left hand. She wasn't wearing any rings. So that was the point of the tea. They'd found her another single pregnant woman to talk to. The only difference was that Louise looked old enough to be her mother.

Louise

Dear God, she's a child! Louise thought. She's barely into puberty! Little Gemma Hamilton was about five foot two and fine-boned, with long, straight blonde hair. She had no figure to speak of . . . Rachel had told her Gemma was a dancer, and she had the straight waist and flat chest that comes from years of ballet training. Because she was so tiny, the bump under her white jumper was already very visible. Gemma was staring at her coolly. She's not stupid, Louise thought. She's worked out that we've been set up. Rachel, Richard and David were all standing around the room, watching them warily, like zookeepers who'd put two animals in a cage together and were worried they'd tear each other to pieces. Nobody spoke, and as the silence got longer and more embarrassing, Louise realised she had to do something. 'I'm going to put the kettle on,' she announced abruptly and headed for the kitchen.

Annoyingly, Rachel, ever the perfect hostess, had already laid out the tea tray and put beautiful homemade cakes and sandwiches on plates. There was nothing other than boiling the kettle to keep Louise in the kitchen. She wished fervently for a sink full of dishes to wash, or for any other fiddly domestic task that would save her having to go back into that living room to talk to that poor, sullen child. She spent ages

188

running the tap and rinsing out Rachel's spotless, limescale-free kettle, before filling it with water from the water-filter jug. She contemplated ducking out of the kitchen door, crawling past the living-room window and getting into her car to speed off back to the calm oasis that was Simon's flat. But then she remembered that her handbag, with her car keys, was next to the sofa in the living room. She'd be willing to abandon the bag . . . she could get new credit cards and things, but without the keys, she was screwed. She didn't know how to hot-wire a car. She laughed quietly to herself at the thought and turned back from the sink to put the kettle on its stand, then jumped and almost dropped it. Gemma was standing silently in the kitchen doorway, watching her. 'I said I'd come to help you,' she said. She had a very soft, breathy voice, and an accent that came from thirteen years of achingly posh private schooling.

'Not much to do,' Louise said, holding up the kettle and gesturing at the table of teatime goodies, 'my sister is a domestic goddess.'

'And you were hoping to hide in the kitchen,' Gemma observed. 'Me too. What a fuck-up.'

Louise, veteran of a thousand business meetings, didn't let her face betray her shock at the teenage girl's swearing.

She resorted to the eternal conversation of pregnant women everywhere. 'So, how far along are you?'

'Fourteen weeks. You?'

'Eighteen weeks on Tuesday. How are you feeling? You been sick?'

'Not at all. Just hungry all the time.'

'Oh my God, I know! Me too,' said Louise and laughed. 'I've been looking at those sandwiches and wondering how many I could nick if I rearranged the plate so Rachel wouldn't notice.'

Gemma smiled for the first time. She was really very pretty, Louise thought, and everyone would see it if she could get rid of that permanent teenage pout. That said, she had good reason to pout: her life wasn't going very well right now.

'Maybe we could just take the whole plate and duck out of the back door,' she said. 'They wouldn't miss us.'

Just then, Rachel came into the kitchen. Clearly, Louise could be trusted to put a kettle on, but not to actually make the tea. She started bustling about, putting things straight that were already perfect. Louise and Gemma stood side by side by the sink and tried not to get in her way. Suddenly, she looked up and looked at them both. Her eyes were very bright. 'Gosh!' she said gaily. 'Look at all the preggie tummies in here! Isn't that lovely!' Then she grabbed two platters of cake and sandwiches and swept out into the living room. Louise could hear her being bright and bubbly to Richard and David.

'What was that about?' Gemma asked.

'She, um . . . she's been struggling to fall pregnant. I think seeing the two of us, pregnant by mistake, is just a bit hard for her.'

Gemma turned to look at her. 'Oh, I'm not pregnant by mistake,' she said calmly.

'You . . . what?' Louise was sufficiently

190

stunned to forget her manners.

'I decided I wanted to be a mum more than anything. My boyfriend and I talked about starting a family, and I got pregnant. So here I am.'

'And your boyfriend . . . '

'He's saying now that he didn't really mean it. We've broken up. But he loves babies. I think he'll come round eventually. I honestly believe everything will be okay.'

Louise was shocked. She couldn't help it. She had come to Rachel's, thinking she could be the one impartial, non-judgmental adult this girl met. But she hadn't expected to hear this. Louise was flummoxed. She'd expected a tearful, frightened young girl. Instead Gemma was self-possessed and graceful, and, mad as it was, she'd had a dream and now it was reality. Nevertheless, it made her heart ache. Gemma was such an innocent. The situation was totally insane, and Louise was not quite sure how to get that across to her. She went for the subtle approach.

'You do know that what you've done is crazy, don't you?'

Gemma looked at her. 'Is it?'

'Well, yes. You can't just get pregnant and think it'll solve all your problems. What about the other people involved? Ben, is it? And the baby?'

'I wanted to do it at first because I really, really wanted to hold on to Ben. But I'm not so sure about that now. He's being pathetic, so if he's not around I'm not sure I'm all that fussed any more. As for the baby, I'm going to love it, and be there for it always. I want to be a mum. I wish people would just understand that.'

'And what about your parents?'

'My mum's either busy doing charity stuff or getting her hair done. My dad's always at work or busy with recreational activities. They haven't noticed me in years.'

She pulled a face when she said 'recreational activities'. There was no doubt what she meant, Wow. Louise had never thought this would be easy, but she had no tools at all to deal with someone who was as blunt as this.

'And what about you?' Gemma asked.

'What about me?'

'My dad said you're on your own. Where's your baby's father?'

'He's, er . . . he's up in Yorkshire. We're not together.'

There was an awkward pause. 'We really should go through and talk to the others,' Louise said.

'Okay,' said Gemma, looking for all the world like the perfect, obedient teenage daughter. 'Let's go and be polite. I'll pretend you gave me a good talking-to and that I feel so much better, and you can tell them that I've got a good head on my shoulders. What do you think of that?'

★ ★ ★

When Louise got back to the flat, she told Simon all about Gemma.

'She sounds utterly terrifying,' Simon said.

192

'She was. It's that growing-up-posh thing. She's so self-possessed. I don't think she's nearly as confident as she pretends to be, but she decided she'd be honest with me, and she was. She's got into this situation and she's dealing with it. Amazingly, she seems really happy about it. And despite all his millions and his power and influence there's nothing her dad can do about it.'

'Sounds like she quite likes putting one over him.'

'She implied he's unfaithful to her mother a lot.'

'That doesn't surprise me,' Simon said. 'He's got the look of a man who thinks he's entitled.'

'Entitled to what?'

'Anything he wants. So I don't suppose you gave her too many facts about your situation?'

'Knocked up by accident by a married man? Having the baby without telling him? No, I didn't think it would do her any good to know that.'

'Well, when you put it like that it does sound pretty rotten,' said Simon. Louise recoiled like he had slapped her. She didn't expect criticism from Simon. Not him, of all people.

'Thanks, Simon. I know. I really do know. But this is my lot, and I'm just trying to get on with it.' She stood up to leave the room. Her face felt hot, and she thought she might cry.

'Relax, Lou. I wasn't having a go. It's just when you put it in such bald terms . . . '

'That's rich, coming from you.'

'What do you mean?'

'Well, you're the reason I'm doing this. I was going to have an abortion, and you talked me out of it.'

'Come off it, Lou. Nobody talks you into or out of anything. You've always done exactly what you were going to do. All I did was say aloud what you were already feeling in your heart.'

There is nothing more infuriating than someone being absolutely right in the heat of an argument. There was a long moment of silence, then Louise did what every sane, rational adult would do. She said, 'Yeah, well, sod you!' and stormed off to her bedroom. Simon, wisely, left her to it.

Subject: Bloody Siblings

Dear Toni,

I hope you can forgive my endless bleating, but I've had one hell of a day with both of my siblings. Tea with the pregnant teenager was predictably awful for three reasons. 1. She's not terrified or regretful, she wanted to fall pregnant and she's really happy about it. She's scarily determined and I had nothing of value to tell her at all. 2. Rachel walked into the kitchen and looked at us both all teary-eyed and said something about 'all those preggie tummies', making me feel grade-A Awful. So yes, the principle of limited good is alive and well in Surrey, as you suspected. And 3. Well, there isn't a 3. I can't even complain about there not being enough cake . . . there was a mountain of superb cake. My sister should bake for England.

Anyway, I came home and just had a stupid row with my wonderful brother Simon, because I'm feeling all oversensitive, and he said something that was true, but not what I wanted to hear.

Sorry for the offload. Hope your weekend was better than mine.
Love,
Lou
X

A reply came back within minutes:

Subject: Re Bloody Siblings

Dear Lou,
Go and make Simon some tea and say sorry. Blame your hormones. I blow up about four times a day at James. I have to make a lot of cups of tea.

I also had a fairly rotten weekend, details too long to share here.

Listen, I've got a mad idea . . . tell me if you think this is overstepping the mark, but why don't we have lunch tomorrow? I know you'll be moving to Surrey soon to start your new job. You'll be living in the same neck of the woods as us, more or less, and maybe we could be more than digital friends? So while you're still a lady of leisure, why not come into the West End and meet me for a sandwich? There's a

nice place near my office called Jack's,
corner of Kingsway and Great Queen
Street. If you're free, I take my lunch at
one, and it would be great to meet you in
person.
Love
T
xx

P.S. If you say yes, I'll be the short blonde
with the belly which may be pregnant or
may just be a bit fat.

Toni

When I woke up in the morning, I remembered my spur-of-moment email to Louise. I regretted it a bit. Would she think I was some kind of freaky internet stalker? It seemed odd to be taking a friendship from the anonymous safety of the online world to the really quite intimate realm of sitting opposite one another in my local sandwich shop. What if she was a psycho? Or a fifty-year-old bloke who got off on pretending to be a pregnant woman? All of these options seemed fairly unlikely, but who knew? I'd never done internet dating, but I had lots of mates who had, so I knew to take precautions. I should let someone know where I'd be and who I'd be meeting, in case she chopped me up into little bits and left me in rubbish bags around the West End.

I fired up my laptop in the kitchen while I ate my breakfast and checked my email. There was a message from Louise. 'I'd love to meet you. I'm tall with short, reddish-dark hair and a tummy like half a football. See you at one.' Ah. Well, then this was definitely happening. James came in from the shower with a towel wrapped around his waist. His hair was wet and he smelled of sharp, lime-flavoured shower gel. In years gone by, I would have checked the clock and if we had a few minutes I'd have whipped off his towel for a naughty pre-work quickie in the kitchen. But things were still fragile between us. We'd had a massive row the day before. I'll spare you the details, but it came down to James pointing out that we'd barely had sex since the day I'd found out I was pregnant, and me trying to explain how I didn't feel my body was my own and I felt uncomfortable about sex, and him saying did that mean he was going to be a born-again virgin, because I had at least twenty-five weeks to go, and me saying that it wasn't fair for him to pressure me, and him saying 'Oh, for heaven's sake', and me bursting into tears, and then him saying that I'd started using tears as a weapon and storming out. Whoops. Those were the details. Now you have them. Sorry for not sparing you.

Anyway, he came home after about an hour, and we'd made a tentative kind of peace, and I said I would try, and he said he would do his best not to be a pushy bastard. We didn't actually do the deed on the Sunday night, but we did a bit of cuddling and kissing on the sofa, and that was okay. So things were fine between us, just a bit delicately balanced, if you know what I mean.

I smiled at him, and he gave me a sweet grin back, then went to the fridge to get some juice. It was an odd feeling, feeling awkward around James. He's my best friend, and I can normally say absolutely anything to him, but this was new. Sex has always been something easy and comfortable for us: it's never been an issue before. I knew I'd caused the problem . . . I'd been avoiding it for weeks now. I'd worked up quite a repertoire of excuses. I was tired, my back was sore, I felt sick. Or I'd just go to bed first and pretend to be asleep. It wasn't that I didn't fancy him . . . it was just that sex was the last thing on my mind. All my attention was turned inwards, focusing on the busily multiplying cells in my uterus. I knew James had noticed . . . he could hardly have missed it. We'd gone from several times a week to pretty much nothing for the past ten weeks. I also know it must have taken a lot for him to say something. James just isn't a confrontational guy. He'll usually do anything to avoid a row. He must have been very frustrated indeed. Oh, and let me tell you, I wasn't ignorant . . . I knew perfectly well that it wasn't dangerous or bad for the baby . . . I just didn't want to do it.

But I was smart enough to realise that I was going to have to get over myself or my relationship with James was going to end up in trouble. I wished I could just have a few glasses of wine to relax, and then get on with it, but the wine was out of bounds.

All of this ran through my head as I showered and got dressed for work. James left before me, and he gave me a very sweet and tender (non-sexy) kiss and a hug before he left, which made me feel a bit better. But he was gone and I was halfway out of the door before I realised I'd not told him about my lunch with Louise. I would have emailed him, but I knew he was out of the office all morning at a client pitch. Ah well. Jack would keep an eye out for me, and hopefully Louise wouldn't be a serial killer.

It was Sod's Law that my phone rang at twelve

199

fifty-five. It was a client who needed some gentle reassurance, so I was a good five minutes late walking into Jack's. It was quite busy, and every table was occupied. Would I know her, I wondered? It hadn't occurred to me that it would be impossible to spot a pregnant belly if the woman was sitting down. I looked around the tables, and there was only one woman on her own, and sure enough, she had short, dark-reddish hair. She was sitting with her back to me. I walked over hesitantly.

'Lou?' I asked. The woman looked up and smiled. She had a great, wide grin and twinkly, laughing eyes. She stood up quickly. 'Toni!' she said, and gave me a friendly kiss on the cheek. Suddenly, all my silly fears seemed ridiculous. She seemed lovely and I felt an instant connection. She was right about her tummy . . . it did look like half a football.

'Sorry, I'm late,' I said. 'Nervy client.'

Jack came over and we ordered a couple of sandwiches and fruit juices.

'I don't actually know what you do,' Louise said. Her Manchester accent was noticeable.

'PR,' I said.

'Ah . . . silly me . . . PR–Girl. Of course. What kind?'

Out of the industry, no one ever asks that. They assume there's only one kind.

'Consumer PR: I work for a big firm with lots of different accounts, but my speciality is the cosmetics industry.'

'Ah. I've always loved those amazing terms they come up with for the new ingredients in

200

cosmetics. 'New! With added elasto-plastin!' Do you get to make up the names?'

I laughed. 'No, sadly not. I wish that was my job, but I just get to spin the exciting, all-new story about elasto-plastin and try to get the magazines to buy it!' Jack brought our sandwiches, and we fell on them, chatting between bites.

'Come to think of it, I might have printed some magazines your work was in.' She named a couple of big women's titles. 'We did all of those at one point or another.'

'Sounds like you left a pretty successful career.'

'Well, these things are all relative.'

'Are they?'

'No, not really, but I keep telling myself they are. I'm so grateful to Adam Harper for giving me the job I've got, not to mention a place to live. It would be really petty to worry that it's a bit of a step down from the work I was doing before.'

There was something about the way that she said Adam Harper's name that made my ears prick up. But we weren't proper friends yet, so it didn't seem right to press her for girly confidences. Talking about work seemed to be a safe middle ground.

'I suppose it's human nature to think like that,' I said. 'I mean, I'm thrilled to be pregnant, but at the same time, my career was just taking off. And if I do come back to work I'll be way behind my contemporaries. I can't help being a bit miffed about that.'

'I guess PR is a young person's career too, isn't it?'

'Like all media, I think you're right. If you haven't made it by the time you're thirty — '

Louise laughed. She had a fantastic, loud infectious laugh that matched her grin. 'Well, I guess I'd better scrap my plans for a career change!'

Before I had time to think if it was polite to ask, I blurted out, 'Why? How old are you?'

'Thirty-eight. And you?'

'Twenty-six?' I felt a bit bad saying that. Maybe she thought I was too young and immature, and she wouldn't want to be friends with me. But she just grinned again, and then we were off talking about something else. When I glanced at my watch, it was already after two.

'Oh wow! Look at the time! I have to get back to the office.' Louise looked at her watch too. 'Sorry . . . so busy nattering. Hope you don't have far to go.'

'No, it's just around the corner.' I stood up. 'Without making this sound like a really cheesy first date, I had such a nice time. It was great to finally meet you.'

She stood up too. 'Me too. Let's try and hook up again before I start work, and then you and James must come down to the farmhouse once I've settled in. Adam's place is really pretty . . . it's right on the river.'

Often when you meet someone, and they say 'Let's get together soon', you think: Yeah, right. They'll never call. Or you hope they won't. But I knew it was different with Louise. I'd made a

202

new, real friend, and I knew we'd be friends for ages.

I gave her a quick hug and headed for the door. As I walked out, I noticed a skinny, dark woman of about forty standing on the street outside the shop. She was staring in through the window of the sandwich shop, with a shocked expression on her face. When I looked back into the shop I saw she was looking at Louise. I didn't have time to stop and ask her who she was, or to go in and tell Louise what I'd seen, but I made a mental note to tell her when we next spoke.

That night, I excitedly told James all about my meeting with Louise. He told me off for not mentioning it beforehand.

'I know, I know, she might have been a psycho or something. I should have told you. But she wasn't. She's really nice and now I have a friend who's also pregnant.'

'That's great. I hadn't thought about it, but I suppose that would be quite useful. You can compare notes and go shopping for baby stuff.'

'Or you and I can go shopping for baby stuff.'

'True.' He laughed. 'Or maybe let's make that a qualified yes.'

To be fair, James really does hate shopping, I'm not one of those girls who love to go out and spend, but I'm not actually allergic to it like he is. When we moved in together he handed responsibility for his wardrobe over to me, and I like to think he's better dressed as a result.

'I'm happy to do the big stuff like cots and pushchairs. But I'm not going to stand around

203

Babies R Us comparing little pink sleepsuits,' he said warily.

'Your son will look really interesting in a little pink sleepsuit!'

'So you think it's a boy?' He looked excited.

'Oh, James, I haven't a clue. It's only a few weeks till our twenty-week scan. Do you want to find out the sex?'

'No. Definitely not. Definitely, definitely not.'

'Okay' I was a bit surprised he was so adamant, but if he felt like that, I was happy to go with it. He drew me towards him, and gave me one of his finest, warm James hugs. I swear, if I could bottle them and sell them, I'd be a rich woman.

He was being very nice and gentle with me, and I was grateful for that, after our awful row the night before. But at the same time, I had a sneaky thought — was he being so nice because he was trying to get his leg over? I felt awful for thinking that. James is anything but sly. And anyway the problem was mine, not his. I had to get over this silly no-sex thing. After dinner, I went and had a lovely long candlelit bath, then moisturised all over and put on a little of James' favourite perfume. I tried very hard to relax. James was sitting in front of the telly, and I went and snuggled next to him in my dressing gown. I slipped my hand under his shirt. I felt his body stiffen a little . . . it was an old signal between us, but I could see he wanted to be sure not to misread it. I kissed his ear softly and he turned and took me in his arms.

It was really nice. It was. It took me a bit of

time to get in the mood, and I maybe wasn't as acrobatic or enthusiastic as I used to be. But James was very patient and gentle, and we managed to do the deed. He looked so happy afterwards . . . he gets a particular look after sex . . . his face relaxes and his eyes go very dark. He grinned at me, then gathered up his clothes and went to shower before falling into bed. I put my dressing gown back on, tidied up the living room and put off all the lights. And I put to one side the terribly guilty thought that I'd got that out of the way and I wouldn't have to do it again for at least a week.

*   *   *

About ten days later, I was sitting at my desk at work, typing a very carefully worded email to a client who had complained about something. They spend a lot of money with us, and even though the problem wasn't our fault, I couldn't really say that. So I had to say sorry, without taking any responsibility, if you know what I mean. I tell you, it's like the United Nations. I should get a prize for writing that kind of stuff.

I was concentrating, so at first I scarcely noticed . . . then I had a half-formed thought that my tummy felt a bit fluttery . . . a bit like the butterflies you get when you're nervous. Then, as I finished the email, I gave the sensation my full attention. What was it? Could it be . . . ? But wasn't it too early? I looked up 'baby kicking' on the baby website. They said with a first baby, you'd probably only feel something around eighteen weeks. I was just short of sixteen weeks. But what else could it be? I hadn't been thinking about it or looking out for it, so I didn't think I could be imagining it. I grabbed my mobile, went off to the loo and rang Louise. She answered, sounding a little distracted.

'Hi there . . . it's Toni. Do you have a minute?'

'Er . . . sure. Hang on a second . . . ' I heard her put her hand over the mouthpiece and murmur something to someone. Then she came back on the line.

'Hi.' From the background noise, it sounded like she'd moved outside.

'I feel awful,' I said. 'You're obviously busy. I didn't mean to disturb you.'

'It's no problem, really. I'd tell you if it was. Adam and I are just out for lunch, chatting about . . . work things.'

'Lunch? It's four o'clock!'

'Is it?' She sounded guilty. 'Anyway . . . what did you want to ask me?'

I described what I'd felt. 'Yup, that's definitely it,' she said. 'I felt it for the first time the other day. And every day, the feeling gets a little stronger.'

I laughed. 'It's amazing!' I said. 'Oh, I wish it was strong enough so you could feel it from the outside. I want James to feel it too.'

'I'm sure in a few months we'll be complaining that they're booting us too hard all the time.'

I put my hand on my tummy again and felt the tiny little flutters. Like wings. 'This is the craziest feeling I've ever had in my life. There's another

206

whole person inside me, moving independently.'

It was Louise's turn to laugh. 'Isn't it mad? I know billions of women do this, but I keep feeling like I'm the first one ever to go through it.'

'I won't keep you. You'd better get back to your lunch,' I said.

'Yeah,' she said. 'And Toni . . . thanks for ringing. It's great to have someone to share this stuff with.'

That night, James and I lay together in the dark and I tried to explain to him what it felt like.

'I'm so jealous,' he said.

'Jealous? Why?'

'Well, I'll never, ever know what it feels like to have someone kick me from the inside.'

'That's probably a good thing. You wouldn't be doing well at all if someone could do that.'

'I'm being serious. You have all this stuff going on inside your body. You're making those little curly bits on its ears, and eyelashes and things. And then you get to give birth. And breastfeed.'

'I wish you could do some of those things. Especially the giving birth. You can definitely have that one.'

'I'm serious. I mean . . . I've done my bit. And very nice it was too. But the rest of this is all up to you.'

We lay there in silence for a while and I thought about what he'd said. I remembered the message I'd got on the baby website when I very first found out I was pregnant, when the woman asked me if this was bringing James and me closer together. Were we closer, or further apart? Yes, there were a million little niggly things, but we'd get over those, right? I heard James' breathing change and I knew he was asleep. I turned on my side and looked at his lovely profile. This man was the father of my child. And deep in my pelvis, I felt the tiny quiver once again. The tiny person inside me was half me, and half him. And that was the most amazing thing of all.

Louise

She was moving in very dangerous waters. Very dangerous indeed. Every day she spent with Adam Harper, she found herself more attracted to him. Yes, he was good-looking, but there was more to him than that. He was a fair, consistent and generous employer. He expected a lot from his team, but he treated them with respect and gave them autonomy and made them account-able. As a result, he ran a tight shop, and everyone who worked for him was intensely loyal. He was also well-read, witty and clever. His conversation was wide-ranging, and, unusu-ally (Louise thought) for a middle-aged man, he listened. He really listened to her when she talked, unlike a lot of the blokes she'd worked with before, who always had seemed to be waiting for her to finish so that they could say the much more important thing they were thinking about.

There was one pressing question that occurred to her — why the hell was he single? He didn't share many details about his personal life, but she had worked out that he was divorced, and had been so for at least ten years. His ex-wife lived in Chelmsford with his two teenage children, and he spoke to his kids most days and saw them every weekend. She'd heard him have a few conversations with his ex-wife, and they seemed to have a civil and friendly relationship, and seemed to be committed to parenting their kids together.

Her cynical heart knew there had to be something wrong with him, but she couldn't see anything. She really tried. She was desperate to give herself some kind of aversion therapy . . . she wanted to dislike him, or find something repulsive about him. But it was no good. She had it bad. When they leaned over a document together and she could smell his warm skin, she felt positively faint.

She was used to acting professionally in a work context, so she didn't think she was giving anything away. She treated him coolly and tried to keep a physical distance between them at all times. She kept another thing front of mind . . . she imagined his look of horror if she made a play for him . . . a single, pregnant woman in her late thirties . . . she was scarcely a first-class catch. He'd asked a few general questions about her situation. She'd told him she was single and raising the baby alone, and made her tone of voice sufficiently brisk to discourage further questions. He soon got the hint and stopped asking.

But no matter how formal she tried to be, they were definitely getting closer. They were spending all day every day together as he brought her up to speed on every aspect of the business. They ate meals together and she learned how he liked his coffee and that he was allergic to nuts.

He offered to set up one of the spare bedrooms so she could stay and not commute back to London each evening, but she knew that was far too dangerous. Dinner, a small glass of wine sitting close to one another on the sofa, seeing him in the morning fresh from his shower . . . she'd never manage to keep her professional distance under that kind of pressure.

She counted the days to his departure . . . feeling both desperation that she wouldn't see him for months and months, and relief that the sexual tension she could cut with a knife would be relieved. Somehow, the days crept past and it came to the day before he was due to leave. She'd agreed to move in that day and had driven to Surrey with her worldly possessions piled high in her little car. He helped her carry everything in and left her to settle in in a pretty bedroom that faced on to a little enclosed garden on the side of the farmhouse. She stood looking out of the window at the crazy profusion of daffodils in the garden outside, and beyond at the green hills. She could be very happy here.

There was a soft knock at the door. She turned, and he was standing there. 'Kettle's on,' he said and smiled. 'And I got some lemon cake in town today to celebrate your moving in.'

'Ah, Adam,' she grinned, 'you know the way to a woman's heart!'

What a thoroughly stupid thing to say! She found herself blushing like a schoolgirl, so she put her head down and walked towards the door as if she was headed briskly for the kitchen. But he didn't move out of her way. He laughed, and said lightly, 'Funny, I've always been told that the way to a woman's heart was through her

211

sternum with a bone saw.'

She looked up, shocked, and saw he was grinning from ear to ear. 'Kidding,' he said softly. 'I have all the lines, don't I?'

He still wasn't moving. Louise couldn't get past him, so she just stood and looked into his lovely face. And then, finally, he kissed her.

She'd imagined that kiss every night since she'd met him. She'd lain in bed at Simon's flat like a breathless teenager, and thought what it would be like to kiss Adam's full, firm lips. She'd never fantasised about a man like that before. It was so unlike her that she'd put it down to raging pregnancy hormones. She'd imagined a splendid, blood-roaring-in-her-ears, fireworks-going-off-behind-the-Disney-Castle, full-orchestra-playing kind of kiss. But it wasn't like that. It was better. Dear God, the man should write a bestselling book about kissing. He should get the Nobel Prize for kissing. He should be granted the Freedom of Kissing City. It was gentle and tender, but probing and sexy, and kissing him meant being pressed against his lovely body and smelling him and running her hands over his broad, muscled back. She felt a melting, pulling sensation between her legs, and then the tattoo of tiny limbs deep inside as the baby moved within her.

He pulled away first. His eyes were unfocused and his face looked blurred and changed with lust. But then he shook his head and took another step backwards. 'I'm so, so sorry, Louise. That's the most unprofessional thing I've ever done. I'm . . . oh my God.' He turned and walked quickly away, and she heard him go into

212

the kitchen and start bustling around making tea.

They both needed a minute, that was clear. She went back into her room and combed her hair and took a few deep breaths. He had certainly been excited — there was no doubt about what she'd felt when she pressed up against him, and she was sure he would want a few minutes for things to . . . calm down. She sat on the bed for a little while, but she couldn't hide in her room forever. She smoothed her clothes and walked briskly into the kitchen.

He was sitting at the table, his hands around a mug of tea. He'd put her tea at the far end of the table, and put slices of the lemon cake on a plate in the middle. It made her smile: neither of them could reach the cake if she sat where he'd put her tea. Well, that wouldn't do. She scooped up her mug, walked around the table and shoved the cake plate towards him, then sat down beside him. Neither of them spoke for a while. She decided to be brave.

'Please don't feel awkward . . . you didn't do anything that I didn't . . . want you to do.'

'Well, that's a relief. I just . . . well, this is possibly the most complicated situation I've found myself in in a long time.'

'I agree. I mean, I'll be here, running your business, and you have to feel you can trust me . . . '

'That's not what I mean. Louise, I trust you completely. You've shown that you're more than equal to the task professionally. It's just that . . . '

'I'm pregnant?'

213

'Well, yes. That's part of it, and I'm going away . . . and when I come back you'll have the baby . . . not that I mind . . . oh God. This is all coming out wrong. I've just wanted to kiss you since the moment I saw you, and I've told myself every day that it's a terrible, terrible idea. But today I just . . . well, I didn't want to go away without telling you how I feel.'

She left a pause, and asked quietly, 'How do you feel?'

He thought about it, and then spoke hesitantly.

'I feel like . . . like meeting you was significant. Very, very significant. Like I drove up to the station to pick you up that first day, and when I saw you, I felt like you were coming home.'

Well, there really was nothing to say to that. Louise drew a ragged breath and put a hand over his. His skin was warm under her palm, and he flipped his hand gently so their palms were pressed together.

They talked until the sun went down, then she cooked them big bowls of pasta with chilli and tomato. Then they went into the living room and talked some more. They sat close together on the sofa, and Millicent came to sit on his knee. She purred and extended one paw on to Louise's knee, almost as if she were offering a truce.

Later, much later, they went to sleep together in Adam's big bed. They didn't have sex . . . they'd both agreed that no matter how much they wanted to, it would make things even more complicated than they already were. She fell asleep with her hand in his.

The room was still dark when his alarm bleeped softly, and he got up and walked quietly to the shower. Louise lay on her side, looking at the mountainous piles of bags and backpacks arranged against the wall of his bedroom. He was going, and that was it. They had made no definite plans. He'd asked her to wait for him to come back from the sailing expedition, and they'd agreed to see where they stood then. No promises, just a door left open.

Their last few hours together were quiet. So much had been said the night before, and so much could be said to damage the tiny, fragile beginnings they had built. They held hands over cups of steaming coffee at the kitchen table, and then he loaded up the car. He came into the kitchen and held her, at first gently, as if she might break, then fiercely, as if he needed her strength to be able to go. They didn't say goodbye.

Once he had driven away into the grey, early morning light, she crept back into his bed and let herself cry a little, resting her head on the pillow where he had slept. It hurt that he was gone, but at the same time it was a good pain, if there was such a thing. She had so much to deal with at the moment ... the baby, running a new business ... amazing though Adam was, it wasn't the right time to be falling in love and losing her head. After a little while, she fell asleep again. It had been a long, emotional night and she was very tired.

The knocking sounded like someone hammering on a castle door. She began to dream a

215

confused dream about being in a palace under siege, hiding in the kitchens. It took several minutes to realise the knocking was real and that she was in Adam's house in Surrey. She stumbled out of bed, looking around wildly for something to put on. She found a ratty old dressing gown of Adam's on the back of the bedroom door and ran barefoot through the house. The hammering and doorbell-ringing was coming from the front door. She'd never come in through the front door, it didn't look like it had been opened in ages. She struggled with the locks, yelling pointlessly, 'I'm opening it! Don't go away!' Then she wrenched the door open to reveal . . . Brian.

★　★　★

She would have stood there, shocked and dumbfounded, but he started yelling the moment the door was open and pushed past her to get into the house. All she could do was follow him into the living room as he ranted. He'd obviously been working up to a boil on the drive down from Yorkshire, and the steam was going to have to escape somehow.

It took a while to work out how he had found her. Toni had mentioned in an email that the day they'd met for lunch in town she'd seen a woman staring at Louise as if she knew her. It transpired, from Brian's rant, that that woman had been Jane, his PA. She'd been in London to see a show with her sister and had delighted in going back to Leeds to tell everyone that worked

216

for Barrett and Humphries that she'd seen Louise Holmes in a coffee shop and she was 'wearing her apron high'. The news had reached Brian's ears, and he had quizzed Jane about how far along Louise was. Jane, along with every other staff member at Barrett and Humphries, had suspicions about what had happened between Brian and Louise at the awards ceremony in Manchester, so she was more than happy to fan the flames.

Brian had heard through the management grapevine that Edward had helped Louise to get a job near London, so it took one phone call to get an address. And here he was. Louise couldn't help thinking that if he'd got there a day, or even a few hours earlier, he'd have been yelling at Adam, not her. There were some small mercies.

There wasn't a lot for her to do or say. Brian was in full flow. The gist of what he was saying came down to three words: 'How could you?'

And to be fair, in the chilly grey light of that early April morning, what Louise had done seemed fairly appalling, even to her. She stood in the living room, naked under Adam's dressing gown, her arms crossed over her body, and looked at Brian. She'd persuaded herself that she felt nothing for him other than disgust, that what had happened between them had meant nothing to him, and that his moving on to another affair was justification enough for leaving without telling him that he was to be a father. She had begun to believe that the baby she was carrying was hers and hers alone, nothing to do with him. But that wasn't true. It wasn't his anger that persuaded her . . . it was seeing him. Looking at his familiar face, she thought for the first time that her child might have Brian's blue eyes, or coppery hair. Would the child be tall and slim like her, or chunkier, like Brian? Genetically, the baby was half his, and that meant he had a lifetime's emotional claim on this child, and a lifetime's link to her. She couldn't believe that she hadn't thought this all through. And, insanely, not three hours before, she'd parted from a man she thought she might be falling in love with. A man who was not the father of the baby she was carrying.

She felt a bit weak, and sat carefully on the edge of an armchair. Brian was saying, 'And what about Lisa? And my girls? How am I going to tell them?' He kept talking, but Louise found she was fighting an overwhelming urge to go back to Adam's bed and fall into a deep sleep. If she was asleep, none of this would be happening. But then, out of the torrent of Brian's rant, one word rang out — 'abortion'.

'What?' she said. It was the first time she'd spoken since he had arrived.

'I think you should have an abortion. This is ridiculous. We're middle-aged people. This is going to ruin our lives.'

'Brian, I'm nineteen-and-a-half weeks pregnant, almost at the limit for a legal abortion. I doubt I'd find a doctor in England who'd condone it. And, secondly, no. I want this baby.'

And, suddenly, Brian sat down on the sofa opposite her and started to cry.

Brian was tough, businesslike and practical,

often a bit dogmatic, to be fair. In a work context, he was known to be quietly forceful, and sometimes, very dramatically, he yelled. He didn't cry. Yet here he was, sitting on the edge of Adam's faded gold sofa, with his head in his hands, sobbing like a child. She hesitated, then went to sit beside him. She patted his back awkwardly and felt his sobs heave through him. It was absolutely awful to watch. He did stop eventually and excused himself to go to the bathroom. She used the time to dash to her own bedroom and put on some clothes. She heard him blow his nose like a trumpet, and then heard water running as he washed his face. When he came out, his eyes were red, but he looked relatively normal.

They sat down again in the living room, side by side on the sofa. After a long silence, Brian said, 'I'm sorry. That's not like me at all.'

'I know.'

'I just feel so totally out of control. Like you've put my life under the wheels of some juggernaut and you're going to destroy it.'

'That was not my intention, Brian, believe me. I left Leeds, hoping you'd never find out, that I'd just be gone. I'm just trying to make the best of the situation.'

'Like I'd believe that.' His face twisted into an ugly sneer.

She was too shocked to say anything more than, 'What?'

'Look at you,' he said. 'You're nearly forty. Biological clock ringing like a fire alarm . . . you did this on purpose.'

'I . . . what?'

'You were trying to trap me. I see that now.'

'Oh, for the love of God, Brian, listen to yourself! You sound ridiculous. If you remember, you came to my room, that night, not the other way round. It was your condom we used, and you knew then that it split. Was that my fault? Do you think I did a speedy Ninja trick where I cut it with a razor blade I had concealed somewhere? Don't be absurd.'

He looked stung, and it slowed him down for a minute, but he was soon back on the attack. 'You didn't have to keep it though.'

'No, you're right. I didn't. But I decided to. And I knew you'd want no part in this baby's life, so I left, hoping I could make it easier for you.' She paused, and then said hesitantly, 'In hindsight . . . in hindsight I should have told you. And I'm sorry. I suppose deep down I just couldn't bear the thought of having this very argument with you.'

'But now I know, and now we're having the argument. And it's too late to change what's happening.'

'You're right. But I'll do my best to make things okay. I'm willing to sign some kind of legal document absolving you of any involvement, financial or otherwise.'

'Does such a thing exist?'

'I don't know. Can we find out?'

'I'm sure it doesn't. But anyway, it wouldn't be worth the paper it's written on. One phone call to Lisa and you could destroy my life.'

'To be fair, Brian, one phone call to Lisa and I

could have destroyed your life at any point in the last four months. I gave up everything. My job, my home . . . I moved hundreds of miles. I know you don't feel like trusting me now, but I really, really don't want to ruin things for you.'

'And what about . . . ' he gestured in the direction of her belly. He clearly couldn't bear to say 'the baby', or 'the child'. 'You can't promise me . . . it . . . won't come looking for me.'

'No. I can't promise that, you're right. But I would discourage that, if you want me to.'

'Of course I'd want you to discourage it,' he said, as if any other choice was crazy.

She was suddenly, so, so sad. Over the past weeks, she'd come to love the tiny soul developing inside her. She'd got excited at the thought of meeting him or her, of getting to know her child. She'd pored over the fuzzy ultrasound pictures, trying to glimpse a recognisable feature. And here was the other parent, and as far as he was concerned, 'it' was an inconvenience in which he wanted no part. What made her saddest was that, for all his faults, Brian loved his two daughters. And this child, as much his offspring as Emily and Charlotte, would never know his love at all.

'You know what, Brian? I'd really like you to go now. I've made my promise to you. I shan't be contacting you, and as far as I'm concerned, if I never, ever see you again, it won't be too soon. So, please, have some dignity and just go.'

'Fine,' he said, standing. 'I'll speak to my lawyer and see if we can't make that promise legal in some way. Goodbye, Louise.'

221

She didn't bother to say goodbye, or to see him to the door. He walked out and she heard him pull the front door closed behind him. Very soon after that, she heard a car start up and roar away. She curled up in a ball on the sofa. The pain in her heart was intense. It had been an awful, horrible day. One of the worst she had ever experienced. But for the sake of her child-to-be, she had to keep going. It was midday on Sunday, and on Monday morning at 8 a.m., she had to be on the shop floor, acting like a manager. So whatever it took, she'd have to do it to cope. For Adam, for the baby, and for herself.

Toni

A phone call from Louise in the middle of a Sunday afternoon was the last thing I expected, to be honest. It was quite a new friendship . . . I mean, don't get me wrong, I liked her a lot . . . but I kind of thought we'd progress with a few lunches, then maybe a dinner out with James too. Now, I know that sound silly. It sounds like we were dating and she was moving too fast. But in a funny way, it is kind of the same. You don't really know someone, and you want things to move at the right pace so you have lots of warning if they're about to unleash the full weight of their craziness on you. My gut instinct said that Louise wasn't crazy, but what did I know? My mobile rang as James and I walked into the garden at our local pub. It was the first halfway warm day of the year, and we'd gone for a lovely stroll by the river in Richmond, and now we were planning to have a drink (lime and soda for me, pint for James), then go home and make dinner. I took out my phone and saw it was Louise. James gestured to say he'd go to the bar and see me outside in the garden, and I answered the call.

'Hi, Lou . . . everything all right?'

'It's not been the best day . . . just thought I'd check in with you and see . . . how things were.'

To be honest, she sounded absolutely terrible.

'Are you sure you're okay, Lou? Do you want

223

to tell me what happened?'

'Is it okay if I don't? Not right now. Can you tell me what you've been doing instead?'

So I told her about James' and my walk, and how we were at the pub. She asked me to tell her about the pub, so I told her how we come here most weekends in the summer, and how we hope once the baby's born we'll be able to eat Sunday lunch here with our little sprog in the pushchair out in the garden. Out of nowhere, she said, 'I like the way you say 'we'.'

'What do you mean?'

'You talk about you and James as a unit a lot. You don't even think about it.'

Shit. Was I rubbing it in that she was alone? 'I'm sorry,' I said, 'I don't mean to . . . '

'I'm not being sarcastic, Toni, I really like it. It's so great that you think of yourselves as a team. What a great environment for a baby to be born into.'

I asked again, 'Lou, are you sure you're all right? Are you out at the farm? Can I come and see you?'

'No, no . . . I'm fine. Got to get ready for the big day at work tomorrow . . . I'm the boss now. And I really am fine. Just talking to you and hearing about your day has made me feel so much better. Go and enjoy your drinks, Toni. Have a lovely day. Lots of love.'

And then she was gone.

I didn't know what to make of it at all. I went and found James in the garden and told him about the conversation. 'She sounded really down,' I said. 'I'm really quite worried about her.'

224

'Hang on,' he said, sipping his pint, 'you've met this woman once, right?'

'Well, yes . . . ' I said dubiously. I could see where this was going.

'And you found each other online?'

'It's not as simple as that. I know you think she's showing her true colours as some kind of internet freak. But she's not like that.'

James didn't look convinced at all. I felt I had to defend Louise.

'I admit it was a bit weird, her ringing out of the blue like that. But I think there's maybe more to her circumstances than meets the eye. She hasn't told me anything about the father of her child, just that he's not in her life any more. It just . . . well, it has to be difficult, going through this whole baby thing on your own.'

'I suppose,' James said, but he looked unconvinced.

'I would hate to be doing this without you,' I said, and took his hand. 'Nobody else in the world cares as much as we do about this baby.'

Just then, I felt a little one-two kick. I think the surprise showed in my expression. James laughed and pointed at me.

'I know that face. That's the 'I just got booted in the bladder face'!'

'You see? Louise has no one to share her face with!'

He took my hand. 'Thousands would find what you just said very confusing, but I understand.'

'I know you do.'

'That's how I got your father's permission to

225

marry you. I told him I spoke fluent Toni, and he said, 'You have my blessing, young man'.'

'My father doesn't talk like that.'

'To be fair, he does a bit.'

And, as with many things, James was right about that too.

Gemma

Samantha came home from the clinic when Gemma was twenty weeks pregnant. In her time away, she'd lost her glossy tan and let the grey roots grow out in her hair. She'd even put on a little weight. Gemma was a bit horrified to see her mum looking so . . . well . . . mumsy. It was a bit depressing. Although, in a funny way, she looked much better. Not so strained. Less like a nervous whippet.

Samantha didn't seem to know what to do at first. She clearly wasn't going to rush straight back into her usual mad round of committee meetings and lunches. Gemma could see that she knew perfectly well that the gossip machine had been busy in her absence, and everyone, but everyone, knew where she had been. She spent a lot of time wandering around the house rather vaguely, or paging through magazines, without actually seeming to see the pages. She seemed somehow softer, fuzzier around the edges, as if she were slightly out of focus.

In the week that Samantha came home, Gemma left school for the last time. She was officially on study leave before her exams in early June. So, for the first time in years, they were both home at the same time, pretty much all day.

Samantha did everything she could not to mention Gemma's pregnancy, and she even seemed to avoid looking at her. The bump was unmissable now. The baby had started to move quite a bit, and Gemma wished she could ask her mother to feel her tummy. The little kicks and punches and funny little rollercoaster rolls felt so strange from the inside, but she had no one to ask what they felt like from the outside. She'd read on a website about babies that later on in the pregnancy people would be able to see the baby move, and even see elbows and knees poking out. But she couldn't imagine it.

Then the date rolled around for her twenty-week scan. She'd asked Ben if he'd go with her and he'd muttered something about college. He hadn't come for the twelve-week one either. She didn't want to go alone. Now that her mother was home, her father had gone back to his fourteen-hour days in the office and frequent nights out, so she knew there was no point in asking him. Eventually, the day before the appointment, she plucked up the courage and caught her mother in the kitchen as she made her morning smoothie. She knew Samantha couldn't escape, not with all those strawberries and goji berries whirring around.

Gemma launched in without small talk. 'So, I have an ultrasound scan tomorrow at the hospital. Will you come with me?'

She'd thought about saying 'Would you like to come with me?' but decided against it. She knew the answer to that. Samantha looked in turn horrified, a bit cross, and scared, then she said briskly, 'Yes of course. What time?'

'It's at two.'

Samantha nodded, and poured out her

228

smoothie. There was a lot left in the blender jug, and she hesitated for a second, then grabbed another glass and poured the remainder out for Gemma. When she handed her the glass, Gemma couldn't help noticing that for the first time in her memory Samantha's nails were unmanicured and free of polish.

Her mother went out shortly after that, calling up the stairs that she would be gone for most of the day. That afternoon, Gemma was sitting in her room, revising the poems of W.H. Auden when her mobile rang. She looked at the screen and saw with a shock that it was Ben's home number. Maybe he'd changed his mind and wanted to come after all.

'Hello?'

'Gemma?' A woman's voice, not Ben's. 'It's Hannah.' Ben's mum.

'Oh,' said Gemma, trying to hide the disappointment in her voice. 'Hi, Hannah.'

'I hope you don't mind me ringing . . . it's just that Ben, well, he said something last night about you having an ultrasound.'

'Tomorrow, yes.'

'Well, I don't know how you feel, but . . . I'd, well, I'd really like to come with you. I'm going to be this baby's grandmother so I'd love to see it.'

Gemma was speechless. She'd never expected this. She'd always liked Hannah, but when Ben seemed not to be interested she'd never thought that Hannah would have feelings about it too. She was right. She *would* be the baby's grandmother.

229

'Well, my mum's coming to the scan . . . ' she started to say.

'I'm sure she wouldn't mind if I came too,' said Hannah briskly.

Gemma didn't know what to say. How she would work this out, she didn't know. What would Samantha say? What if the grandmothers ended up having an argument? Too late to worry about that now. She told Hannah which hospital to go to and arranged a meeting point.

Hannah sounded absolutely thrilled. 'That's fantastic. It really means a lot to me, Gemma.' She paused, and then said, a little awkwardly, 'I know Ben hasn't been too . . . you know . . . supportive, but he's young, and a bloke. They're a bit thick at this age. He'll come round. He's a good guy, Gemma.'

'I know,' said Gemma. She didn't really. As far as she could see, Ben was just being a prize twit. But his mum would view it differently.

★ ★ ★

Her mum came home in the early evening as Gemma came downstairs to make herself some tea. She stopped short when she saw Samantha because, in the space of a few short hours, she'd been transformed into her former self. Her hair had been cut, coloured and styled, she was wearing a new outfit, and her nails were a subtle and expensive shade of pearly pink.

'Wow, you look . . . amazing, Mum!' Gemma said.

'Thank you, darling,' Samantha said briskly. 'I

230

thought as I'm going to be meeting my first grandchild tomorrow I'd better smarten up!'

She'd come back into focus, Gemma thought. She'd got her hard, brittle edge back, which was sad in one way, but in another was a good sign. Samantha was always at her best when she had a purpose and a task to accomplish. If the scan had given her a mission, then that was a good thing. Gemma decided she'd leave the issue of Hannah for the next day. Better to spring it on Samantha when they were already at the hospital.

The one time the mothers had met, when Hannah and Ben had come to the house, had not gone well. Hannah was defensive, and Samantha had been days away from her breakdown and more than a little unstable. Gemma was pretty sure they would never be bosom buddies. She didn't want Samantha to be rude when she saw Hannah, so she hesitantly told her on the way to the hospital that Hannah had asked to be there.

'Well, at least she has some sense of responsibility, unlike that gormless idiot of a son of hers. I don't know what you were thinking, Gemma, I really don't.'

Gemma smiled secretly to herself. The way her mum said it, if Gemma had got herself pregnant by someone with a bit more gorm, things would be fine. How things had changed. From this baby being the worst possible thing in the world, it had become something tolerable . . . manageable. And when Samantha and Hannah were sitting in the ultrasound room watching the

231

grainy images resolve into hands, feet and, astonishingly, a picture of the baby's heart, four perfect chambers, beating steadily, the baby became more than that. She saw their faces soften, and they turned to each other for a brief second and smiled. She felt a surge of triumph. She had known all along that having the baby would make everything all right. Hannah and Samantha would be wonderful grannies, now Ben would come round and fall in love with her again . . . it was all going to be perfect.

'Would you like to know the sex?' The ultrasound technician asked.

'Yes,' said Gemma. She hadn't thought about it before, but in that moment she knew she wanted to know so she could imagine the child more clearly.

'Good idea, darling,' said Samantha. 'Always helps when planning the decor of the nursery.'

Hannah looked sideways at Samantha, and Gemma could see she wanted to laugh. Hannah turned to the ultrasound technician and said, 'Can you tell for sure? When I had Ben, they were only right about half of the time, so they didn't like to say.'

'Oh, this little one has presented the goods. I'm certain. Sure you want to know?'

Gemma nodded, but she knew, even before the woman spoke.

'It's a girl. You're going to have a daughter.'

Louise

What with one thing and another, Louise didn't go for her twenty-week scan until she was twenty-four weeks along. She was extremely busy at work and had to move her original appointment, and then the clinic rang to cancel the revised appointment because the sonographer was off ill. She finally got to go one rainy Wednesday morning. Rachel came with her. Louise thought long and hard about inviting her, knowing how difficult it would be for her sister, but also knowing Rachel would be hurt and offended if she wasn't invited. So, firmly sat between rock and hard place, she asked her if she was free. Rachel said she was thrilled, but Louise was prepared for fallout.

The baby was much bigger than at the twelve-week scan, so they couldn't see all of it on the screen at once. But the sonographer was very good and pointed out each part so they would know the baby was all right. Rachel held Louise's hand very tightly and kept giving little gasps. 'Do you want to know the baby's sex?' asked the sonographer.

'Of course,' said Louise, just as Rachel said, 'Oooh, no!'

'Yes, I do,' said Louise, a little more firmly.

'Oh Lou, don't. You'll jinx it. You'll spoil the surprise!' said Rachel. Typical Rachel, thought Louise, spouting phrases that didn't actually mean anything. She would normally have let something like this go . . . a fight with Rachel was never worth it. But this was her baby and her only chance to find out the sex. She had to stand her ground.

'Jinx what? And spoil what surprise? I may know what sex the baby will be, but I still won't know anything else. It'll be like meeting a total stranger.'

Rachel didn't say anything else, but she sat back in her chair, with two hot little circles of pink on her cheeks. She looked as if she might cry. Louise felt awful. She knew that Rachel was living this experience vicariously, and, in choosing to know the sex, she was choosing something Rachel would not have done herself. She knew asking her sister to be there would be a mistake. There was nothing to be done, though. The sonographer waited patiently, her transducer poised over Louise's taut stomach. Louise looked at her and nodded. She moved the probe slightly and then pointed at the screen.

'See for yourself.'

Louise burst out laughing. 'Well, that's the tiniest meat-and-two-veg I ever saw!'

Rachel leaned over her and peered at the screen. 'Oh my God, Louise . . . it's a boy!' she shrieked, ever one to state the breathtakingly obvious. 'You're having a little boy!'

After the scan, they went out for lunch, and Rachel chattered away at a million words a minute. Her colour was high, and she barely touched her food. She went on and on about private schools, football clinics, and how she'd be going home to look on the internet for tiny denim dungarees . . . so eighties, but really fashionable again, didn't Louise know. 'What about names?' she said suddenly. 'Are you going to go with the 'grandpa chic' fashion?'

'The what?'

'Oh, it's very trendy these days to go with a little-old-man name . . . like Charlie, or Alfie, or Sid.'

Louise laughed at this. 'I haven't even thought about names, Rach . . . maybe we should go for 'Dad' chic . . . think of all those names no one uses any more. I could call him Alan . . . or Dennis . . . or Colin!'

Rachel looked truly horrified, changed the subject and started prattling on about push-chairs. She'd done extensive research, and was willing to give her folder of reviews to Louise . . . on loan of course. She took a quick sip of water, and then stared hard at her plate. Definitely time to call it a day, Louise decided. Through Rachel's barrage of conversation, she'd barely had time to absorb the news she'd got at the scan herself. And she could see that Rachel was trying so, so hard not to cry. She made an excuse about work, they paid the bill and went their separate ways.

On the drive back to the farm, she began to think about the little boy she was carrying. She was glad she'd found out the sex . . . suddenly it made him seem very real. She imagined a red-faced baby, a little curly-haired toddler, a gangly ten-year-old. My son. She thought: Hello, I'm Louise, and this is my son.

Her phone bleeped as she drove, and when she stopped at the motorway services (as always, for a pee break), she checked the message. It was from Simon. 'You didn't ring!' it said. 'Waiting in breathless anticipation. Am I an aunt or an uncle?'

She typed a quick message in reply. 'Well done, Uncle Si. You'll have to teach him about show tunes and football. All's well, by the way. Ring me later.'

She got back on the road, and was in the office by mid-afternoon. Everything was running smoothly . . . a big job had just gone out and the schedule was clear for the rest of the day. She checked her emails, and there was one from Adam. No subject line, and just one word. 'Well?'

She sent him a single-word one in response. 'Boy.'

He must have been at his computer — they were in port somewhere in Spain that week — because he replied immediately.

'I wish you great joy with him, my lovely. In my experience, boys adore their mums. They'll give you grey hair jumping out of trees and running around like animals, but they're just great. Grazed knees and all, he's going to own your heart.'

She smiled at this. Her fledgling relationship with Adam was being conducted via email, and the odd echoey telephone call when he could get an internet connection and hook up via Skype. Oddly though, it felt close and easy . . . she couldn't explain it, but in the two weeks they'd

236

spent together and the four weeks since, she felt as if they were really intimate. Funny how she could feel that way about a man she'd never even seen naked, and yet the father of her child was pretty much a stranger.

She answered a few more emails, and then wandered around the shop floor and made sure everyone was happy and had what they needed. Then she went back to the office and rang Toni to tell her about the scan. Toni was thrilled for her, and wanted to know all the details about head circumference and whether her dates had changed. They got off the phone after about twenty minutes, and Louise found herself straightening pencils on her desk. She really didn't have anything to do. She thought about packing up for the day and going to make some tea and stroke Millicent. And then she found herself doing something she wasn't expecting to do at all. She opened an email and entered Brian's email address. She typed quickly: 'Had my scan this morning. All is well, and the baby is a boy. Just thought you might want to know. L.'

She hit Send before she could think about it, then shut down her computer and left the office.

THE THIRD TRIMESTER

Toni

'Honest to God, Lou,' I said, as we sat having lunch on the South Bank one sunny Saturday in June, 'I'm a heifer! The size of me! I'm two weeks less pregnant than you are, and look at me! I've got fat fingers . . . I can't wear any of my rings, my belly's the size of St Paul's, and look at my cankles!'

Louise laughed and helped herself to another chip. She can eat anything, and not gain weight. It's bloody annoying, but she looks like a model for a pregnancy catalogue. She's still all tall and slender and her bump is this neat little thing that looks like she pops it under her T-shirt every morning like a fashion accessory. The rest of her is still the same. Slim legs, slim arms, slim face . . . whereas I am the Michelin woman, all rolls of chubbiness and water retention and permanently red in the face because I'm so damned *hot* all the time.

'You're blooming, Toni,' Louise said. 'You're like a gorgeous, blossoming milkmaid, and for your information, you couldn't be a heifer. Heifers are virgin cows who haven't had a calf. And what are cankles, anyway?'

'I have no ankles. My water retention is so bad my calves go all the way down to my feet. Hence cankles.' I looked down at my puffy legs. From our stroll along the South Bank on the way to lunch they seemed to have got bigger, if that was possible. I sighed. 'It may be worse than that. I think I may have thankles.'

'You may be uncomfortable, but you look lovely. I'm your friend; I'd tell you if you looked hideous. I bet James says you're gorgeous.'

'James is no fool. He's not going to mess with an unpredictable pregnant woman. He tells me I'm gorgeous several times a day and then stands well back in case that's become one of the things he gets yelled at for saying.'

'Do you yell at him a lot?'

'Not yell, as such.'

'Shriek? Whine? Nag?'

'A bit . . . '

'Which one?'

'All three, pretty much. I like to mix it up.'

I was joking with Louise, but I'm afraid it was all true, to a certain extent. At twenty-six weeks, I was already horrendously uncomfortable. I was hot, hot, hot all the time and it was only the beginning of June. With another fourteen weeks to go, through the heat of summer . . . well, it didn't bear thinking about. On top of that, I wasn't getting a summer holiday this year. I'd be too far gone to fly anywhere by July or August, and anyway I was trying not to use any holiday days so I could tag them all on to my maternity leave and get away from work a bit earlier.

Every year James and I had been together we'd had a cracking summer holiday. One year we went to Greece, and the next we had two weeks in Egypt. We'd been clubbing in Spain and one year we'd splurged all our cash and gone to Australia. We're both total sun bunnies, so the hotter the location the better. That summer holiday was the highlight of my year. Now I couldn't imagine wanting to go somewhere hot . . . even the watery spring sunshine in June was making me swelter.

I'd stayed home in April when James went snowboarding . . . it had been a bit of a sore point, but there was no point in my going and sitting around the chalet for days. We'd lost quite a bit of money on the deal, and I'd sulked for a week when James got back. He pointed out, logically, that we'd have lost even more money if he hadn't gone, and I pointed out even more logically that it wouldn't have been all that much if he hadn't spent heaven knows what on copious drinks every evening. I mean, for heaven's sake, he had a Jägermeister in his hand in every picture on Facebook! He tried to say it was because he missed me so much, but I gave him the frozen stare and he stopped talking.

Louise looked at me closely. 'Are things okay between you guys?'

'Well . . . things are a bit strained. I mean . . . joking aside, I know I'm being difficult, and totally focused on myself, but I'm pregnant, for heaven's sake! My body's been taken over by an alien life force! James is doing what he can but he's, well, he's James. Don't get me wrong . . . he's sweet and funny and loyal, but maybe . . . no, never mind.' I stopped myself.

'Maybe what?' Lou said quietly.

'Maybe our relationship was supposed to be all fun and romance . . . and now we're facing real, grown-up hard stuff it just isn't strong enough.'

'Do you believe that?'

'I don't know. It never used to be this hard.'

'I'm going to sound like your grandmother now, but was he your first serious boyfriend?'

'Well no, I had this boyfriend all through uni . . . '

'Uni boyfriends don't count. That's not real life. Not work and rent and pressure and . . . '

'And babies.'

'Exactly.'

'Well then, James was my first serious real-life boyfriend. Why? Do you think that's a problem?'

'Oh God,' said Louise laughing, 'I'm the last person to give romantic advice. I'm a walking disaster area when it comes to men.'

'Have you ever been married?' I asked tentatively. We'd never talked about Louise's romantic life. I knew nothing about the father of her baby except that they'd broken up.

'Never married, no. I had two long-term relationships in my twenties. When the last one broke up, I went travelling, then I worked and studied and worked some more. And then suddenly, I was in my late thirties and . . . ' She stopped.

'And?' I was really intrigued now.

'And . . . well, I was in a brief relationship that didn't work out. And here I am.'

'What was his name?'

'Brian.'

'How did you meet him?'

'Work.'

Boy, did she look prickly. I decided not to keep questioning her, but there was something odd

244

about the situation, that was for sure.

To be honest I was a bit miffed, because I'd shared quite personal stuff with her about my marriage and my feelings. We hadn't been friends for long, but we'd got close very quickly. Because we were both going through our first pregnancies, we were experiencing all sorts of things for the first time and it was all so intense . . . it was great to have someone you could ring or text about every little thing. She also went on the baby forums, like I did, and we often joked about people who posted there. That was something James really didn't get . . . this massive online community of women, all chatting to one another for no other reason than because they were pregnant. But Louise got it, and it was nice to have a real friend to share it with.

Even though we had quite a bit in common, I felt that with Lou, there was always a wall. There was stuff she just didn't want to talk about. She'd told me a little bit about the guy whose company she was running and I'd got the feeling that maybe she liked him more than you would normally like your boss, but she'd only met him recently, and he wasn't the mysterious Brian. And she told me about her brother who was gay and very cool, apparently, and her sister who was a posh housewife and desperate to get pregnant, and her sister's friends whose teenage daughter was also pregnant . . . That seemed like a safe topic of conversation, so I went with that.

'How's the teen mum?'

'Who, David and Samantha's daughter? She's

okay, I think . . . having a girl. She must be about twenty-four weeks now.'

'Do you speak to her?'

'We email. She's also in Surrey, some super-posh bit of Weybridge, I think. She seems really happy at the moment, her mum went off the rails for a while but she's back home now and stable, and the mother of the baby's father seems very involved. She seems pretty happy with how things have turned out, to be honest.'

'Who'd have thought it, eh?' I said thoughtfully. 'James and I thought we were too young for this at twenty-six and twenty-eight . . . and she's what, seventeen?'

'Eighteen.'

We'd decided not to find out the sex of our baby, but I was soooo tempted to ask in the twenty-week scan. Most people in our group on the baby forum were finding out, and changing their profile signatures . . . they'd sometimes put something twee, like 'team blue' or 'team pink', or they'd announce the name they were planning to call the child, and put the signature in pink or blue. There were others, like me, who didn't know, and some of them used 'team yellow', but that sounded too much like a baby with jaundice to me. So I just left my signature as it was: 'PR–Girl, Toni, married to James, expecting 14/9'. But, to be honest, now Louise knew she was having a boy and the teenager . . . Gemma, I think her name was, was having a girl, I kind of wished I knew.

But there you are. It was the one thing James was adamant about. He said he was the last of three boys, and if his mum had known she was having yet another boy maybe she'd have been disappointed and not have wanted him. I couldn't imagine Eileen feeling like that, but when he said he didn't want to find out, it seemed like an easy compromise to make. Except now I really wanted to know. I was musing on this and chewing my way through another slice of pizza, so I didn't hear what Louise said. I just caught, ' . . . dessert down by the river. What do you think?'

'Think about what?'

'You're a million miles away!' she observed. 'I was saying, did you think you and James might like to come down to the farmhouse and I'd invite Gemma too? Be nice to have a bumps party.'

'That would be great, thanks.' It would also be a good opportunity for James to meet Louise. He thought it was funny that we'd become so inseparable so quickly, but so far all of our meetings had taken place when James was busy with something else . . . either we'd caught a girls' lunch during the week if Louise had to see clients in town, or we met up at weekends when James was playing five-a-side or going to the pub to watch football. To be honest, he hadn't made too many noises about wanting to meet her . . . he seemed to think our friendship was a pregnant women's thing and nothing really to do with him. But she had become important to me, and I wanted to share that with him. What he'd think of being the only bloke at a party with three pregnant women, I wasn't sure . . . but

247

we'd cross that bridge when we came to it.

We made an arrangement for the following Sunday, and when I told James, he said that the weather was supposed to be lovely and it would be nice to be out in the countryside. To be honest, I kind of glossed over who was going to be there . . . I just said a few friends.

We took the train there, and Louise came out in her car to pick us up from the station. When we got to the farmhouse, I was impressed. 'Wow. You certainly got yourself a cushy number here, Lou!' It was a beautiful, old, rambling house, and the grounds were amazing. Louise had obviously also thought about James being the only guy there, so she'd invited her brother Simon, as well as a bloke called Alan, who was her second-in-command at the printing firm. He was about twenty-five, earnest and ginger, and obviously totally in awe of Louise. We went through to the back garden, where Louise had set out a jug of Pimm's and some snacks, as well as soft drinks for us. There was a Foo Fighters song playing on the radio, and that gave Simon, James and Alan something to chat about. Even though they'd never met, they seemed happy to talk music and sport, and we left them to it.

We went into the kitchen so Louise could carry on with making lunch. She gave me a cheeky grin. 'Lord, woman. You never told me your husband looked like that.'

I couldn't help laughing. 'I know. I've kind of got used to it, but he really is insanely gorgeous.'

'How do you keep your hands off him? Most women would never let him out of the bedroom.'

248

'Well, try carrying seven pounds of baby and seventy-two other pounds of water, placenta and general flab. It'd put you off sex, no matter how tasty the bloke.'

Louise wrinkled her nose. 'The last time I got to do it was the time I got knocked up. To be honest, most blokes are starting to look good to me.'

'Even Alan?'

She laughed her big, loud laugh. 'Can you imagine? He'd die of fright.'

Louise was cooking an enormous roast with all the trimmings. She buzzed around the kitchen very efficiently, basting things and chopping things. I leaned against a counter and tried not to get in the way (difficult when you're four foot wide), and nibbled on raw green beans and carrots.

'So is Gemma coming?' I asked.

'Yes . . . she's just got her licence and Daddy bought her a Mini, so she's very proud that she'll be driving herself.'

'That's quite brave, for someone who's probably not driven much alone before.'

'She says she's got sat nav and music. She's very determined. She said she'd ring if she got into any trouble.'

I looked around at the big, open kitchen with its scrubbed table and stone counter tops.

'So, tell me about the guy whose house this is.'

'Adam?' Louise looked up and caught my eye as she said his name. There was definitely something there. 'He's, well . . . ' She seemed lost for words, unusually for Louise. Eventually, she finished lamely with, 'Well, he's Adam.'

'Oooh, *Adam*?' I teased breathlessly, like we were in junior school. And, to my absolute surprise, she giggled like a schoolgirl. I thought she wouldn't say anything more, but in a way, I think she was just dying for someone to ask. She wanted to talk about him (as you do when you really, really like someone), and once she started, she just couldn't stop.

'He's amazing. He's away on this Tall Ships Race, working with kids and helping them to learn to sail. But then he's also built this amazing business here, and all his staff love him. He's moral and strong, but also funny and clever. And hot. My God, so hot.'

'And he feels the same about you?'

'I know . . . it's bizarre. Even though I'm . . . ' she gestured at her belly. 'He still seems to care about me. We only met two weeks before he left, and only realised we had feelings for one another the day before he left. So the whole relationship has been conducted by email and the odd phone call when he's in a port. It's kind of old-fashioned . . . courting by correspondence. I quite like it.'

'And he comes home . . . ?'

'In a month. Four weeks, actually. Not that I'm counting.'

'And the baby? And the job? And staying here?'

'I know. There's a lot to work out. We haven't actually talked through all the logistics of it. We've just been getting to know each other, really.'

She turned away from me and stirred

something, but I could see her profile, and honest to God, she was blushing! She really did have it bad. But there was still that elephant in the room (and I don't mean me!). After all, she didn't get pregnant by herself. I decided just to come out and ask.

'So Lou . . . what about this Brian bloke . . . the . . . father?'

Her lips tightened. 'He really isn't interested. He doesn't want anything to do with us. He wanted me to have an abortion. So . . . well, I've written a letter to say he has no legal responsibility for the child and I won't ask him for anything.'

'Can you do that?'

'Strictly speaking, if I wanted to I could send the child-support people after him. But I'm not going to. He's got . . . ' she paused. 'Well, he's got his own life.'

I had a lot more questions, but before I could ask anything, a midnight-blue Mini convertible pulled into the driveway. Louise looked out of the window. 'Ah, Gemma's here,' she said, and I could hear the relief in her voice. The discussion was clearly over.

Gemma

Gemma loved her little car. She felt invincible in it . . . like it was her own small kingdom. She'd taken to driving from her first go and passed her test after just fifteen lessons, and her dad, as he had promised, had bought the Mini. 'There you are, pumpkin,' he said indulgently, handing over the keys. 'Now you can buzz around town and give lifts to all your mates.' He didn't seem to notice that she didn't have mates any more. Even if she had, she wouldn't have wanted them in her car. She didn't want anyone in her car. When she got in and shut the door, turned the key and heard the satisfying roar of the engine, when the music came pouring from the speakers and the seatbelt was snugly tucked under her bump, she felt she had everything she could ever need in the world. When the bass was thumping particularly loudly, the baby responded by kicking more firmly. She'd looked forward to the drive to visit Louise for days, as much for the drive as the chance to see Louise.

She stepped out of the car, and Louise came out of the front door to welcome her. Behind her was another pregnant girl, with a round, very pretty face and a wide smile.

Louise kissed her quickly on the cheek. 'Glad you made it in one piece,' she said. 'This is my friend Antonia.'

'Oh, call me Toni, please!' the girl said, and

impulsively came forward and kissed Gemma too.

Gemma took a last quick look at her car, and the other two bustled her through the house. She only had a moment's impression of the rustic farmhouse. All the furniture looked a bit scruffy and old. Then they were out in the back garden. There were three men there: Louise's brother, a skinny ginger bloke, and a tall, blond guy who looked like a movie star. They all greeted her really politely, but a bit nervously. She was used to that. People, especially guys, didn't know where to look when they met a pregnant teenager. She'd always looked a bit young for her age anyway. The pregnant belly seemed to make them very uncomfortable indeed. Louise went inside to finish the lunch, and the other girl, Toni, stayed outside to chat. She was really nice and bubbly, and asked lots of questions. How far along was Gemma? It seemed Toni was only two weeks further along . . . twenty-eight weeks. How was Gemma feeling? She looked amazing! Toni made fun of her own size and water retention, and called herself a whale. She seemed to like to put herself down, which was odd, because she really was a pretty girl, and she was married to a totally gorgeous guy who kept glancing over as if he wanted to make sure she was all right. If that was me, Gemma thought, I'd feel amazing about myself.

Louise yelled from the kitchen window for help, and her brother went in to help her serve. Together, they brought out dish after dish. It looked like she had cooked a whole cow, with a mountain of potatoes and more vegetables than

Gemma had ever seen in her life, as well as great crusty Yorkshire puddings and a massive jug of gravy. They set everything down on the big, old wooden table outside. Everyone started passing dishes around and sharing. They didn't know each other well, but the chat seemed to flow easily. Gemma served herself the smallest portion she could without looking rude, and started cutting things into tiny bites. She didn't feel nervous: she was used to being the youngest person at a dinner party. It had been that way her whole life. Her father had always expected her to be able to hold a conversation and be polite. But this was different. Here she was an equal. One of the pregnant women.

She was sitting between Simon, Louise's brother, and Toni's husband, who was called James. Now they'd got used to her, they both made a big effort to be friendly. She knew about Simon, because her mum and dad had met him at Richard and Rachel's. Her dad had been quite rude about him. 'I didn't know Richard was going to invite his wife's brother . . . ' he'd said. 'Definitely light in his loafers, that one.' Her father was a real, old-fashioned homophobe. But she thought Simon was really nice. He asked her about school. He did something in the government, and he seemed to know a lot about education. He asked her serious questions about going on to university, and how her generation felt about the increased debt they faced, and whether they'd find jobs. She liked how he took her answers seriously. 'It's a lot harder now,' he observed. 'You can't always follow a creative dream. If you're going to start your working life with tens of thousands of pounds of debt, you'd better be able to get a job that pays well.'

'You're not kidding,' James chipped in. 'I'm twenty-eight, and I'm still paying off my student loan. So's Toni.'

'You don't look twenty-eight,' Gemma said before she could stop herself.

'Thanks,' James grinned, 'it's my dewy complexion, and reflected youth from your good self!' And he gave her a cheeky wink.

Gemma felt herself blush. How silly. She knew he was just being nice to her, as if she were one of his mates' little sisters. He was clearly crazy about his wife. But he was just, so, so good-looking and well dressed and charming. Next to him, Ben would look like a scruffy, gawky teenager.

She looked down and was surprised to see she had cleaned her plate. Louise got up to clear things away and the blokes leapt up to help her. She brought out a big apple crumble and a jug of custard, and they all sat around eating dessert in the warm afternoon sun. Toni swapped places with Simon, so she, Gemma and Louise were all grouped around the head of the table. Toni tucked in to her dessert, but then suddenly paused and waved her spoon at Louise. 'Lou! I forgot to tell you . . . on the site this morning, there was a whole discussion about packing hospital bags.'

Gemma realised that she must have looked confused because Louise said, 'It's a baby website, with discussion forums. It's how Toni and I met.'

'She's my dodgy internet-dating bump buddy,' Toni smiled.

'Anyway,' Louise said, 'you were saying — hospital bags?'

'Loads of people were saying they'd got theirs all packed. Nighties, toiletries, clothes for the baby, the lot!'

'But I've got ten weeks to go! You've got twelve . . . Gemma . . . '

'Fourteen weeks yet,' said Gemma. 'If I pack mine now, my moisturiser will be past its use-by date before I open it!'

Toni and Louise chuckled loudly at this and Gemma felt absurdly pleased to have made them laugh.

'I mean,' Toni said, helping herself to another portion of dessert, 'I can understand wanting to be ready in case you went into labour early, but three months ahead of time? That's ridiculous. If I go into hospital early, I'll just give James a list and he can bring me what I need.'

'I'll need to pack mine well ahead of time, though,' said Louise. 'If I go into labour and nothing's ready, I'm screwed. I can't expect Simon to rifle through my underwear drawer or go out and buy me sanitary towels.'

'My mum wouldn't be much use either,' said Gemma. 'She's given me gift vouchers or money for every birthday and Christmas since I was seven. She'd probably come into the hospital with an Evian face spray and a John Lewis gift card and expect me to get everything online or something.'

'So what sort of stuff are we supposed to have

packed?' Louise asked.

'Well, clothes for the baby and nappies obviously, then nighties for yourself, ones that open in the front if you're going to breastfeed. Underwear, something to wear in labour . . . '

'What sort of thing do you wear?' Gemma asked. 'I mean . . . whatever it is, you'll need to take the bottom half off when . . . '

'When the bleeding and screaming starts,' Louise said wryly. 'I guess the answer is — something you're unlikely to want to wear again. It's going to get messy.'

'And I had my Stella McCartney jumpsuit all picked out!' giggled Toni. 'Gemma, there's still a tiny sliver of apple crumble there. You have to eat it, or I'm going to. Save me. Please.'

Gemma laughed and put the apple crumble on her plate. She felt more relaxed than she had in months. She wished she could stay at Louise's sun-warmed table forever. Here she wasn't the girl Ben had dumped. She wasn't David and Samantha's embarrassing pregnant daughter, she wasn't the scandalous centre of gossip at Lady Grey's . . . she was just Gemma, mum-to-be, scoffing dessert with the other mums-to-be. It was lovely.

Simon went in to the house to use the loo, and James brought a chair around to sit between Louise and Toni and took Toni's hand. He seemed happy to sit with her while she gossiped. Gemma turned to try and engage with the ginger chap, who was called Alan, who had been left on his own across the table from her. He was really uncomfortable with her, and obviously didn't know what to say, so he talked boringly about the printing work he did with Louise. After years of listening to her dad's friends waffle on, Gemma knew how to smile and nod silently, and she did it patiently, while watching James rest his hand lightly on Toni's shoulder. Toni didn't seem to notice, she was chatting animatedly to Louise, waving her hands around as she told a story about some weird woman she worked with who seemed to stalk everyone in the office.

At first, Gemma thought someone was chopping wood somewhere else on the property, but then she heard the yelling. Everyone else seemed to hear it at the same time too.

'What's that?' said Toni.

'Sounds like maybe there's someone at the front door,' said Simon, coming out of the house. And Louise went white.

Louise

Déjà vu. She'd lived through this moment before
. . . the hammering on the door, the sinking
feeling . . . but it couldn't possibly be. Could it?
Not again. She smiled at everyone, excused
herself and went to open the front door. And
horrifyingly, unbelievably, it was. Brian. On the
doorstep, looking distraught, his hair all over the
place, and even worse, at his feet, an enormous
sports bag. She stood staring at him in silence
for a moment. What the hell had he done?

'I told Lisa everything. I had to. I couldn't take
it. The lying. She threw me out.'

'And you came here?'

He looked astonished. 'Of course! I had to.
Our son . . . '

'Our *son*? *Our* son?' Without meaning to, she
was almost shouting.

'Yes. Our son,' he said obstinately. She was
utterly furious.

'Since when is this *our* son? This was the *thing*
you wanted me to get rid of . . . like it was
nothing. You made me promise 'it' wouldn't
come looking for you.'

'Yes, but that was before I knew it was a boy.'

That took Louise's breath away. She stared at
him for a moment, then laughed. 'Well, you must
have known there was a fifty per cent chance. It
had to be one or the other.'

'I know it sounds crazy. At the time I just

didn't think about it. It wasn't a child to me, just a threat. But now I know. It's the son I always wanted. And I want to be a dad to him. I really do.'

'What?'

'Louise, I thought you wanted me to be a part of his life. I'd have thought you'd wanted me to . . . well, that's why you emailed me, isn't it? So we could all be together?'

'No!' she said vehemently. But why had she emailed him? To get his attention? To hurt him for rejecting his child? Never had she so regretted sending an impulsive email. Brian took another step into the hallway and said calmly, but firmly, 'Louise, this is a boy. It's my son. Carrying on the family name, the line . . . '

'For fuck's sake, are you completely insane? You've driven two hundred miles to spout some archaic Victorian crap at me about the sacred genetic line . . . you made it perfectly clear that you didn't want to know this child, let alone for him to have your name. And let me tell you, he won't. Not as a surname, not on the birth certificate . . . ' She was shaking with fury.

Brian's face darkened. He spoke harshly. 'Listen to me, you bitch, I've lost everything because of you. My wife, my children, my home, my job . . . '

'Your job?' Oh God. This was worse than she thought. Suddenly, she heard a voice behind her.

'Louise, is everything all right?'

She spun around. Toni was standing in the kitchen doorway. How long had she been there? What had she heard? Then Simon appeared

260

behind her. In a split second, he took in the situation. 'Ah, this must be Brian,' he said smoothly, stepping around Toni. 'I'm Louise's brother, Simon. Come through to the living room; let me get you a drink. Louise . . . you've got guests to look after.' He scooped up Brian's bag and ushered him through the living-room door, pulling it closed behind him. Louise was left staring at an incredulous Toni.

'It's getting late,' said Toni, faintly. 'I . . . James . . . we'd better get going.'

'Of course,' said Louise quietly.

Within ten minutes, Toni and James had talked Gemma into giving them a lift to the station, and Alan, sensing things had somehow gone badly wrong, had also said goodbye and headed off to his mum's place in Hersham. Louise spent a few minutes carrying dishes from the garden back into the kitchen. She was tempted to stay hidden in the kitchen, washing up, restoring order, pretending that Brian wasn't sitting in her living room. Oh God . . . not in *her* living room, in *Adam's* living room. What would Adam say? How would she explain? Everything she'd run away from had come crashing into her new, freshly formed little life, scattering friend-ships, possibly her new relationship, and quite likely her job as well. What had Brian said when he appeared the last time? She'd put his life under the wheels of a juggernaut? Now she knew how he felt.

She couldn't hide forever, though. She washed and dried her hands, spent a little more time smoothing on some hand cream and then walked

261

purposefully into the living room. Simon and Brian were sitting in two armchairs, each nursing a large whisky. Brian was leaning forward on his knees, running one big hand through his already dishevelled auburn hair. Simon was sitting back coolly, letting him talk. They had turned the chairs so that they were sitting facing one another. There was nowhere for Louise to sit and join them, so she hesitantly perched on the edge of the sofa, some way away. Brian barely acknowledged her. His attention was focused on Simon, and he kept talking.

'Well, when I broke down and told Lisa, that's my wife, that I'd fathered a child with someone else, she told me to go. I told her it was just one night, just a terrible mistake, but she was furious. She kicked me out.

'It was about seven in the evening, so I just flung a few things in a bag and went to a hotel. I thought I'd give her a few days to cool off and then try to talk to her. Anyway, the next day I went to work as normal. I was down on the shop floor talking to the print foreman, when I heard a racket in the gallery above. I looked up and Lisa was standing there. She started to scream at me. I could see my PA trying to pull her away, but she wouldn't go. She was effing and blinding, which isn't like her at all, calling me every name under the sun. And then she started yelling that she wanted to get her hands on Stephanie.'

'Stephanie?' Louise, said, a little surprised. Brian looked up at her and blinked. He had obviously forgotten she was there. He looked mildly annoyed that she had interrupted his flow.

'Yes, Stephanie.' He turned back to Simon. 'Stephanie is my assistant manager . . . '

' . . . that you've been shagging on the side since your liaison with Louise. I'm familiar with the story,' said Simon coolly. Brian looked as if he might be ready to argue the point, but seemed to decide against it and carried on with his story.

'Yes, well. Lisa seemed to think it was Stephanie that was pregnant.'

'You didn't tell her who it was?' said Louise disbelievingly.

'I only said it was someone from work. She was so upset there wasn't really time for more detail.'

Louise and Simon exchanged a glance. Simon was clearly enjoying this horrifying story. 'So Lisa was screaming from the gallery, wanting to get her hands on the woman she mistakenly believed to be the mother of your child . . . ' he prompted.

'It's not funny,' said Brian, affronted. 'She was screaming and calling Stephanie every name under the sun, and saying things about my . . . manhood. Then she lifted up a bag she had with her, and she said, 'Here's the rest of your stuff, bastard.' And she emptied it down on to the shop floor. She'd cut all my clothes up into little bits and they just went everywhere. All over the wet print laid out to dry, into the presses. It was a terrible mess.'

Simon sat back and put his hand over his mouth as if he didn't trust himself to speak. Louise slid off the arm of the sofa and pulled a cushion on to her lap to hug.

'Stephanie was very traumatised and had to be signed off for stress . . . ' said Brian.

Of course she did, thought Louise. Lisa might have gone for the wrong woman, but everyone would know that there was no smoke without fire. Stephanie would be lying low, hoping to salvage something of her reputation and career.

'And you?' asked Simon in a small, strangled voice.

'Edward, our GM, asked me to take indefinite leave of absence.'

'Gosh,' said Simon quietly.

'So I have no home, no job, and exactly one suit, two shirts and three pairs of pants and socks to my name,' finished Brian. Finally, he looked at Louise. 'You ruined my life. What are you going to do about it?'

There was a long silence. A million retorts ran through her head. She thought about getting up and walking out, about hitting him, about laughing hysterically. Again, he said, 'Well, what are you going to do?'

'Buy you some socks?' she said.

Toni

I felt like crying, to be honest, pretty much all the way home. James didn't say much, thank heavens. He just held my hand, and when we got home he made me a cup of tea, then came and sat next to me on the sofa.

'So did you know the father of her baby was a married guy?' he asked gently.

'Of *course* I didn't!' I said indignantly. 'She never said anything about him being married. All she ever told me was that his name was Brian and that they'd broken up and he didn't want anything to do with the baby.'

'Wow,' said James softly.

'I just didn't think she was . . . that type,' I said, taking a big sip of my tea.

'What type?'

'The other-woman's-husband-shagging type. It's just such a bloody rubbish thing to do. I mean . . . what about the code of the sisterhood?'

'The what?'

'The unwritten rules that all women should look out for one another. Support each other. Don't backstab, don't nick your mate's boyfriend, don't bitch behind her back.'

'Well, sweetheart, I've never met a woman who signed up for that,' laughed James. 'Not even your own so-called best mates. And certainly not your work colleagues. You've experienced a fair

265

bit of bitchiness since you got pregnant. I'm surprised you still have such faith in your gender.'

'I just thought Louise was . . . you know . . . different. She's older than me, and she seemed so sorted. Like someone I could trust.'

'This doesn't mean you can't trust her,' said James. 'She did a stupid thing. A very stupid, very wrong thing, but it doesn't make her a bad person.'

'Doesn't it? If you went and asked Brian's wife and children today whether they thought she was a bad person, what do you think they'd say?'

'They'd probably say she was,' James agreed. 'But maybe it's easier for them to do that than hating Brian. After all, he's the one that made promises to them and then broke them. Not Louise.'

'Well, she should have!' I sat up suddenly. 'I make that promise to every woman I meet! I silently promise them, 'I will not shag your husband!' '

James nearly fell off the sofa laughing, but that didn't stop me. 'I mean, what if she decided she'd taken a fancy to you? She did tell me she thought you were hot.'

'Well, she's only human,' James said smugly. I punched him for that.

'But what if? I mean, I chose her for a friend without knowing she was the type to go after other women's husbands. What if she'd put moves on you and squeezed your bottom in the kitchen?'

'What if she did? Do I get a say in this at all?'

266

'Are you saying you don't fancy her?'

'I don't fancy her one bit, my love. I fancy you. You are my type, and you alone.' He kissed me extravagantly and I hugged him back. I love him when he's all silly and loving like that. I couldn't resist teasing a bit, though.

'Now that's bollocks, because I know you fancy Megan Fox and that tall one off *Strictly Come Dancing*.'

'Fancying celebrities is allowed,' said James. 'I'm never going to meet them, and they're never going to squeeze my bottom in the kitchen.'

'And if they did?'

'I'd have to say, 'I'm sorry, Megan, but I'm an old, married dad-to-be. Get away with your saucy behaviour and small denim shorts. Oh, and pass me my pipe and slippers on your way out.''

★ ★ ★

Going on the baby forum, I learned a whole new vocabulary. A lot of it consisted of cutesy acronyms I'd never use, like DD for 'Darling daughter', or DS for . . . well, you get the picture. But I also learned that there was a whole world of shopping I never knew existed. You can't believe how long a group of seemingly smart women can spend debating which pushchair to buy. Mind you, as a new, posh pushchair costs more than some cars, it's a purchase worth serious consideration! But there were other things too: in my third trimester, I learned that the two most important words in my life should be 'birth plan'. For lots

267

of the women on the site, birth plans took up about half their waking thinking time.

It seems you have to make a plan, and write it down, and make multiple copies to give to anyone who comes anywhere near you in the hospital. I didn't really know what to put in my plan, to be honest. I didn't have very strong feelings one way or another about most aspects of labour. Despite the intense debate on the site, I thought I'd just go with the flow, see how I felt, maybe have drugs if the pain was bad, maybe not have them if I was coping. Or that was what I was thinking when I went for my first antenatal class. But then I met the other women. Our poor teacher, Donna was her name, the nicest Scottish midwife you're ever likely to meet . . . well, she ended up with the stroppiest, most opinionated, argumentative antenatal group in the history of pregnancy. The later classes were to include husbands and birth partners, but the first one was supposed to be just for the women.

At first, I was the youngest one there, for certain. All of the women looked like they were in their thirties, and one or two looked even older. Where we live is nice, but some of the surrounding bits are crazily posh, and I'm sure loads of the women were bankers or traders or lawyers or something. Lots of them were in business suits, neatly tailored over their bumps, and a few were expensively dressed in lovely summer maternity dresses. I felt a bit scruffy in my maternity jeans and flowery top, but I'd got to the point where I was just living in the few things that were comfortable, and sod fashion.

I say I was the youngest there at first because about five minutes into the class, little Gemma, the teenage mum, arrived. She was with a tall, dark, older woman. At first I assumed it was her mum, but they looked, I don't know, kind of awkward together, and when everyone introduced themselves, the woman said her name was Hannah and her son was the baby's father. I knew she was a lawyer because Gemma had told me she was when we were at the disastrous lunch at Louise's. And she wasted no time wading in when the arguing started, which it did pretty much straight away.

You'd think that in most antenatal groups, the women, who are generally all having their first babies, would sit quietly and listen to the midwife telling them what to expect and what their choices are. But these women had come prepared. They all seemed to have typewritten lists of questions (or they read them off their phones or iPads). They weren't going to listen to a lecture. They all knew what they wanted from their birth experience, and, basically, they wanted to know if they would be allowed to do it, and what they had to say to get it.

They all had very different expectations. One beautiful blonde woman, who was wearing a floaty, white dress that I was sure cost more than my monthly Travelcard, said she wanted an elective Caesarean. 'I've done my research,' she said, 'and one in four births needs medical intervention. Those odds are too high for me. I want the highest level of control. Also, I have family coming over from Sweden for the birth, and I need to be able to predict the date of the birth so they can book flights.'

James always teases me that my face hides nothing. I thought she sounded barking and that what she'd just said was, frankly, hilarious, and I'm sure that opinion was written all over my face in big capital letters. I looked around the room, sure I would see expressions of disbelief to match my own, but quite a few women were nodding in agreement. Some were looking at her in disgust, as if she'd suggested something obscene. Then one of the business-suit women looked up from her laptop and said coldly, 'Don't you think, by undergoing major surgery for no reason other than your own flakiness, you're putting you and your baby at more risk?'

Donna, the midwife, tried to get her to take the 'flakiness' comment back, but Floaty Dress waded in with a flood of statistics, and then Business Suit started yelling other statistics back about the process of natural birth clearing the baby's lungs, and health risks to mothers and babies from caesareans. And she finished by using the dreaded phrase 'too posh to push'. Well, I thought Floaty Dress was going to drop her baby right there, right then. Donna the Midwife was wittering gently, trying to get them to calm down, and then another business suit, who looked like she was about forty, fiercely organised and as if she probably ran a country, chipped in. 'I've done all my research,' she said, 'and none of the pain-relief options seem completely risk-free to me. What's your view on water birth and hypnobirthing?' Well, Donna the

Midwife never got to give her opinion, because at least four other women had opinions and statistics about that. Hypnobirthing sounded a bit weird to me . . . like I'd have to give birth on stage with some dodgy bloke swinging a watch and telling me I was a chicken, but it seemed there was more to it than that. I'd never read about it on the baby website, but I made a note to find out more.

After a while, Donna the Midwife stopped trying to run the class and just let the women argue with one another. It wasn't like she could have stopped them. I used the chance to edge my way over to talk to the woman who had asked about hypnobirthing. She looked a bit intimidating: she was very tall, with quite a severe face, but when I hesitantly asked her if she could tell me something about it, her expression got soft and she looked all enthusiastic and much younger.

'I'm so not a self-help book person,' she said, 'but a friend who gave me a whole heap of maternity clothes also gave me a book on hypnobirthing, so I read it out of curiosity. It makes so much sense, not in a hippie, New-Age way, but just sensibly. You trust your body to give birth, and you work with it. And it's painless, or it can be.'

'Painless? Are you joking?'

'I'm serious!' she said. 'Search for it on You-Tube. There are all these videos of blissed-out women, breathing their babies out. I saw one video of a woman asleep on the sofa, and the baby just came out.'

'Asleep? I'll have some of that!' I laughed.

She smiled at me, then dug in her bag. 'Here's my card — I'm Susie, by the way. If you want to know more, drop me a line and I'll give you the details of my hypnobirthing coach.'

Gemma was sitting across the room, listening to all the women yell and argue. She hadn't said anything yet. Hannah, Gemma's baby's grandma, seemed to think she should shout louder than everyone, as she had actually had a baby. She seemed to be very much in support of the pain-relief argument. 'It's there,' she yelled at some poor pro-waterbirthing mother-to-be. 'It's been invented. So use it! What do you want for doing it with no pain relief? A medal? Some kind of bravery award? That's just stupid!' I smiled at Gemma then, and she grinned back. I was sure Hannah must be telling Gemma how she should give birth all day, every day.

At the end of the class, Donna finally wrestled control back and told us firmly what we'd be doing in each of the following classes. There was one on pain-relief options (and when some of the natural-birth lot started muttering she just spoke straight over them). Then we'd be doing the stages of labour, a class on breastfeeding (cue more muttering), and a beginner's nappy-changing-and-bathing-the-baby class, using dolls. 'Unless one of you has popped by then and wants to bring in your baby for us all to practise on!' said Donna brightly. Well, that went down like a lead balloon with the humourless crowd. I felt sorry for her, I really did. It was like trying to teach a class of grumpy, pregnant velociraptors.

Everyone sped off as soon as we'd been

dismissed, tapping on their phones and jumping into 4x4s, no doubt hurrying to take over companies or knit their own duvet covers or something. Susie waved goodbye to me and waggled her fingers like she was typing, to remind me to email her. Hannah was having a very forceful phone conversation in reception, so as I faffed about packing my stuff it was only Gemma and me left in the room. She came over and sat elegantly on the arm of the sofa as I shoved things into my bag. I struggled to get up, half rolling onto my knees and hauling myself up, panting slightly. I was grateful that she didn't try to put a hand under my elbow or anything.

'What bloody sadist holds a class for heavily pregnant women on squishy sofas?' I said, to cover my embarrassment. If Louise makes me feel awkward and hefty, Gemma's about a million times worse. She is so tiny and fine-boned, and so graceful. She doesn't waddle at all when she walks, and she'd just leapt up off the sofa like a slightly startled gazelle or something. I didn't really know what to say to her. We'd shared pregnancy chat at Louise's disastrous lunch, but I don't have a clue what to talk to a teenager about. It seems a bit silly, because it's only seven years since I was a teenager myself. And in fact, Gemma is closer in age to me than Louise is. Still, I thought I'd make some polite excuse and duck out. I'd have to walk out into the street and catch a bus.

'I must be going . . . ' I started to say, but she interrupted.

'You don't have a car, do you?'

273

'Er, no, actually. I was just headed for the bus stop . . . ' I pointed vaguely in the direction of the main road.

'Only I came in my own car and met Hannah here. If I say I'm giving you a lift home, we can leave now and I don't have to wait for her. Please. I don't know what to say to her and I don't want to be the last loser left hanging around here.'

I remembered her smart new Mini. 'Are you sure? You don't really have to take me home . . . you can just fling me out at a bus stop along the way. I'm pretty spherical, so I roll quite easily.'

'Where do you live?'

'Kingston. Down towards the river. It's not too far, actually, if you're in a car.'

'Well then, I'll take you home. I'm sure you'd rather not have to walk from the bus stop at the other end.' She started to walk towards the door.

'It's not too bad, actually,' I said, waddling behind. 'We've never had a car, so I just don't really think about it.'

As we walked through the reception area, Gemma did complicated sign language to tell Hannah she was going and driving me home. I waved goodbye to her, but she looked right through me and turned away, barking something about lost briefs. I was pretty sure she didn't mean knickers.

We got into Gemma's cute little car and she punched my postcode into the sat nav. She was a good driver, as far as I could tell. She certainly didn't seem jumpy or inexperienced. We drove in silence for a bit, and she suddenly burst out laughing.

'What?' I said.

'Oh, I was just thinking about my mum saying the antenatal group would be a wonderful place to make friends. She says everyone she knows stayed friends with their antenatal friends for years after the babies were born.'

'Everyone she knows didn't end up with the antenatal class from hell like we did.'

'Oh my God!' Gemma squealed, and for the first time, she sounded like a girl her own age. 'They're awful! They're like sharks.'

'I was thinking carnivorous dinosaurs.'

'I'm sure most of them will just eat their babies if they misbehave.' She giggled again. I liked it when she laughed . . . it made her seem less like a fairy princess and more like a normal human being.

I found myself prattling on. 'They're just all so *definite*! I mean, I just haven't made up my mind about the birth yet. And I don't know enough about babies to be absolutely sure how I'm going to do everything once it's born. Am I a bad mum because I don't have my birth plan all laid out and laminated and a nursery all colour-coordinated and fully kitted out?'

'Oh, we've got the nursery, but only because my mum just called in an interior designer and it got done. I didn't really get a say in it at all,' said Gemma, but funnily enough she didn't say it in a snobby way. I suppose in her world everyone has interior designers.

'Wow,' I laughed. 'Well, I have a husband I

275

dragged around IKEA, and a list as long as my arm that I keep scribbling on. I don't have a nursery, I've got a spare room, with some flatpack stuff still in boxes leaning against the wall, five packs of nappies and a giant green teddy I couldn't resist buying that takes up half the room.'

We were about to turn into our road when my phone beeped with a text. It was from Louise.

'Hello, stranger,' it said, a bit tentatively for Louise, I thought. 'Around for coffee sometime?' I just dropped my phone into my lap. Gemma glanced over. 'Not going to reply?'

'Not really.' I hesitated for a second. 'It's Louise. I haven't spoken to her since . . . the lunch, and I'm not sure I want to.'

'Why not?'

'Well, in the whole time we've been friends, she never once told me that the father of her child was married. I just feel . . . '

' . . . that she's a heinous, disgusting betraying bitch?'

I looked at her, very surprised. 'Wow . . . no . . . I was going to say that I feel a bit uncomfortable. But you obviously have issues with it.'

'Women who sleep with married men are scum,' Gemma said harshly.

'So, I'm guessing you're not planning to see Louise again any time soon?' I asked.

'If I never see her again, it'll be too soon,' said Gemma, as she pulled up outside our house. 'I texted her and told her not to call me again . . . ever. She's a witch.'

Gosh, I found myself thinking. Gemma seemed to have forgotten that Louise had helped her and supported her and been a friend. Now she'd made one mistake, it was game over as far as Gemma was concerned. Things are very black and white when you're a teenager. There's no room for someone to have made a mistake, to have been lonely, to have wanted some closeness, and chosen the wrong person . . . and then I remembered that I'd said the same and worse about Louise when I first found out about Brian being married. I didn't feel so good about myself then. And I suddenly remembered Louise telling me something about Gemma's dad. She seemed to think he was a bit of a player. So there was more to this situation for Gemma than met the eye. I wasn't going to get into any psychology with her though. We'd only just met.

Gemma hesitated for a moment, then she said, 'Listen, if you wanted someone to go shopping with for baby stuff, I'd be free, I mean . . . I'd really like to.'

I smiled at her. 'Yeah, me too.' We swapped mobile numbers, and I even gave her a quick kiss on the cheek. She's a bit hasty, a bit judgmental, but she's not so bad.

Louise

Having Brian live in the house with her was an education. Despite the fact that she had seen him naked and from all angles that fateful night in Manchester, she had only just learned that his feet smelled. They hadn't got much sleep that night, so it was also fresh news to her that he snored like a train. Even though he was sleeping down the corridor from her, she could hear him, and the noise set her teeth on edge and kept her awake. She learned that with nothing to occupy him he would get up late and sit in crusty tracksuit bottoms and an old T-shirt on the sofa *all day*. He'd keep the television going non-stop, with the drone of antique shows and talk shows permeating the house, while he clicked aimlessly around sports websites and played endless games of freecell on his laptop. And he was messy. He was one of those people who generated an ever-increasing circle of crumbs, used coffee cups, crumpled tissues and inexplicable bits of paper and fluff. To be frank, it all drove her nuts.

But nothing drove her quite as nuts as his complete lack of movement. He was still asleep when she left in the morning to go to the printing works, and when she came back at lunchtime, he had assumed the position on the sofa and there he would stay. He'd be in exactly the same spot when she got home in the evening. He didn't seem to be looking for a job, making contact with his family or looking for somewhere to live. He certainly wasn't making an effort to be a pleasant and useful house guest. He just seemed to have . . . stopped.

It was impossible to have a conversation with him. If she came in from the office and said, 'Did you have a good day?' he'd stare at her like a sullen teenager and say, 'No.' If she asked him what he was going to do that week, he'd say, 'I don't know. I haven't got a job, or a family, or a home . . . ' and then he'd start whining about how she'd ruined his life.

For a while, well, about two days, guilt won over irritation, and she tried to be pleasant and helpful. But his inertia just drove her batty. On the third morning, she marched into his room at seven thirty, and whisked open the curtains.

'Right, Brian, there's coffee and muesli in the kitchen. I've booted up your laptop. Go and shower. It's time to start looking for a job. And a place to live.'

He rolled over and glared at her. 'I'm on leave of absence, not unemployed. I still have a job.'

'Well, then let's find something for you to do. You can't just lie around here all day. You need to find somewhere else to live, for one.'

'Where would you like me to go?' he said sullenly.

'Well, don't you have friends? Or family?'

'None of them are speaking to me. They've all taken Lisa's side. I just had to get away from Leeds.'

'Well you can't stay here forever.'

279

'But you're carrying my son! I came here so we could — '

'Could what?'

He looked uncomfortable, as if he knew that what he was about to say was patently ridiculous. But he said it anyway. 'Be together.'

'Really? And where exactly would I fit in? You already have a wife, and a girlfriend — do you have time in your schedule for the mother of your illegitimate child?'

'Don't be bitchy, Louise . . . '

'Brian, we've been over this. What happened between us was a mistake. I don't want to be with you. And to be honest, I don't think for a moment that you want to be with me. You didn't want anything to do with this baby . . . '

'I do now . . . '

'I wish I believed you really meant that. But I'm not going to be a solution for your homelessness. You don't just get to trade families. You have to sort your life out!'

'I know. I know. I'm just . . . not ready yet.' He sat on the edge of the bed and looked really hangdog and pathetic. Louise couldn't bear the thought that he might start crying again. 'I'm going to work,' she said hastily, and left.

Most worryingly, she hadn't spoken to Adam about him. Adam was in the final weeks of the Tall Ships Race and was too busy to send anything but the briefest of email messages. And being the coward she knew she was, Louise responded in the same way. She sent him bullet-point reports on the business, news about Millicent and expressed warm affection, but she

280

neglected to mention that the six-foot-four father of her child was currently squatting in his spare room. She just didn't know what to say. This job had been her fresh start, and it had seemed as if, in that new beginning, there was tentative hope of a new relationship with Adam. But her past had come back to get her and was currently picking its toenails on Adam's sofa.

On top of that, she was accelerating towards the end of her pregnancy with alarming speed. She wasn't worried; as usual, she was prepared. She'd found a reputable website to tell her what she'd need for a baby and bought it all in one fiendish, credit-card-scorching online spree. It was neatly packed up in boxes in the garage. As soon as she found somewhere to live (and it would have to be soon, Adam was now due back in a matter of weeks), she could unpack her instant nursery and be ready to be a mum in a matter of hours.

As far as antenatal training was concerned, she had booked into classes at the local hospital. Because she was usually so superbly prepared she was extremely annoyed when she opened her electronic diary one morning and realised that what with Brian and all the stuff going on at work she'd missed the first class the night before. Never mind, it had probably just been an introduction. She'd catch up.

The next week, she got there good and early so she could collect any notes she'd missed from the previous class. However, it seemed she wasn't there as early as some . . . the room was already half full of women about her age, who all

281

seemed to be doing business; talking on their phones, typing busily on laptops or reading and annotating sheaves of notes that looked like work rather than antenatal preparation. She found the class organiser, a pleasant Scottish midwife, and got the introductory pack from the previous week. 'It's a pretty vocal group,' said the midwife, Donna. 'You'll find the discussion . . . lively.'

Louise found a corner and began skimming through the notes. The start time was nearly upon them, and more people were starting to arrive. It didn't seem as if they'd be covering anything she didn't already know at least something about, but it would still be good to be part of a class where she could ask questions. She could also find out the procedure for booking in and . . .

She was really surprised at how shocked she felt when she looked up and saw Gemma and Toni walk in together. It hadn't occurred to her that they would all be attending antenatal classes at the same hospital. Thinking about it, it was obvious: they were all booked in there, and their due dates were close together. They looked pretty shocked to see her sitting there too. Gemma's face hardened and shut down. She was obviously quite happy to cut Louise stone dead and not speak to her at all. Toni stopped, looked extremely uncomfortable for a moment, then made up her mind and marched over. She bent with some difficulty and kissed Louise on the cheek.

'Lou! How are you? Just a few weeks to go now.'

Louise struggled to her feet . . . she felt very

vulnerable sunk in the sofa while the other two stood over her. 'Yeah. Four weeks to go for me now. So six for you?'

'Yeah,' said Toni, 'although it feels like I've been pregnant forever.'

Gemma had her arms folded and a stony, sulky, very-teenage expression on her face. To be frank, after her rude text, Louise didn't feel very warm towards Gemma. She'd been shocked at the discourteous, judgmental tone of the message. Gemma had no idea about her situation. Louise hadn't asked her for her opinion and, to be frank, she didn't want it. Yes, as the daughter of a man like David, Gemma would see a woman who slept with a married man in a different light, but nevertheless. Nevertheless what, she didn't know. But still. She didn't need some snotty teenager judging her. She stared at Gemma until she got her to make eye contact. Gemma curled her lip and looked as if she was about to say something, but Toni jumped in hastily. 'So, Lou, this class is really quite something. There are some very scary women . . . and be ready to yell, or you won't get heard. Never mind survival of the fittest . . . in this class, it's survival of the loudest.'

There wasn't time to say anything more. Donna came bustling in with a laptop, which she connected to a projector, and the class began. Toni hesitated and sat down next to Louise on the sofa. Gemma looked around, obviously intending to sit somewhere else, but all the seats were taken, so she sat down too, leaning as far away from Louise as she could, even though Toni was between them.

Donna the Midwife ran briskly through the pros and cons of all the types of pain relief available at the birth unit. Louise got the feeling that she was talking very quickly so that there would be no opportunity for anyone to interrupt and ask questions. But as soon as she got to the end of her PowerPoint presentation, it was open season and almost every woman had her hand up. Donna laughed, a little nervously. 'I was going to say 'Any questions?', but it seems you all beat me to it.' She chose a woman sitting close to her. 'Francesca? Let's start with you.' Francesca had come prepared, and had not one, but about fifteen questions on a typed sheet. After a few minutes and dark glares from the other women sitting with their hands raised in a pointed manner, Donna said, 'I'm going to have to ask you all to restrict yourself to a single question, or we'll never get through everyone.'

The rest of the class was spent with Donna answering questions, then arguing with women who needed to ask 'Just one more follow-up question', as soon as their turn was up. Donna finally looked up at the clock on the wall, and with visible relief, she said: 'That's it, I'm afraid, ladies, we're out of time. See you next week!'

Ten or so women immediately rushed over to Donna to see if they could get their questions answered on a one-to-one basis. Gemma got up, turned to Toni and said, 'I'll see you outside,' and walked briskly out without saying goodbye to Louise.

After a week of dealing with Brian, Louise wasn't going to put up with another sulky teenager. She walked quickly and caught up with Gemma in the hallway.

'I got your text, Gemma,' she said. 'And I thought it was very rude.'

'Well . . . ' Gemma said, going very pink. 'I was angry.'

'You were angry? What does my situation have to do with you?'

Gemma obviously decided to brazen it out. 'It has to do with the whole world. It's about decent behaviour. How can you sleep with someone else's husband? It's disgusting.'

Louise actually took a step back, as if she'd been stung. She felt tears prick in her eyes, not from hurt, but from sheer fury. 'For what it's worth, and let me tell you I don't owe you an explanation, I slept with him once. It was a mistake, I regret it, and, boy, am I paying for it now.' She turned to walk away, but then stopped. She looked back at Gemma and spoke softly, coldly. 'You know, Gemma, I've always tried to treat you like an adult, but if you're going to talk to me like a nasty, spoiled child, then I'd suggest you toddle off home and throw your toys there.'

Gemma stared at her, her big blue eyes wide and beginning to fill with tears. Then she turned and stormed out without a word. For a second, Louise regretted being so rough on her. But then, no one seemed to be cutting *her* any slack. She turned around, and Toni was right behind her.

She looked a bit pink in the face, but whether

that was anger or embarrassment, Louise couldn't tell.

'Good to see you, Lou,' she said. 'I'll, um . . . I'll see you next week. Gemma's giving me a lift, so I'd better go.'

She gave a little wave and waddled out. Well, that was horribly awkward, Louise thought. She felt tired and really rather sad. Toni had been a new friend, but one she'd really valued. It seemed the relationship had been too new and delicate to survive all the drama. It was just another loss to have to face up to.

She slowly gathered her things and got ready to go. She didn't want to move too quickly and have to face Gemma and Toni in the parking lot. As she headed for the door, Donna extricated herself from the circle of relentlessly questioning women and made her way over to Louise. 'Louise, isn't it? You're the one who missed the first class. Everything okay? Did you learn what you needed to know?'

Louise smiled at her. She felt absurdly grateful for the woman's kindly, uncomplicated interest. 'Yes, thanks. It helped to confirm the choice I've made.'

'Which is?'

'I've already asked for an epidural, it's in my birth plan.'

'Are you sure? You don't want to give it a go without pain relief and see how you go?'

'No, thanks. I don't want to find out I'm too far along to have it and have to go through the whole thing drug-free. Plan ahead, that's my motto,' said Louise firmly.

286

'Well, as long as you're sure,' said Donna, patting her arm. 'See you next week.'

Louise walked out slowly into the parking lot. The sun was setting, but the evening was still warm. Plan ahead. What a laugh. For a woman who'd always prided herself on her organisational skills, she seemed to be living in a state of ever-increasing chaos and uncertainty.

Toni

The weekend after I saw Louise at the antenatal class, James and I were invited for Sunday lunch at my father's house. To those of you who pop in to see your parents any time, that may sound a bit strange, but my dad is really quite formal about these things. He's a university professor, in fact he's a history professor, and his speciality is the ancient civilisations of the Middle East. He's worked for the School of Oriental and African Studies for my whole life, and I'm very, very proud to be his daughter, even if I don't really understand very much about the stuff he researches and teaches.

I'm an only child, and my parents were always wonderful to me. In fact, you could say I had a really old-fashioned happy childhood. Everything started to go wrong when I went to university. My mum was diagnosed with breast cancer. She was very sick indeed for nearly three years, and in the end, my dad had to take leave of absence to look after her. I wanted to leave university, but they were both absolutely adamant that I shouldn't. Just as I was about to graduate, she died. She was just fifty-five years old. It really took its toll on my dad. He moved into a smaller house, very sparsely furnished. It didn't express his personality at all, and there was nothing of our family history, except for one small table where he kept pictures of my mum and me, and eventually a wedding portrait of James and me. But he loved it. As he got older and cut down his teaching load he'd spend hours pottering in his neat garden and even neater shed. James called the house in Hendon the 'monk's cell', and it did feel a bit like that. I didn't worry, though. My dad was as happy as he could be. I think he loved my mum so much that the only way he could manage was to make a new home and a new day-to-day life. I knew he hadn't forgotten her. He couldn't, and neither could I.

So as I say, James and I were invited for Sunday lunch. We arrived in good time, because we knew the routine: drinks at twelve fifteen, lunch at exactly one. My dad wasn't a great cook, but he took great pride in his Sunday roast, and I knew that the timing was everything. If we were early or late, we'd throw out his careful preparations.

We rang the bell, and he came to the door, wiping his hands on his cooking apron. My dad is very finicky about his clothes, and because of that, he's a big fan of aprons. He has a pinstripe-navy one he wears in the kitchen (the above-mentioned cooking apron). Then there's an oilcloth one for the barbecue, a dark-green canvas one for gardening, and a white one with matching hat for pruning. I'm not kidding. He also has a tweed hat for going for walks, and driving gloves. Sometimes I think he time-travelled from the nineteenth century, from a vicarage or something.

He's quite a handsome chap . . . he's still slim

and very narrow ... I think he's terribly English-looking ... imagine an older version of Jeremy Irons. Where I came from, all round and curvy and messy blonde curls, I'm not really sure. I'm definitely his, though ... we have exactly the same hands, and we're both obsessed with correct punctuation.

I stepped in and gave him a big hug. He held me at arm's length and looked me up and down. He gave a little nod, and I saw a tiny smile ... I knew he was completely thrilled about the baby and the idea of being a grandfather. Now I was so enormous, there was plenty of me for him to admire. James followed and shook his hand. They did that gruff man-hello shoulder-patting thing. My dad likes James, but he's very reserved by nature.

'Come through,' Dad said. 'The weather's rather good, so I thought we might have a drink in the garden before lunch.' There was a recording of classical music playing softly in the kitchen, and I could smell roasting chicken and potatoes.

We took our glasses out on to Dad's little patio, and he took me for a short walk around the garden, pointing out the neat rows in the vegetable garden, and the flowers in the tidy beds. When we were right at the bottom of the garden, he said, rather stiffly and formally, 'So, how are you ... feeling?'

'Really well, Dad. Really, really well. We've had another sonogram, and everything seems to be going along just as it should.' I knew he wouldn't want any more detail than that. It's not that he's squeamish, it's just that ... well, he's my dad.

'Good, good,' he said. 'And are you planning to work for much longer?'

'I'll have to stay at work pretty much until my due date. We need to save as much of my paid maternity leave as we can for after the birth. I don't want to waste it on sitting around at home scoffing chocolates and watching daytime TV when I could still be working.'

'Still, you don't want to get too tired. Especially with the commuting. You might start to get a bit uncomfortable when you get . . . larger. Your mother . . . ' But he stopped himself, and then said brightly, 'Shall we go in? I'd better check on my broccoli.'

I followed him into the house, but I was suddenly so sad. I'd have loved to hear a story about my mum's pregnancy: I was still a teenager when she first got ill, so there'd never been a time when we might have shared stories like that. But I knew how hard it was for my dad to talk about her and I didn't want to push him.

We all have jobs at Sunday lunch . . . at the monk's cell, things have to be done the same way every time. He sets the table perfectly, and I bring in the warmed plates and serve veggies and gravy for all of us. He lets James carve the chicken (which, thank heavens, James does neatly and well . . . my old boyfriend, Gavin, got one go at it. He basically ripped the carcass limb from limb with his hands. He wasn't asked to do it again).

We made small talk through lunch — my dad told us about a conference he was planning to go to in Cairo in the summer, and he and James had some banter about cricket. When we finished the main course, Dad went to the kitchen to fetch the cheeseboard. James turned to me when my dad was out of the room. 'So why did you never go?'

'Go where?'

'Cairo. Egypt. Israel. The Middle East. Your dad must have gone all the time when you were growing up.'

'Um . . . I don't know. I don't remember him travelling all that much when I was younger, and I suppose it would usually have been in school termtime. Then I was at uni, and Mum was sick . . . '

'Would you like to go now?'

'What, now? This afternoon?' I joked.

'I'm serious. I mean . . . I wouldn't want to go in summer, when it's forty degrees, but maybe January or February . . . '

'*What* January or February?'

'Next year,' he said, like that was a perfectly reasonable thing to say.

'With a three-month old baby? Are you mad?'

I didn't mean to sound so shrill, and James looked shocked.

My dad came back into the room, carrying the cheeseboard. He looked at James and me, staring at one another, and I could see he sensed a bit of an atmosphere. I know how much he hates a scene, so I tried to defuse it by making a joke about it.

'Listen to this, Dad, James thinks we should head off to the Middle East in January, baby and all!'

As soon as the words were out of my mouth, I knew it was the wrong thing to say. It sounded like I was asking Dad to gang up on James with me.

Dad's never a man to be hurried, though, so he thoughtfully put down the cheeseboard and went to the sideboard to get the knives and plates before he spoke. I could feel James seething beside me. 'Well, it would depend on where you went, but I don't see why not — ' Dad began. But James, who is never rude, cut in.

'You see?' he spat at me, then turned back to Dad. 'When we first found out Toni was pregnant, we said it wouldn't change our lives. That we could still travel. Still do things — '

'No, *you* said that!' I interrupted. 'You had some harebrained scheme about shoving our baby in a backpack and going to Thailand.'

'It was an example!' said James sharply, and I was mortified to realise we were yelling, and we were doing it in front of my father. As calmly as I could, I said, 'Can we talk about this later?'

James caught himself. I knew he'd also seen how awful the situation was, and he said, very coldly, 'Of course.'

He turned back to Dad and tried to make a polite comment about the Camembert, but the afternoon was ruined.

We left soon after that, and started walking down to the Tube station in grim silence. James was walking too fast for me so I had to run and skip like a little girl to keep up. Eventually, I had to say, 'Can you just slow down?' and there we were, fighting again.

'Jesus, Toni, was that really necessary?'

'Was what necessary? Asking you to stop when you picked a massive fight in front of my poor dad?'

'I didn't pick a fight!' James really was furious. He stopped in the middle of the pavement. 'I was just talking about plans for the future. Our future. Things we might want to do together.'

I touched my belly. 'This is our future, James.' And that was exactly what he'd been waiting for me to say, because he went ballistic then.

'Is it? Is that it? Our whole future? We can never think about anything else, plan anything else, want anything else?'

'I don't understand . . . '

'Don't get me wrong, Tones, I'm thrilled as anything we're having a baby, but sometimes . . . I think about all the things we . . . I . . . haven't done.'

'And you think I don't?' Well, right then I wanted to scream at him like a fishwife, or punch him right in the face, or storm off, all of which are not things it's right to do in a rather nice bit of north-west London, where lots of people I went to school with still live. So instead, I said as calmly as I could, 'You know what, James, I can't have this conversation with you right now. I'm tired, and my feet hurt, and what happened at lunch was . . . diabolical. And we're very bloody far from Surrey. So can we just get home? Please?'

James seemed to come to his senses and he nodded. We walked in silence to the station. We didn't say a word on the way to Waterloo, or all the way home to Kingston on the train, which, let me tell you, is a bloody long time not to talk.

When, finally, we were back in our own little house, James went into the kitchen and made two mugs of tea. I curled up in a miserable ball on the sofa, and he came to sit by me, putting my tea within easy reach.

'I'm sorry — ' he began.

'Well, you should be!' I butted in, but then I saw his nostrils flare, and I knew I'd said the wrong thing. 'Sorry,' I muttered. 'Why don't you finish?'

I could see he was holding back a lot of anger, but he said, as calmly as he could, 'I'm sorry we ended up rowing in front of your dad. That wasn't my intention. But Toni . . . sometimes I feel . . . well, I feel like you don't see me any more. Or hear me. I feel like everything is changing, and while it's wonderful and amazing that we're having this baby, there's, well, there's other stuff.'

'Like what?'

'Well, like the fact that we can never go to the Middle East.'

'I didn't say never, just not three months after the baby's born. And since when have you had this yearning to go to the Middle East?'

'I don't! But I might have. Or I might have a yearning to go to South America. Or to chuck in my job and be a painter. And now I can't do any of those things.'

I hate to say it, but it sounded to me like he was whining. I tried very hard to be reasonable.

'It isn't the baby that stops us doing those

295

things. It's having a mortgage. It's not having won the Lottery. It's real life.'

'I know, I know,' he said. 'But I'm not even thirty yet, and sometimes I feel like I'm going to spend every holiday for the rest of my life at Centreparcs, and every weekend going to those horrible soft-play places that smell of wee and chips.'

Well, then I really let rip. 'Every holiday for the rest of your *life*? Spare me the melodrama, James, really. And I don't see why you're the one who's so worried about making all these sacrifices. At least at the end of it all, you'll still have a pelvic floor and a career!'

'It's not a competition, Tones . . . ' he began.

'Bloody right, because you'd lose!'

He stood up then, and walked to the door. He turned back to look at me and his face was really bleak. 'I'm sorry; I can't fight with you about this. Tones, you're my best friend. The only person I ever tell my secrets to. And if I can't tell you how I'm feeling, how I'm really feeling . . . who can I tell?'

And then he left, closing the door softly behind him.

It was the worst row we'd ever had, and to be honest, I was quite scared he wouldn't come back. I didn't have the first clue how to fix it or how to take back the horrible things I'd said. The truth is, James had touched a nerve. What if our lives as we knew them were over? I wasn't ready for us to be that couple we'd seen in the coffee shop all those months ago, ignoring each other, expending all their energy controlling their feral children. James had kicked off about travel, but what about ordinary, day-to-day stuff? Would I never again be able to put on a sparkly dress and gorgeous shoes and go on the lash with Rob and Caro? Would we ever go to the cinema again? And was Kate, my boss, right? Was I throwing my career away? If I took a year off, would I be past it and out of the game?

But that was ridiculous. Of course our lives weren't over. Millions of people have children and careers, and social lives. We'd be fine. We just had to decide what our priorities would be. It was a tiny, helpless little baby, for heaven's sake. It would have to fit in with our lives, not the other way round. We'd be hip, cool parents who took their baby everywhere. I'd once seen a couple with a baby of about six months old at a festival. The mum was carrying the baby in a sling and they'd put those giant ear protectors on it, like road-construction men wear, and they were dancing right up front to 'Thirty Seconds to Mars'. We'd be like that. Only with better taste in music.

James came back an hour or so later. He felt awful for yelling at his pregnant wife and storming out, and I explained how I was scared too which was why I had yelled back. We managed to patch things up, and spent the next few days being extra-carefully nice to one another. We'd be fine, I kept telling myself. And the thought that something 'patched up' still has cracks . . . well, I pushed that to the back of my mind.

Gemma

Toni was eating her way through a bag of mini muffins. Her appetite for sweet goodies seemed just endless. After fifteen years of ballet, Gemma couldn't remember the last time she'd eaten one muffin, let alone a whole bag. They'd spent the morning shopping for baby things for Toni, and they were now resting their aching feet in a little coffee shop.

Toni took a sip of her hot chocolate. 'So if it isn't too weird a question, who's your birth partner? Will Ben be there? Or your mum?'

'It's not a weird question, just one I hadn't thought about. I mean, I imagined I'd do it on my own.'

'On your *own*?'

'Well, I suppose there'll be doctors and nurses and things, but I don't really want anyone I know to see me, you know . . . '

'Screaming and swearing?'

'Well, I'm more worried about the thing Donna told us in last week's class.'

'Oh my God . . . that you might poo when you push the baby out? How did I never know that?' Toni went pink with horror.

'I think it's one of those secrets they only tell you when you're already pregnant.'

'Do you think if women knew before, none of them would do it?'

'Exactly. And I really don't believe what

298

Donna said about it,' said Gemma firmly.

'What, that when you're in the middle of it, you won't really care? Me neither. I've ordered James to stay next to my head at all times. I don't want him seeing me squeezing out a poop and a baby at the same time. He'll never look at me in the same way again.'

Toni looked closely at Gemma. 'Which brings me back to my original question. Are you serious about not having a birth partner? Won't you be scared? If I were you, I'd want my mum with me.'

Gemma laughed out loud at this. 'Have you met my mum? You might think differently if you had. She's glamorous and very, very busy. And she's had some . . . problems of her own.'

'Firstly, I can't believe *anyone* is so busy they wouldn't want to be there for the birth of their grandchild, and secondly, maybe this is what she needs. Something positive to focus on. Something to look forward to. And if not her, what about Ben? He is the baby's father.'

'Really? You'd never believe it. He hasn't shown any interest in it so far at all. He's avoided me as much as he can, and hasn't come for a scan or anything. He's been next to useless.'

'How do you feel about that?' Toni popped another little muffin in her mouth. 'Sorry, that makes me sound like a therapist, but you know what I mean. I mean, I suppose you love him very much.'

'I did . . . ' said Gemma slowly. 'I loved him so, so much. When I got pregnant I thought it would be a way to hold on to him. But I feel different now. He's been so hopeless, and that makes me think he's a bit rubbish . . . not a proper grown-up man, just a silly little boy. And also, it's much more about the baby for me now. I'm going to have my own baby. I don't need a stupid boy in my life if I have my little girl.' It sounded so brave when she said it aloud. She wished she could believe it. Now that it looked pretty certain that her dream of a little house with her and Ben as the perfect parents was never going to come true she didn't want to seem pathetic. She'd just have to keep putting on a brave face.

Toni smiled sympathetically. 'It would be nice if your little girl had a dad, though.'

'That's true, but if Ben's not going to step up and do the job, I'll meet someone else in a few years. I'm young. I've got lots of time.'

Gemma wished she felt as confident as she sounded. But Toni's questions had made her uncomfortable and a little bit scared. Maybe she did need more help and support. She dropped Toni off at her house and drove slowly home. Samantha was sitting in the kitchen with a magazine. She had her laptop and phone beside her, and she was simultaneously texting, typing on the computer and paging through the magazine when Gemma walked in.

'Hello, dear,' she said briskly, and went back to tapping on her keyboard, her long nails clicking. 'Did you have a nice time at the library?'

'I was shopping,' Gemma said. 'I told you, I went shopping with my friend Toni.'

'Tony who? Do I know him?'

'Her. Antonia. A girl Toni. And no, you haven't met her. She's also pregnant.'

'That's nice,' said Samantha vaguely, but she was busy looking at her phone, and Gemma wasn't sure her mum had heard her.

She swung herself up on to one of the stools opposite her mother.

'Listen, Mum, I've got something to ask you.'

'Hang on a second, dear,' Samantha said, tapping away on her phone screen. 'Right!' She clicked the Send key and put her phone down, then folded her hands and looked at Gemma brightly. 'What did you want to ask? Do you need money for something? I do keep asking your father just to get you a credit card so you can buy what you need.'

'It's not money,' said Gemma, already regretting the conversation she'd begun. 'It's just . . . well, I wasn't going to have a birth partner, but Toni says maybe I should, and I was wondering . . . '

'Oh Gemma,' said Samantha, leaning as far back on her stool as she could without actually tumbling off backwards. 'I, er . . . '

'Well, I thought maybe you could . . . '

'It's not, well, it's not really my thing, sweetheart,' said Samantha, her tone still brittle and bright. 'You know how squeamish I am. I go all funny if someone even mentions blood.'

'You could stay up at the head end,' Gemma said, remembering what Toni had said about James.

'Oh dear . . . ' said Samantha, clearly horrified that Gemma was serious about this. 'Really,

301

darling, I do think this is one of those things that's best left to the professionals. I'll be right outside, and I'll rush in with a pretty nightie for you and loads of pressies for the baby the minute it's all over.'

Samantha's phone beeped and she swept it up and began tapping away. Clearly, the conversation was over.

Gemma had been Samantha's daughter for far too many years to be upset by this interaction. She'd been surprised and grateful when Samantha had come to her scan, but she knew hands-on parenting (or indeed grandmothering) wasn't really her mum's style. She slipped off the kitchen stool and went upstairs. She sat quietly and thought for a while, then quickly took out her phone and rang Ben's number. She'd just ask him straight out. The phone rang and was answered within just a few rings. Hannah spoke briskly. 'Ben's phone, hello!'

Shit. Gemma couldn't exactly ring off now, her name would have come up on the screen. 'Hi, Hannah,' she said brightly. 'Is Ben there?'

'He's just in the shower,' Hannah said (and I bet he won't be thrilled to know you're answering his phone, Gemma thought). 'Anything I can help you with?'

'Oh, no, it's fine . . . just ask Ben to call me,' Gemma said. She was desperate to get off the line before Hannah asked her about the next antenatal class. She really, really didn't want to go with her.

But Hannah wasn't going to let her off that easily. 'Gemma, I've been meaning to ask you.

What are you planning to do about the birth?'

'What do you mean 'do' about it?' said Gemma, playing for time. How did Hannah know that was what she had rung about?

'Well, I assume you'll be in the hospital rather than at home,' Hannah said, as if a home birth was the most ridiculous thing she could imagine. 'I wanted to know who would be there? Your parents?'

Gemma almost laughed. If her mum had been a long shot, the thought of her father watching her give birth was truly insane.

'Well, I was actually ringing to ask Ben . . . '

' . . . Oh I can't imagine Ben would do it. But I would just love to — '

'Listen, could you just get Ben to call me?' said Gemma firmly. 'Thanks,' and she rang off.

Of course Ben didn't call. She didn't really expect him to. He'd been such a lame idiot about the whole thing, why should it change now? Maybe she was just being ridiculous. She'd planned all along to do it by herself. She'd just keep planning it that way. It would be fine.

LOUISE

She shouldn't have been surprised when Adam called. But of course, she was caught utterly off guard when her office phone rang at nine sharp on Monday morning. 'Louise,' he said briskly, and from that one word, she knew he knew about Brian. 'I've just had a chat with Alan. He has some concerns about what's been going on at the house.'

Alan. Of course. Alan had been at the ill-fated lunch party and would have seen that Brian's car had remained in the farmhouse driveway ever since. She wasn't sure what Alan had heard of the fight she'd had with Brian, but whatever it was, what he had had to report to Adam would not look good. With the splendid clarity of hindsight, she realised that, no matter what, she should have got to Adam before Alan did to tell him what had happened. There really was nothing, nothing at all she could say that didn't paint her in a completely awful light. She took a deep breath.

'I'm very sorry, Adam. My personal life has . . . somewhat overtaken me. The father of my baby arrived out of the blue and needed somewhere to stay. There's nothing going on between us, but it's unforgivable that I didn't speak to you beforehand.'

There was a long, crackly silence on the line.

'You're right,' Adam said, and with a sinking

304

feeling, she realised his voice was as cold as she'd ever heard it. 'You should have spoken to me. It seems to me you've overstepped boundaries, both in terms of personal trust and professionalism.'

There was no intimacy or affection in his voice at all. Louise began to shake a little. He continued. 'I should be back a fortnight from today, and I'd appreciate you finishing up your time in the office. But I would prefer it if you and your . . . man would move out of my house immediately. Alan has said he will move in for the last couple of weeks to look after Millicent.'

What he was asking was perfectly fair. She couldn't argue at all. It was her own stupid fault. To be honest, though, she'd spent so much time kicking herself for stupidity and bad decisions recently, she was surprised she could still walk. 'Fair enough. I'll have my stuff out by the end of today,' she said. 'And Adam . . . I'm sorry. So, so, sorry.'

There was a long pause on the line, so long she thought the call might have been cut off, and then he said, 'Me too.'

The click on the line sounded horribly, hollowly final.

Well, the very least she could do was do what she had promised Adam. She checked her diary: there were no meetings until the usual staff catch-up at midday. She rang Brian, waking him up, and briskly told him to pack up all his things and tidy the house.

'Why?'

Louise hesitated. Then she said, 'The boss, the

man whose house it is, well, he found out you were staying there, and he's not happy about it. He wants us both to move out.'

'Good God. What an unreasonable bugger! Why shouldn't you have a house guest? Do you want me to speak to him?' said Brian.

That was the very last thing she wanted. 'Well, to be fair, you're a bit more complicated than just a . . . house guest . . . ' Louise said. She hadn't expected Brian to ask questions, and she didn't have answers. She didn't want to tell him about her fledgling relationship with Adam, not right now. But Brian, it seemed, was quite keen for an argument.

'That's none of his business! You could take him to tribunal for this.'

'Look, Brian, the job is one thing, but staying in his house was an . . . informal arrangement. He feels I've overstepped a mark by having you to stay without letting him know, and I'd like to put things right. So could you pack your things and be ready to move this afternoon, please? Now I have to go. Goodbye.' She hung up with relief, and prayed that Brian would do as she asked.

She did a quick web search for estate agents, made a few phone calls and set up viewings on three short-let apartments relatively near to the hospital for that afternoon.

Throughout the midday meeting, she avoided meeting Alan's eye, but when she glanced at him, she could see he had his head down and was blushing furiously. She felt quite sorry for him. He'd done the right thing, there was no doubt about it, but he wasn't a very brave chap and it must have taken all his courage to shop her to the boss. After the meeting, as everyone filed out of the boardroom, she called him over. She could see he was shaking in his boots, obviously expecting her to tear a strip off him. Instead, she said calmly, 'Alan, I'll be out this afternoon for a couple of hours viewing apartments. Could you hold the fort, please? I don't have any meetings but I am expecting a call from the vinyl company about that late order.'

Alan nodded, obviously not trusting himself to speak.

'I should be back at about four,' continued Louise. 'And I'll be out of the house this evening. I'll feed Millicent before I go, so you don't need to stay the night there if it's not convenient for you.'

'It's, er . . . it's fine,' said Alan. 'I've got my stuff with me.'

When Louise popped back to the house, she discovered to her enormous relief that Brian had done a fine job of packing and cleaning. 'I'm going to meet some estate agents,' she told him. 'I know you don't have anywhere to go, so for now, you can stay with me. But Brian . . . we need to sort out what's going to happen long-term.'

She expected another argument, but to her surprise, he just said, 'I know.'

She took fifteen minutes to pack her own clothes, toiletries and books, and then hopped into the car to meet the first of the estate agents.

The first flat she saw was dark, absolutely tiny and none too clean. The second was lovely, but expensive, and up two flights of stairs. There was no lift in the building. She felt the climb, heavily pregnant as she was, and she didn't relish the thought of lugging a baby and a pushchair up and down the stairs every time she went out.

The third flat was sparsely furnished, a bit corporate and cold, but it was clean, there was a lift in the building and it had two double bedrooms. Best of all, it was empty, and the landlord was keen to get someone in immediately. She went back to the estate agent's office, paid an eye-watering sum as deposit and first month's rent, and signed all the paperwork.

The reference checks would take a couple of days, so she drove back to the farm and informed Brian he was paying for two rooms in a hotel until they could move into the flat. He meekly agreed and carried all of her bags and boxes out to her car. He drove off in his own car to check them into the nearby business hotel, and Louise took one last, slow walk around Adam's house. She tidied away a few things in the kitchen, loaded the washing machine with bed linen and towels and set it going. Then she sat down on the window seat and stroked Millicent's smooth fur. When the tears began to drip on her, Millicent gave a human-sounding moan, stretched and stalked off. Louise blew her nose, took one last look around, and then left, locking the door. Silly, she thought, so silly. How can you be so sad to lose something you never had?

★ ★ ★

Louise was busy unpacking the very first of the nursery boxes in the new flat on the Saturday morning when her mobile rang. Her heart sank a tiny bit when she saw it was Rachel.

'Louise, I'm here at your farmhouse and some nice young red-headed man tells me you've moved out. You didn't tell me!' Rachel's voice was unnaturally high . . . she never responded well to surprises or the suspicion that she'd been left out.

Louise decided to go with absolute remorse. It was the only way. 'I'm so sorry, Rach. It all happened so quickly. I haven't even told Simon.'

'Oh,' said Rachel, sounding slightly soothed. 'Well, I'm standing here with bags of sleepsuits and the sweetest little teddy. I was in John Lewis and I just couldn't resist. Where are you? I'll bring them round.'

'Oh . . . ' said Louise. It was a Saturday morning, how could she possibly put Rachel off? 'Well, we're in the middle of unpacking right now . . . ' the word was out of her mouth before she could stop herself. Might Rachel have missed it? But no.

'We?' said Rachel suspiciously.

Oh Lord. What was she going to do now?

'You might as well come round,' Louise said. 'The flat's in the middle of Kingston.' And she gave Rachel the address.

She had about fifteen minutes. She knocked on Brian's bedroom door, expecting him still to be asleep, but he was up and showered and

309

dressed, and was sitting at his computer.

'My sister's on her way over,' Louise said without preamble. 'It might be better if you're not here.'

Brian turned to look at her. He looked different somehow, as if he had got some of his spirit back. 'Why shouldn't I meet your sister?'

'Because . . . ' She couldn't believe they were having this conversation. 'Because she doesn't even know you exist, let alone that you're here, and I don't feel like explaining it all to her now.'

Brian's expression darkened. 'So she thinks this baby was an immaculate conception? Wow. Only the second one in history. You'd think you'd have been on the news or something.'

'Brian . . . I don't have time to have this argument with you now. She's on her way over. I will explain to her who you are and what the situation is, I'd just rather not do it . . . '

'With me here?' Brian was still sitting down. Did he not get the urgency? Why was he not up and finding his keys?

'So, tell me, Louise, what *is* the situation? You didn't mention me to the man whose company you were running, you haven't mentioned me to your sister. You seem to be trying very hard to pretend I don't exist. Meanwhile, I've given up my whole life, not to mention my job and my family, to be here for you and our baby.'

Louise knew she and Brian were due a discussion about their situation. She just desperately wished it didn't have to be now, with Rachel practically on the doorstep. But he'd provoked her now, and she was going to say her piece.

'That's complete bollocks, and you know it! You're here because you didn't have anywhere else to go, not because you want to be here. You wanted me to have an abortion, remember? We had a one-night stand, Brian. I am not the love of your life, and this baby is not your convenient new family. You don't even like me, let alone care for me or this child, and to be honest, if I never saw you again, that would be fine with me.' She glanced at her watch. 'Look, Brian, I really can't have this argument with you now — '

'Because your sister might arrive and it all might impact on *your* family? Forgive me if I'm not full of sympathy.'

At that moment the door buzzer sounded. Brian looked bitterly satisfied. 'There she is now. Well now, I'll have to meet her, unless you expect me to hide in the bathroom or jump off the balcony.'

The balcony sounded like a good option, except for the fact that they were only two storeys up. Louise went to buzz Rachel in. She made one last attempt to plead with Brian.

'Look, I'm sorry. I know we should have talked more, but can I just get through this morning with my sister? Things with her are difficult enough as it is. You and I can sit down this afternoon and thrash everything out. Please.'

Brian looked ready to argue more, but then his face softened a little. He could hardly miss her distress. 'Okay. I'll say hi and go out for a coffee.'

Rachel came bustling in, her arms full of shopping bags. She looked around at the chaotic living room, with its stack of boxes and a pile of

311

Louise's clothes on the sofa. 'Wow! This is . . . nice. I'm sure you'll make it cosy in no time at all!' She looked for somewhere to dump all of her bags. Every surface was covered with boxes, so she piled the parcels below the window. Brian chose that moment to emerge from his room, with his jacket on. Freshly shaved and with his hair combed for the first time in days, he looked presentable. In fact he looked better than presentable, he looked downright handsome. 'You must be Louise's sister,' he said smoothly, offering his hand.

'Rachel,' she said, breathlessly, smiling up at him. 'And you are?'

'Brian. Do excuse me, I was just going out. Lovely to meet you.' He nodded politely to Louise, swung his laptop case on to his shoulder and was gone.

Louise took a deep breath and turned to her sister, prepared for a barrage of questions, but Rachel was silent, staring at the door where Brian had gone out. Her face was suddenly pale. 'Is that . . . ' she said quietly.

'The baby's father. Yes. He arrived the other day. We're not together, but . . . '

'He's married, Louise. He's wearing a wedding ring.'

He was? Louise couldn't remember Brian having worn his ring since he arrived. He must have put it on that morning. The bastard. Knowing that women always notice that sort of thing, it was his way of getting at her through Rachel.

'Rachel — ' she began.

'Don't you speak to me. You're having a baby

312

with someone else's husband. I . . . I don't even know where to start.'

Louise took a deep breath. 'I'm sorry you found out this way. I didn't want you to — '

'You think it matters how I found out? What about you? About what you're doing? It's disgusting.'

With anyone else, Louise would have lost her temper. She would have torn a strip off the person in question, as she had with Gemma, and told them to mind their own business. But this . . . this was her sister, with all the baggage that brought with it.

'Rachel . . . ' she said again, in her most conciliatory tone. But her sister turned on her with the speed of a snake.

'Don't talk to me like that.'

'Like what?'

'Like you feel sorry for me, like I'm some kind of simple-minded charity case that you and Simon snigger about. I'm so, so sick of it.'

Louise was floored. She tried to speak, but Rachel ploughed on.

'You know, I cannot believe you and I come from the same family. You seem to hate everything I believe in. Everything that matters to me. Sometimes I think you do this stuff because you hate me.'

Louise found herself raising her voice to Rachel's level, just to be heard. 'What the hell are you talking about?'

'I always knew I wasn't clever like you and Simon. Even when I was small. I knew I didn't want a big important career, or to be able to make clever, unkind jokes at dinner parties like you do.'

'Is that what you think I do?'

Rachel ignored her. 'I just wanted a husband to love, and a nice home and a family. I know you think I married Richard for money, like some kind of tacky little gold-digger, but for your information, I married him because I love him very much.'

'I know . . . ' Louise tried to say.

'Do you? Do you know? Or do you just think you know all about me? Silly little Rachel, staying at home, going out to get her hair done and her nails done. Someone to laugh at. Someone stupid.'

'I've never laughed at you,' Louise said firmly.

'You've also never really listened to me either,' said Rachel, her voice softening slightly. 'You know I've been trying for a baby for years now, and I think you think I'm just being silly, that it's Rachel's little obsession, wanting a baby to keep her occupied.'

'I don't think that — '

'But you have no idea what it feels like to want something so much that every part of you hurts. To spend every single month praying . . . *begging* your body not to bleed. I used to love making love with my husband. Now it's this horrible, sad, mechanical thing we do on the right days of the month. I can't remember what it's like to have sex for the pleasure of it any more.'

'I'm sorry . . . '

'Are you? Are you? You've never even *wanted* a baby, and here you are, three years older than me, and pregnant without even trying. And you never even bothered to tell me that the father was someone else's *husband*.'

'It's not exactly something I'm proud of.'

'Tell me, does he have other children?'

'Two daughters.'

Rachel snorted and walked away. 'It's like you're trying to make a mockery of everything I've ever wanted. It's repulsive.' Then she turned, and said very softly, 'Do you know what my biggest fear is? That Richard will find some young, gorgeous bit on the side, and she'll get pregnant. I think . . . no, I know . . . I would kill myself. Do you have any idea what women like you do to women like me?'

Finally, Louise exploded. 'For fuck's sake, Rachel, can you cut back a bit on the histrionics? For once, this situation is not all about you. And what do you mean women like me?'

'Women like you who sleep with other women's husbands.'

'There's no point in my trying to defend myself. No point in my trying to tell you the story of what happened with Brian and me, or what happened with Brian and his wife. You've made up your mind that I'm this evil, awful person, and the reasons why have nothing at all to do with me, it's all your own personal stuff. Now if you'll excuse me, I'm thirty-six weeks pregnant, what life I have is all in boxes and I've had enough of you and everyone else crapping on me for today, thanks. The door's there.'

Rachel looked as if Louise had slapped her. She went white, and then very red. She scooped up her handbag and stalked out of the door, leaving it open behind her. Louise went to close it and make sure it was locked. Then she went back into her bedroom and sat on the bed.

It would have been a good time to have a cry, if she'd been that kind of woman, but she wasn't. She wished she could ring Simon, but he'd gone away for the weekend with friends to a cottage in remotest Wales. Even if he had a mobile signal, which she doubted, it wasn't really fair to ruin his weekend by ringing up to whinge that she'd had a fight with her little sister. They weren't six any more after all. Right at that moment, things felt very bleak. Toni wasn't speaking to her, Adam wasn't speaking to her. She felt terribly, terribly alone. For the first time since she decided to keep the baby, she found herself wondering whether the price was too high. She'd given up a very successful career, her home and her social circle in Leeds to sit alone in a rented flat in Kingston without a single friend to talk to.

She knew she should get on with unpacking, but she just didn't have the energy. So she turned on her laptop and clicked through to the baby site. She was a fairly regular visitor to the forum, although she seldom posted. It was nice to read everyone's news . . . she recognised lots of the user names, and quite a few women had posted pictures of their growing bellies. It was odd to think of the thousand-odd women across the UK who had joined this group, who would all give birth in September and raise babies of the same age, experiencing all the same milestones. At the moment, it was the closest thing to friendship she had. Pathetic. She considered writing a post about her awful week, but then she imagined how it would read to others: 'Got kicked out of the house by my new boyfriend (and boss), got snubbed by my friends and yelled at by my sister. Now sharing a flat with a smelly squatter, a.k.a. the father of my unborn child.' It made her sound like a character on one of those terrifying morning chat shows. They'd assume she lived in a caravan and was missing some of her teeth. Besides, Toni was a member of the group too, and a frequent poster, and Louise was not going to give her the satisfaction of seeing how low she was.

She curled up on the bed and considered just going to sleep, but then she heard Brian's key in the lock. She shuffled down the bed and gently kicked her door closed. After a while she could hear him moving around in the living room. It sounded like he was heaving boxes around. She couldn't leave him to do her unpacking, so she dragged herself off the bed and went through. She smelt fresh coffee, and Brian was kneeling on the floor, pushing books into the bookcase. He looked up and said, 'I made a pot of decaff for you, and there are some nice pastries. There's a great bakery just around the corner.' Even though he'd been an arse and caused her row with Rachel, it felt like the first nice thing anyone had done for her in a very long time. If it were anyone but Brian, she would have hugged him. Instead, she said, 'Thanks', and bit into a sugary bun.

Toni

I met Robyn and Caro for brunch one sunny August morning. We hadn't got together for ages, but I think they were both feeling bad about how they'd been a bit useless when they found out I was pregnant. It was a bit strange, but I appreciated the fact that they were both making such an effort.

'We got you pressies,' said Caro, sitting down at the table and dumping an enormous bag in front of me. 'This is going to be the best-dressed baby south of the river. Hell, it's going to be the best-dressed baby outside of Brangelina's nursery.'

And she wasn't kidding. She'd obviously got some baby-fashion guru to advise her, and there were gorgeous white quilted satin sleepsuits and delicate knitted cardigans, and even a sweet little sailor suit. 'I know you don't know the sex so I went for gender-neutral stuff. It's all very retro this year,' said Caro helpfully. 'You should get one of those old-fashioned Silver Cross perambulators with the great big wheels.'

Robyn chipped in. 'And maybe get an Edwardian frock and a big hat for yourself, Tones. Seriously, Caro, a baby isn't a fashion accessory.'

'I know,' said Caro, slightly hurt. 'But that doesn't mean it can't have a signature look.'

'Well, I haven't met 'it' yet,' I said, 'so I'm not

too sure what its look is going to be. At the moment, I think it may be 'premiership footballer' or 'Riverdancer' . . . it spends enough time booting hell out of my bladder.'

'Well, my presents are a bit more practical,' said Robyn briskly. 'I got you a bottle of champagne for afterwards and an ice pack for your fanny.'

'I appreciate the thought, Rob, but I'm very much hoping my fanny will be fine.'

'Well, if champagne is being bandied about, I suggest we get some!' said Caro, flagging down a passing waiter. 'Still not drinking, Toni?'

'Sorry, no . . . not for a long while yet, especially . . . ' I stopped myself. I was going to say ' . . . if I breastfeed', but that wasn't a conversation I wanted to have with those two. I could just imagine their views on breastfeeding. The waiter brought the bubbles and poured for Rob and Caro. I sipped my fruit juice.

'I have to say, darling, you're being very brave about all this. I'd be terrified!' said Caro, taking a huge gulp of her champagne. 'You hear such stories!'

'I don't want to listen to — ' I started, but Caro wouldn't be stopped.

'There's a woman I met at work whose baby got stuck, so she had to have one of those epi-things . . . '

'Episiotomy,' I said warily. This was definitely not a story I needed to hear.

'Anyway, apparently they normally only make one cut, but it was so stuck they had to cut her four ways. She was in a wheelchair for weeks afterwards. She couldn't stand up or everything would have fallen out through her pelvic floor!'

Robyn leapt in with her own lovely story. 'There's a girl I met snowboarding, anyway her sister had to have the baby sucked out with a plunger thing . . . '

'Ventouse,' I said, wishing I could just put my hands over my ears and sing 'La-La-La' till they stopped.

'And then there are the epidurals that don't work . . . '

'And tearing! I heard of someone who tore right through to her bum . . . '

'Stop!' I yelled. 'My God, I thought we were getting together so you two could be supportive! How is this supposed to help me? I have to give birth to this baby. I don't have a choice. Hearing every gruesome horror story you can think of doesn't make it any easier!'

They both looked suitably hangdog. I hadn't really missed drinking during my pregnancy, but right about then I could have poured myself a bucket of the lovely champagne they were drinking and slurped it up in one go.

I tried to get the conversation off babies and giving birth, and soon Rob and Caro were sharing all the gossip from their jobs and their far more interesting lives. It was just like old times, and Rob told a completely filthy story about her and a co-worker and a middle-of-the-work-day shag behind the screen in the training room that had me laughing so much I nearly peed myself. I'd really missed this. Of course I couldn't join in and drink like I used to, but then

I'd always been the good girl in our group, always in a long-term relationship, always quite well-behaved, so not much had changed. I was just happy there would be brunches like this in the future, and that there'd be space for a pushchair next to the table. Little babies sleep pretty much all of the time, I'd read on the baby website, so I was pretty sure that within a few weeks of the birth we'd be back, chatting and gossiping.

I had to go just before midday because I had to get to the first of my hypnobirthing classes. I kissed Caro and Rob and promised them that James had their numbers to text the moment the baby was born.

So, hypnobirthing. I read the book Susie, the woman I met at the antenatal classes, recommended, and it turns out it has nothing to do with a dodgy bloke with a ponytail saying 'Look into my eyes'. It's all about deep breathing and relaxation, and trusting your body to do what it's designed to do. I was so inspired after reading the book, I wanted to tell everyone. Pain-free birth with no drugs! It was the most amazing thing I'd discovered since eyelash extensions. Anyway, the book says you have to do the course, so I emailed Susie, and she sent me details of the teacher she'd been to. It wasn't cheap, but I figured you can't put a price on a pain-free labour . . . and after I'd watched those YouTube videos of women giving birth in blissful silence, I would have paid double for the course!

I'd asked James to read the book, and he said he'd get round to it. He's not much of a reader, so I wasn't holding my breath. He raised an eyebrow when I told him what the course was going to cost, but he could see I was certain about it so he didn't argue. He'd gone off to play football first thing, but he did remember to say 'Good luck!' before he went.

The course was in a wonderful old Victorian house, with a big plum tree in the front garden. I was a few minutes late because I walk a lot slower than I used to, so everyone else was sitting in a circle already when I huffed and puffed my way in. I sat down and fanned myself with the thick wodge of course notes that had been left on my chair. I had a vague feeling that I'd forgotten something. Let me think — loose comfortable clothes, pen and paper, water bottle — I had all of those. Then I looked around the room. I was right. I had forgotten something. My husband. Everyone else was paired up. There were four pairs who looked married, or at least like conventional heterosexual couples, one gay female couple and a pregnant girl of about my age who was there with a woman who had to be her mum. And then there was little old me, there all on my own. I wanted to crawl into a hole. I couldn't leave now, and I couldn't even ring James and beg him to come, as he was running around on a football pitch and his phone would just ring and ring in his bag in the changing room.

Our hypnobirthing teacher, Jenny, who I'd spoken to on the phone, was a tall, lovely, soft-spoken woman with thick, red hair down to her waist. She welcomed me, and said, 'So glad you're here, now, Toni. We were just going to go round the circle and say our names and what we hope to get out of the hypnobirthing experience. Tell us your story.'

'Um . . . I'm Toni. I'm thirty-six weeks pregnant, and me and my husband James . . . I do have a husband . . . ' (Oh God, listen to me, what if the woman who's here with her mum doesn't have a husband? Does it make me sound judgmental?) ' . . . Um, not that you need a husband, well, you do a bit, someone has to provide the sperm . . . ' (Stop talking, Toni, there's the lesbian couple here, where did they get their sperm?) ' . . . Anyway, James isn't here because I didn't know we were supposed to bring our husbands, but, um, anyway . . . I want to have a pain-free birth so I hope I can do it without him. I mean, not without him at all, just without him here today! He'll be here next week. I guarantee it!'

I was relieved when I stopped talking, but I bet not as relieved as the other people in the room were. Jenny took a deep breath and said, 'Well, I'm sure we'll all enjoy meeting James at our next session. And do remember, hypnobirthing doesn't guarantee a pain-free labour, it just helps you to connect with your body's natural processes.'

We spent three hours doing breathing exercises and guided meditation. Whenever the pregnant one needed a partner to help them, Jenny came over and did the exercise with me. After a while I stopped feeling awkward and self-conscious, and I really got into it. In the last

323

meditation, with Jenny's soft voice describing a sunlit beach, and the gentle music playing in the background, I actually drifted off to sleep. I learned a lot. But the most important thing I learned was that you can't do hypnobirthing without a partner to help you.

I walked home slowly, thinking about it. James hadn't said he wouldn't help me, he just hadn't been very interested, and I had a feeling if I asked him to do some of the exercises with me he would think they were silly and that they wouldn't work. Jenny had told us that for hypnobirthing to work for us, we needed to be positive and committed and to avoid negative people and people who told us birth horror stories (that was Rob and Caro off my list till after the birth too, then!). But how do you avoid someone negative when they're your husband and birth partner?

When I got home, he was lying on the sofa, covered in mud, with a pack of frozen peas on his leg. He wanted to tell me all about the disgusting bad tackle that had taken him down and the massive bruise coming out on his shin. After what felt like an hour of football talk, he remembered to say, 'How was your course?'

'Fine,' I said vaguely. It didn't feel like the right time to start a major, serious discussion about it. I'd bring it up with him well before next Saturday's class and hopefully everything *would* be fine.

Gemma

She didn't recognise the number on her phone. Normally, when that happened, she ignored the call and let it go to voicemail, but for some reason, she answered it. 'Gemma?' said a female voice she didn't recognise.

'Yes?'

'This is Kat. I'm Ben's girlfriend.'

Somehow, Gemma knew this was the short, dark-haired girl she'd seen Ben with all those months ago. She didn't know what to say. It was one thing knowing Ben didn't want to be with her, but another thing altogether to know he was with someone else.

'Gemma?' Kat said into the silence.

'Yes. What do you want?'

'Can we meet?'

'Why would I want to meet you?' Gemma knew she sounded rude, but she didn't care. She was hugely pregnant, uncomfortable and hot, and she didn't need Ben's new girlfriend rubbing her nose in how she'd lost him.

'I know you probably don't want to talk to me,' Kat said. 'But I only just found out about you. I mean I knew Ben had a girlfriend before, but he's only just told me you're pregnant.'

'So?'

'Well, I was a bit freaked out. A lot freaked out, actually, but then I heard that he's hardly seen you since he found out. I told him he hasn't treated you right. I've spoken to him about it, and I think he wants to try again.'

'Try again?' Gemma felt her heart lurch.

'To be a good dad,' said Kat. Gemma swallowed hard. So, not to try again with her. Kat continued, 'He hardly ever sees his own dad, and he doesn't want that to happen to his little girl.'

'I still don't know why I have to meet you,' said Gemma stonily.

'You don't, if you don't want to. But I thought you might not answer a call from Ben, after he's been so shit to you. He'd like to see you.'

'Okay,' said Gemma dubiously. 'Get him to call me. But I still don't get why you're doing this.'

'Ever heard that saying, 'Keep your friends close, but your enemies closer'?' said Kat. 'Not that you're my enemy. But I love Ben, and I want to keep him in my life, and you're too important to ignore.'

And then she hung up.

Ben rang later that afternoon, and they arranged to meet for coffee on the high street. She hadn't seen him for ages, even though she'd seen Hannah almost every week, and he looked downright shocked when she walked into the coffee shop.

'Wow, Gem, you look . . . '

'Pregnant?' she said, sitting down.

'Very. Very pregnant.'

'Well, the baby's due in six weeks. She could be born today and she'd probably be okay.'

'Six weeks.' Ben wiped a hand over his face. 'Wow.'

'So your girlfriend makes your phone calls these days.' Gemma couldn't keep the bitterness out of her voice.

'I'm sorry. I would have phoned, but I thought you probably wouldn't speak to me. I've been really shit.'

'You have been, but I'd always speak to you. You're my baby's dad.'

'Kat says that no matter what happens, I'll always be her dad. She says it's really important that I have a relationship with her, even before she's born, and then from the minute she's born.'

'Kat says? What do you say?'

'I say . . . that Kat's right. I was so angry with you for doing this to me that I wasn't thinking right. I was thinking about me, and about you and how you'd messed up my life. I wasn't thinking about the most important person.' He gestured awkwardly at her belly.

'Sounds like Kat talked some sense into you, finally,' said Gemma.

'Kat is . . . ' Ben seemed to be struggling to find the words. 'Kat is amazing.'

'And you're happy with her?' It was such a difficult question to ask, but Gemma had to ask it.

'Really happy,' said Ben, and awful though it was to see it, Gemma had to admit he did look happy when he spoke about her.

They talked more easily after that. Gemma told him about the scans she had had and promised to email him pictures. He asked to come and see the baby's room and asked her if

327

there was anything she needed. She hesitated then. 'I suppose you haven't changed your mind about . . . being there.'

'Being where?'

'There. When she's born.'

'What, like . . . in the room? I thought you . . . well, I thought you wouldn't want me to.'

Gemma looked stung. 'I asked you! I rang your mobile weeks ago and spoke to your mum. She said she'd talk to you, and then you never rang back, so I assumed — '

'My mum answered my *mobile*?'

'She said you were in the shower.'

Ben stood up and walked away from the table. Gemma could see he was very, very angry. He came back and sat down. 'She never told me. I swear, Gem. I know I've been flaky, but I would never not ring you back about something as important as that.'

'So do you want to?'

'Yes,' said Ben firmly. Then he nodded his head vigorously. 'Yes. If you want me there, and I can be there to see my little girl born, then yes.'

Gemma smiled and squeezed his hand. He looked uncomfortable for a moment, then he reached under the table and came out with a crumpled plastic bag.

'I got her something,' he mumbled. Gemma opened the bag, and inside was a soft, brown teddy bear with a pink bow around its neck. 'I chose it,' Ben said. 'Not Kat, or my mum. I chose it for my girl.'

Gemma stroked the bear's soft fur. She was

close to tears. How could he be in love with someone else? It was just awful. Still, even if he wasn't hers, it looked like he was going to be there for his daughter. And that was the most important thing.

Louise

When she got to thirty-eight weeks, Louise stopped work. Adam had not returned from sailing — he'd initially planned to be back a few weeks before she was due, but for some reason he had stayed on the boat. Louise hoped it wasn't just a ploy to avoid seeing her. She'd done her handover via email, sending him a final report and balance sheets, and handing on day-to-day running of the firm to Alan until Adam got back. She was proud of the work she'd done: it hadn't been as challenging as her work for Barrett and Humphries, but she'd given it her all, and she knew she'd done a good job. She reasoned that even if Adam thought she was a terrible person, he couldn't fault her managerial skills.

And now it was just a waiting game. It felt very strange. Louise had got her first job straight out of uni, and she'd always worked. Other than the few weeks before she'd gone to work for Adam, she'd never had time off that wasn't a holiday with a predetermined end date. For the first week or so, she rushed around, organising the flat and buying all the little things she hadn't thought of before. Because she wasn't going out to work every day, it grated on her even more that Brian was still there and still showing no signs of moving on. His every little habit grated on her; the way he ate, the way he hummed under his breath when he was concentrating, his sloppy washing up. She'd tried a few times to ask him if he had plans to move on, but he kept saying that he wasn't ready. They'd had a few blazing rows, but most of the time they lived side by side in a monosyllabic, uneasy truce. She didn't have the energy for anything else.

She went into town a few times to have lunch with Simon, who was very excited about the birth and looking forward to being there. Every time she met him, she came back laden with more bags of gifts for the baby.

'I wish you lived closer,' he said one lunchtime, handing over a Mothercare bag full of tiny vests and socks.

'I wish *you* lived closer,' Louise replied. 'I certainly won't be able to afford a flat in your posh neighbourhood any time soon.'

'Much though I love my nephew-to-be, I'm not relocating to yummy-mummy Surrey, thanks very much.'

'Well, I'll just have to bring him round every weekend to put sticky fingerprints on your glass coffee table.'

'I can't wait. I can't wait to meet him and see his little fingers,' said Simon, squeezing her hand.

'You know, I think you're broodier than I am!' Louise laughed. 'You should have one of your own.'

'Well, I just have to meet Mr Right, settle down, get approved to adopt . . . I should be a dad around the time that I retire. Nope, I'm afraid carrying on the Holmes line is all down to you.'

'And Rachel, if she's lucky.'

'Not likely to happen now, what with the latest development.'

'What development? Rachel's not talking to me at the moment.'

'Didn't she tell you? She found out quite a while ago. She's gone into early menopause.'

'But she's only thirty-five!'

'What can I tell you? Seems her eggs have passed their expiration date.'

'Well that explains it, I suppose.'

'Explains what?'

'She came round to the flat and met Brian. And when she worked out he was married, she really lost it. She pretty much implied my being pregnant made a travesty of her whole life and everything she dreamed of.'

'Harsh.'

'Well, I wasn't very nice back. I've got quite a bit on my plate, in case you hadn't noticed, so I basically kicked her out and we haven't spoken since.'

'Oh dear,' said Simon.

'Oh dear? That's all you can come up with?'

'Well, I've been thinking about it a lot, and I thought you and Rachel could really help each other. I mean, Lou, you're living down here in the sticks, you have no support structure, no grandparents to babysit. I live an hour away and work full-time . . . I'm going to do everything I can, give you all my spare time and as much money as you'll let me, but I was hoping you and Rachel could fill a need in each other's lives. She'd get a baby to cuddle, and you'd get help when you need it.'

'Well, that all sounds lovely, but she hates me. I don't see how it's going to happen.'

'She doesn't hate you. She's just in a lot of pain right now and she lashed out. But you know what she's like. She'll find it so hard to come to you and apologise. I'm afraid you're going to have to be the big sister in this case and try and make the peace.'

'I know. And I will. Not because I want her to be my free babysitter, but because she's my sister. I just have to solve the Brian problem first, though. She's not going to want to come round and be the doting aunt with him sprawled all over the sofa.'

'What's happening with Brian?'

'Well . . . nothing. He arrived, told me I'd ruined his life . . . seems I ruin a lot of lives . . . and sat down on the sofa. It's been weeks and he's hardly moved. He's improved a bit . . . he goes out once a day now for a coffee or a pint, but he's not *doing* anything. And in between wanting to push him off the balcony, I suppose I do feel guilty, so I tend to leave him to it.'

'Are you . . . '

'What? Together? In love? Having sex? None of the above. Separate rooms, no physical contact. And let me tell you, now I've got everything unpacked, I've realised that that flat is really very small. It's bloody small. Definitely not big enough for a heavily pregnant woman and a six-foot-four bloke who is always underfoot. And God knows what it'll be like when the baby arrives.' Louise sighed and took a big sip of her water.

'Well, he's going to have to do something, isn't he? He has to get a job, surely. The man has families to support!'

Louise snorted, spluttering water all over the table. 'Oh dear, Si, I so need you in my life. Every time I think my life is a mess and a tragedy, you find the comedy and I think I might just make it.'

When she got back to the flat, Brian was in his customary spot on the sofa, tapping away at his laptop. As soon as she came in, however, he slammed it shut.

'Hello, there,' Louise said, trying to keep her voice pleasant. Since he'd been kind to her on the day of her fight with Rachel, she had been trying to be nicer to him, although his habits still grated on her intensely. 'Been busy?'

'Oh . . . ' he said vaguely. 'Yeah . . . checking out the job market, you know . . . just in case . . . well, just in case.'

She was fairly certain he hadn't been trawling a job site . . . that wasn't how you found work at his level anyway. But if she'd caught him out watching porn, it was quite sweet that he was so embarrassed.

'I picked up some nice steaks for dinner on my way back,' she said. 'And Simon's bought the baby another twenty outfits.'

'Splendid! Good!' said Brian, jumping up. 'Why don't I nip out and get something nice for pudding then? And one of those grape-juice cooler things you like. Since you can't have wine.'

'That'd be nice,' she said, surprised. It was the

most proactive thing he'd done since he'd arrived on her doorstep. Nevertheless, she couldn't help noticing that he took his laptop through to his bedroom and pocketed his mobile before he left.

The next day, she was shopping on the high street, wondering why it took so damned long to get anywhere and whether once the baby was born she'd walk normally again, rather than rocking from side to side like an obese duck. Her mobile rang and, with a swooping-rollercoaster feeling in her stomach, she saw Adam's name come up. It was his UK mobile number, which must mean he was back from his travels. She took a deep breath and answered. 'Mr Harper. Home from the high seas?'

'Ms Holmes. Not dropped the bairn yet?' He sounded like he was outside somewhere. She imagined him standing on the driveway outside the farmhouse.

'No, still waddling around.' Why, oh why, did his deep, soft voice tie her insides in such a knot? It was crazy. She didn't trust herself to say anything more without her voice trembling and giving away how much his call had shaken her, so she stayed quiet, waiting to hear why he had rung. When he spoke again, his voice sounded uncertain.

'I thought . . . well, now I'm back, we should meet up to er . . . catch up.'

'Were my handover notes okay? Do you need more information?'

'No, the handover was fine, and, may I say, you did a fantastic job. Sales were up, costs seem to be down a bit. You ran my company better than I do myself.'

It was good to hear, Louise thought. She might be messing up every other area of her life, but at least she could still do a good job. But Adam wasn't finished. He dropped the jokey tone, and his next words were quiet and serious.

'Lou, I think there's unfinished business . . . between us. I think we need to meet to . . . resolve things.'

Now that wasn't what she wanted to hear. It sounded all too final. All too much like he wanted to close this chapter of his life and move on. She knew there could be no future, not after she'd let him down by letting Brian move into his house, but she wasn't ready to hear it. He deserved her honesty, though. She walked to a quieter corner of the shopping precinct. 'Adam, my due date is a week away. I'm enormous and uncomfortable. The few friends I had in Surrey are blanking me, my sister won't speak to me and I have to deal with the mess I've made of Brian's life. Do you mind if I take a rain check?'

'I don't want to see you to yell at you, Louise. I was furious with you for letting that guy live in my house without telling me, that's true. But I don't know the full story of what's going on with you and him. I also don't know what I feel about this, about you, about anything, because I haven't actually seen you since the morning I left for the Tall Ships Race. Can we just have coffee? Or decaff tea? And talk? Not have a big serious conversation, just a face-to-face chat, as colleagues — or friends. It's been a long time.'

Louise spied a bench and sat down. There was a long silence, and then she said, 'I think so.'

Adam's voice sounded raw when he spoke again. 'If you think so, can you answer me one question?'

'The answer is no. Brian and I are not together, not in any way. I haven't slept with him since the night I got pregnant and I'm not going to.'

'That wasn't the question, but thank you for that. It's this. I'm on the other side of the walkway, standing outside Boots. I rang you because I could see you. The question is, can I come over and sit on your bench?'

Toni

With hindsight, I should maybe have found out what kind of day James had had at work on the Monday before I launched into my hypnobirthing speech. If I'd known they'd lost a major account and one of the junior designers had been made redundant, I might have picked a different day, or at the very least poured him a big glass of wine before I started talking. But I didn't know, and I'd been sitting at home all day practising my exercises and thinking about it, so I just launched in as soon as he came through the door.

'I should have told you on Saturday, but I didn't. I need you to come to the next three sessions of the hypnobirthing course. I can't do it without you.'

'What do you mean, you can't do it without me?'

'Well, you're the birth companion. You have to do all the readings, and say the affirmations for me, and do the massage.'

'Affirmations? I thought you said this wasn't weird and New Age.'

'It's not! It's not at all! But if you'd read the book, you'd know that. You haven't read even a page of it, have you?' I felt ready to burst into tears.

'Listen, Tones, can you wind your neck in and let me get my coat off before you launch into a

338

full-scale drama?' said James, and there was no mistaking the crossness in his voice. I didn't mean to start crying, honest I didn't. But I sat there on the sofa while he put his stuff down and went to the loo and got a drink, and the tears just started leaking out.

I think I said in the beginning that I've always been a bit of a cryer. Well, pregnancy seems to have magnified that sevenfold, and I'm now officially captain of the weepy team. James just doesn't know what to do, and I can't understand why. To me, it seems perfectly simple. If it's not your fault, put your arms around me. If it is your fault, ask if you should put your arms around me and then do what I say. James usually manages it quite well, but that Monday night was obviously not a good day for him, because he just got really exasperated. 'Oh, for God's sake!' he said, furiously. 'What have I done wrong now?'

Well, that would make you cry more, wouldn't it? It would make anyone cry more, especially if they were the size and shape of a hippo and worried about having a horrendously painful birth experience because their husband wouldn't do the affirmations. I just sat there and sobbed for about five minutes. I could practically hear the steam coming out of James' ears. Eventually, he sat down next to me and took my hand, not as gently as he usually would, but as if he was really trying. 'Stop crying, Toni, and tell me what's wrong,' he said, trying to keep his voice calm. 'I can't do anything if all you do is howl.'

I managed to hiccup that it was the hypnobirthing and that if he was negative and unsupportive I couldn't do it, and he sighed deeply.

'Toni, my love, I'm going to make you a cup of tea. Then I'm going to take the book into the bedroom to read about this hypnobirthing' — I could hear him trying not to say it in a sarcastic way — 'and then when I come out we'll have a calm, rational discussion about this. But I can't have a fight with you about something I know nothing about.'

He did exactly as he'd promised, and he came out of the bedroom forty-five minutes later with a notepad full of notes and questions. I had drunk my cup of tea and then done a visualisation where James and I were walking around a park, holding hands and laughing together, and not sniping at each other like a pair of mean old monsters. I felt better and calmer, and the baby had stopped kicking a tattoo on my ribs. It always knows when I'm upset and seems to get agitated too. I hope it doesn't mean we're going to have a neurotic mad child who flies off the handle all the time like its mother.

'So what do you think?' I asked tentatively.

'It's not as flaky as I thought it would be, but I don't like some of the weird 'Imagine you're in a forest' stuff. But if you want to do it, I'll do it and I promise not to take the piss.'

Well, that was as fair as I could hope for. We sat down then with my course notes, and we did some of the exercises. Doing them with James, some of them did seem a bit silly, and we totally got the giggles doing a thing where I had to pretend I had a silver glove of endorphins on my hand. Jenny had told us to choose the techniques that worked for us, so we chucked the glove in the bin, if you know what I mean, and tried some others. I loved the massage and the stroking, and, if you don't mind my being a bit graphic, it actually made me a bit horny, so we gave up practising and instead we had sex on the sofa, which when you're as pregnant as I am is no mean feat. And when you're having to shag a woman as pregnant as I am, and you still fancy her (or at least say you do), then you should get a medal or something. Or that's what I told James. And he laughed, and stroked my head, and then fell asleep and snored a bit, which in its own way was very sweet.

He came to the hypnobirthing session on the next Saturday, and I swear he was the best birthing companion there. If they were giving hypnobirthing birthing-partner prizes, he would have got a gold star. But then Jenny made us do the silver-glove thing, and James had a coughing fit and had to leave the room, and I said I would lie on my side in the meditation pose, which meant I got to giggle away silently to myself until James came back.

After the session we went out for dinner, and held hands and laughed and talked, and for the first time since I got pregnant things felt the way they used to between us. It was a funny feeling, sort of bittersweet, because while I was very excited about the baby coming, I couldn't help remembering all the rows we'd had since I found out I was pregnant, and I wondered whether nights like this, where James and I could talk and talk over a pizza, just the two of us, might never happen again, or not for a very long time.

Jenny advised us that we shouldn't attend antenatal classes where people were going to go on and on about the pain of labour, or where we might be told too many labour horror stories. After my brunch with Robyn and Caro I tended to agree with her, so I skipped quite a few of the classes at the hospital. One of the last classes was all about breastfeeding, though, and I really wanted to learn about that, so I went along. Gemma had already decided she was going to bottle-feed (and believe me, I tried to persuade her otherwise), so she didn't come.

Quite a few of the women who'd been there at the beginning of the course had already given birth and weren't there. I'd had a text from Susie and she'd had her baby . . . she'd had an amazing hypnobirthing and water-birth experience. She said she'd write me a long email all about it when she had the chance. Louise's due date had come and gone, so I was really surprised when I walked in to see her sitting by the open window on an upright chair, fanning herself with a sheaf of notes and looking none too happy.

'Hi,' I said, going over. We hadn't really been in contact, and I was a bit worried that things would be awkward, but she gave me a big, relieved grin.

'Hello, you!' she said warmly. 'Look, do me a favour, please don't say, 'Why are you still here?', or 'Gosh, thought we wouldn't see you here again,' or definitely not 'Still pregnant?' Because believe me, I've heard them all, a hundred times, this week already.'

'How overdue are you?'

'Five days. Nearly a week. One hundred and twenty hours. Many, many, heavy, hot minutes. I've actually been to this breastfeeding class before, but I am so bored of sitting at home and waiting for something to happen, I thought I'd come and do it again.'

'I'm so sorry. I know it's hard not to focus on the due date you were given, but they do say you should see it as a due month rather than a single date.'

'A due *month*? Oh my God, I'm not having another three weeks of this.'

'They'll induce you, though, won't they?'

'I'm having a sweep, where they loosen the membrane through your cervix, tomorrow. If that doesn't work, I have to wait another five days before they'll induce me.'

'Induction's supposed to be really painful, though, isn't it?' I said, doubtfully.

'Not if you're numb from the waist down!' said Louise cheerfully, and I remembered she wanted an epidural. Well, each to her own, I say.

'Well, I hope it happens soon, or at least if you have to wait I hope it cools down a bit.'

'I know! This has to be the worst possible weather to be heavily pregnant. I'm just sweltering all the time.'

'Me too. I spend hours at home sitting with my feet in a bucket of ice water. Not elegant, but it's the only thing that cools me down.'

'Really?' Louise said. 'That sounds like bliss.

I'll give it a go when I get home.'

'Where's home now?' I asked. She obviously wasn't working any more, so I supposed she'd moved out of Adam's house.

'Ah . . . well, it's not what I'd have chosen, but Brian and I have ended up sharing a flat in the centre of Kingston. It's small. Very small. Way too small for a woman this shape and a man his size.'

'Are you . . . '

'Together? No. He just had nowhere to go. It's an awful situation, but what can you do? He keeps telling me I messed up his life and that I have to help him now.'

'You messed up his life? Louise, he's the one who cheated on his wife and got someone else pregnant. He has to take some responsibility for his actions and get off his arse and do something to change the situation.'

'Ah, we've had that conversation about a hundred times. He keeps saying he needs time, and to be honest, I just don't have the energy to fight him any more. Anyway, it can't go on forever. I think he's starting to do something. He seems to spend ages online and talking on his phone in his room. Maybe he's about to get a job.'

'Is he helping financially?'

'A bit, but I'm okay. I saved practically every penny I made working for Harper Graphics. I can take a good few months off without having to worry.'

I'd forgotten what Louise was like . . . she's so resourceful and independent. It makes me feel like a right ditzy, useless blonde, I can tell you.

'And what about . . . was it Adam?'

Louise smiled a little. 'Adam, yes. Harper Graphics is his company.'

'There was a little something going on between you, wasn't there?'

'Well, kind of, but he was understandably hacked off when he found out Brian was living in the house, so he asked me to move out.'

'Ouch.'

'It was pretty horrible. Anyway, he's back, and I ran into him in town the other day.'

'And?'

'Well, we didn't have any major, life-changing conversations, if that's what you're asking. But we had a cup of coffee, and a chat. I explained a bit about Brian, and I hope . . . well, I hope maybe we can be friends after all. I told him we could meet up again after the baby was born. I just didn't expect to have to wait so damned long!'

Anyway, then the class started, and very interesting it was too. I learned loads, and I got really excited that in a week or so I was going to meet my baby and feed him or her. When the class was finished, Louise struggled to her feet.

'Right, I'm off to find the biggest bucket I can, empty the contents of my freezer into it and stick my feet in.' She picked up her bag and gave me her trademark wide grin.

'Lou,' I said, not sure how to say what I wanted to say, 'I'm sorry. I know I judged you, and, well, I'm sorry. I hope things are okay for you and the sprog.'

'That's okay,' she said. 'I deserved to be judged. I'm living with the consequences of my actions, so I'm doing my best to make things all right.'

'Well, I hope the consequences of your actions will have made you a nice dinner when you get in,' I said, smiling.

'Fat chance,' Louise laughed. 'I'll ring the Chinese on my way home and they'll deliver.'

We said goodbye then, and, on impulse, I went to give her a kiss and a hug. It was a funny old hug, with our enormous bumps getting in the way. But it was nice. 'I'll give you a ring in the week,' I said.

'Do. I'd like that. And I'll let you know as soon as I pop. And don't you dare go and have yours before me!' Then she waved goodbye, clambered into her little car and was off.

Gemma

As the late-summer weather grew muggier and cloudier, Gemma felt less inclined to go out. Her dad handed her his credit card and told her to stock up on DVDs, so she bought a few films and box sets of her favourite US sitcoms and dramas and settled herself on the sofa in the air-conditioned living room every day for hours on end. Ben popped in sometimes, but he never stayed for long, and he spent half his time texting Kat. He'd had a massive argument with his mum about her not passing on Gemma's message. Gemma felt a bit guilty that she'd caused them to row, but the up side was that Hannah had backed off and stopped ringing her and visiting all the time. Now Toni was on maternity leave, she came round too sometimes, bringing biscuits, caramel popcorn and ice cream. Most of the time, though, Gemma was happy to settle on the big sofa on her own, feet up, cool drink close at hand and the remote balanced on her bump.

She knew about Braxton-Hicks contractions: she'd been having a few a day for weeks on end. She knew that the painless but intense tightenings of the muscles of her uterus were just practice contractions, but, one steamy, humid Tuesday, they seemed to be coming more frequently than usual. Maybe it was the heat, or the fact that she had drunk several glasses of fruit juice. She'd noticed the baby got more active if she had sugar.

She had one quite intense one, when her uterus went as hard as a rock, during the title sequence of an episode of *Desperate House-wives*. Then she had another one as the next episode was starting. She picked up the DVD case and idly noted that the episodes were forty-two minutes long. She got up to get another drink, and glanced at her watch. It was two fifteen. When the next Braxton-Hicks came, she checked the time again. Two fifty. Thirty-five minutes since the last one. It was funny, she didn't remember them coming so often before.

She suddenly felt restless, as if her legs were desperate to move, and she couldn't bear the idea of sitting around on the sofa any longer. She went upstairs to shower and change out of her scruffy tracksuit bottoms. Maybe she'd go and sit out in the garden in the shade for a bit, or even go for a little walk. But as she washed in the shower, she glanced down and saw a smear of something on the tiles of the shower floor. When she crouched down to look, she saw it was a blob of mucus, with a little blood in it. Had it come from inside her? It must have. As she stood up to wash her hair, another contraction squeezed her belly, and this time it was mildly painful, like an intense, but brief period pain.

She finished showering and towelled herself. When she dried between her legs, there was an unmistakable smear of blood. Despite the heat of the afternoon, she felt suddenly chilled and began to shake. Was this it? Was the baby coming? It was too early! She was only thirty-seven weeks pregnant. She tried to think. Her father was at work in the City, obviously. Her mother had gone into town too, for an all-day spa break at the Sanctuary. Her mobile would be off, and she'd be unreachable . . . and anyway, she was a forty-minute train journey away too. Ben. She'd ring Ben, and Toni. Maybe Toni could tell her she was just being silly and that everyone had symptoms like this a few weeks before the baby came. Yes, she'd ring Toni first. But Toni's phone went straight to her voicemail, and when Gemma thought about it she remembered Toni had an antenatal appointment that afternoon. She wouldn't be long, though, surely? Gemma rang back and left a message: 'Hi, Toni, it's me. Um, I'm having some pains, and there's been a little bit of blood . . . I think it might be the show. Can you call me? I'm worried I might be in labour, but maybe I'm just being silly. It's too early, anyway, so I'm sure it's nothing. Anyway, it's um . . . about half past three.'

She got dressed slowly, and put a sanitary towel in her knickers, although there was no sign of any more blood. She checked her watch. She hadn't had a Braxton-Hicks, or contraction, or whatever for a while . . . maybe it was all a false alarm. Maybe it was . . . oh God. The next contraction was unmistakable, intense and actually quite painful, and seemed to go on for a good thirty seconds or so. She picked up her phone, her hand shaking, and dialled Ben. Thank God, thank God, he answered on the first ring.

'Ben . . . ' She didn't worry about polite niceties. 'I think I'm in labour,' she said, and burst into tears.

'Are you at home?'

'Yes.'

'Can you get to the front door and put it on the latch? Do that and go and lie down, and I'll be there as soon as I can. I'm coming right now, Gem, don't worry,' he said, and he rang off.

She made her way downstairs slowly, holding on to the banister with both hands, and did as Ben had asked. She didn't want to lie down or even sit down, so she went into the kitchen and made herself sip some fruit juice. Should she ring the hospital? Not yet. She'd wait for Ben to come. They could ring together. When the next contraction came, it was just ten minutes since the one she'd had upstairs. Things seemed to be speeding up very quickly indeed. This wasn't at all like they'd said it would be in the antenatal classes. 'Seventy-five per cent of first babies are late,' Donna had said reassuringly. 'And, with a first labour, from your first twinge, in most cases, you're looking at at least twelve hours till you see your little one for the first time. So you should have plenty of time to get to the birth unit calmly and slowly.'

Calmly and slowly, my arse, Gemma thought, as another contraction came, just eight minutes later. Where the hell was Ben? That was when she remembered that Donna had also said, 'Every labour is different, though. You might just pop your baby out in three hours, or you might go twenty-four hours and need a Caesarean.

There's no way of knowing.'

When Ben arrived, a few minutes later, she was on all fours on the kitchen floor panting like a dog. She looked up when he rushed in. He was sweating and red-faced, his hair all over the place.

'You look a mess!' she said between breaths. He was kind enough not to comment on what she looked like.

'I ran all the way here,' he said, falling on his knees beside her. 'I waited at the bus stop for about ninety seconds, and I couldn't bear to wait any longer. There's a massive traffic jam up and down the high street in both directions. What's happening?'

'Contractions, basically,' she said sitting back on her knees. 'They're coming closer and closer together, and each one is longer and more painful.'

'How close together?'

'Six minutes apart, the last two.'

'That's close.'

'I think . . . um, I think you should call an ambulance, Ben,' she said. He didn't argue, just took out his phone and dialled 999.

He went into the next room, and she heard him giving information to the controller. He came back in to ask her for the postcode, but she was having another contraction. As soon as it finished, she gasped it out and he passed it on. When he hung up, he came to sit next to her on the floor.

'They say there's been a big accident on the motorway, that's why there's a traffic jam, and that most of the ambulances have been called over there. They're making us a priority, she says, but, well, it might be a little while.'

Gemma burst into tears, and Ben awkwardly put his arm around her.

'Do you want to get off the floor?' he said tentatively. 'Maybe go and lie on your bed?'

'I don't want to lie down!' she growled. 'This is the most comfortable position and I like the floor, it's cold.'

'Okay . . . ' he said, 'but can I get you some towels or something? For your knees, and in case . . . '

At that moment, her waters broke, drenching her lower half and making her cry harder. Ben ran up the stairs, opening doors until he found the airing cupboard. He grabbed an armful of thick towels and ran back down to Gemma. He gently helped her to take off her soaked track-suit bottoms and dried her, then wrapped a clean, dry towel around her waist.

Thirty minutes later, and the ambulance still hadn't arrived. With each contraction, Gemma growled and howled. She couldn't believe the animal noises that came out of her. Ben was clearly terrified, but he kept close to her, rubbing her back when she let him, and giving her water when she asked for it in between the contractions. She tried standing for a while, but the intensity of the pain drove her back on to her knees. Ben took Gemma's mobile and rang both her mum and her dad. Both phones went to voicemail and he left messages, hoping he sounded like it was urgent, but not totally panicked.

Gemma, who had been crouching down with her face close to the floor, suddenly straightened up and stared at Ben, her face streaked with tears. 'Ben, I need to push. I need to push now. The ambulance isn't going to get here in time.'

'I'll ring them again,' Ben said, almost crying, reaching for his phone.

'There isn't time,' Gemma sobbed. 'I need to push now!'

'Um . . . wait!' Ben yelled. He was crying too now. 'Don't you need to wait for the contraction? Gemma, wait. I don't know what to do! I don't know what to do! What if something goes wrong?'

'How much more wrong can it go?'

And then, like an answer to a prayer, they heard the front door open.

'Mummy?' said Gemma plaintively, and Ben prayed with all his heart it was a paramedic.

'It's me,' said Toni, rushing in and falling awkwardly on her knees next to Gemma. 'You didn't answer your phone, so I thought I'd just come over.' She looked at Gemma's desperate face and the drenched towels. 'Oh my God!'

'It's coming now, Toni . . . I can't stop it. It's coming right now.'

'Okay,' said Toni, and her voice seemed deep and calm, and very grown-up to Gemma. 'Spread your knees, and let's wait for the next surge.'

'Surge?'

'Contraction. In hypnobirthing they say 'surge' to separate the muscle action from the idea of pain.'

'It's not an idea! It fucking *hurts*! It feels like I'm going to split in two!'

'Okay,' said Toni. 'Take a deep breath, and I want you to breathe out into your bum, with the sur — contraction.'

'Breathe into her bum?' said Ben.

'Shut up,' growled Gemma, 'I know what she means.'

And she did. It felt like there was an earthquake in her body, a cataclysmic event so huge that every muscle was straining together. When the contraction built to a peak, she focused all her attention down.

'I can see her head,' cried Toni. 'Keep going!'

'Should she still be on all fours like that?' asked Ben, his voice high and scared. 'Shouldn't she lie down?'

Both women ignored him. Gemma suddenly let out all her breath in a big whoosh and flopped forward on to her arms.

'She's coming out with the next one, lovely. You're doing amazingly,' said Toni, patting her on the hip. It seemed to Gemma that she had only taken two or three ragged breaths when she felt the force building again.

She heard Toni's voice from far, far away, 'Breathe down!'

Through the hammering in her head, she heard Ben say 'Oh my God!' and there was a rushing, tearing agony between her legs, and Toni cried, 'I've got her!'

Gemma toppled over sideways. Ben caught her and laid her down on the pile of towels, and Toni placed a slippery, bloody little body in her

354

arms. Gemma looked down at her daughter's beautiful little face. The baby hiccupped and sobbed, and then let out a healthy yell. Gemma couldn't speak, but a high noise, half-giggle, half-sob escaped her.

'We need to keep them warm,' said Toni, and began swaddling Gemma and the baby in towels.

'There's so much blood,' said Ben. 'It keeps coming out of her.'

Gemma looked between her legs, and there was a massive puddle of blood and gunk. 'I'm very tired,' she said faintly.

'Don't go to sleep!' Ben said urgently, but she wasn't sure why she shouldn't. She wanted to, so badly. As she closed her eyes, she was vaguely aware that the kitchen was filling with large people in yellow high-visibility vests clattering about. Her mum would be furious about the floor.

Toni

I didn't even notice that I had blood on me, but when I walked in the door at home, James went white. 'Jesus Christ!' he said, rushing to me. 'What happened? Shall I call an ambulance? Are you having contractions?'

'What? No!' I said, shocked. 'I'm fine! Why are you panicking?'

'I got home and you weren't here. And look at the state of you!'

I looked down then, and saw that I had Gemma's blood all down my trousers, and, when I looked in the mirror, there was a smear of something unidentifiable on my cheek too. The taxi driver must have thought I was a right weirdo.

'It's not my blood,' I explained. 'It's Gemma's.'

'Gemma?'

'Gemma's baby was born . . . on the kitchen floor . . . and I delivered it!'

'You what?' James took my hand and led me over to the sofa, and, in my usual muddled way, I told him the whole story.

'I never thought that the first birth I'd see, and the first newborn baby, wouldn't be ours! But it was amazing. Totally amazing. I can't wait now, love. I'm so, so excited to do it myself!'

'You weirdo!' James laughed. 'So there was loads of blood and screaming, and Gemma got rushed off to hospital, and you can't wait to do it?'

'Ours won't be like that. Ours will be calm and beautiful. I just know it.'

'And is Gemma okay? And the baby?'

'She's fine. She bled quite a lot, but the paramedics arrived about two minutes after the baby was born, and her mum got there about five minutes after. They took her off to hospital, and they said she might need a transfusion, but she'd be okay. And the baby . . . well, she's tiny, and perfect and absolutely beautiful. Just like her mum. Ben, the dad was there, and he couldn't stop crying looking at her.'

James put his arms around me. 'Well, all I care about is that you're okay. I'm sure you're not supposed to be kneeling on kitchen floors delivering babies when you're thirty-nine weeks pregnant.'

'I'm fine, honest. It was the most incredible experience I've ever had. And Gemma was amazing! It was a freakishly quick labour . . . from her first proper contraction to a baby in her arms, it took just over four hours.'

I was still on a high. I talked and talked about it. I know millions and billions of women have had babies, and if you haven't had one yourself or been there when one was born, you've seen it in the films. But honest to God, it *is* a miracle. There's no other way to describe it. One minute there's this woman straining and pushing, and the next there's another person in the room. A whole complete, breathing other person. James just let me talk and talk, but after a while, I could see he'd heard enough. I suddenly thought of Louise. I know she and Gemma weren't speaking, but I'm sure she'd want to know that the baby had been born . . . not that she'd be all that thrilled . . . Gemma was due four weeks after she was.

I grabbed my mobile and dialled her number. It wasn't till it was ringing that I looked at my watch and realised it was already nearly 10 p.m. A bit late to be ringing someone, especially an overdue pregnant woman who probably wasn't getting much sleep anyway. I was about to cut off the call when she answered. She must have been really fast asleep, though.

'Hello,' she said, 'Louise's phone.' Her voice sounded incredibly gruff and deep.

Then I realised that of course it wasn't Lou, but a man answering her phone. Why was a man answering her phone?

'Why is a man answering Louise's phone?' I blurted. I really should learn to ask questions properly.

'This is Brian,' the voice said. 'Who am I speaking to?'

'This is Lou's friend, Toni. Can I speak to her?' I didn't want to spend my time chatting to the faithless husband. And anyway, why the hell did he have her phone? Sometimes I'm really thick, because it should have been perfectly obvious why he had her phone.

'She can't talk right now,' he said. 'She's feeding.'

'She's feeding? Oh my God, she had the baby? When? How?'

'About an hour ago. She went into labour this morning. Everything went according to plan, she had the epidural and Peter was born at 9 p.m.'

'Peter? She's calling him Peter? How was the labour?'

He sighed. I could hear he didn't really want to talk to me . . . I'm sure he was a bit wary of speaking to Louise's friends. Would they know who he was? And want to kill him?

'The labour was fine, as far as I know. Simon, her brother, was in with her.'

'And the weight? And what does he look like?' I thought if I just kept asking questions, he'd have to keep answering. But he cut me off.

'Look, why don't you ring back in the morning, and speak to Louise? Or to Simon? They'd be able to tell you more.'

It wasn't till I'd rung off that it occurred to me that he didn't sound as thrilled as a man should be who'd given up everything to be there for the birth of his only son.

So Louise had Peter, and Gemma had Baby Girl Hamilton (I didn't know what her name was, if she had one yet), and I had the biggest belly south of the Thames, and not a single sign of labour. But there was no point in sitting around brooding and paying too much attention to every tiny twinge, so the next day, I went baby gift-shopping, and then went to get acquainted with the two new arrivals.

I went round to Louise's first. She'd only spent one night in hospital and then taken her baby home. It turned out her new flat was about a ten-minute walk from our house. Brian let me in, muttered hello and disappeared into another room. I found Louise settled on the sofa with baby Peter fast asleep in her arms. Something had changed in her face. She looked softer, somehow. Maybe it was just tiredness. But she gave me her lovely big grin when I came in.

'Look what you did!' I said, sitting down beside her. He was a big chap, that was for sure, and there was no doubt he was going to be a fiery red ginger of note.

'What did he weigh?'

'Just on nine pounds,' said Louise proudly.

'Ouch!'

'Well, I was lucky and I only had a little tear. It's a bit sore to sit down, but I didn't need stitches and they reckon it'll be all healed up in a week or so.'

'And the feeding?'

'Don't let anyone lie to you. It bloody hurts! But the midwife's been coming round every day and she tells me it will get easier. We're getting better at the latching on, and he seems to have the idea, so it's all good.'

Brian pottered in. 'Tea, anyone?' he said.

'Not for me, thanks,' said Louise. 'Although I'd love some more iced water if it's going. What about you, Toni?'

'Iced water for me too.'

Brian brought two glasses of water from the kitchen. He put them down and, briefly, gently touched Peter on the head, then went off to his bedroom again. Well, I didn't need Louise to tell me there was nothing going on between her and Brian. I've never seen two people with less of a spark between them. It wasn't like they hated each other or anything, they just didn't seem to really . . . see each other at all, if you know what I mean.

'So how's he been?' I whispered.

'Who, Brian? Okay, I suppose. He's had two kids so he's better at things like nappies and bathing than I am. But I don't know . . . his heart doesn't really seem to be in it. I mean, he's gentle with Peter and everything, but I'm so totally head over heels in love with my baby and he seems . . . I don't know. Not so excited.'

'Well, this is his third time.'

'I know. And the circumstances are not really ideal. But still. My brother Simon was amazing at the birth . . . really supportive and calm, and then when Peter came out, he just sobbed and sobbed, and sat holding him and gazing at him for absolute ages. And he's only an uncle. Brian's the dad and he doesn't act like that at all.'

'Maybe it's hard for Brian to bond because he wasn't there at the birth.'

'I don't think he saw his other two born either. Still, I shouldn't complain. He's been very helpful.'

'Helpful' sounded like . . . what was that expression my dad always used . . . damning with faint praise? I didn't say so, though.

Peter picked that moment to open his eyes and make the sweetest little snuffling noise. His eyes were unfocused, but they were the most amazing navy blue. He yawned and spread his little starfish hands and gazed up at his mum, and I swear, I thought Louise would just burst with

361

pride. 'Are you hungry, little egg?' she said softly, and went through a whole rigmarole of hoiking out a boob, laying Peter on her special support cushion, lining him up and getting the nipple in his mouth. It took quite a few goes, and when he started sucking, she jumped and breathed in sharply.

'Bloody hell. I have such admiration for the mums I've seen breastfeeding who just sling the baby into their laps and plug them on . . . it's such a mission for Peter and me. Still, we're doing it ten times a day . . . practice must make perfect, I suppose!'

Now he was latched on, Peter looked like he was going to be on there for quite a while, and Louise's whole attention was focused on him. I finished my water, had a wee, called a quiet goodbye to Brian and let myself out.

★ ★ ★

I went round to see Gemma the next afternoon. She was settled in her lovely girly bedroom in the big Hamilton house, with the baby in a Moses basket next to the bed. Now she was cleaned up, the little girl was even more beautiful than she had been when I saw her born. She looked absolutely tiny compared to great bonny Peter, although considering she was three weeks early, she'd been a reasonable weight: six pounds, eight ounces. Gemma still looked pale and a bit peaky, but she seemed rested and cheerful.

'My mum and dad have paid for a night nurse for the first ten days or so. She has Millie in her room and she does all the night feeds so I can sleep.'

'Millie? Is that her name?'

'Well, I call her Millie, but she's really Emilia. Um . . . if it's okay with you, Emilia Antonia.'

I got all teary at this, not really a big surprise. I've never had anyone name a baby after me before (although I did have a boyfriend in junior school who called his goldfish Toni). 'That's fine with me,' I managed to say. 'Emilia Antonia Hamilton? She's destined to marry an earl at the very least, with that name.'

'She could be Prime Minister,' said Gemma proudly. 'She can do anything she wants. I'm not going to dress her in pink or make her do ballet. She's going to study physics and languages and we're going to travel together.'

'Wow . . . giving birth has turned you into a feminist!' I said, surprised.

'I want her to be braver than me,' said Gemma softly, touching the lacy blanket that Millie was swaddled in.

'Are you regretting this?'

'No, not at all!' She looked shocked at the suggestion. 'But now I understand why people turn into pushy parents, sort of. I just want the world for her.'

I stayed with Gemma for an hour or so, but Millie stayed asleep. Then Ben arrived to spend some time with them. They both gazed adoringly at their daughter. Ben seemed all right . . . just, and I know this sounds stupid . . . very, very young. I suppose I'd got used to Gemma's age, but, looking at Ben, he really is just a kid. Half an hour later, the night nurse arrived and started bustling around and organising things. That was my cue to go, so I set off home.

That evening, I told James all about it. 'It's amazing . . . both Lou and Gemma seem quite different, like the whole experience of having a baby has changed them.'

'In a good way?'

'I think so. I suppose it's that weird thing of realising there's someone in the world who matters more to you than yourself.'

'You matter more to me than myself,' said James.

'Thank you, love, that's the right thing to say, of course, but it's, you know, conditional. If I murdered someone, or shagged your best mate or stole all your money, you'd stop loving me. You can't stop loving your child . . . ever.'

'No, I suppose you can't. Even if they grow long hair and listen to terrible music, or support Manchester United.'

I giggled at that. 'Oh, I forgot to tell you the best bit!' I said suddenly. 'Gemma has a night nurse.'

'What, like the cold medicine, or like the song?'

'Neither. It's a special maternity nurse who comes in at night and takes care of the baby so Gemma can sleep.'

'Wow, what does that cost?'

'A lot to the likes of us, pennies to the Hamiltons, I'm sure. Anyway, I met her. She's a large, northern woman with a bosom like a shelf and a proper, old-fashioned nurse's uniform.'

'I bet poor little Millie's too scared to cry at night,' said James.

'I'm sure she is. But the best part is her name. She's called Sister Nethercleft.'

'You made that up!' said James.

'I did not. She had a name tag and everything.'

'Nethercleft?'

'Nethercleft.'

'Sister Bumcrack?'

'Indeed,' I said, and we started to laugh.

And that was when I felt the very weird sensation inside, like a swelling. And even though I'd never felt anything like it before, I knew it was my waters breaking. I jumped up with great agility, and made it to the bathroom and slammed the door before the flood poured out of me. James was right behind me. I heard him tapping on the door.

'Toni? Are you OK?'

'My waters have gone,' I said, in a faint, sick voice. 'There's a big mess.'

'What do you need me to do? Shall I ring the hospital?'

'James, there's greenish stuff in the water. And it smells awful.'

'What does that mean?'

'It's meconium. Stuff from the baby's bowels. Basically, It's done a poo.'

'Is that bad?'

'It can be, especially if there's a lot of stuff.'

'Well, is there? Is there a lot?'

'I don't know. It looks like a lot to me. James, come in.'

He opened the door then and came into the

bathroom. He took one look at the puddle of gunk on the floor around my feet, and he said, 'I'm calling an ambulance.'

Things happened very quickly after that. James rang, and I was luckier than Gemma, an ambulance was there in minutes. As it was late evening, we got to the hospital really quickly. Through everything, I just kept doing my hypnobirthing breathing and holding on to James' hand like it was my lifeline. I wasn't in pain or anything, but I also couldn't feel the baby moving very much. Maybe now the waters were gone he or she was a bit more squashed.

They examined me and put on a foetal monitor. I could see that the midwife didn't look happy. She kept checking the readout, and then she went off and came back with a young doctor. The doctor looked at the printed sheet, then stood watching the paper spooling out of the machine for another minute or so. She was young and Asian . . . very pretty, but she looked even younger than me. Gemma's age, if that was possible, which of course it wasn't.

'Okay, Toni,' she said in a very calm voice. 'It looks as if your baby is in some distress. I'm going to recommend an emergency caesarean, and that we prep you for theatre right away.'

'But I'm doing hypnobirthing!' I said. 'I can't — '

'Do it.' I've never heard James sound so firm. 'Take her to theatre right now. Can I come too?'

'A nurse will take you to clean up and get scrubs and a mask,' said the doctor.

Before I knew it, James was gone, and my bed

was being wheeled down the corridor, very quickly it seemed. I tried to keep doing the breathing, but I was so, so scared. I remember seeing those circular theatre lights above my head, and hearing a kindly voice as I was hoisted off the bed and on to an operating table. I kept breathing and counting in my head, trying to visualise my special, calm place, but then I felt a needle go into my arm, and everything went . . .

★ ★ ★

Waking up from an anaesthetic is very peculiar, because it just feels like waking up at any other time. Except you didn't go to sleep, and you're not in your bed, and there's pain and noise and lights and nausea, and more than anything, you want to ask someone where the hell you are, but you feel so damned sore and sick that you can't.

It took me a good few minutes (not to mention a bit of retching into a kidney bowl, while crying and holding my stomach), to work out I was in a hospital bed and the birth I'd been looking forward to for nine months had happened, and I'd missed it. First I realised that the person holding the bowl for me to throw up into was James. Then I realised that the stomach I was holding was a mass of wobbliness and not a big taut ball any more. And then I sat up as best I could and looked around wildly.

'Where's my baby?'

'He's okay,' said James soothingly. 'He's breathed in a bit of the meconium stuff so they're keeping an eye on him. But he's going to be fine.'

'He? It's a boy?'

'He's bloody gorgeous,' said James. 'Lots of blond hair.'

'I want to see him!' I started to cry.

'I know, sweetie. As soon as they let me, I'll put you in a wheelchair and wheel you over.'

'I have to hold him! We have to have skin-to-skin contact to bond. Did you do skin-to-skin? Please tell me you did.'

'I couldn't,' said James. 'They had to take him straight away to clear his lungs. But we'll hold him every minute as soon as we can.'

I lay back on the pillows, and the tears just kept falling. This was so not how I imagined it. Me, full of stitches, lying in a hospital bed, my baby somewhere else, sick, alone, without me.

The hospital staff were amazing, though. Within a few minutes, a nurse came and helped me into a wheelchair. She gave me a big handful of tissues to mop up the tears, and she and James wheeled me through to the baby ICU. And there he was, my little son, with a tube up his nose and his scrawny little chest struggling for breath. It was the most heartbreaking thing I've ever seen.

'Don't worry,' said the lovely nurse. 'He's a big, strong boy. This is just a little setback. He'll be right as rain in a day or two.'

I stroked his hand and he grabbed hold of my finger. 'Wow! His grip is so strong!' I gasped.

'He's a fighter,' said the nurse.

James pulled up a chair on the other side of the little crib and took hold of our little boy's other hand. And together we sat and watched him fight.

THE FIRST THREE
MONTHS

Toni

The lovely nurse was right. He was as right as rain. For the first two days, I basically sat next to his bed 24/7 with a breast pump attached to one of my boobs. At first, I produced little teaspoonfuls of colostrum (that's the first, yellowy milk — you only get a tiny bit, but it's very important that the baby gets it), but then my proper milk came in. Now let me tell you, I might have been a bit rubbish at giving birth, but I was born to breastfeed. I woke up on the third morning, and I swear I'd swapped boobs with Jordan. Without putting too fine a point on it, they were sodding enormous! Blimp enormous. 44-EEEnormous. When I showed James, he laughed out loud, and then looked like a little boy whose Christmas and birthdays and tickets to the Cup Final had all arrived on the same day. I felt a bit sorry for him . . . it wasn't like he was going to get to play with them any time soon.

When I sat down to express, well, the milk started to just pour into the bottle. When one of the nurses saw, she asked if I'd like to donate some for the sick and premature babies in the neonatal ICU. 'Okay,' I said dubiously, 'as long as there's enough for Harry.'

And there I go again, getting things in the wrong order. That's his name. Well, it's Henry, actually, but as soon as that was decided, it got shortened to Harry. He weighed seven pounds and ten ounces at birth, and he's got this sweet little quiff of blond hair. Because he was born by C-section, he didn't have that squished look lots of newborns do. As far as James and I were concerned, he was quite simply the most beautiful baby every born. And possibly a genius too. The pinnacle of evolution.

Those days in the hospital, while they were scary and worrying, were actually quite cool. Gemma and Louise couldn't come in because you're not supposed to bring tiny babies back to the hospital, but they texted all the time. Caro and Robyn rushed over with balloons and booze and all sorts of inappropriate gifts and made me laugh so hard I feared for my stitches. James' parents and my dad came and gazed at their new grandchild with all the love in the world. There were loads of people around, and I was this big star because I was doing so well at feeding Harry (and about three other babies too, with my donated milk). He soon lost the tubes, and I could hold him as much as I liked, and feed him myself instead of expressing. And within a few days, he was so much better that we got sent home. Those first days at home were fun too . . . James was on paternity leave, and loads of people came to visit, and everyone brought food and presents and wanted to cuddle Harry.

But then James went back to work, and the visits slowed down and then stopped. And I was on my own at home with Harry, all day long. And then Harry got colic.

I never really knew what colic was before I had Harry. It's just a little word. Five letters.

C-o-l-i-c. I'd heard people talk about 'colicky' babies, and I thought it meant they were a bit irritable. I remembered 'colic' as something horses got, from those pony stories I used to read when I was about eleven. But when it happens to your baby, well . . . then it's more than just a little word. I suppose there are lots of things like that, words that seem small and manageable until they directly affect you. 'Doctoral dissertation'. 'Parachute jump'. 'Root-canal surgery'. Well, 'Baby with colic' is right up there.

Harry was fine in the mornings . . . he'd lie quietly in his carrycot, looking at the world, or feed, or sleep. But like clockwork between 2 and 3 p.m., he'd start to grunt and pull up his knees, and then he'd begin to scream. And he wouldn't stop until he fell asleep, exhausted, at about 8 p.m. It was just awful. I tried everything . . . walking up and down with him, jiggling him on my shoulder, holding him very still across my knees. Sometimes, holding him face down so his belly rested on my forearm would work for a little while and he'd stop and whimper, and even doze for a while. But it never worked for long, and besides, I'd get tired and so sore from standing and holding him. My C-section scar would start to pull, my back would ache and I always seemed to need the loo. Because of the screaming, I couldn't go out, and I didn't want visitors to come round either. It wasn't like I could chat politely to a visitor while poor Harry howled his little lungs out. So every afternoon became this endless, endless torture for both of us. By five thirty, I'd be standing by the window, praying that somehow James would have got off work early and would be coming down the road. But of course it would be another hour before he finally came through the door, at which point I'd thrust Harry into his arms and dash off to the loo. I needed to do that firstly because I was bursting to pee, but secondly because then I could bury my face in a towel and sob for a minute or two.

I looked it up, and there's no cure for colic. There are some drops and medicines you can try, but they didn't help Harry at all. The health visitor, or as James and I learned to call her, the total moron, suggested that maybe my breast milk disagreed with him, so against my better judgment I offered him a bottle of formula. Well, that made it ten times worse, so the formula went in the bin and the health visitor went on the shit-list. The best anyone could offer me was to say — 'It usually gets better after twelve weeks.' Which, when your baby is two weeks old, means you have at least seventy days of watching him scream for six hours at a stretch, and you can't do a damned thing to stop it. And that's *if* it got better at twelve weeks, because there's no guarantee of that. It can go on longer.

So that was my life — completely overtaken by the monster, Colic, a five-letter word that I'd never given a moment's thought to before. I'd imagined brunches in the sun with Gemma or Louise and their babies, strolls by the river with Caro and Robyn pushing the pushchair and stopping at every pub, proudly taking Harry into the office to show off to everyone there. I'd imagined handing Harry over to a babysitter and going dancing, for heaven's sake! The reality was, I often didn't even get to brush my teeth or eat anything more complicated than a slice of bread with nothing on it, let alone dress up and go out. If you'd told me a year ago that this was where I'd be this September, I'd have laughed at you. Well, let me tell you, nobody's laughing now.

Louise

Rachel, polite as always, sent a beautiful display of flowers with a blue teddy bear to the hospital when Peter was born, but she didn't come to see him. Louise wasn't surprised that Rachel didn't come to visit her in the flat . . . she wouldn't want to do that while Brian was there. So, one sunny Wednesday, when Peter was just over a week old, she spent an hour packing an enormous bag of nappies, spare clothes, muslin cloths, blankets and other paraphernalia. She carefully strapped him into his car seat and gingerly carried him down to the car. Brian came along to help her strap the car seat into position. She got into the car and pulled out into the traffic cautiously. She'd always been a confident driver, but she had never driven a car with a more precious cargo. The journey to Rachel's house should have taken fifteen minutes, but as she crawled along it took more like half an hour. She even stopped twice to check on Peter, who slept peacefully through the whole rigmarole.

She got out of the car, and was wrestling the car seat out of the seatbelt when Rachel came out of the front door. Louise stood up. She couldn't read Rachel's face at all; it was a blank mask.

'Hey, Rach,' she said warmly. 'I didn't know if you'd want to see me, but your nephew really wanted to meet you. He's so excited, he's fast asleep.'

Rachel didn't say anything, but she came round to the passenger side of Louise's car. Louise stepped back so Rachel could see, and she peered in at Peter's serene, sleeping face.

'He's beautiful,' she said, and touched his cheek gently. Peter huffed and sighed in his sleep.

'Can we come in?' asked Louise gently.

Rachel said nothing for a bit. She just kept looking at Peter's sleeping face.

'Okay,' she said finally. 'Will he wake up?'

'He's due for a feed soon, so I'm sure he will.'

Louise followed Rachel into the house, and when Rachel went into the kitchen to make tea, she settled herself in the living room. Peter began to wriggle in his car seat, so she took him out. As soon as he smelt her, he immediately began to root. When Rachel came back in with a tea tray, he was busy feeding. A spasm passed over her face. 'So you're breastfeeding,' she said. 'I didn't think you would.'

'It was difficult at first, but we're getting the hang of it.'

Rachel poured tea and served biscuits. 'So how was the birth?'

'Surprisingly calm. Simon was amazing . . . very strong and supportive. Although he did cry like a big girl when Peter was actually born.'

'He said it was the most amazing thing he's ever seen,' said Rachel.

Louise could see how very, very hard this was for Rachel. She wished she could make it easier . . . make the pain and the envy go away, make the awkwardness between them disappear. But she didn't know how. She leaned forward to get her tea and Rachel pushed her cup closer. They sat in silence for a time while Peter fed, then he unlatched and Louise gently winded him over her shoulder.

'Would you like to hold him?'

'Er . . . not yet, if that's okay,' said Rachel.

'That's fine.' Louise took a blanket out of her bag and spread it on the floor in a patch of sun by the window. She laid Peter on the blanket, and let him gaze at the trees outside and wave his arms and legs. After a while, Rachel came to sit beside them on the floor. She waited a few minutes, and then held out a finger to Peter. He grasped it and turned his fuzzy gaze on her.

Later, as Louise drove home, she thought that it had been a reasonably good first visit. Rachel hadn't thrown her out, or picked a fight, or even asked about Brian. She hadn't been full of love and forgiveness either, or melted and cuddled her nephew. But it was a first step.

Gemma

Gemma wasn't kidding herself. She knew she had it good. Millie was a very sweet, placid baby, who very quickly settled into a predictable routine, feeding every four hours during the day and every six at night. The formidable Sister Nethercleft helped a lot in getting things organised. Ben came round every day, and wanted to spend time holding and playing with his daughter, so if Gemma was tired she could go off for a nap, and, amazingly, her father, always an early riser, had got into the habit of taking Millie into his study in the morning to give Gemma an hour's extra sleep. She had never expected him to be an involved granddad, but he seemed to love having Millie beside him in her little bouncy chair as he checked the progress of the Asian markets. Samantha was less involved, and didn't seem to want to hold the baby or feed her, but if Gemma needed anything she was happy to buy it for her. She was going to be the grandmother who threw money at the problem, it seemed.

Hannah and Ben's relationship had been strained since their row about her answering Ben's phone, and Ben wanted to stop her seeing Millie at all, but Kat eventually calmed him down. Then Hannah started going round to Gemma's every day, staying for ages and commenting on everything that Gemma did with Millie.

'Isn't she a bit cold?' she'd say, when Gemma

379

put Millie down on her sheepskin in just a vest and nappy so she could kick her legs. And when Gemma winded Millie, Hannah would say briskly, 'You haven't got all the air out. Give her to me. Nanna will fix it.'

At her wits' end, Gemma spoke to Ben and said his mum was stressing her out, and that led to another massive fight between Ben and his mum. Eventually, though, they negotiated a truce with Hannah, and she visited Gemma and Millie every Friday and had Millie over to visit without Gemma on a Sunday afternoon for a few hours. Gemma was enormously relieved: Hannah was a big help now she wasn't hanging over her, criticising her every parenting decision.

Gemma went round to see Toni in her first week home from the hospital with little Harry. Toni looked shattered . . . the emergency Caesarean and Harry's worrying first days had obviously taken their toll. She was very proudly breastfeeding, and seemed to have Harry plugged on to a boob all the time. Gemma was a bit grossed out . . . she had never wanted to breastfeed. She thought it was animalistic and a bit primitive, but Toni kept going on about how breastfed babies were cleverer and never got sick and were generally superhuman. For Gemma though, she liked the fact that she could just give Millie a bottle and be done with it (or in fact *anyone* could give Millie a bottle, it didn't even have to be her). Also, from what Toni said, she was up half the night feeding too. James was there, looking after Toni and bringing her cups of tea and biscuits and generally being really, really sweet. He was such an amazing guy, always kind, always smiling and making a joke, and he was so, so good-looking. He really was the best-looking guy Gemma had ever met — not a handsome boy, like Ben, but a proper, hunky man.

After that first visit, she didn't go and see Toni for a while. It was so easy for the days just to drift past in a haze, playing with Millie, sitting out in the garden with her, reading or watching TV while she slept. But one rainy Thursday, she realised that she hadn't heard from Toni in quite a while. She sent off a quick text, saying 'Hi, fancy a visit tomorrow? Can Millie and I come for afternoon tea?'

There was no reply for ages, then Toni's response came: 'Prob not, sory . . . Hry has COLIC. afternoons bad.'

Gemma knew then that things had to be really awful. Toni was a stickler for punctuation and correct spelling, even in texts — they'd had a conversation about it. For her to send a message like that, Toni had to be in a really bad way.

After what Toni had done for her, delivering Millie, she wanted to do something, however small, in return, so she decided she'd ring that evening. She'd wait till Harry would be asleep.

Once Millie was tucked up at seven, she made herself a cup of tea and went to sit in the kitchen. She rang Toni's mobile, but it went straight to message, so she dialled her home number. Toni answered, and she could hear Harry yelling rhythmically, without stopping, close to the phone.

'James?' said Toni, a real edge of desperation

in her voice. 'Are you nearly here?'

'It's Gemma.' Toni sounded so out of control, she half-regretted ringing at all. 'Are you okay?'

'Gem!' said Toni, trying to sound cheerful, although Harry was still screaming. 'How are you? How's Millie?'

'We're fine. Millie's asleep. Things don't sound so good there, though. Shall I come over and help? My mum's here, she can watch Millie.'

'No, no! James is on his way . . . he was just held up at work. It'll be fine.' There was a heartbreaking catch in Toni's voice.

'Why is he screaming like that?' Gemma couldn't help asking.

'It's colic. He starts mid-afternoon and screams until he falls asleep.'

'When will that be?'

'Another hour, maybe?'

'Oh my God, that must be awful! Toni, how are you coping?'

There was a pause, not a silence, because Harry's squawking continued without a gap, then Toni said, 'Barely. I'm barely coping, to tell you the truth. Oh wow!' she said suddenly. 'I'm looking out of the window and I see James hurrying up the road. My knight in shining Levi's. Gotta go. Thanks for ringing, Gem, honestly.' And she rang off.

Gemma was worried, but she didn't have a clue what to do. She owed Toni so much, but she had no idea how to help her. There was no point in asking Samantha, she'd hate having a conversation about emotional stuff, and then she'd probably just suggest writing Toni a cheque. So

Gemma did something she thought she'd never do. She rang Hannah for advice.

'Ben was colicky,' Hannah said. 'It was hideous. Your poor friend.'

'What can I do to help her?'

'She needs practical help. Do her housework. Take food around. Have you got a pen? I'll dictate you a list of things to buy.'

For once, Gemma was glad Hannah was so bossy.

The next day at two, she knocked on Toni's door. As soon as Toni opened it, Gemma marched in, Millie's car seat in one hand, a large M&S carrier bag in the other. Toni clearly hadn't showered and was still in trackie bottoms, her hair scraped back in a ponytail. Harry was asleep, slumped against her breast. She looked mortified.

'Gem, I wasn't expecting . . . sorry, everything's in such a state.'

'Don't worry about it. I heard how you sounded last night, and I thought, if Toni's going to have a rough afternoon with a screaming baby, she's going to do it with a bucket of chocolate mini-rolls.'

Toni looked like she might cry. 'Gem, you didn't have to.'

'I owe you my baby's life, and probably my life too. Now shut up, sit on the sofa, and tell me what I can do to help.'

Toni protested a lot, but Gemma wore her down. She held Harry while Toni had a shower and got dressed, then she washed up all the dirty dishes in the kitchen and wiped down all the surfaces and put on a load of laundry. Along with sugar and carbohydrate-laden treats, she'd followed Hannah's suggestions and brought soup, bread, fresh pasta and tubs of sauce: things that could easily be shoved in a microwave or prepared one-handed while holding a baby. She made Toni have something to eat (she hadn't had anything but a cup of tea all day), and made her promise she'd get James to make some pasta for their dinner.

She gave the sitting room a quick hoovering, then put down the playmat and let Harry and Millie kick side by side for a while. And when Harry started to scream, she stayed, and she and Toni swapped babies every half an hour or so. She kept chatting, kept joking, kept sending Toni into the other room to give her a break.

She wasn't surprised Toni was at the end of her tether . . . the screaming was just heartbreaking, and when Toni was on her own she couldn't get a moment's peace. But Gemma was proud that with her and Millie there to act as distractions the afternoon seemed a bit easier for Toni.

There was a noise in the hallway, and Toni glanced at her watch.

'Good grief!' she said. 'That's James, home already! Gem, you've been a life-saver. That's the best afternoon I've had since this started. Thank you. Thank you from the bottom of my heart.'

James came in then, tall, breathtakingly handsome, smelling of outside air and a very sexy lemony aftershave.

'Hey, Gemma!' he said, exuberantly kissing

384

her cheek. 'Let's see your little tadpole. Wow, she's a beauty. Just like her mum!'

Then he went over to kiss Toni. 'Love, you look amazing!' he said tenderly.

'You mean, dressed and not smelly. All thanks to Gemma,' said Toni. 'Here, this is yours,' and she shoved Harry into his arms. 'Gotta pee!' And she dashed to the bathroom.

'There's pasta and sauce for your dinner,' said Gemma, gathering up Millie's things and packing her bag. 'Just something easy, so you and Toni can relax.'

James came over and put his free hand on her arm. 'Gemma, I can't thank you enough. I've been worried sick about her, here all day on her own with him. But you've worked a miracle today.'

'It's nothing.' Gemma blushed. 'Compared to what she did for me.'

James pulled her to him and gave her a big one-armed bear hug. It took her breath away, being so close to him. He smelled so good, and he was so big and muscular. She stepped away sharply, and stammered, 'I'd better go. Tell Toni I say . . . um . . . goodbye. I'll come again on Monday, if she likes.'

She grabbed her bag, scooped up Millie's car seat and left as quickly as she could.

Toni

Mornings used to be different. Well, I know that's a really obvious thing to say . . . of course they did. I used to wake up to an alarm clock and spend the first half-hour of my day showering and getting ready to rush off to work. Now I'm woken up by a snuffling, squawking baby, anytime between 5.30 and 7 a.m., and I spend the first half an hour sitting in bed with him latched on to my boob. But that's not what I mean. I used to like waking up . . . I've always been a morning person, and I used to drive James nuts by being relentlessly cheery first thing. But now I dread mornings. It's not even as if I'm sleep-deprived — Harry may scream all afternoon, but he's very good at night and I'm getting a reasonable amount of sleep. It's just that I don't want to open my eyes. Harry starts to stir, and I get this feeling of dismay, like I've only just got into bed and I could sleep for another twelve hours. Like I'd do anything, anything at all to have Harry and James and everyone leave me alone in bed for the whole day.

But of course that doesn't happen, and I drag myself out of bed and gather up my baby. Every morning, James gets up and looks at Harry and me, propped up on the pillows, cuddled together, and he says, 'Ah, that's the life.' And I think . . . is it? Is this my life?

This past week was really bad. Gemma kept coming round . . . she came Monday, Wednesday and Friday. I know she means well and she's trying to help, but when she's here, I have to get dressed. I have to talk to her. And she makes me eat. That's another thing. I've always had the sweetest tooth, and it got worse during my pregnancy. I put on way too much weight, I know. But now, I'm not interested at all. If Gemma wasn't around pushing sandwiches at me and making me eat biscuits and drink cups of tea, I wouldn't eat at all. I just don't think about it.

Things are bit better when James is home in the evenings and over the weekends. He loves spending time with Harry, and he makes us get out of the house and do things. He takes us out shopping, or out for lunch, and he invites friends around, or his parents, or my dad. Our weekends are very full and busy, and they should be the most fun, but . . . well, it's hard to explain. Do you ever feel like everyone else around you is living in full-colour high definition, and you're living in a slightly fuzzy, black-and-white VHS version of the same world? Maybe not. Maybe it's just me.

I know what you're thinking . . . what an ungrateful cow. Harry's a miracle baby, probably one in a million, and probably my only chance at being a mum, and here I am, thinking miserable thoughts. Every day he grows and changes, and I know I should be beside myself, watching each new development, cherishing every moment of his babyhood. But I'm too busy wishing I could go back to bed and sleep. Or not so much sleep as lie very still and not have anyone ask me for anything.

And I feel guilty. I feel guilty about everything. I feel guilty about being a grumpy, rotten wife to James and a joyless, grumpy mum to Harry. I feel guilty about Harry's colic and the fact that I can't fix it. I feel guilty about his traumatic birth and the fact that I failed utterly at having the wonderful hypnobirth I wrote about in my birth plan. I feel guilty about my unscrubbed bathroom and unhoovered carpet and unwashed dishes, and the fact that all Gemma seems to do when she comes round is my housework. I feel guilty for hating Gemma a little bit for already being back in her jeans, and for having Millie, the perfect baby who never cries and is beautiful. I feel guilty for hating all my other friends for never coming to visit, and I feel guilty because I never ring them either, and secretly, I don't want to see them anyway. And most of all, I feel guilty because while I know all of this is wrong and I shouldn't feel like this, I don't know what to do about it. Every day I promise myself that tomorrow will be better. It's just the baby blues, and soon my hormones will sort themselves out. But there've been quite a lot of tomorrows, none of them better. I'm in a very much light-free tunnel right now.

Louise

It wasn't until she got beyond the first few weeks that Louise realised what a dream world she'd been living in. She'd lost all sense of time, and spent hours just sitting holding Peter, often forgetting to get dressed properly or eat regular meals. He tended to be very wakeful at night, so the days often drifted by in a haze of exhaustion. Gradually, as she mastered breastfeeding and she and Peter established a routine of sorts, she started to emerge from her trance. It made her smile to think back on it . . . for someone usually so sharp and on the ball, she'd developed a first-class case of baby brain. Brian did his best to help, making meals and keeping the flat relatively tidy. But when Peter was three weeks old, he told her he'd been offered a week of consulting work in London, and Louise found herself alone in the flat all day for the first time.

She was sitting on the sofa late on the Wednesday afternoon, cuddling Peter, when she heard a text tone. Her mobile was lying on the coffee table in front of her and she checked it, but there was no message. Besides, the tone she'd heard was not the one she had set on her phone. She looked around and couldn't see another phone lying around, so she felt between the sofa cushions and found a small, cheap phone, the type you buy with a pay-as-you-go SIM card. She'd never seen it before. Brian, like her, had a smart phone, so she knew it wasn't his, and no one had been to visit for days. She clicked on the message icon to see the text that had come through on the phone. 'Missing u, sexy man, Lx', it said. The message had come from a mobile . . . there was no name saved in the phone for the number, and in fact no names in the directory at all. She opened the inbox, and there were about fifty texts, all from the same number. There were no messages from anyone else.

She scrolled through, reading some of the messages. Some were affectionate, quite a few were variations on 'missing you', and one or two were downright filthy. From the anatomical detail in one of them, Louise knew that the sender had definitely seen Brian naked, and from a certain angle. But who was the mysterious 'Lx'? She read a few more messages, and then she found one that read, 'Em & Char miss u too'. Em and Char? Emily and Charlotte? Brian's daughters? Louise laughed out loud, startling a dozing Peter. Brian was having a clandestine text affair with his own wife!

An hour or so later, Brian came home. She heard him running up the stairs and hastily unlocking the door. He called a quick hello and went straight to his room. She could hear him rummaging around, looking for something. She sat calmly on the sofa, with Peter in his bouncy chair beside her. After a few minutes, he came out of his bedroom, looking stressed.

'Looking for this?' Louise asked, holding up the phone. Brian started to bluster.

'Ah, there it is! It's er . . . my work phone . . . '

'A text came through for you. Which of the executives is it who's 'missing you, kiss-kiss'?'

'Louise . . . '

'Oh my God, Brian, you're such an idiot! Do you thrive on having some kind of secret life? I've been *begging* you to get on with your life, and here you are hiding it from me like I'm some kind of jealous harridan! It's Lisa, isn't it?'

'Er . . . yes.'

'Are you . . . thinking of getting back together?'

'It's early days . . . we're talking, that's all.'

'Would you move back up north?'

'Well . . . ' She could see he had something to say, but he was too nervous to say it. He hated surprises, and she'd really put him on the spot.

'Brian, for heaven's sake! I can see you're up to something. You don't owe me fidelity or eternal love, but you do owe me a bit of honesty.'

'The consulting work I've been doing . . . well, it's for an affiliate company of Barrett and Humphries. They want me to go back to Leeds and take a management role. It's a kind of sideways move from where I was before. I've not said yes because of you and Peter. I know you need me . . . '

Louise laughed so hard that Peter jumped and started to cry. She shushed him, and standing and holding him, she said, 'Brian, stop right there. With all the love in the world, we don't need you. You've been a great help, but we'll be fine. I always planned to do this on my own.'

'I'd like to see him . . . '

'Whenever you like.'

'And I'd like to give you money for his upkeep. We can draw up a formal agreement.'

'How does Lisa feel about that?'

'Well, she agrees that I have to take responsibility for him. She doesn't want to meet him, not yet, anyway. But she understands.'

Louise got up and impulsively hugged Brian.

'Well, I never thought I'd say it, but I think we may have the best possible outcome for this funny old situation,' she said. 'Bri, I really do wish you all the best. I hope you're very happy.'

'You too, Lou,' he said, patting her back fondly. 'Now, shall we take this small boy out for some dinner?'

'I'd like that.'

They enjoyed an early dinner at the local Italian restaurant, then, once Peter was settled, chatted long into the night. Brian had decided to head back up north within a fortnight. For the first time since he had arrived on her doorstep, things felt easy between them, and Louise felt an enormous sense of relief that Peter might be able to have a good relationship, if a little distant, with his dad.

The next day, Louise couldn't help chuckling over the whole story. It really was absurd, Brian sneaking around behind her back, romancing his own wife. It occurred to her that Toni would find the story hysterical. She felt quite bright and full of energy . . . maybe Toni would like to meet her for brunch or lunch, and they could take the babies for a stroll. She rang Toni's mobile, but it went straight to message, and the disembodied voice told her that the voice mailbox was full and that she couldn't leave a message. How odd, she thought. She dialled again, and got the same thing. She didn't have a home number for Toni, so she sent a text saying 'Your phone's being odd, can't leave a voicemail. Ring me!' After an hour or so Toni hadn't rung back, so she dialled one more time. This time, Toni answered, her voice husky and confused, like she had been asleep.

'Hey, Toni, it's Lou. Sorry, did I wake you?'

'Hmm? What? Er . . . no. I don't think I was asleep.'

She didn't *think* she was asleep? What a strange thing to say, Louise thought. But she pressed on. 'Listen, there've been some . . . developments in my situation. I wondered if you and Harry fancied brunch and a walk and a gossip?'

'Oh . . . thanks, but we can't.' Louise felt a first twinge of concern. Toni didn't sound like herself at all. She was vague and dreamy, and her voice had a flat, dead quality that Louise had never heard before.

'Listen if today's not good, how about tomorrow? Or any day this week? It'd be great to meet up,' said Louise persistently.

'Thanks, but no. We don't go out.'

'What do you mean you don't go out?'

'Harry and me. We don't go out. It doesn't work for us, so we stay home.'

'Can I bring Peter round to yours then?'

'Probably better not,' said Toni.

'Toni, are you okay?'

'Fine,' said Toni, sounding anything but fine.

'Look, I'd better go.'

'Okay,' said Louise uncertainly. 'Listen, there's something funny going on with your phone . . . I rang and it said your mailbox was full. Maybe let your service provider know there's a fault?'

'I don't think it's a fault. I just haven't listened to my messages. Listen, Lou, thanks for calling, but I really have to go. Bye.' And she was gone.

It was all very worrying. Louise scooped up Peter and held him close while she walked around the flat going over the conversation in her head. She was pretty sure that it wasn't because Toni was angry with her: their last few meetings had been friendly and warm, and she'd felt their relationship was back on track. No, something was very wrong with Toni. About half an hour later, Brian came home, and in the spirit of their new, easier relationship, Louise told him about her conversation with Toni. 'Sounds to me like your friend might have post-natal depression,' said Brian.

'Do you think so?'

'Lisa had it with Charlotte. She wouldn't leave the house, cried all the time, didn't want to see anyone. Sounds like Toni's going through something similar. You want to get your friend some help,' said Brian.

Cradling Peter against her shoulder, she sat down at her computer and went onto the baby website to look up post-natal depression. There were several articles, and on the forum there was a big group for sufferers of PND, with thousands of members, as well as smaller ones for each birth month: there was already a September

394

PND group which had forty members. If that was what Toni had, she certainly wasn't alone.

Some of the things she read in the articles suggested Toni was a prime candidate, like the fact that she'd had reproductive issues, then a difficult birth. Her lethargy, her lack of interest in going out all pointed to the possibility of post-natal depression. But what to do with that thought? She was certain that if she rang Toni again, assuming Toni even answered her call, she wouldn't be open to a discussion that she might be mentally ill. She wished she had a way to speak to Toni's husband . . . James, was it? But she'd only met him briefly at the awful lunch party that Brian had gatecrashed, and she had no way of reaching him. It was a real problem. She really had only one way to get the message to James. She didn't like doing it, but her concern for Toni overrode her misgivings. She popped Peter in his bouncy chair and began to type an email.

Subject: Toni

Dear Gemma,
I'm sure you're surprised to see an email from me, and I hope, reading the subject line, you'll at least read it before you junk it. I know you and I have little to say to one another, but I am very worried about Toni. I know you and she have got close in the last few months.

I just spoke to her on the phone and she sounded very down indeed. I tried to arrange to see her, but she won't go out and won't let me go round to see her. I'm worried she may be suffering from post-natal depression. I've looked up symptoms, and many of them seem to fit her behaviour. Have a look and see what you think.

(Here she copied and pasted a number of web links)

I don't expect to hear back from you, but if you're in a position to speak to Toni's husband, or even to suggest gently to her that she might want to look for help, it would be a good thing.
Best,
Lou

Louise hit Send before she could have second thoughts. Gemma was just a kid, and a judgmental one at that. But she cared about Toni. She had to just hope and pray that Gemma would do the right thing.

A few days later, she got a call from Adam. When she saw his name come up on her mobile she couldn't control the little rollercoaster-swoop feeling she got in the pit of her stomach, but she hoped she had managed to sound calm and cheery when she answered.

'Ah, Mr Harper! To what do I owe this pleasure?'

He sounded a lot less confident. In fact, he sounded quite hesitant. 'Er, hi. Um, well, I hope things are going well with Junior . . . '

'Fine, yes. Sorry I haven't been in touch, but, well, you know about the post-baby mush-brain. I've really just been sitting staring at him adoringly.'

'As you should, as you should. Listen, do you remember the Nicholson contract?'

'Fifty banners in a very odd size, could they have a discount? Yes, of course.'

'I've been looking at the numbers and I'm not sure I understand what you did with the purchasing on that job.'

'Ah, well, even though it was an unusual size, I worked out if we printed landscape rather than portrait, I could fit five banners into the width and buy the vinyl more efficiently.'

'Oh,' said Adam, sounding slightly disappointed.

'Were you hoping for a better explanation than that?'

'No, it's a perfectly good explanation. I was just hoping for one that was more than a sentence long so you'd have to come out to the farm for a meeting to explain it to me.'

'I could come out to the farm to visit my old workmates and introduce them all to my baby.'

'That would also be a good reason for you to come. I approve of that reason.'

'When would be convenient for you?'

'Well, purely from a workplace-efficiency point of view, I'd say lateish on Friday afternoon.'

'Sounds good. I wouldn't want to impact negatively on productivity.'

'And I wouldn't want a new mum to wear herself out driving back home on an empty stomach so maybe you could explain the Nicholson-contract thing to me one more time over a bite of early dinner?'

'I'm sure I could come up with some more details to make the explanation worthwhile.'

'I look forward to it,' said Adam. 'See you Friday.'

He rang off, and Louise sat clutching her phone to her chest, grinning at Peter like a giddy teenager, and wondering where she could buy some good tummy-shaping underwear before Friday afternoon.

She spent ages choosing outfits for her and Peter on Friday. Peter was easier: he had loads of gorgeous little tops and trousers, thanks to Simon and Rachel. She dressed him in a green, long-sleeved jumper that showed off his auburn hair, and a very sweet pair of leggings with frogs on them. Her own outfit was trickier. She wasn't quite back to her pre-pregnancy weight, and her waistline was definitely nowhere near what it used to be, so many of her old clothes simply didn't fit. In the end, she went for a long, white skirt (with an elastic waistband), with a pretty pale blue blouse over the top, to cover any muffin-top-type bulges at the waistline.

She got to the farm at about 4.30, and took Peter, sleeping angelically, out of the car in his car seat. Anita, the Australian receptionist, came out to meet her. 'Hi!' she said enthusiastically, 'wow, what a stunning little fella! And, Louise, you look amazing!' The uncomplicated warmth of Anita's welcome made Louise a little less nervous. She walked in with Anita, had an

398

awkward moment saying hello to Alan, who clearly didn't know what to say to her, or indeed what to say about a baby. The guys on the floor stopped what they were doing to say hello, and the dads among them asked her questions about Peter's eating and sleeping. There was no sign of Adam. Anita took her up to the offices on the first floor and made her a cup of tea, and they sat chatting. Peter woke up, and she took him out of his car seat and let Anita have a cuddle. She had thought about it, and she wasn't sure she wanted to breastfeed at work, in front of all the guys, and definitely not in front of Adam, so she'd expressed a bottle of breastmilk. She warmed it in a jug of water and gave it to Anita, who sat feeding a contented Peter, cooing and smiling.

Suddenly, Adam's office door flew open and he burst in. 'So, so sorry,' he said, looking flustered. 'I got stuck on the phone talking to a supplier in Ireland. The man had definitely kissed the Blarney Stone; he wouldn't shut up!'

He was a big man, and his presence seemed to fill the room. Louise stood up and turned to face him. It was the first time she'd seen him since their chat in the shopping precinct, when she was heavily pregnant. They stood looking at each other for a while, and something electric passed between them. Guiltily, she glanced at Anita, but the Aussie girl seemed totally focused on little Peter.

'You look . . . great,' said Adam and if Louise didn't know better, she would have thought he'd come over all shy.

'Thank you.'

He stared at her for a while longer. 'So where's the little man?' he said, suddenly.

'Oh, he's lost his heart to Anita,' Louise laughed, and Adam went over to kneel down and look at her baby.

'He's a solid little chap.'

'He's finished eating . . . want to hold him?' said Anita, and handed Peter to Adam.

Adam stood up, expertly cradling Peter against his shoulder, and rubbing his back. Peter let out an almighty burp.

'Wow!' said Louise. 'How did you do that? It usually takes me ages to wind him.'

'It's not my first time,' Adam smiled. 'It's been a while, but it's definitely one of those riding-a-bicycle things.'

Because it was Friday everyone who worked at Harper Graphics was keen to get off home, and within fifteen minutes the offices and printing floor were deserted. Adam and Louise walked over to the house. He'd obviously planned ahead, and had a chilled bottle of white wine in the fridge and a big salad already made. 'I thought we could have a sort of ploughman's for dinner, if that's okay,' he said. 'Cheese and pickles and bread and salad. Sound okay?'

'Sounds lovely,' said Louise. It was her turn to feel shy . . . being back in Adam's house reminded her of their intense last night together before he went sailing, and also, more uncomfortably, of Brian's time there and the mess it had caused.

'Wine?' Adam said.

'I'd better not,' she said regretfully. 'I'm

driving and breastfeeding, two things best not mixed with alcohol.'

'What if I make you a very weak spritzer?'

'Now that sounds good!' said Louise.

'When I saw Anita giving him a bottle, I assumed you were bottle-feeding,' said Adam, pouring the drinks. She noticed he poured himself a rather large glass of wine. She was pleased . . . at least she wasn't the only one who was nervous.

'Nope, he's getting the good stuff. I expressed some to bring with me. I wasn't sure I wanted to be whipping a boob out on the factory floor.'

'Fair enough,' said Adam, and she could swear he was blushing. Maybe she shouldn't have said 'whip a boob out'.

He brought her her drink, and then busied himself preparing their dinner. Millicent came strolling through from the living room and sniffed at Peter in his car seat with great suspicion. Then she let out one of her human yowls and stalked out of the cat-flap in high dudgeon.

'Oh dear,' said Louise.

'Millicent has never liked competition,' observed Adam. She'll punish me all weekend for letting someone smaller and cuter than her into the house.'

He set dinner out on the table and they kept the conversation on safe topics, chatting about Harper Graphics and Adam's sailing trip. Every moment, however, she was aware of him, the warmth of his arm close to her own, the way his hair curled above his ears, the deep burr of his voice. Peter sat in his car seat, watching them contentedly, happily awake.

When they had finished eating, they went through to the living room and Louise settled in an armchair, Peter on her lap. She wondered how long they could make polite small talk. She wasn't sure she was ready for a heavy discussion, but there seemed to be so much that was unsaid. Was Adam avoiding talking about it because he now saw her as just a friend and a colleague? Was he just being nice to the unemployed new mum?

She didn't get a chance to ask him, though, because Peter chose that moment to do his characteristic hunch, grunt and push. An ominous rumbling issued from his nappy area, like a stampeding herd of buffalo, heard from afar. Adam looked surprised, then realised what had happened and laughed out loud. His loud guffaw made her laugh too, at least until she felt warm wetness spreading across her thighs. She lifted Peter up, and to her horror, neon-orange-breastmilk poo had leaked around the nappy, through his leggings, and liberally all over her carefully chosen white skirt. 'Oh no!' she cried. Peter squirmed in her hands, and a little more poo dripped into her lap. Adam was doubled over, laughing so much he was crying.

'Help me!' she cried, starting to laugh too.

'Your baby went off!' he roared.

'I'm aware of that. Don't just stand there, help me!'

Adam came over and took Peter away from her, holding him at arm's length.

'Well done, little buddy,' he said. 'That's a crap any man would be proud of!'

He carried Peter to the bathroom, and Louise

402

followed. Grabbing some loo roll, she mopped the worst of the poo off her skirt, and together they stripped Peter and showered him with warm water, then wrapped him in a towel.

'I assume you've got spare clothes,' said Adam. 'For him, not for me.'

'Ah, rookie mistake. I'll lend you something. Get your skirt off and hop in the shower. I'll pop something into your bedr — into the spare bedroom.'

'And Peter?'

'Are the spare clothes in your nappy bag?' She nodded. 'I'll dress him,' he said calmly.

Ten minutes later, she came into the living room wearing a pair of Adam's old jogging bottoms and a soft grey jumper. He was sitting on the sofa. Peter, dressed in clean, dry clothes, was fast asleep in the crook of his arm. He patted the sofa cushion next to him with his free hand, and she went to sit next to him. He took her hand easily, companionably.

'That was a bit shitty, eh?' he said, and they started to laugh again, softly though, so as not to wake Peter.

'Thank you,' she said finally.

'For what?'

'Dinner. Jogging bottoms. Finding this funny.'

'I can't believe *anyone* wouldn't find it funny.'

'Well then, thanks for not making me feel awful about it. And also, thank you for so much else.'

They started to talk then. She told him the story of her and Brian, and explained her feelings of guilt and inertia when he had arrived

403

on the doorstep. She didn't hold anything back. He told her about the break-up of his marriage and his wife's infidelity, and how hearing Brian was in the house had brought feelings of betrayal flooding back.

She took Peter from him. He smelled her and began to snuffle and root, and it seemed the most natural thing in the world to put him to her breast and feed.

After a while, Adam said softly, 'And what now?'

'Well, 'what now' is a big and complicated question,' she said, looking down at Peter.

'Does it have to be?'

'Well, Brian is going back up north, but he hasn't gone yet. I think in the interests of keeping things clean and simple, I should wait for him to go, and I should also tell him about you.'

'I agree. But what will you tell him?'

'What do you think I should tell him?' she said, batting the question back to him.

'Tell him you've met someone you're interested in. I hope that's true. And tell him we're going to take things slow. A kind of old-fashioned courtship, if you like. I'd like to take you and Peter out for dinner, have the two of you over for lunches at the weekend, maybe take walks in the park with the pushchair.'

'I never imagined I'd find a man who wanted to date me *and* my baby,' she said, smiling.

'Are you joking?' he said, squeezing her hand. 'A wee man that can produce a weapon of mass destruction like that . . . I'm going to want to stay on his good side!'

Gemma

Gemma sat and stared at the email for a good long while. She had junked it twice, then moved it back to her inbox. She didn't want anything to do with Louise. But at the same time, she couldn't shake the niggling feeling that Louise was right. There was something very wrong with Toni at the moment.

Gemma had made a resolution to go and visit Toni at least three times a week, and for a few weeks, she had, but Toni was very resistant, and would use any excuse she could think of to stop Gemma from coming. When Gemma did go, they'd sit in Toni's none-too-clean living room, and they wouldn't *do* anything. Toni didn't neglect Harry, but she didn't seem very interested in him. She'd feed him and change him and hold him, but she didn't seem to want to play with him, and she definitely wouldn't go out. No matter how many times Gemma tried to persuade her to go for a walk, or even just pop down the road for a coffee, she wouldn't. It became such hard work that Gemma had kind of stopped trying. When she rang Toni's mobile these days and it went to message, as it invariably did, she felt a guilty relief, and went off with Millie to do something else instead. She told herself that she had tried, and that if Toni didn't want company, she couldn't force her.

She clicked on the first of the links Louise had

included in her email. It was a list of possible symptoms of postnatal depression. Exhaustion, lack of interest in the baby, taking no pleasure in day-to-day activities, changes in eating habits . . . Toni had shown signs of all of those. She hated to admit it, but Louise was right. And she was also right that the best thing to do was to speak to James. She knew if she tried to talk about it to Toni herself, she'd just turn away and say 'I'm fine', in that strange, colourless voice she'd started to use.

Gemma waited till after eight o'clock that night and dialled Toni's home number. She was taking a chance . . . if Toni herself answered she could always say she was ringing to make an arrangement for the next day. But she was in luck, James picked up the phone.

'James, hi, it's Gemma.'

'Oh, hi, Gem,' he said warmly. 'Sorry, Toni's already gone to bed. Can I take a message for her?'

'Er . . . I actually rang to talk to you.'

'You did?'

'James, I'm worried about Toni. She seems very down.'

'She is. I know. Well, Harry's not an easy baby, what with the colic, and she's still recovering from the Caesarean . . . '

'I think it might be more than that. Louise . . . Well, you know Toni's friend, Louise?'

'The one on the farm? Embarrassing end to a lunch?'

'Yes. She spoke to Toni on the phone, and she got very worried and emailed me. She thinks it might be post-natal depression.'

'Post-natal depression? Oh, I, er . . . ' James sounded really uncomfortable. But Gemma wasn't going to let him brush her off.

'Look, what's your email address? Can I send you some links?'

James gave her his address. 'I'm sending them now,' she said. 'And James, if you don't believe me, ask yourself, would the Toni you know normally be in bed, asleep, by eight fifteen?'

There was a long silence, then James spoke. He sounded tense and a bit angry. 'Look, let me read the stuff you sent through and I'll ring you back. What's your number?' Gemma gave him her mobile number and they rang off.

She sat on her bed, watching Millie sleep, her perfect little face in repose, her arms flung above her head. Poor Toni. It must be awful to be in such a dark place in these precious first days with your baby. But James would make things okay. James was amazing . . . strong, caring, compassionate. Toni really was the luckiest girl to have him.

After half an hour or so, James rang back. He didn't bother with hellos or chit-chat. 'So if this is what she's got, what do we do?'

'I suppose you have to speak to her. She won't talk to me, or to Louise apparently. Maybe she'll listen to you if you say you think she needs help.'

'I feel like such a bastard . . . I've just been annoyed with her lately, to be honest. I keep coming home to her in tears and the house in a mess, and then she wants me to take Harry the minute I walk through the door, and I kept

407

thinking — well — I keep thinking that surely it can't be that hard. Other people manage with new babies. Why not Toni? But this . . . this makes sense. Thanks, Gemma.'

'It's nothing, really . . . '

'It's not nothing, You're amazing . . . you've been such a good friend to Toni. And I can't believe how brilliantly you're doing with your own baby. You're my hero, girl!'

Toni

Remember that sick feeling you got in the pit of your stomach when you were at school and there was some piece of homework you were supposed to have done or something you should have brought to class, and you hadn't? You knew you'd get found out and that you'd be in trouble, but you just had to wait it out until the trouble hit? Well, I'd been feeling like that for weeks. I've been feeling like I left my metaphorical PE kit at home, and someone was going to crap all over me. Except it's not PE kit, it's my ability to be a mother. Yes, I know, no one can mix a metaphor quite like me. But in all seriousness, if someone were to mark me on this whole maternal thing, I would definitely get a failing grade. I'm trying. I really am. But it's so hard. Deep, deep down, I know I love Harry, but what with the screaming and pooping and endless feeding, it's all so thankless. And every day is the same. I really don't see the point in trying, so I do less and less every day. I hardly ever get dressed, and I can't face the idea of going out. I keep the curtains closed, because the light is too bright. I used to watch loads of telly, but the noise felt like scratching on my skin, so now I don't even turn it on. I tried reading when Harry was asleep, but I can't retain information, so as soon as I turn the page, I forget what I've read and I have to go back and read it again. I know if people come here and see me, and see me ignoring Harry and sitting staring at the wall, they'll know I'm a terrible mum and they'll take him away from me, or yell at me, or something. So I've stopped answering the phone, and if people try to come round, I tell them not to. With James, I try to go to bed as soon as I can after he comes home, and I pretend to be asleep until after he's left for work, and for the times that he's here and I'm awake, I use all my energy trying not to look like the dead-inside zombie psycho that I know I really am.

It's a funny thing, that PE-kit feeling, because when the teacher finally says, 'Why haven't you changed yet, Antonia?', under the fear, there's a feeling of relief that it's all over and out in the open. You've been found out, and you'll be scraping chewing gum off the gym floor for the next hour. So, when I woke up that morning, and James was sitting on the bed watching me, holding Harry in his arms, and his face was sad and angry and full of love, under the awful feelings, I was relieved.

I looked at the clock, and saw it was 9 a.m. I sat up quickly.

'You should be at work! Why are you still here?'

'I took the day off. Toni — ' I couldn't let him start talking, so I interrupted, instantly on the defensive.

'I would have woken up when he cried. I would have.'

'I know you would have. I was glad to let you sleep in a bit.'

410

'I'm fine!' I swung my legs out of bed. 'If you're here and you can hold him for a bit, I'll jump in the shower.'

James put his hand on my arm. 'Can you sit down for a sec? I want to talk to you.'

'I really should shower. I should have fed him an hour ago.'

'Toni . . . '

I sat back down. I might as well face the music now, I thought. 'Do you want a divorce?'

'What?' said James, his face a picture of shock. 'No! What gave you that idea?'

'You've stayed home from work, you're hanging on to Harry like you can't trust me to hold him . . . '

'Toni, I'm worried about you.'

'I'm fine.'

'You're not fine. You know you're not fine. Your friends know you're not fine.'

'What? Who? Who have you been speaking to?'

'Gemma rang me. She's worried, and she passed on an email from Louise — '

'Louise emailed *Gemma?* She hates Gemma. And Gemma hates her.'

'Well, that's how concerned about you they are.'

'Seriously . . . Louise and Gemma talked to each other?'

'Toni, can we focus on you?' said James, and I could hear he was using his 'patient' voice. I decided just to shut up and let him talk.

'I know you've been very . . . down since Harry was born.'

So much for keeping quiet. I jumped right in.

'That's not true . . . I was okay when we were in the hospital, and when you were on paternity leave.'

'Well, since then,' said James, jiggling Harry, who was starting to whimper.

'What do you mean 'down'?' I said, playing for time.

'Gemma tells me you don't leave the house.'

'Harry cries. He's got colic.'

'He's much better now, though. And he always only cried in the afternoons. Did you not want to go out in the morning?'

'I . . . ' I didn't know what to say. What I wanted to do, most of all, was lie back down on the pillows and go back to sleep. James patted my hand.

'Toni, my love, you're not on trial. I love you, and I'm very worried that you're feeling alone and very unhappy.'

'So what if I am? I *am* alone. And how can you change that? You can't give up work to stay with me. Harry exists. He's not going away. I'm here alone with him for the next eighteen years and there's nothing I can do about it.'

James tried not to smile. 'Well, the authorities might wonder why you didn't let him go to school, but okay. My love, the point is, you're not alone. You have friends, and family, and support if you ask for it. But you're not asking. You're hiding.' He paused, and I could see he was nervous about what he was going to say next.

'Louise and Gemma think you may have post-natal depression.'

There it was. Someone had said it. The words

I'd been too scared to say to myself. I'd kept telling myself that I don't get depressed. I'm Toni. Bubbly Toni, always smiling. How could I possibly be suffering from depression? I didn't say any of that to James, though. Very intelligently, I said, 'What?'

'Gemma sent me some information, and I think you should look at it. If the symptoms look like something you recognise in yourself, we can look for help for you.'

I blathered on for a while more about how I was fine, just a bad day, etc., etc., but I just felt such relief. Someone had recognised the dark, dark tiredness that was my whole life. It had a label other people knew. There were web links. Support groups. I wasn't a bad person, just someone who needed help. After a while, without thinking, I took Harry from James and popped him on the boob for a feed. When he was full up and sleepy-drunk, I handed him back and went for a shower. Then I sat down at James' computer to read the information he had gathered. After about half an hour, I turned to him.

'I could have written this myself. It's exactly how I feel. So what do I do?'

'What do *we* do, you mean. We'll work together.'

'So what do we do?'

'We go and see the GP. He or she can recommend whether you take medication or see a therapist or whatever. But it's a good place to start.'

I shrank back a bit at that. I hadn't left the

house in over a fortnight. But James was ahead of me.

'You won't be going alone. I'm going with you, and I'm not going to let go of your hand the whole time.'

'And when . . . ?'

'Two o'clock. I made an appointment already.'

We saw the doctor, and she was a lovely warm lady, very maternal, who was quick to tell me she had had postnatal depression after the birth of her second child. She spent ages with me, and we drew up a plan. I wrote everything down, and when I looked at it later, it still looked like quite a sound arrangement. This is what we worked out:

1. Antidepressants. I was really scared at the thought of taking mind-altering medication, especially as I wanted to keep breastfeeding, but she promised me it was perfectly safe and wouldn't harm Harry at all. She explained that the tablets would help the really extreme mood swings and would just let me see things a bit more positively.

2. Company. She made me promise to ring friends and set up a roster, so I had someone coming round pretty much every day. So Gemma said she'd come round on Mondays and Wednesdays, Louise said she'd take Tuesdays and Thursdays, my dad said he'd come down and spend Friday afternoons with us, and Robyn and Caro said they'd split Saturdays — when

James was at football — between them. Gemma had also told James there were groups online, so I was going to join the September PND group . . . I'd be able to chat to women I knew from the site already, who were going through the same thing.

3. Therapy. The lovely doctor recommended something called cognitive behavioural therapy, which isn't about lying on a sofa and thinking about your childhood, but more tackling each negative thought and trying to turn it into a more positive one. She gave me the name of a therapist she often worked with, and I booked in to see the woman once a week for six weeks.

4. The last bit of the plan was what we called 'baby steps'. The doctor said that if I made a tiny bit of progress every day, managing to do something I couldn't before, that would be very positive. So, for example, I'm going to try to get Harry and me dressed every morning. That's my first baby step. Then maybe a little bit of housework each day. Then maybe a trip to the shops every couple of days. She made me promise not to try and do too much, and also not to beat myself up if I didn't do something every day. 'Remember,' she said, 'eighty per cent is still an A!'

So that was The Plan. To be honest, just admitting there was a real problem and taking steps to do something about it had made me feel a million times better already. It wasn't a miracle cure, far from it, and I still had some really bad days. But it was all out in the open. I wasn't crazy about the fact that James had been talking to Gemma behind my back, it seemed like I was some kind of invalid that people were gossiping about, but I was grateful that they'd helped me. Honest I was.

The first week, it was as much as I could manage to have someone come round for half an hour a day. The good thing about admitting I had PND was that I could actually say, 'Sorry, I've had enough, can you go now?' without sounding like the rudest woman in the world. Gemma was happy just to sit with me and be quiet, and Millie, the perfect baby, just sat in her bouncy chair and stared at things without making a sound. Gemma was such a head-girl type . . . she always made sure she stayed till James got home, and he always walked her down to her car. I knew she was giving him a report on me, and I tried not to mind.

Louise wanted to chat more, which was more work, but good. She pushed me a bit harder to do things, like go out to the shops, even if it was just to buy a pint of milk. She was so no-nonsense and jolly about it, that I managed to do it without too much anxiety, and Harry seemed to love being out. He peered around him at the outside world with big eyes.

One night towards the end of the second week of the execution of The Plan, Harry woke for his 2 a.m. feed and I went to pick him up. In the dim glow of the night light, he saw my face as I bent over the Moses basket and he gave me a big, gummy grin. There was no doubt about it, it was a real smile. His first one. Well, I woke James up straight away, and the two of us danced around the Moses basket like a pair of demented monkeys, trying to get him to do it again. When he did, we clutched each other and laughed, and James wanted to run and get a camera. 'Poor little thing,' I said, laughing. 'We're so busy trying to get him to perform, and all he wants is his feed. Come here, little frog.' I scooped him up and sat down in the rocking chair to feed.

James came to sit on the floor beside me, and rested his hand on my knee. 'I don't want to jinx it, Tones, but that's the first time since Harry was born that I've seen you laugh. It's wonderful.'

I didn't say anything, just stroked his thick hair. Baby steps.

Louise

Even in her fuzziest baby-brain moments, Louise never missed her weekly visit to Rachel. Every Wednesday morning, she'd drive round to Rachel's house and spend an hour or so there. Rachel was very frosty for the first few visits, but Louise persisted. Her sister was too polite to ask her not to come, or to be inhospitable, so they sat and sipped tea, and Louise cradled Peter in her arms or let him sit beside her in his car seat. She took care to dress him in an outfit Rachel had bought every time she took him for a visit. One Wednesday, her fourth visit, she noticed that Peter, sitting on her lap, seemed to be staring fixedly at Rachel.

'Look how he's looking at you,' she observed.

'He is staring, isn't he?' said Rachel, almost smiling.

'I think it's your blouse.' Rachel was wearing a silk blouse with a dramatic black-and-white geometric print. 'Tiny babies like black-and-white patterns.'

Louise sat Peter up, and he tried hard to hold his head steady while he goggled at the pattern. She could see Rachel hesitate and fight her natural urges, and then she saw her lose the fight.

'Let me hold him, then he can see it better,' Rachel said.

Without comment, Louise handed him over,

and watched her sister melt as she took hold of Peter's warm, sturdy little body. They stayed longer that day, and for that extra hour Rachel sat holding her nephew close. When Louise packed up to leave, Rachel patted her arm awkwardly. 'See you next week,' she said. 'I'll get one of those playmats for him to lie on, one with nice black-and-white checks. He'd like that.' The battle was won, but not the war. Rachel remained frosty towards her, even if she had warmed to Peter and liked playing with him and holding him.

Things were a little better at the weekends when Simon was also there. Once Brian had packed up and gone back to Leeds, Simon got into the habit of coming down on a Friday night and staying with Louise for the weekend. It meant she could have a lie-in on a Saturday and Sunday morning, and on Sunday afternoons, she and Simon would take Peter over to Rachel's or meet Rachel and Richard somewhere for a meal.

Simon was the proudest and most devoted uncle Louise had ever seen. He bought three different varieties of sling so he could carry Peter close to his body. He discovered that Richard had once been a keen amateur photographer, a hobby he'd not had much time for in recent years, and he bullied him into getting a good digital camera in order to take pictures of Peter on a weekly basis. He was very good at putting everyone at their ease, and, week by week, he gently teased Rachel until she started to loosen up a little.

Things often worked best when they all went

out. There was more to talk about, and Rachel couldn't buzz neurotically around her perfect house, straightening things and tidying around them. One crisp autumn afternoon, they ate a splendid pub lunch and then went for a walk by the river. Peter could now hold his head up pretty reliably, so Simon wore him in a sling that let him face outwards to see the world. Richard walked with him, every now and then running ahead a few steps so he could take another picture in the golden afternoon light. Rachel and Louise strolled a little way behind. Louise laughed and said, 'I wonder what people think, seeing us. Do you think they're trying to work out who Peter belongs to?'

'I'm sure they think Simon is the dad,' said Rachel.

'Unless they think Richard is . . . he's doing proud-daddy photographing.'

Rachel gave a naughty giggle. 'Maybe they think Peter has two dads . . . and that Simon and Richard are a couple!'

'And we're their fag-hags!'

They walked on in silence for a bit, then Rachel said, 'Peter's very sweet, Louise. He's a real blessing to you.'

'He is,' Louise said quietly. 'I know the circumstances weren't ideal. Not at all. And I know it caused a lot of pain, and some things, well, some things can never be fixed. But however it came about, he's the best thing that ever happened to me. I love him. I do. And none of it is his fault.'

'Of course not.'

Simon suddenly turned back to them. 'Lou! Rach! Look at this!' He did a silly little dance and jiggle, and Peter, excited by the movement, gave a goofy little grin. 'Richard got a picture of it!' Simon said excitedly.

'Ah, proud dads,' said Rachel, smiling.

'What?' said Simon, puzzled.

'We were just speculating about passers-by thinking you and Richard were a happy couple out with your baby,' explained Louise. 'We thought people might be wondering who Peter belongs to.'

'He belongs to all of us, doesn't he?' said Simon pragmatically. 'We all love him, after all.'

Rachel and Louise looked at one another and nodded.

'Now I'm freezing,' said Simon. 'Even with this little hot-water bottle strapped to my front. Let's go and get a coffee.'

* * *

Later that evening, Simon and Louise sat chatting after Peter had gone down for the night. 'Today was better with Rachel, wasn't it?' said Simon.

'I think we made a bit of a breakthrough,' agreed Louise. 'She still totally disapproves of me, but she loves him. That's all I really care about.'

'She is softening towards you, though. You've made a real effort to spend time with her, and I know she appreciates that.'

'Glad she tells you that. She doesn't tell me much of anything.'

'She will. She'll open up. It just takes time.'

'Has she told you any more about what the doctor said?'

'Just that they reckon she's almost certainly not going to conceive a baby naturally.'

'Because she's gone into menopause?'

'Yes. The equipment's apparently all fine, just the ingredients are not up to scratch.'

'So could she have IVF?'

'Not with her own eggs. And she feels that she doesn't want to use donor eggs because then the baby wouldn't be her blood.'

'So what now?'

'I don't know. If she doesn't want a baby that's not hers, I don't know that she'd consider adoption.'

'Poor Rachel.'

'I know,' said Simon. 'But you're doing the right thing. If she can't be a mum, giving her the chance to be a very involved aunt is a wonderful thing.'

Gemma

An email came through, inviting her to the antenatal-group Christmas party. She was in two minds about it . . . she didn't really want to see any of those women again, but Toni had tentatively said she would like to go. Gemma was happy to be there to support Toni, who was making small but significant steps towards recovery, but then Toni told her Louise would be there too. She was grateful to Louise for her support for Toni, but she wasn't sure she wanted to have to speak to her. They'd been alternating days, spending time with Toni, so she hadn't seen Louise at all, and had never seen her baby. In the end, it was Santa who persuaded her. Toni told her that there would be a Santa Claus at the party, and she wanted a picture of Millie with Santa to make into a Christmas card. She'd ignore Louise if she had to. There'd be enough other people there so they didn't have to talk.

The antenatal unit had declared the waiting area to be a pushchair car park, and by the time Gemma and Toni arrived, it was already crowded with Bugaboos and iCandy Apples. 'I'm too embarrassed to park mine here. It cost less than a thousand pounds,' said Toni. 'Do you think they'd mind if I hid it out in the hallway?'

Gemma laughed and lifted Millie out of her own top-of-the-range pink pushchair. 'You can pretend mine is yours if you like.'

'Put my butch son Harry in a pink pushchair? That's the way to give him an identity crisis!' laughed Toni. She was much more herself these days, cracking jokes and laughing, although she still had dark times and days when she wouldn't leave the house.

They carried their babies into the room, and the full range of motherhood was revealed before them. There were mothers breastfeeding, other mums offering their babies bottles, mums whose babies were strapped to their fronts in slings, others whose babies sat in car seats or bouncy chairs while they texted or talked on the phone. Having seen all these women pregnant, it was odd to see what they had been hiding inside their bumps. A quick glance around the room satisfied Gemma that Millie was the most beautiful baby there. Some of them were downright scary: fat, spotty, bald, or very red in the face, although there was one rather sweet chap, about twice Millie's size, with the face of a cherub and a shock of flaming red hair. She glanced up to see who he belonged to and blushed as she caught Louise's quizzical gaze.

'There's Louise and Peter!' said Toni happily, and headed over to join them.

She didn't have to talk to Louise. There was plenty of other chatter going on. She went and queued up to have Millie's picture taken with Santa, and then made her way back across the room, chatting to people as she went. Everyone wanted to tell everyone else their birth story, although Gemma's giving birth on the kitchen floor was by far the most dramatic. People kept coming over to ask her about it, and she was proud to tell them all that it was Toni who had actually delivered Millie. Toni blossomed under all the admiration and attention, and for the first time since Harry was born, she had real colour in her face. Gemma was glad they had come.

A woman holding a baby with a perfectly round, bald head came over and sat down next to Toni. Toni introduced her as Susie, the woman who'd told her about hypnobirthing. It seemed Susie had had a brilliant waterbirth, and now all the midwives wanted to be trained in hypno-birthing because of her experience. Gemma thought she was a bit smug, to be honest. It wasn't a competition, but if it were, Susie clearly thought she'd get first prize for the best birth. Well, at least Millie had hair and didn't look like a potato. Being born on a kitchen floor didn't seem to have done her any harm.

Donna the Midwife came round and said hello to everyone. She had been on duty for Susie and Louise's births, but was very interested to hear about Toni and Gemma's experiences.

'You were both incredibly lucky,' she said. 'It doesn't always end so well . . . ' She stopped herself.

'What do you mean?' asked Toni.

'No, no, nothing,' said Donna. 'I'm just so happy you both have such beautiful, healthy babies.'

She moved on to talk to the next group of women.

'I wonder what that was about?' said Louise.

'She was talking about Penny,' Susie said.

'Penny?'

'Penny was also in this group. You might remember her . . . very businesslike. Always wore a suit.'

That could be any one of ten women, so Gemma, Louise and Toni just nodded.

'She went into labour, but when she came in to have the baby, they couldn't find a heartbeat. He'd died, and she had to give birth to a baby she knew wasn't alive.'

'Oh my God, that's awful!' said Toni, her eyes filling with tears.

'I've just remembered we have to leave!' said Louise firmly. 'Susie, it was lovely to meet you. Gemma, remember we have to get to that thing.' She stood up and scooped up her baby. 'Toni, let's go.'

Gemma was about to protest, but she could see what Louise was trying to do. In her fragile state, Toni didn't need to stay here listening to stories of women who had lost their babies.

Together, they hustled Toni out, and Louise led them to a nearby coffee shop. She went to get drinks, and Gemma sat patting Toni's shoulder. Toni was shaking a little, and she held Harry tightly. 'That poor, poor woman!' she said. 'I keep imagining what it must have been like. A whole pregnancy and then the labour, and all for nothing! And having to come home to a nursery all ready, but with no baby to put into it . . . I don't know how she bears it.'

Louise sat down with the tray, and handed Toni a plate with a big slice of chocolate cake.

'Get that down you,' she said briskly, 'and I

got you hot chocolate too. I can't buy you wine, but we can medicate with the cocoa bean.'

'I'm okay, really I am,' said Toni. 'It was a shock, hearing it, but I'm not going to have a relapse or anything.'

'As long as you're okay,' said Gemma doubtfully.

'I'm not a fan of your friend Mrs I'm-the-first-person-to-have-given-birth-ever-in-the-world-and-I-did-it-better-than-you Susie,' said Louise acidly. 'A little less talking about herself and a little more sensitivity to others would do her no end of good.'

Gemma laughed out loud, it was so exactly what she'd been thinking. But because it was Louise who'd made the joke, she stopped herself. Toni turned to look at her.

'This Penny thing puts things in perspective, doesn't it?' said Toni. 'I mean, look at the three of us. None of us had the perfect experience. Pregnancy, birth, whatever. We all had lots of doubts, lots of issues, lots of problems. But look at these three!' she said, indicating Harry, sleeping pressed against her chest, Peter, gazing curiously around the room and chewing his fist, and Millie, lying like an angel in her pushchair, her little starfish hand by her cheek. 'They're healthy and perfect. They have great futures ahead of them. And we're alive and well too. It just makes all the other petty crap look like . . . well, like petty crap, don't you think?' She stared hard at Gemma and Louise. 'Now I love you both, and you've both been amazing supportive friends, but it really gets on my wick that you won't speak to each other. Gem, I wouldn't even know you if it wasn't for Louise. I love seeing you both individually, but I feel like the tug-of-love child in a divorce. I want to see you together. Can you get over your argument and be friends again? Please?'

There was a long and awkward pause. Then Louise spoke. 'Gemma, I was really hurt by your text message. You made assumptions about my situation, and I know you're young and you might have your reasons, but it was hurtful. I'm sorry I yelled at you at the antenatal class that time, but I'd just been getting it from all sides that week.'

'Fair enough,' said Gemma. 'I'm sorry for the text message. It was mean and unnecessary. I have big issues around married men who sleep around, because of my dad. I took it out on you, and I'm sorry.'

'Apology accepted,' said Louise, and then she smiled. Gemma remembered that warm, lovely smile and she was secretly pleased to be on the receiving end of it again. 'Right, well, I'm glad that's sorted, as we're going to be in-laws.'

'What?' said Gemma, confused.

'Well, that's a beautiful girl you've got there. I'm putting in a claim now for Peter to marry her. After all, they were born on the same day.'

'Oi!' laughed Toni. 'Back off! Harry's had his eye on her for ages! And who knows? She might like a younger man.'

'I think Millie's going to play the field for a while before she settles down,' smiled Gemma. 'Now, Toni, are you going to eat all of that cake, or can I have a bite?'

She loved Toni, she really did. They'd become incredibly close, and she had nothing but admiration for her friend's daily battle with depression. But there were other emotions churning in Gemma's heart . . . feelings she could do nothing about. Feelings she couldn't deny, couldn't control, and definitely, definitely couldn't do anything about. She was in love with James.

Every day she spent with Toni, she made sure she stayed until James got home from work. Then, while Toni went off to the bathroom to have a minute to herself, she and James would chat and she'd give him a report on Toni's state of mind. He always made time to ask how she was, to comment on how beautiful Millie was, to ask about her plans for the days to come. She knew he was just being nice. Of course that was the case, but he was just so . . . amazing. Funny, good-looking (oh my God, so good-looking), and talented! Toni had shown her some of James' design work, and he really was brilliant. He'd recently done the design for a shampoo billboard ad, and whenever Gemma drove past the billboard, she got a little thrill that she knew him.

Things might have been different if there was any hope of something happening between her and Ben. But Ben was head over heels in love with Kat. He'd recently asked if he could take Millie out for the day, just him and Kat, and so far, Gemma had said no, but she knew she was just doing it to be spiteful. Ben was very good with his baby daughter. Millie would be perfectly safe. She just couldn't bear the thought that people might think Kat was Millie's mum.

She knew it was ridiculous having a crush on James. He was her best friend's husband, for God's sake, and she'd just spent months hating Louise for going for a married man. It was just . . . well, next to James, no one else seemed really good enough.

When he'd rung her that first time to talk about Toni's PND, she'd saved his mobile number, and of course she had his email address. When the new iPad came out, she read a report about it, and, on impulse, sent him a quick mail with the link. He sent a warm response, so the next time she read something about design she thought he'd like, she mailed it too. When Ben told her a particularly silly joke she texted it to James, and he sent her one back about two penguins in a bar. After a while, they were exchanging an email or a text pretty much every day. It was just a harmless friendship, she told herself. But she couldn't help imagining what it would be like to have James in her life, making her laugh every day, looking after her like he looked after Toni.

Toni

It started as a niggle. Every time James came home and Gemma was round for the afternoon he would walk her out to her car and chat to her. I wouldn't have minded, but, firstly, he seemed to stay out there ages, and, secondly, he didn't do it for anyone else. Not Louise, not Rob or Caro, just Gemma, like she was this delicate little flower who needed to be handed into her fairy carriage. I started looking out of the window when he went outside with her, and they'd stand next to the car and chat. It wasn't like they snogged or anything, but I couldn't help hating the fact that James always seemed to laugh when he talked to her. He didn't laugh like that with me any more . . . he was too busy being concerned and careful.

I suppose I just had too much time on my hands to worry about it, because it really started to bug me, and one evening, after he'd been out there for sixteen minutes (and yes, I timed it), I did something I never, ever thought I'd do. Something I know other women do all the time, but I've always thought was the height of craziness. I waited till James had gone to shower, and I went through his phone. Sure enough, there were texts from Gemma, and texts from James to her. I felt like throwing up, but then I read the messages. They were all just friendly messages, jokes, mostly. All of Gemma's ended with xxx, but she does that on every message she sends me too.

I didn't say anything to James in case he thought I had the crazies again. Was I being paranoid? Was I reading too much into their friendship? I just didn't know. Well, the best way to decide would be through close observation.

'So here's my plan,' I said to James excitedly. 'I'm going to throw a party!'

'You're going to what?' he said, disbelievingly.

'I want to say thank you to Gemma and Toni for all their support over the last while, not to mention my dad and Rob and Caro. So I thought we could have them all over for Christmas drinks and mince pies.'

'Are you sure? I mean, doesn't it sound a bit stressful?'

'For who? You or me?'

'You. And me. You know I'm not very good at parties.'

'You always say that, and then you end up being the life and soul, and having a splendid time, and I have to prise the lampshade off your head and drag you home at dawn.'

'Ah, but if the party is here, I'm already home!'

'I knew you'd come round to my way of thinking!' I said, grinning at him.

'Seriously, though, Toni, are you sure you're up to it?'

'I won't know unless I do it. But I have to re-enter the real world. Harry's three months old now, his colic is so much better, and I'm much better too. I really do want to do it.'

We fixed a date, and amazingly, everyone we invited said yes, even Rob and Caro (although Caro was going to have to dash off early to go to something much more glamorous). Louise even rang up and said, 'Can I be incredibly cheeky and have two plus ones?'

'Two? You and Peter, plus two?'

'Well, as the party is a Saturday night, I'll have Simon staying with me. And, well, I thought I would like to invite Adam. So you could meet him.'

'The handsome and mysterious Mr Harper? Of course! And we'd love Simon to come too.'

I kept things simple and we just did canapes, most of which I got from M&S, and mince pies, and James got a recipe at work for mulled wine and did an enormous saucepanful. My dad was first to arrive, and in no time at all our little living room was full of people. Gemma arrived with little Millie, and we put her in our bedroom in her carrycot. Harry was already fast asleep in his Moses basket. 'We've got the monitor so we'll hear them if they wake up,' I assured her. She looked very pretty, and definitely a bit overdressed for a small party at a mate's house . . . she'd got her figure back in no time at all, and she was wearing a very classy black dress, which was a little bit too old for her, and very high heels.

Louise arrived with her 'plus two'. The mysterious Mr Harper was quite a hunk, a little bit older, but clearly besotted with Louise. He'd brought a couple of bottles of nice bubbly (so I knew Rob and Caro would approve of him!).

Simon had little Peter in a sling on his front, fast asleep, and he proudly refused to take him off. 'He loves to sleep like this,' he insisted. 'I'm happy to wear him all night.'

Soon, people were chatting away . . . and I was surprised at who hit it off with whom. Simon stood by the mulled wine in the kitchen, and was having an uproarious time giggling away with Robyn, then shushing her because of the sleeping baby. After a glass or two, he got quite camp, and they seemed to be having a whale of a time. Adam was in serious conversation with my father about the Mesopotamians, or some other ancient seafaring nation, and my dad looked pleased as punch to have someone knowledgeable to talk to. Louise and Caro had monopolised the sofa and seemed to be talking fashion. And, surprise, surprise, James was sitting at the kitchen counter, talking intently to Gemma. I handed around a plate of warm mince pies, and then James called me over.

'Toni . . . listen to this! Gemma's had an amazing idea.' I went over, and Gemma looked up at me and smiled.

'James has got all excited because I told him I'm going to study next year.'

'Are you?'

'Yes. I've thought about it, and I think I want to become a midwife. It'll mean doing a three-year course, but I think it's such an amazing thing to do. As you would know!'

I laughed. 'Try not to deliver too many babies on kitchen floors when you're heavily pregnant, though. That's my advice. So when will you start?'

'Next September, when Millie's one.'

'Wow, I'm really proud of you, Gemma. That's an amazing plan. And I think you'll be great at it.'

'Won't she?' said James, flinging his arm around her shoulders and giving her a squeeze. Gemma blushed bright red. I felt my stomach tie itself into a knot, but I smiled and forced myself to walk away and mingle.

Rob and Simon called me over to say that the mulled wine was running low. Entirely due to their efforts, I might add! I yelled for James, and he dragged himself away from Gemma, grabbed a couple more bottles of red and went to make more.

Caro came over to kiss me goodbye. She had a cab waiting to take her to another party. 'Glad you're still, you know . . . you, darling,' she said, wiping her lipstick off my cheek. 'We'll get those eyebrows seen to in the New Year and you'll be right back to the Toni I know and love.'

Everyone had a drink and they'd had plenty of snacks, so I went to sit with Louise on the sofa for a bit.

'This is quite a hit!' she said, looking around the room.

'Well, your Adam, who is lovely by the way, has made a friend for life. My dad loves anyone who'll let him talk shop.'

'Is your dad a sailor?'

'Historian. But Adam knew something about Phoenician biremes, so he's in there.'

'A man of hidden depths. I didn't know he knew about that stuff.'

'So how are things going?'

'Slowly. Well. But slowly. We have a date about once a week, and we're getting to know one another. He's a nice man.'

'He's a silver fox!'

'Well, that too. But I'm in no rush to hurry things along. I've made enough spur-of-the-moment mistakes to last a lifetime. And besides, with Peter, I have to be sure. I'm taking care of two of us now.'

'Oh, speaking of taking care, have you heard Gemma's thinking of training as a midwife?'

'Really? Well, it's good to hear she's got some direction. She's a smart girl. She'll do well.'

'Won't she just? Beauty and brains, and the perfect baby. She's got it all.'

Obviously I hadn't hidden the vitriol in my voice, because Louise looked at me sharply.

'What's going on?'

'Oh, you know, the usual. Teenage sirens hitting on my husband.'

'Really?' said Louise. 'But James can't be taking it seriously, can he? Not your James.'

Ah. My James. I looked over at him. He was measuring brandy to pour into the mulled wine, and laughing at something Gemma was saying. He'd put on his glasses to read the recipe, but then he peered over them at her like an old professor and they both burst out giggling again. In the course of this mad, mad year, I hadn't paid James as much attention as I should have. He'd stuck by me through my pregnancy, through the stress of Harry's birth and all that came after. He'd been loving, supportive and

436

dear, and even nice to my friends. And since Harry was born, he'd never once complained about what he might be missing out on . . . going out, holidays. Even sex. And before you ask, no we hadn't, not since a few weeks before the birth. After the caesarean, my mid-section had been very tender and the post-natal depression had completely removed my libido. And he'd never once asked, or nagged, or even hinted. I knew how high his sex drive was, but he had been incredibly patient and understanding.

'Wow,' said Louise softly, beside me.

'Wow, what?'

'You're right. Gemma's staring at him with those big cow eyes. Sorry to say it, but that is one smitten kitten.'

Yes, there was lissom, slim, nineteen-year-old Gemma, staring at my husband with undisguised adoration. My handsome husband, who hadn't had sex in four months, and whose wife seemed to take him totally for granted. The room seemed very small then, and very dark. Had I wanted a baby so much that I'd gambled away James, the best thing ever to happen to me? Was I going to lose him? I thought about going over and hanging on his arm, or warning Gemma off, but I was too scared to. What if they laughed at me? What if he turned to me and said, 'Well, now that you mention it, I *do* prefer Gemma, with her thirty-inch hips and her perfect girl baby who never cries.'

So in the end, I spent the rest of the party sitting right there on the sofa, glaring at them both and wishing death and destruction, or at least boils and cellulite, on Gemma.

It was a successful party, but it didn't go on late. At about ten, Louise pulled Simon away from his new BFF Robyn, and they headed off home with little Peter and the lovely Adam. Robyn persuaded my dad to drink a shot of Jägermeister, and they tottered off together to get a train.

I got up then, and started tidying up in a kind of frenzied way, chucking cans and bottles into a bin bag and clinking glasses together, making far too much noise. Sure enough, one of the babies woke up and squawked, and that woke the other one up. James and Gemma went upstairs together to settle them, leaving me standing staring miserably into the sink.

'All right, little fella,' I heard James say over the baby monitor, and I heard a rustle as he picked Harry up. Gemma shushed Millie, and I could hear her moving around, packing up their stuff. I don't think they realised the monitor was still on and that I could hear them. I heard James say, 'Relax, I'll sort all of that and carry it down to the car. You just worry about that lovely little girl.'

'Thanks, but what about Harry?' said Gemma.

'He's gone straight back to sleep,' whispered James, and I heard him put Harry back into the Moses basket and tuck him in. 'Just wanted a little cuddle.'

'Thank you so much for tonight,' said Gemma. 'I had such a great time.'

'Really? All you did was chat to me!' said James, walking right into the trap. Here it comes,

I thought, and gripped the edge of the sink like it was Gemma's throat.

'That was the best bit,' said Gemma. 'I like talking to you. You're . . . you're amazing.'

Well that's it out in the open, I thought. Now I have to listen to them snog over the monitor, my heart breaking . . .

And then something happened that I hadn't bargained on. You see, I may have mentioned that James is gorgeous. Yes, I know that everyone thinks their man is dazzling, but James' hotness has been independently verified by over a hundred of my friends and family. He really is drop-dead stunning. As a result, women hit on him all the time, and he is a master at letting them down gently and politely. And this is what he said.

'Gem, you're the amazing one. You've had a baby all on your own, you're doing a great job of raising her, and you're planning to go into a challenging career. You've got your whole life ahead of you, and I just know there's a super guy who's going to wake up every morning, thanking his lucky stars he's got you.'

'He won't be you, though,' said Gemma in a small voice, and to my surprise, I felt sorry for her. She really is just a lonely little girl.

'No, it won't be me,' said James, walking her towards the door. 'It won't be me, because I'm in love with . . . '

And then, because they were moving towards the door, his voice got muffled and strange over the monitor, so it sounded like he said, 'I'm in love with Mabel Whiton.'

Mabel Whiton? Who the fuck is Mabel Whiton? And was I going to have to kill her too?

No need to panic, though, reader. I'm not as stupid as I look, because by the time they'd come downstairs, Gemma had called out a quiet goodbye and James had seen her out (and *not* walked her to her car this time), I'd worked out that what he'd actually said was this: 'I'm in love with my beautiful wife Toni.'

James came back in, and stood behind me at the sink and held me gently. It was then that I realised he probably did know the monitor was on, and that I would hear what he and Gemma said in the bedroom. We went upstairs then. We didn't speak, but we went into the bathroom together and undressed, and had a slow, lovely shower together, like we always used to in the old days. I washed his hair and he soaped my back, then we dried each other lovingly. He turned off the light then, and in the dim glow of the hallway light, he put me in front of the mirror, and stood behind me. For the first time in months, I looked at the reflection of my naked body.

James stroked my hair, which was longer than it's been in years. It curled crazily, and he wound one tendril around a finger and then bent to kiss it. He ran his hands over my shoulders, and then gently down over my breasts. They weren't so enormous any more, but they definitely sat a bit lower than they used to. My nipples were bigger and darker, and each breast was covered in a network of blue veins. But as James gently lifted and stroked each one, I could see they were beautiful. They'd changed because they were doing what breasts were designed to do — feeding our baby, and I liked them for that.

James slid his hand down to my waist, or where my waist used to be. I'd never been slim, but the bit that used to go in now went out. But as he stroked my sides, I could see that there was a certain lush beauty in that curve. Not size zero, but lovely in a different way.

With infinite tenderness, James ran his hand over my belly, still a bit jellified, and marked by a few purple tiger-stripe stretch marks. They would show if I wore a bikini but then I'd never worn a bikini in my life so that was no loss. Finally he slid his hand down to the edge of my pubic hair and traced the line of my caesarean scar with one finger. It wasn't sore any more, and the hair hid it almost completely, but it was there. A mark on my body that would never go away. Did I care? Not at all. It was nothing compared to what we had gained when that cut was made.

And then he slid his fingers lower, and I was amazed at how powerfully my body responded. I turned around to face him, and he drew me into his arms. I buried my face in the curve of his neck, and it smelled of home.

EASTER

Louise

After the crazy turmoil of the previous year, the first three months of the new one were remarkably kind and gentle to Louise. Peter started sleeping a little better and grew into a bonny, chubby, laughing baby. She started tentatively looking for work, and found a part-time opportunity, lecturing in business and management at a local further-education college. She loved the work, spending two mornings and one afternoon a week there. It didn't pay a fortune, but together with her savings, it meant she didn't have to look for anything more full-time until Peter was at least a year old. Rachel looked after Peter when she worked, and they had become much closer, losing the awful combative edge to their relationship.

As for Adam, they had kept on with their slow, careful dating, until one rainy Wednesday evening, they had lost all self control and ended up ripping one another's clothes off on Louise's sofa. Adam, with enormous presence of mind, had condoms with him, and after the initial desperate coupling, they had gone to the bedroom for several more leisurely attempts. Peter woke up bright-eyed and early the next morning to two very bleary, but very happy adults. So things had moved on, and she was almost ready to admit to herself, and to him, that she loved Adam.

As the weather warmed up and blossoms and flowers began to appear, she admitted that she was beginning to love Surrey too. She had given up her home and her career up north, and it had seemed like an enormous loss, but, unexpectedly, she had found a real home down south ... she loved being closer to Simon and Rachel and having a sense of family for the first time since their parents had died. Her friendship with Toni was strong, and she found she got along famously with Toni's friend Caro too. There was no doubt, she had blessings, and possibly too many to count.

Rachel invited Louise and Peter, Adam and Simon over for lunch on Easter Sunday. The weather was glorious, so Richard wheeled out his enormous barbecue and the men all gathered around it and made an enormous fuss about grilling a few bits of meat. Rachel and Louise stood on the patio, looking out over the beautiful garden. Peter, who had recently learned to sit up by himself, sat on a soft rug at their feet, shredding one of Rachel's expensive magazines.

'Oh, I nearly forgot! I bought Peter a little inflatable pool,' said Rachel. 'It's probably not warm enough for him today, but I thought during the week he might like to have a splash and play with some toys.' She went round to the other side of the patio and came back dragging the brightly coloured pool, already filled with water.

'He loves his bath,' said Louise. 'I'm sure he'll be thrilled with it.'

'I won't leave him for a second,' said Rachel anxiously. 'I'll make sure he doesn't get chilled, and I'll cover him in sunscreen, or get one of those little wetsuits.'

'I know you will. I trust you absolutely. Still, as it's all set up, it seems a waste not to use it. If it's too cold for Peter, we could put our feet in it and sip Pimm's, and pretend we're on holiday in the Bahamas!'

'I like it!' said Rachel, giggling a little. She went to get them each a glass of Pimm's from the jug on the table. She had loosened up so much, thought Louise. It was lovely to see her having fun.

They pulled chairs closer to the splash pool, moved Peter nearby and kicked off their shoes. Louise wiggled her toes in the cool water and sipped her drink.

'This is definitely the life. We just need a few fine-looking lifeguards to jog by and my happiness would be complete.'

'Get your handsome Adam to whip his shirt off,' suggested Rachel.

'Oh, he's much too dignified for that,' smiled Louise, allowing herself a private moment to think about Adam with his shirt off, and what a lovely thing that was. 'Nice pedicure, by the way,' she said, looking at Rachel's toes.

'My beautician Lara is an artist,' said Rachel, extending a foot and admiring it.

'I can't remember the last time I had a pedicure,' Louise said sadly, looking at her own chipped polish.

'I'll treat you. One Saturday morning, you can go to Lara and Peter and I will go for a walk around the shops.'

'Sounds like heaven.'

'Look at our feet, though,' Rachel observed. 'They're exactly the same. You've also got that twisted little toe.'

'They are the same, you're right. I've never noticed that before.'

'So, how's your friend Toni? The one who had PND?'

'She's doing great. Harry's a sweet little chap. Had a few problems in the beginning, but she's really got into the whole motherhood thing. She's still friends with loads of women from our antenatal classes, so she's started running a mums and babies group, and she's always trying to drag me along. Peter and I don't really go in for group activities, though. I'm too old to sing, 'Wind the bobbin up', and Peter's too cool.'

Rachel smiled down at Peter. 'You all right, sweetheart?' she said, stroking his flaming red hair. 'Oh, Lou, next Easter, he'll be twenty months old. He'll be running everywhere! We can have an Easter-egg hunt for him in the garden. It'll be lovely.'

They sat in silence for a bit. The men's conversation, inevitably about sport, drifted across to them. Peter babbled happily to himself as he set about eating a picture of Penelope Cruz. Taking a deep breath, Louise turned to her sister. 'Rach, I want to ask you something. Can you let me say my piece before you stop me?'

'Okay.'

'We haven't spoken much about your problems trying to conceive lately, and I know you probably still think I'm the last person you want to talk to about it . . . '

Rachel took a breath, as if to interrupt, but Louise kept talking. 'Simon's told me some of what you've been going through. I know you don't want to have a baby that's not yours, but how about having a baby that comes from your genetic pool?'

She reached into her handbag and drew out a magazine. 'There's an article in here about women who have been egg donors for their sisters. I know it sounds weird when you say it like that, but read the stories. I think . . . well, I think it could work for you.' She took a deep breath. 'Rachel, would you let me be your egg donor?'

'Lou, I — '

'Don't say anything now. Don't decide now. Read the article. Do some more research. Talk to Richard. The offer stands, whenever and whatever you decide.'

Rachel nodded, clearly unable to speak. Louise sat and looked at her for a moment longer, then scooped Peter up and went over to join the men at the barbecue. She glanced back, and Rachel was sitting staring at her own feet in the water, as if she'd never seen them before.

Gemma

Gemma stood in the doorway of the church hall, clutching the handle of her pushchair tightly. The noise level seemed astonishing, maybe because the hall was so large and echoey. There were four or five boisterous little boys, who looked about three years old, racing around the room on push-along cars. Two other children seemed intent on scattering Lego over the entire floor surface, and there was a screaming match between an angelic blonde girl of about two and a thickset little boy over a set of plastic power tools. The mums all stood clustered around a table at the far end of the room, sipping coffee and chatting, seemingly ignoring their rampaging offspring. It was all terrifying, and Gemma was suddenly sure she didn't belong there.

She was about to back out of the doorway and go back home when a smiling woman with grey hair and bright green eyes came hurrying over. 'Hello, new ones! Welcome to St Gerard's baby-and-toddler group,' she said brightly. 'I'm Diana.'

'I'm Gemma, and this is Millie,' Gemma said. It seemed she wouldn't be able to leave now. But Diana made her feel a bit easier when she glanced ruefully around the room and said, 'I know it all looks a bit raucous, but I think you'll find it a bit more peaceful in the baby corner. You can leave your pushchair here in our buggy park.'

Gemma unstrapped Millie, and holding her close followed Diana to the other side of the room. Next to the table where the women were having coffee there was a little circle of chairs and sofas. Someone had put a rug down in the middle of the space and covered it in colourful baby mats. There were a few other women with smaller babies sitting there, and they all smiled welcomingly as Gemma approached. She sat down hesitantly, holding Millie on her lap. Diana rattled off a list of names, pointing at mums and babies, but Gemma didn't catch any of them.

A woman with dark, curly hair and beautiful eyes, who had a fat little baby on her breast, leaned over to say hello. 'We were just talking about weaning. Gemma, is it? How old is your little one?'

'Six months,' said Gemma.

'Really? She's a small one. But I suppose you're a small-boned girl too. This little bruiser's also six months, believe it or not. So, have you started weaning?'

'A bit of baby rice and some mashed fruit,' said Gemma hesitantly.

'She eats fruit?' Another woman sitting opposite chimed in. Her baby was sitting in a bouncy canvas chair opposite, and she was dangling a turtle toy just out of his reach. 'Mine won't touch any fruit, just spits it out. What have you given her?'

'Some banana, and a bit of papaya. She liked that.'

'Wow!' said the first woman. 'I hadn't thought of papaya. Good thinking!'

The conversation barrelled along, and Gemma

was mainly content to listen. Every now and then the dark-haired woman, who was called Vicky, would ask her a question, drawing her into the chat. She felt oddly at ease. She could contribute intelligently to the talk about babies, and even though the other women were a bit older than her, they talked about the same kind of things Gemma's other friends might talk about: what had been on TV, celebrity gossip, a book several of them had been reading. She'd been very reluctant to come to a baby-and-toddler group with a bunch of strangers, but she'd been worried that Millie wasn't getting enough stimulation. She was glad now that she'd been brave enough to give it a go.

Millie, who had sat quietly on her lap for a while, was now leaning over precariously, staring at the brightly coloured jungle-animal mat on the floor. The mat looked clean enough, so Gemma put her down on her tummy. Millie immediately grabbed the loose ear of an elephant, which had a cellophane crinkle to it, and began to chew on it. She seemed content.

'While she's happy, go and grab a tea or a coffee,' Vicky said. 'I'll keep an eye on her.'

Gemma would have said no, but the coffee table was right beside the baby corner and she would be able to see Mille the whole time. She picked up a paper cup, popped a teabag in, and waited her turn for hot water from the urn.

'Biscuit?'

She looked up and a gawky young man standing behind the table was holding out a plate of digestives. 'Um, no thanks,' she said.

He seemed out of place at a toddler group: he was too old to be a big brother, but too young to be a dad. Although, as Gemma reminded herself, most people would say she looked too young to be a mum. Maybe he was a single dad. He seemed to read her enquiring expression, because he said, 'I'm Seamus. I'm here to help my nan today . . . Diana. She runs the group.'

Now he said it, she could see he was related to Diana — he had the same amazing sea-green eyes and curly hair, although his was sandy-coloured and too long. He was very tall.

'I'm Gemma, and that's Millie.'

'Looks like Millie's almost on the move,' Seamus said, and she turned to look. Millie had got herself up on all fours and was rocking back and forth determinedly.

'Oh, she's been doing that for a while, but she never goes anywhere,' Gemma said.

'She's likely to go backwards before she goes forwards,' Seamus said wisely. It seemed an unlikely thing for a young guy of — what was he? Twenty? Twenty-one? — to know.

'Have you got a baby of your own?' Gemma asked.

'No, I'm studying early-childhood development as part of my degree. I'm going to be a junior-school teacher.' Then he laughed and said, 'Go on. Have a biscuit. I took them out of the packet myself! It took great skill and ingenuity.'

He was really goofy-looking, not ugly, but definitely not handsome like Ben or James. He did have a nice smile though, and lovely straight teeth. Gemma found herself taking a biscuit.

EPILOGUE

Rachel

Baking is easy, Rachel told anyone who complimented her on her feather-light cakes, delicately flaky pastry or melt-in-the-mouth macaroons. It simply requires the best ingredients, consistency in method and absolute accuracy. To this end, she had a state-of-the-art oven, highly calibrated scales for measuring her ingredients and a stainless-steel, digital, to-the-second kitchen timer. It was this last instrument she needed today.

She programmed it for three minutes and set it on the counter, ready to go. Then she unwrapped the plastic probe and put it in the beaker of liquid. She set the timer going and it began to count down.

Three Minutes

She looked out of the window into the garden. The swing set was plonked in the middle of her immaculate lawn. It spoiled the sweeping lines of her carefully designed garden, but she didn't mind: the way Peter chortled when she pushed him on the swing made it totally worthwhile. He was standing unsteadily now and loved to waddle along holding on to her fingers. He'd be walking any day soon. She loved having him with her on the days when Louise was at work. He filled her days and kept her busy. Still, it took a lot of energy, and she'd been feeling rather tired this past week or so.

Two minutes

She turned to look at her kitchen. It was usually spotless, but she noticed that there were some grubby fingerprints on the lower cupboards and the bottom of the fridge door. That wasn't just Peter, though. They'd had a first-birthday party for him the week before, and Louise's friend Toni had come with her husband and their little Harry, an insatiably curious little blond chap who was already walking, or rather running, everywhere. Louise had also invited David and Samantha Hamilton's daughter and her little girl who had the same birthday as Peter.

Louise had told Rachel that Gemma had made a play for Toni's husband at Christmas time, and Rachel was frankly amazed Toni would be in the same room as the teenager. But, to her surprise, Toni was very kind and jokey with Gemma, and seemed to go out of her way to put Gemma at her ease. To be fair, Toni and her husband did look happy together. They held hands a lot, and at one point when Rachel was carrying plates into the kitchen she caught them kissing while their little boy played around their feet. She cleared her throat and they leapt apart, but she just smiled. She'd come in to get another pot of coffee. She had to hold her breath carrying it back out into the garden, though, the smell was so strong and it made her feel a bit nauseous.

Gemma had brought her new boyfriend, a tall, shambling boy with curly hair who was at teacher-training college. He was nice enough, not exactly glamorous, but he seemed really serious about Gemma, and very committed to her and Millie. Gemma was about to start her training at the hospital. So it seemed quite possible Gemma would end up as a midwife married to a teacher. Probably not quite what David and Samantha had imagined for their daughter with all that expensive private schooling. Still, as long as she was happy.

One minute

Rachel smoothed her T-shirt. It was a new one, a bright floral print. Now that she looked after Peter so often, she wore a lot less white. She still liked to look smart, but there were only so many times a day you could change when you got smeared with jam, or someone got a bit enthusiastic with the finger paints. Peter had certainly taught her to relax. Come to think of it, maybe the T-shirt hadn't been such a good buy. She'd only washed it once, but it seemed to have shrunk. It was definitely tight across her breasts.

Zero

The timer finished with a discreet electronic 'ping'. Was that three minutes gone already? Time seemed to have gone faster these past six months, ever since Louise had made her astonishing offer to be Rachel's egg donor. They'd gone through a battery of tests, then counselling, then Louise had had a series of injections to stimulate her egg production. Time had just zipped by, especially since the eggs had been harvested and mixed with Richard's sperm and Rachel had had the implantation. And here she was, in her kitchen, with a beaker of wee, a timer and a pregnancy test. She hadn't told anyone that she was doing this today. She wanted to find out alone, before she shared the news with Richard, or Louise, or anybody. And now it was time. Rachel took a deep breath, picked up the pregnancy test, and looked.

Thanks and Applause

This is the bit where I step out from behind the puppet theatre, sweating and smiling awkwardly, and show you my own rather disappointing face.

I wish I were able to dash off an Oscar-accepting-style comprehensive and witty list of thanks and acknowledgments, but to be honest I'm the working mother of a toddler and a teenager, I've got a shepherd's pie in the oven and a deadline to meet, and this is as good as it gets. If you should be on this page and you're not, I'm so sorry. You only have me to blame.

Great heaps of gratitude and squishy hugs to the many people who had a hand in *Babies in Waiting*. You wouldn't be holding it in your hands if it weren't for:

Caroline Hardman at Christopher Little, my splendid agent. Thanks for your long investment in me, for your patience and endless faith, and your tenacious hard work and attention to detail.

Charlotte van Wijk and all at Quercus for quite simply making my life's ambition a reality.

Dr Annabelle Clerk, who read the manuscript to make sure I hadn't made any massive medical errors. If there are any mistakes they are all mine and entirely due to my reliance on those snake-oil merchants, Dr Google and Professor Hearsay.

My friends — Corrinne and Alli for the title, and all my Facebook mates for their many, many

461

suggestions, both serious and ridiculous. Also the early readers: Denise, Heather and Marian, who were all so encouraging and supportive. Many friends off- and online whose experiences, anecdotes and scare stories inspired so many bits of the book.

And finally, and of course, my thanks and my heart are always with my boys, Tom, Matt and Ted — for tea — and everything, really.

We do hope that you have enjoyed reading this large print book.

Did you know that all of our titles are available for purchase?

We publish a wide range of high quality large print books including:
**Romances, Mysteries, Classics
General Fiction
Non Fiction and Westerns**

Special interest titles available in large print are:
**The Little Oxford Dictionary
Music Book
Song Book
Hymn Book
Service Book**

Also available from us courtesy of Oxford University Press:
**Young Readers' Dictionary
(large print edition)
Young Readers' Thesaurus
(large print edition)**

For further information or a free brochure, please contact us at:
**Ulverscroft Large Print Books Ltd.,
The Green, Bradgate Road, Anstey,
Leicester, LE7 7FU, England.
Tel:** (00 44) 0116 236 4325
Fax: (00 44) 0116 234 0205

Other titles published by
The House of Ulverscroft:

NIGHTWOODS

Charles Frazier

In the lonesome beauty of the forest, across the far shore of the mountain lake from town, Luce acts as caretaker to an empty, decaying Lodge, a relic of holidaymakers a century before. Her days are long and peaceful, her nights filled with Nashville radio and yellow lights shimmering on the black water. A solitary life, and the perfect escape. Until the stranger children come. Bringing fire. And murder. And love.